2011

October 3, 2011

ROSEMARY
ROGERS
BRIDE
for a NIGHT

ISBN-13: 978-1-61793-080-5

BRIDE FOR A NIGHT

To my family, my loyal readers.
Thank you for always being there!

BRIDE *for a* NIGHT

CHAPTER ONE

SLOANE SQUARE WAS not the finest neighborhood in London, but it was respectable and comfortably situated next to the more fashionable areas. As a rule it was occupied by members of the *ton* who clung to the fringes of society, or those who preferred to avoid the bustle that spilled throughout Mayfair.

And then there was Mr. Silas Dobson.

Claiming the largest mansion on a corner lot, Mr. Dobson was what was delicately known as an "upstart." Or for those less kindly disposed, as an ill-bred mushroom who reeked of the shop despite his fortune.

He might eventually have been forgiven for his unwelcome intrusion among his betters had Silas been willing to fade quietly into the background and accept that he would always be inferior to those born into the aristocracy.

Silas, however, was not the sort of man to fade into any background.

As large as an ox, with a barrel chest and meaty face that was ruddy from the sun, he was as loud and crass as any of the hundreds of men who worked in his numerous warehouses spread throughout the city. Even worse, he made no apology for the fact he had crawled out of the gutters to make his fortune in trade. The youngest of twelve children, he had started as a dockhand before beginning to invest in high-risk cargos and eventually purchasing a number of properties that were rented out at an exorbitant fee to various shipping companies.

He was a bully without manners who had managed to insult nearly every resident in Sloane Square at least a dozen times over the past ten years.

And while he wasn't stupid enough to believe he could ever pass as a gentleman, he was willing to use his obscene wealth to foist his only child onto society.

An impudence that did nothing to endear him to members of the *ton*.

Of course, their ruffled feathers were somewhat eased by the knowledge that, for all of Dobson's wealth and bluster, he couldn't make his tiny dab of a daughter a success.

Oh, she was pretty enough with large emerald eyes set in a perfect oval face with a delicate nose and full, rose-kissed lips. But there was something quite…earthy in her gypsy curves and unruly raven curls.

It was, however, her awkward lack of charm that ensured that she would remain a wallflower.

After all, there were always those gentlemen of breeding who were notoriously short of funds. Being a member of nobility was an expensive business, especially if one was a younger sibling without the benefit of large estates to offset the cost of being fashionable.

With a dowry well over a hundred thousand pounds, Talia should have been snatched off the marriage mart her first season, even with a boorish father who promised to be a yoke of embarrassment around the neck of his prospective son-in-law.

But, when a man added in the fact that the female was a dreaded bluestocking who could barely be induced to speak a word in public, let alone dazzle a gentleman with practiced flirtations, it all combined to leave her a source of amused pity, someone who was avoided like the plague.

Society members took pleasure in Talia's failure. They smugly assured themselves it would be a blow to the odious Mr. Dobson and an example to other encroachers who thought they could buy a place among the aristocracy.

They might not have been so smug had they known Silas Dobson as well as his daughter did.

The son of a mere butcher did not acquire a small financial empire unless he possessed the unbridled determination to overcome any obstacle. No matter what the sacrifice.

Well aware of Silas Dobson's ruthless willpower, Talia shuddered at the sound of her father's bellow as it echoed through the vaulted rooms of the elegant house.

"Talia. Talia, answer me. Damned, where is the child?"

There was the muffled sound of servants rushing to provide the master of the house with the information he desired, and with a sigh Talia set aside the book on China she had been studying and cast a rueful glance about her temporary haven of peace.

Arched windows overlooked the sunken rose garden and a marble fountain that sparkled in the late May sunlight. Heavy shelves filled with leather-bound books lined the walls, and the coved ceiling high above was painted with an image of Apollo in his chariot. At one end a walnut desk was set near the carved marble fireplace that was flanked by two leather chairs. And the floor was covered by an Oriental carpet that glowed with rich crimson and sapphire.

It was a beautiful library.

Rising from one of the chairs, Talia smoothed her hands down the teal skirt of her simple muslin gown,

wishing she had changed into one of the fine silk dresses
that her father preferred.

Not that he would ever be pleased with her appearance, she wryly acknowledged.

Silas's disappointment in not having a son and heir
was only surpassed by his disappointment in possessing a daughter who looked more like a gypsy than one
of the elegant blonde debutantes who graced the London
ballrooms.

Braced for her father's entrance, Talia managed not
to flinch as he rammed open the door to the library and
regarded her with an impatient glower.

"I might have known I would find you wasting your
day hiding among these damnable books." His disapproving gaze took in her plain gown and lack of jewelry.
"Why did I spend a fortune on your finery if not to be
out preening yourself like the other silly chits?"

"I never asked you to spend your money on my clothing," she softly reminded him.

He snorted. "Oh, aye, I suppose you would as soon
go about looking like a charwoman and have all of society think me too clutch-fisted to properly provide for
my only child? A fine thing that would be."

"That is not what I meant."

With heavy steps, Silas moved beside the desk, his
face more ruddy than usual, as if the white cravat tied
around his thick neck was choking him.

Talia felt a flutter of unease. Her father only allowed
his valet to wrestle him into that particular tailored gray
jacket and burgundy striped waistcoat when he intended
to mingle among society rather than devoting his day to
his business. A rare occurrence that typically ended with
her father in a foul mood and various aristocrats threatening to rid the world of Silas Dobson's existence.

"Is it not enough that you embarrass me with your clumsy manner and dim-witted stammering?" he growled, pouring himself a generous amount of brandy from a crystal decanter.

She lowered her head, a familiar sense of failure settling in the pit of her stomach.

"I have tried my best."

"Oh, aye, and that's why you're alone on this fine day while your fancy friends are attending an alfresco luncheon in Wimbledon?"

Her heart dipped in familiar disappointment. "They are not my friends, and I could hardly attend a luncheon for which I did not receive an invitation."

"You mean to say you were slighted?" her father rasped. "By God, Lord Morrilton will hear of this."

"No, father." Talia lifted her head in horror. It was bad enough to be ignored when she was forced to attend the events to which she was invited. She could not bear to be a source of resentment. "I warned you, but you would not listen. You cannot purchase me a place in society, no matter how much money you spend."

The anger suddenly faded from her father's face to be replaced by a smug smile.

"Now that is where you are wide of the mark."

She stilled. "What do you mean?"

"I have just returned from a most satisfying meeting with Mr. Harry Richardson, younger brother to the Earl of Ashcombe."

Talia recognized the name, of course.

A handsome gentleman with brown hair and pale eyes, he possessed a reckless charm and a talent for shocking society with his outrageous pranks and notorious passion for gambling. He was also infamous for being deeply in debt.

Watching from the fringes, Talia had secretly concluded that the gentleman's wild behavior had been a result of being so closely related to Lord Ashcombe.

Unlike his younger brother, Ashcombe was more than passably handsome. In fact, he was…breathtaking.

His hair was the palest gold that shimmered like satin in candlelight, and his lean features were so perfectly carved that he appeared more like a god than a mere man. His cheekbones were high and sharply chiseled, his nose was narrow and boldly arrogant, and his lips surprisingly full. His eyes…

A delicate shiver raced through Talia.

His eyes were a pale silver rimmed with black. They could glitter with cold intelligence or flare with terrifying fury. And his lean body was hard with the muscles of a natural athlete.

He was grace and power and cunning all combined together, and while he rarely made an appearance at the various gatherings, he was all but worshipped by society.

How could Harry not feel as if he were forever in the shadow of such a man? It seemed perfectly natural he would rebel in whatever manner possible.

Aware that her father was waiting for a response, Talia cleared her throat.

"Did you?"

"Well, don't sit there gaping like a trout." The older man gave a wave of one meaty hand. "Ring for that hatchet-faced butler and tell him to bring up a bottle of that fancy French swill that cost me a bloody fortune."

Feeling a chill of premonition feather down her spine, Talia absently tugged on the bell rope near the fireplace, her gaze never leaving the self-satisfied sneer on her father's face.

"Father, what have you done?"

"I have purchased you a place in that stiff-rumped society, just as I said I would." His smile widened. "One they can't ignore."

Talia sank onto the edge of the nearest chair, a growing sense of horror flooding through her.

"Dear lord," she breathed.

"You can thank *me,* not the Almighty. He could never have performed the miracle I achieved over a boiled beefsteak and a bottle of burgundy."

She licked her lips, trying to quell the rising panic. Perhaps it was not as bad as she feared.

Please God, do not let it be as bad as I fear.

"I assume you were at your club?"

"I was." Silas grimaced. "Bastards. It is nothing less than barefaced highway robbery to demand that I pay a fee just to rub elbows with the tedious idiots who believe themselves above us honest folk."

"If you find them so repulsive, then I cannot imagine why you bothered to join the club."

"For you, you pea goose. Your mother, God rest her soul, wanted to see you respectably established and that's what I intend to do. Not that you make it an easy matter." Her father ran a dismissive gaze over the curls escaping from the neat bun at the nape of her neck, then at the dust that marred her skirt from climbing among the bookshelves. "I hired the most expensive governess and a dozen other instructors who promised to polish you for society, and what did I get for my money? A lump without the least appreciation for all I have sacrificed."

Talia flinched, unable to deny her father's accusations. He had paid an enormous sum of money in the attempt to mold her into a lady of quality. It was not his fault that she lacked the talents expected of a debutante.

She could not play the pianoforte. She could not paint

or do needlepoint. She had learned the steps to the various dances, but she couldn't seem to perform them without tripping over her own feet. And she had never been able to capture the art of flirtation.

All of these failures might have been excused had she possessed the sense to be born beautiful.

She knotted her fingers in her lap. "I do appreciate your efforts, Father, but I truly believe Mother would have wished for my happiness."

"You know nothing," her father snapped. "You are a silly chit who has spent too much time with your head stuck in a book. I warned that governess not to allow you to read that dodgy poetry. It's rotted your brains." He paused to glare at her in warning. "Thankfully, I know what is best for you."

"And what is that?"

"Marriage to Mr. Harry Richardson."

The room briefly went black, but Talia grimly battled back the urge to faint.

Swooning would do nothing to sway her father. Perhaps nothing would. But she had to try.

"No," she whispered softly. "Please, no."

Silas scowled at the tears that glittered in her eyes. "What the devil is the matter with you?"

Talia surged to her feet. "I cannot marry a stranger."

"What do you mean, a stranger? You've been introduced, haven't you?"

"Introduced, yes," Talia agreed, willing to bet her considerable fortune that Harry Richardson could not pick her out in a crowd. Certainly he had never bothered to take notice of her since their brief introduction during her first season. "But we have exchanged barely half a dozen words."

"Bah, people do not wed because of ballroom chit

chat. A man seeks a female to provide him with a pack of brats...."

"Father."

Silas snorted, his eyes narrowed. "Don't be giving me your missish airs. I know enough of the world to call a spade a spade. A man has one need of a wife, while a female needs a man who can provide her with a home and a bit of pin money to keep her happy."

The panic once again flared through Talia, and she sucked in a deep breath, pressing a hand to her thundering heart.

Dear Lord, she had to stop this madness.

"Then I fear you have made a poor choice," she managed to murmur. "From what I've heard, Mr. Richardson is a reckless gambler and a..." Her words faltered.

"Aye?" her father prompted.

She turned to pace across the carpet, unwilling to admit that she often used her position as a forgotten wallflower to eavesdrop on the latest gossip. It made it difficult to explain how she was aware that Harry Richardson was a lecher who kept a string of beautiful and extremely expensive mistresses.

"And a gentleman incapable of providing either a home or pin money for his wife," she instead pointed out.

Silas shrugged, obviously willing to overlook his potential son-in-law's numerous faults so long as he could provide the necessary pedigree for his grandsons.

"Which is why I have informed him that I will be using a portion of your dowry to purchase a suitable house in Mayfair as well as to set aside an allowance for you." He deliberately paused. "There, now you can't be saying I haven't done my best by you."

Best?

Talia abruptly turned to meet her father's belligerent

glare, anger burning through her at the ridiculous words. It was bad enough that Silas was willing to sacrifice her to satisfy his frustrated lust for social acceptance. But to hide behind the pretense that his only thought was for her was beyond the pale.

"Why would you choose a younger son? I thought you were determined that I should wed a title?"

"After three seasons of waiting for you to bring even one gentleman up to snuff, I accepted I had set my sights too high." He drained the last of his brandy, his gaze sliding from her too-pale face to study the tips of his boots. "Just like when I wished to sell that chestnut nag this past spring. A man has to bear the occasional loss when he's bartering."

She flinched. Her father was always willing to trample her pride as well as her feelings to force her to do his bidding, but he was rarely so cruel.

"I'm not a nag to be bartered."

His jaw tightened with determination. "Nay, you are a young lady who has a great deal too many sensibilities considering you're close to being put on the shelf."

"Would that be such a tragedy?" she asked softly.

"Don't be daft, Talia," he barked, lifting his gaze with an expression of impatience. "I have not acquired a fortune only to have it end up in the hands of some nitwitted nephew when I cock up my toes." Stepping from the desk, he stabbed a finger toward her. "You will do your duty and provide me with a grandson who will be the flesh of my flesh and blood of my blood. He will attend Oxford and, in time, become a member of parliament. Perhaps he will even become prime minister." A smile of smug anticipation curled his lips. "Not bad for the son of a butcher."

ROSEMARY ROGERS   19

"I am surprised that you do not demand a throne," she muttered before she could cut off the words.

"I might have if you hadn't proven to be such a disappointment." Silas turned to stomp toward the door, clearly finished with the conversation. He had made his decision and now he expected Talia to meekly obey his command. "The wedding will be held the end of June."

"Father—"

"And Talia, you will make certain that it is the social event of the season," he said, overriding her soft plea and glancing over his shoulder to offer a warning glower. "Or you will pack your bags and join your Aunt Penelope in Yorkshire."

Talia's stomach clenched at her father's stark threat.

Penelope Dobson was her father's eldest sister. A bitter spinster who devoted her life to her incessant prayers and causing others misery.

After her mother's death, Talia had spent nearly a year in her aunt's decrepit cottage, treated little better than an unpaid servant and rarely allowed to leave her cramped rooms. That might have been bearable if the horrid woman had not taken pleasure in striking Talia with a horsewhip for the tiniest infraction of her rigid rules.

Her father was well aware that she would toss herself in the Thames before she would once again be imprisoned in Yorkshire.

Heaven help her.

CHAPTER TWO

Much to Talia's astonishment, her wedding day dawned with a glorious sunrise that painted the cloudless sky in shades of pink and gold. It promised to be a perfect summer day. She had expected a gray, dismal morning that would have matched the impending sense of doom that had haunted her for weeks.

Even more astonishing, she appeared almost pretty in her ivory silk gown overlaid with silver gauze and sprinkled with diamonds along the low-cut bodice and the hem that stopped just above her ivory satin slippers. Her dark curls were carefully arranged in a complicated knot on top of her head and held in place by a large diamond tiara that matched the heavy necklace draped around her neck and shimmering earrings.

Gifts from her father, of course.

He was determined that her wedding would be the talk of the season, impervious to Talia's pleas that a lavish wedding would be in poor taste considering that all of society knew that the bridegroom had been purchased with Talia's vast dowry.

So far as Silas Dobson was concerned, discretion was for those who could not afford to toss about their money in gaudy displays of extravagance.

Reluctantly accepting that the earth was not going to open up and swallow her whole, Talia silently entered the glossy black carriage and allowed herself to be driven to the small church where the private ceremony was to take place. After the ceremony they were scheduled to return to Sloane Square for an elegant wedding breakfast with two hundred guests.

It was only when she was standing at the altar that the disaster she had been anticipating the entire day at last struck.

The rector was attired in his finest robes with a somber expression on his round face. Talia's father was standing at her side wearing his finest black jacket and silver waistcoat. And on the other side was Talia's only friend, Hannah Lansing, the daughter of a baronet who shared Talia's miserable fate as a wallflower.

But there was one notable absence.

Mr. Harry Richardson was nowhere to be found.

For nearly two hours they waited for the missing bridegroom to make his appearance, while the increasingly bleak silence that had filled the church echoed in Talia's heart.

She felt...numb. As if the humiliation of being abandoned at the altar was happening to some other unfortunate lady.

It was a sensation that refused to be dismissed even when her father had stormed from the church, swearing that the bastard would suffer for having made a fool of Silas Dobson. And when she had been forced to return to the house and announce to the two hundred avid, twittering guests that the wedding had been regrettably postponed.

Or now, as she sat in her private sitting room decorated in soothing shades of lavender and ivory.

Perched on the edge of the window seat that overlooked the rose garden filled with guests still reveling at being in attendance at the greatest scandal of the season, Talia understood she should feel something.

Anger, humiliation, heartbreak…

Anything but the awful emptiness.

Absently she watched as Hannah paced across the Persian carpet, the swish of her rose satin gown the only sound to break the thick silence. The poor girl was clearly at a loss as to how to handle the awkward situation.

"I am certain there must have been an accident," Hannah at last muttered, her round face flushed and her frizz of brown curls escaping from silver combs.

Talia shrugged, unable to stir an interest in why Harry had failed to appear at his own wedding.

"Are you?" she asked, her voice dull.

"Yes, indeed." Hannah's dark eyes held a sympathy she couldn't entirely disguise. "No doubt the carriage overturned and Mr. Richardson and his family were knocked unconscious."

"Perhaps."

"Oh." Hannah pressed a hand to her plump breasts. "Not that I would wish for the passengers to be injured."

"No. Of course not."

"But it would explain…"

"Explain why I was left at the altar?"

Hannah grimaced in embarrassment. "Yes."

An uncomfortable silence filled the sitting room, and with an effort, Talia searched her mind for a means to be rid of her companion.

It was not that she didn't appreciate Hannah's attempts to offer comfort, but for the moment she desperately wished to be alone.

Clearing her throat, she glanced toward the door. "Has my father returned?"

"Do you wish me to discover if he is here?"

"If it is no trouble."

Hannah gratefully latched onto the small task, obviously pleased to be of service.

"Not at all. And I shall bring you a tea tray."

Talia shuddered at the mere thought of food. "I am not hungry."

"Perhaps not, but you are very pale." Hannah's soft brown gaze lingered on Talia's face with obvious concern. "You should try to eat something."

"If you insist." Talia managed a smile. "You're very kind."

"Nonsense. I am your friend."

Hannah left the room and softly closed the door behind her. Talia heaved a sigh of relief. Later she would appreciate Hannah's staunch loyalty. After all, the young lady could easily have used her position in the center of the brewing scandal to elevate her status among the gossipmongers still cluttering the rose garden.

Instead she had stayed at Talia's side, anxious to provide comfort.

It was not her fault that Talia was incapable of weeping and wailing and wringing her hands like a proper bride who had just been publicly jilted.

With a frown, Talia reached to push the window open, hoping for a breeze to stir the air. The room felt…stifling. Too late, she realized that two of the unwelcome guests had strayed from the banquet tables and were currently standing just below her window.

"Good heavens, Lucille, you appear quite flustered," one of the ladies was exclaiming.

"Have you heard the latest?" the second woman demanded.

Talia froze on the point of sliding shut the window.

It was absurd. What did she care what rumors were

swirling about society? The gossip could be no more humiliating than the truth.

Still, she found herself unable to curb the destructive urge to know what was being said.

"Tell me," the first woman breathed, her voice vaguely familiar.

"Lord Eddings is said to have been with the missing bridegroom last eve at some horrid gambling establishment."

"That is hardly news. It is Harry's fondness for the cards that forced him to become engaged to Dowdy Dobson in the first place."

Talia's hands clenched in her lap. Dowdy Dobson. It was an insult she had endured since her first season.

"Yes, well, last eve he was heavily in his cups and he confessed that he never intended to wed the vulgar chit."

"Never?" There was a malicious giggle. "But why become engaged at all? Surely it was not just a cruel hoax?"

"According to Eddings, the naughty boy insisted on a portion of the dowry to purchase a suitable townhouse he discovered in Mayfair." There was a dramatic pause. "Instead he intends to take his windfall and disappear."

The first woman sucked in a scandalized breath. "Good...heavens."

"Precisely."

Talia knew she should have been equally scandalized.

Despite the fact that Harry had all but ignored her since the announcement of their engagement, he had appeared resigned to the notion of taking a wife. Certainly she'd had no warning that he intended to deceive her father into handing over a small fortune and using it to flee from London.

And from her.

"A daring scheme, but Harry cannot possibly imagine

that he can hide from a man such as Silas Dobson," the first lady said, her tone edged with revulsion at the mention of Talia's father. "The brute no doubt has a dozen cutthroats on his payroll."

"True enough."

"Besides, think of the scandal. Lord Ashcombe will have his head on a platter."

Would he?

Talia was not nearly so confident.

From the whispers that had circulated throughout society, the earl had washed his hands of his younger brother when he had announced his intention to wed the daughter of Silas Dobson.

"Not if Harry escapes to the Continent," the unknown Lucille insisted.

"In the midst of a war?"

The woman's sudden laugh drifted on the breeze. "Obviously the danger of being shot by a Napoleon is preferable to marrying Dowdy Dobson."

"And who could blame him?" her companion swiftly agreed. "Still, he cannot intend to remain exiled forever?"

"Certainly not. In a year or so the scandal will have faded and Harry will make his glorious return."

"And be welcomed as the prodigal son?" There was the sound of a fan being snapped open. "You have a very odd notion of the earl if you believe he will forgive and forget. The man terrifies me."

"He may be terrifying, but he is so wickedly handsome." Her soft sigh was filled with the feminine appreciation shared by most women. "Such a pity he has so little interest in society."

"Well, at least *polite* society."

"I would be as improper as he desires if only he would glance in my direction."

The two shared a giggle. "Shocking, my dear."

"Oh, there is Katherine. We must tell her what you have discovered."

There was a rustle of silk as the two women slowly moved away, their conversation muted but still clear enough for Talia to follow.

"Do you know, I almost have it in my heart to pity poor Miss Dobson."

Talia grimaced. Despite her words, there was a decided lack of pity in the woman's tone. In fact, it sounded remarkably akin to gloating.

"Yes," her companion purred. "One thing is for certain, she dare not show her face in society again."

"She should never have forced her way among her betters to begin with." Talia detected a sniff of smug disapproval. "Nothing good ever comes of getting above your station."

Despite the heat, Talia shivered.

She remained safely cocooned in her odd sense of detachment for the moment, but she wasn't stupid. Eventually the protective shell surrounding her heart would shatter, and she would be laid bare to the endless disgrace of a woman scorned.

She couldn't even console herself with the thought that her father would have the decency to allow her to withdraw from society until the scandal had passed.

No. Silas Dobson would never comprehend the notion of a dignified retreat. He would insist that she face her tormentors regardless of the pain and embarrassment it might cause her.

She was brooding on her bleak future when the door was opened, and Hannah crossed the threshold carrying a large silver tray.

"Here we are then," she said in the overly bright tones

that people used in a sickroom. "I have brought a small dish of poached trout in cream sauce and fresh asparagus, as well as a few strawberries."

"Yes, thank you," Talia softly interrupted, her stomach rebelling at the smell of fish.

Perhaps sensing Talia's distress, Hannah moved toward the low cherrywood table near the white marble fireplace.

"I'll just leave it here, shall I?"

Talia managed a weak smile of gratitude. "Did you locate my father?"

"No. It is..." Hannah broke off her words, gnawing on her bottom lip.

"What?"

"I was told that Mr. Dobson has not been seen since he left the church."

Talia shrugged. Her father was stubborn enough to search for Harry Richardson until hell froze over.

"I see."

Hannah cleared her throat. "No doubt he will soon be returning."

"No doubt he will," a dark, sinfully dangerous voice drawled from the open doorway. "Mr. Dobson is rather like a cockroach that scuttles about the shadows and is impossible to be rid of."

Talia went rigid with horror, as she easily recognized the voice. How could she not? As much as it might embarrass her to admit, there was no denying that she had used her position among the shadows to spy upon the Earl of Ashcombe like a lovelorn schoolgirl.

He had fascinated her with his golden beauty and predatory grace. He was like a cougar she had seen illustrated in a book. Sleek and elegantly lethal.

And of course, his aloof manner of treating society

with barely concealed disdain had pleased her battered pride. He obviously had no more regard for the frivolous fools than Talia did.

Now, however, it was not breathless excitement she felt as she turned to regard the stunningly handsome face and the frigid silver gaze.

Instead it was a chill of foreboding that trickled down her spine.

CHAPTER THREE

GABRIEL, THE SIXTH Earl of Ashcombe, made no apology for being a cynical bastard.

His cynicism had been hard earned.

After inheriting his father's title at the tender age of eighteen, he had shouldered the burdens of several vast estates, hundreds of servants and a mother who refused to leave her bed for weeks at a time.

And then there was Harry.

Six years younger than Gabriel, his brother had always been outrageously spoiled by Lady Ashcombe. Gabriel had done what he could to mitigate the damage, but he was often away at school, and when he did return to Carrick Park, his ancestral home in Devonshire, he'd been expected to devote his time to his father, learning the complex duties of being an earl.

As a result, Harry had been allowed to indulge his worst impulses. He'd been sent down from school for cheating on his exams, he'd gambled away his generous allowance, and he had fought at least two duels. All before traveling to London.

Since his arrival in the city, his wild excesses had become even worse. Gambling and whoring and risking his neck on every ludicrous dare that might be uttered in his hearing.

Gabriel had tried to impose a few limitations, only to be constantly undermined by his mother. In desperation he'd at last warned the countess that he would have her beloved Harry banished to Carrick Park if the boy didn't learn to live within his allowance.

Christ. He had suspected that Harry would plead, lie and even cheat if necessary to avoid being forced from London, but it had never occurred to him that he would become engaged to an upstart female who could only bring shame to the family.

His mother, of course, had taken to her bed with the vapors, demanding that Gabriel do something to rescue her darling son from the clutches of the evil Dobson chit. Gabriel, however, had grimly refused to interfere. If his brother wanted to toss away his future by wedding a female who was a social embarrassment—and worse, related to Silas Dobson—then Gabriel washed his hands of him.

A grim smile touched his lips as he stepped into the private salon. He should have known Harry would find a means of saving his own damned hide while leaving Gabriel to clean up his mess.

Shrouded in the icy composure he had honed over the years, he cast a quick glance around the room, absently noting a plump female with brown hair before turning his attention to the female perched on the window seat.

Miss Talia Dobson.

Gabriel was braced for the frustrated rage that clenched his heart. Any man would be ready to commit murder at having been so neatly trapped. But what he did not expect was the odd sense of recognition that stirred in the pit of his stomach. As if during his rare social appearances he had actually taken notice of Miss Dobson's silky black hair that was forever slipping from its pins and the eyes that shimmered like emeralds in the afternoon sunlight. That he'd contemplated how soft the ivory skin would feel beneath his fingertips and the precise manner her inviting curves would fit against him.

The mere thought only intensified his anger.

The female might have played the timid wallflower to perfection, but the past hour had proved that she was as greedy and conniving as her boorish father.

"Oh…" The unfamiliar female fluttered in the center of the room that was surprisingly decorated with the simple elegance that he preferred. Unlike the public rooms that had been a garish combination of lacquer furnishings covered in a crimson velvet. "My lord."

He waved a dismissive hand, not bothering to glance in her direction.

"You may leave us."

"But…"

"I am not in the habit of repeating myself."

"Yes, my lord." He heard her faint gasp swiftly followed by the sound of the plump female hurrying to obey his command.

His gaze never shifted from Miss Dobson regarding him with an expression of frozen shock. Rather like a mouse watching a hungry cat suddenly approach.

Did the wench think he would accept being blackmailed?

If so, she was in for a bitter disappointment.

By the end of this meeting, Miss Talia Dobson would regret ever having dared to force him into this unbearable situation.

As if sensing his dangerous fury, Talia leaned backward, unwittingly pressing open the window behind her.

"If you are considering a tragic leap to bring an end to this farce, I would suggest that you wait until the guests have taken their leave," he mocked, folding his arms over his blue jacket that he had matched with an ivory waistcoat and buff breeches. He had intended to spend the day at Tattersall's in the hopes of acquiring a new pair of bays to pull his carriage. A convenient means to avoid his mother's hysterical ranting at his refusal to prevent Harry's imminent wedding. When Dobson had so rudely intruded into his townhouse, he had not considered the necessity of changing into more formal attire. "This travesty of a wedding has caused quite enough gossip."

She blinked, shaking her head. Almost as if hoping that he was an unwelcome vision she could make disappear.

"Lord Ashcombe, why are you here?"

"I believe you are well aware what has brought me here."

Her brows drew together. "Is there word of your brother? Has there been an accident?"

He narrowed his gaze, not at all amused by her pretense of bewilderment.

"Please don't play coy with me, Miss Dobson. I have already spoken with your father." His lip curled in disdain. "A shockingly unpleasant experience, I confess."

Talia jerked to her feet, her hand pressed to her enticing bosom.

"My father?"

Gabriel clenched his hands at his sides. Could a woman deliberately drain her face of all color?

"I will admit you play the role of wounded martyr quite convincingly," he said in biting tones. "My jaded heart might be touched if I was not aware that you and your father are shameless charlatans who will use any tactic, no matter how vile, to acquire a place among society."

"I am aware you disapprove of your brother taking me as his wife."

His sharp burst of laughter echoed through the room. "Not nearly so much as I disapprove taking you as my own wife."

"I..." She swayed, and for a moment Gabriel thought she might sink into a predictable swoon. Then, with a visible effort, she sucked in a deep breath and squared her shoulders. "*Your* wife?" She shook her head in denial. "Is this a jest?"

"I do not jest about the next Countess of Ashcombe."

"Dear God."

"Prayers will not help you now, my dear."

"Please," she said softly. "I do not understand."

Gabriel fiercely told himself he would not be swayed by a pair of wounded emerald eyes.

Damnation. The woman was as great a fraud as her bastard of a father.

Was she not?

"Determined to act the innocent?" he rasped. "Very well. After an hour spent enduring your father's crass insults and his boorish bullying it has become obvious I have been neatly cornered. I might have admired his cunning if I weren't the poor sod being coerced into marrying a female who could only hope to force a man down the aisle."

Long moments passed, the silence broken by the tick of the ormolu clock on the mantel and the distant twitter of lingering guests.

"This makes no sense," Talia said at last. "I am to wed Harry."

"In his typical fashion, my brother considered nothing beyond his selfish need to indulge his every desire. And, when it came time to pay the piper, he disappeared, leaving me to take responsibility yet again."

"But…" She licked her dry lips. "Surely you must have some notion of where he has gone?"

"I have several notions, but it no longer matters where he is hiding, does it?" He didn't bother to disguise his bitterness.

She wrung her hands, her face tight with unexpected desperation.

"I suppose there is no means to disguise the fact he did not arrive at the church this morning, but if he could be found and compelled to return to London…"

"You would wed him after he abandoned you at the altar?" he snapped, oddly annoyed by her insistence to have Harry as her bridegroom.

Did the female have feelings for his wastrel of a brother?

Or was this just another clever ruse?

Neither explanation gave him pleasure.

"It is what my father desires," she muttered.

"Perhaps he did before he had the means to capture an earl. Now I can assure you he has no intention of settling on a mere younger son."

She appeared to struggle to follow his harsh words, a pulse fluttering at the base of her throat like a tiny bird caught in a cage.

Heat pierced through him at the thought of pressing his lips to that tender spot. Would she taste as sweet as she promised? Or was that yet another deception?

Thankfully unaware of his treacherous longings, Talia regarded him with a furrowed brow.

"I am aware that my father has acquired influence among some members of society, but how could he possibly force you to marry me?"

"Sordid blackmail."

"Blackmail?"

"He has threatened to sue my brother for breach of promise, ensuring that my family name would be kept on the front pages of every scandal rag in England for months, if not years."

She flinched at his harsh explanation, her ashen face suddenly flooded scarlet.

"Oh."

"Yes, *oh*," he said, sneering. "Your father is well aware I will pay any price, no matter how obscene, to protect my mother from becoming a public spectacle."

"I..." She gave a helpless lift of her hands. "I am sorry."

Barely aware he was moving, Gabriel prowled to stand directly before her, breathing deeply of her warm scent. Lilac, he noted absently, combined with an earthy perfume that was uniquely her own.

"Are you?" he growled.

"Yes." She shivered beneath his brooding gaze. "I know it is difficult to believe, but I am just as appalled as you by this farce of a marriage."

"I do not find it difficult, Miss Dobson, I find it impossible," he countered, assuring himself that his stab of ire was at her continued charade and not at her horror at the thought of marrying him. "I am all too familiar with women like you."

"Women like me?"

"Vulgar females who are willing to use whatever tactics necessary to acquire a husband." He deliberately lowered his gaze to take in the soft curves modestly hidden beneath her silver gown. Had she been bold enough to display her charming wares she might have had more success on the marriage mart. "Of course, their tactics are usually more—"

"Attractive?" she said, an unexpected hint of bitterness shimmering in the emerald eyes.

"Polished," he corrected.

"Forgive me for being a disappointment. It seems to be my lot in life," she said, her voice so low he could barely catch the words. "But in my defense, I never desired a husband enough to polish my tactics."

He frowned. So, there was a hint of spirit beneath that mousey demeanor.

"That would be a good deal more convincing if you had not offered my brother an embarrassing sum of money to take you as his bride, even knowing he had no desire to be tied to you."

"It was my father—" She bit off her words, giving a resigned shake of her head. "What does it matter?"

"It does not." He grasped her chin, peering deep into the eyes that held such remarkable innocence. "Even if I were idiotic enough to accept you are nothing more than a victim of your father's machinations, it does not make the thought of having you as my bride any less unpalatable."

He felt her quiver, her thick tangle of lashes lowering to hide the pain that flared through her eyes. Gabriel gritted his teeth against the sensation that was perilously close to regret tugging at his heart.

Dammit. He had nothing to regret.

"You have made your point, my lord," she said. "Why are you here?"

"Obviously we must discuss our…" He struggled to force out the word. "Wedding."

"Why?" She hunched a shoulder. "It is obvious that you and my father are capable of planning my future without bothering to consult me."

His grasp tightened on her chin. "Do not press my temper, Miss Dobson. Not today."

Her lips thinned but with a resigned obedience. She pulled free of his grasp and waved a hand toward a nearby chair.

"Will you have a seat?"

"No, this will not take long."

She gave a slow nod, her face pale but composed. "Very well."

"On Monday I will request a Special License from the Archbishop of Canterbury. He is a personal friend, so there should be no difficulty."

Her lips twisted. "Of course not."

"The ceremony will be held in the private chapel at my townhouse," he continued. "I will arrange for the rector as well as two servants to serve as witnesses."

It took her a moment to comprehend the meaning of his words. At last her eyes widened.

"My father..."

"Is not invited." His expression warned he would not compromise. "Nor will you include any other guests."

"Do you intend to keep our marriage a secret?"

"A futile wish, unfortunately, but I am determined that it will not become a ridiculous farce." He glanced toward the window where he could view the guests still taking full pleasure in the current scandal. "For the next week you will remain silent and away from society. You may also warn your father that any boasting that he has captured an earl as his son-in-law will greatly displease me."

Her expression remained suitably chastened, but she couldn't disguise the pulse that hammered at the base of her throat. Inwardly she was no doubt seething with the urge to slap him.

"And after the ceremony?"

"I beg your pardon?"

"Am I to remain hidden from society?"

"Not hidden, but you will be enjoying an extended visit to my estate in Devonshire."

She blinked at his frigid explanation. "I am to be banished to the country?"

"If my terms of marriage do not suit you, Miss Dobson, then perhaps you should devote the next few days to convincing your father to blackmail some other fool into becoming your husband."

With an abrupt movement she turned on her heel, staring down at her unwelcome guests with a haunted expression.

"If I had the ability to sway my father I would never have been forced to wed your brother and we would not be in this mess."

Gabriel stiffened in anger as another twinge of pity threatened to undermine his resolve.

Bloody hell. Was it not hideous enough to be coerced into marrying Silas Dobson's daughter without offering her the opportunity to play him a fool?

"Then it would seem that we must both resign ourselves to the inevitable," he bit out, turning on his heel to head toward the door.

"So it would seem," she whispered behind him.

Halting on the threshold, Gabriel glanced over his shoulder.

"Oh, Miss Dobson."

"Yes?"

"I would prefer you refrain from smothering yourself in such a gaudy display of jewels." He flicked a disdainful glance toward the massive diamonds draped around her neck. "The Countess of Ashcombe does not need to make an exhibit of herself."

His parting shot delivered, Gabriel continued out of the room and down the hall, wondering why the devil he didn't feel the least satisfied.

TALIA WAS IN the laundry room sorting through the linens that needed to be mended when her father's butler appeared in the doorway.

As always, she was struck by the sight of the slender, gray-haired servant attired in an immaculate black uniform. He carried himself with a regal dignity that his employer could never hope to emulate.

The irony of the situation was not lost on Silas Dobson, who found it a source of coarse amusement to taunt his prim and proper butler. Anderson, on the other hand, was careful to keep his own opinion hidden behind his facade of frigid efficiency.

Hardly surprising. For all of her father's faults, he was a shrewd businessman who was willing to pay his employees a generous salary that instilled far more loyalty than any amount of personal charm.

Impatiently brushing a stray curl from her forehead, Talia regarded the servant with a faint frown. It was rare for Anderson to enter what he considered the female domain.

"Yes?"

"The Earl of Ashcombe has called," Anderson informed her in formal tones. "Shall I say you are receiving?"

The bed sheet slipped from her nerveless fingers as she surged to her feet. Lord Ashcombe? Here?

Despite the fact the man had been her fiancé for nearly a week, Talia's mind struggled to accept that he had actually come to call upon her. No doubt because she had spent the past days assuring herself that the Earl of Ashcombe had no more intention of making her his bride than his younger brother had.

In truth, she had expected every morning to awaken to the announcement in the *London Times* that Lord Ashcombe had cancelled the absurd wedding, even if it did mean further scandal for his family.

So why was he here?

Had he come in person to cancel the wedding? And if so, why would he bother? It would surely have been easier for all of them if he had sent a message to avoid this unpleasant encounter.

Acutely aware of the silence that had abruptly filled the laundry room, Talia nervously cleared her throat.

"Did you inform him that my father is not at home?"

Anderson dipped his head. "He specifically requested to speak with you, Miss Dobson."

"I see." With no choice, Talia tugged off the apron that covered her sprigged muslin gown. "Please show him to the parlor."

The butler offered a stiff bow. "Very good."

The servant was stepping through the door when she realized that she had nearly forgotten her duties as a hostess. Odd, considering that they had been drilled into her by her numerous governesses over the years.

Of course, she rarely had an opportunity to display them, had she?

Who would desire to visit Silas Dobson or his awkward daughter? So far as London was concerned they were blights on civilized society.

"Oh, Anderson."

"Yes?"

"Could you request Mrs. Knight to prepare a tray of refreshments?"

"Certainly."

Although the butler's gaunt face remained impassive, there was a suggestion of approval in his faint nod before he disappeared down the short hall.

Talia paused long enough to wash her hands and straighten the sapphire ribbon that was threaded beneath the empire style bodice. Then, she reluctantly followed in the butler's path.

Her heart was thundering and her palms sweating by the time she reached the formal parlor, but she did not allow herself to pause as she stepped into the room heavily decorated with lacquer furnishings and crimson velvet. The slightest hesitation would allow her cowardice to take hold, and she would be fleeing to her room in terror.

The idea of flight remained a distinct possibility as her gaze landed on the tall, golden-haired man who always managed to make her heart leap with a dreadful excitement.

This morning he was attired in a pale blue jacket and silver waistcoat that was fitted to his body with flawless lines. Standing confidently near the ornately carved chimneypiece, his elegant style only emphasized the gaudy opulence of the gilded ceiling and massive Chinese vases that were arranged about the carpet.

He stiffened at her entrance, his expression unreadable as his gaze ran an unnervingly intimate inspection over her disheveled appearance.

Talia flushed, acutely aware that the lace of her gown was worn and her simple braid was better fitted for a servant than a lady of breeding. She had no notion that the steam from the laundry room had made the thin gown mold provocatively to her feminine curves. Or that the glossy curls that had strayed from her braid only emphasized her earthy beauty that would tempt any man, particularly one jaded by the frigid perfection of most society ladies.

And she most certainly would never have considered that any man could be imagining her spread on a bed of wildflowers as he ripped away her worn dress to reveal the smooth purity of her ivory skin.

She only knew that his unflinching survey made her feel hot and flustered in a manner she did not understand.

Licking her dry lips, she offered a clumsy curtsy. "My lord, I fear I was not expecting you."

Almost as if her words had jerked him from an unwelcome spell, Lord Ashcombe stepped from the fireplace, a sardonic expression hardening his handsome features.

"I surely do not need an appointment to call upon my fiancée?" he mocked.

Her flush deepened. "Of course not, but I was not prepared to receive visitors. If you do not mind waiting I will change…"

"But I do mind." He cut short her babbling. "I am a very busy man, Talia." His lips twisted in a self-derisive smile. "Besides, we both know I was not driven here by the overwhelming urge to catch a glimpse of my beautiful bride-to-be."

She flinched, wounded by his scorn despite her determination to remain immune to his taunts.

"There is no need to be insulting," she said, her voice barely more than a whisper. "If you have come to cancel the wedding, then I would appreciate you completing the task so I can return to my duties."

"What the devil?" His brows snapped together,

shocked by her words. "You believe I have come here to cancel the wedding?"

"Why else?"

Something dangerous glittered in the silver eyes. "Has your father decided to end his threat to sue my brother?"

"I…" She gave a shake of her head. "My father has not discussed his intentions with me."

"And you have no reason to suspect that he has lost his desire to acquire an earl as his son-in-law?"

She hunched a shoulder. "No."

The prickling threat that had filled the air eased as Gabriel gave an impatient wave of his hand.

"Then, barring a miracle, it would appear the marriage will take place as scheduled."

She clasped her hands together as she sought to comprehend his odd mood. What was the matter with him? He seemed almost…angered by her mention of canceling the wedding.

Or perhaps he was simply angry that she had reminded him of the distasteful event.

Yes, that was much more likely.

"May I ask why you have come?"

He gave a shake of his head before reaching for the stack of papers he had left on the mantel. With a sharp motion he shoved them into Talia's hand.

"These must be signed by your father before our wedding."

She glanced at the official-looking parchment in bewilderment. "What are they?"

"Legal documents that ensure I am protected."

"Protected?" She frowned, lifting her head to meet his unwavering gaze. "From me?"

"From you, and more important, from Silas Dobson."

"What threat could we possibly pose to the Earl of Ashcombe?"

He shrugged. "They are clearly described in the documents."

She returned her attention to the papers clutched in her fingers, a nasty sense of dread settling in the center of her heart.

Silence filled the stuffy parlor as she attempted to unravel the legal nonsense. It took only a few paragraphs to wish she had not made the effort.

Mortification made her gasp at the cold, methodical dissection of what should be a loving union.

It was not the insistence that her dowry would be under her husband's control, or that she was offered no more than a small allowance to cover her household expenses. Or even that she was to be given nothing in the event of the dissolution of their marriage. Those she had assumed from the beginning of their devil's bargain.

But to know that Lord Ashcombe had discussed her most private behavior with a complete stranger made her sick to her stomach.

"You believe I would be unfaithful?" she rasped, raising her head to stab him with an offended glare.

He shrugged with an arrogance that made her long to slap his handsome face.

"I believe your morals are questionable at best and I will not be cuckolded in my own home."

She clenched her hands. Unfeeling bastard.

"And am I allowed to insist upon a similar pledge of fidelity?"

His smile was without humor. "Of course not."

"Surely that would only be fair?"

Without warning he strolled forward, his hand cupping her chin in a touch that scalded her sensitive skin.

"I do not intend to be fair, my dear," he murmured, the silver gaze studying her pale face with an alarming intensity. "I am in the position to dictate the rules of our marriage, not you."

"And your rules include the right to parade about town with your mistresses while I am expected to remain at home and play the role of the dutiful wife?"

She shivered as the heat of his body easily penetrated her thin gown. Dear heavens, she had so often dreamed of this man holding her in his arms as they danced across a ballroom, but harmless fantasies did not prepare a poor maiden for the reality of his overpowering presence.

"What do you think?" he growled.

She lowered her lashes, unwilling to give him the satisfaction of knowing how painful she found the thought of him with another woman.

"I think you will do whatever possible to humiliate me."

He lowered his head until she felt the brush of his warm breath on her cheek.

"Would you prefer that I remain at home with you, pretending to be a devoted husband?"

She hastily pulled from his touch, as horrified as she was baffled by the quivering sensations that fluttered through her at the brush of his hard body against her.

"I would never ask the impossible," she muttered, "but it would be a pleasant change…"

"Pleasant change?" he prompted, as her too-revealing words stumbled to a halt.

She wrapped her arms around her waist, as if they could protect her.

"A pleasant change not to be the source of amusement when I enter a ballroom," she forced herself to continue.

He studied her broodingly. "Is that why you insist on becoming my bride?" he demanded. "Do you believe your position as the Countess of Ashcombe will offer you approval among society?"

She made a smothered sound of frustration. "I have told you, I have no desire to marry anyone, let alone a gentleman who holds me in such obvious contempt."

A muscle in his jaw knotted. "Do you blame me?"

Guilt pierced her at his reminder that he was as much a victim to this hideous fate as she.

Perhaps even more so.

What had he done beyond attempting to protect his family? Now he was trapped with a woman whom he would never, ever have chosen as his bride.

"No," she breathed. "No, I do not hold you to blame."

He appeared caught off guard by her soft agreement, then his face tightened with annoyance.

"You will see that your father receives the papers?"

"Not until I finish reading the terms of my imprisonment," she muttered with a grimace.

He frowned. "What did you say?"

"I think I should at least comprehend what is expected of me as a wife," she said with a shrug. "Otherwise I am likely to be even more of a disappointment."

The silver eyes narrowed. "You will not be a disappointment, my dear."

"No?" A humorless smile curved her lips. "How can you be so certain?"

"Quite simply because I will not allow it."

With his arrogant threat delivered, Lord Ashcombe performed a graceful bow and turned to leave Talia standing alone in the parlor, the hateful papers still clutched in her hand.

Lord Ashcombe's townhouse was as oppressively elegant as Talia had feared.

Built along grand lines in the midst of Grosvenor Square, it was constructed of pale stone and had seven bays with brick archways that led into an alcove hiding the double oak doors. Banks of imposing windows overlooked the street, and alighting from her carriage, Talia had the unnerving sensation that there were dozens of hidden eyes trained upon her.

Her unease was not lessened as she was led through a white tiled foyer and up a sweeping marble staircase to the back of the house where the gothic chapel was located. She might not have been raised as an aristocrat, but she had spent enough hours in the library to recognize the stunning masterpieces that lined the paneled walls of the long gallery and the impressive Italianate ceiling in the formal salon that was painted with miniature scenes from Greek mythology. Certainly she had no difficulty in recognizing the priceless Venetian chandelier that hung just outside the chapel.

It all served to remind her that Lord Ashcombe's title was not simply a mark of his social standing. It was more important an inheritance that came with overwhelming responsibility. Not only to his vast number of tenants and servants who depended upon him for employment, but to his family and the dignity of his position as the current earl.

For all her father's wealth, she was unprepared to enter a world where a person was judged on their ancestry and the purity of their bloodlines. Even if she weren't an awkward wallflower, she would never be capable of bringing pride to her role as Countess of Ashcombe.

These dark thoughts might have made Talia crumble into a ball of terror if she had not still been protected by the numbing sense of shock that had managed to survive their last humiliating encounter.

Certainly she would never have been able to walk down the short aisle to stand beside Lord Ashcombe waiting at the scrolled wooden altar.

As it was she stiffly marched past the worn pews, only briefly glancing at the vaulted ceiling and the exquisite stained-glass window before shifting her attention toward the man who was to become her husband.

Her breath caught in her throat at the sight of his golden hair shimmering in the light from the silver candelabrum and the arrogant features that were so perfectly carved they did not seem quite real. His lean body was attired in a black jacket that clung with loving care to his broad shoulders and black breeches that seemed more appropriate for a funeral than a wedding. And his silver eyes—

They held the ruthless power of a predator.

He had never appeared more godlike, and despite her layers of protection she shivered in fear.

Gabriel made no move to touch her as she halted at his side. In fact, he did not glance in her direction during the brief ceremony. Not even at its close when they signed the marriage certificate and shared a glass of sherry with the visibly curious rector and the rigidly composed butler, as well as a woman who Talia assumed must be the housekeeper.

Then, with an imperious nod of his head, Ashcombe gestured her to leave the chapel, following behind her with obvious impatience.

Distantly Talia was aware that her entire life had just been irrevocably altered. She was no longer Dowdy Dobson, the painfully shy daughter of a mere merchant. She was the Countess of Ashcombe.

Not that her elevated status offered her any comfort, she ruefully accepted.

How many years had she longed to be rid of her father's oppressive rule? Even after it had become obvious that she was never going to attract a bevy of eager suitors, she had continued to dream that a kind, decent gentleman would appear to whisk her away. A man who would treat her with dignity and respect.

But now her hopes were forever crushed.

She had just traded one tyrant for another.

As if to ensure she understood her submissive role as his bride, Gabriel cast a dismissive gaze over her demure attire. Her rose gown was threaded with silk ribbons around the high waist, and a single strand of pearls circled her neck.

"Mrs. Manning will show you to your chambers," he informed her icily, a gesture of his hand bringing forward the plump woman with gray hair tidily knotted at the back of her head. Her black gown was as spotless as the townhouse, and her movements brisk. The housekeeper, just as Talia had suspected. "Let her know if you prefer a dinner tray in your private salon or if you desire to eat in the dining room."

"You will not be joining me?" The question tumbled from her lips before she could check them.

"I have business I must attend to."

Acutely aware of the housekeeper's presence, Talia felt her face flame with color. Was it necessary to shame her by abandoning her before the ink had dried upon their license?

"What of your mother?"

"Her ladyship is visiting her sister in Kent."

Safely tucked away from her ill-bred daughter-in-law.

"I...see."

The silver eyes briefly darkened as he gazed down at her, but his expression remained aloof.

"You are welcome to explore the house and gardens, but you will not leave the grounds."

"Am I to be a prisoner here?"

"Only until tomorrow." A humorless smile curved his lips. "Do not bother to unpack, my dear. You leave for Devonshire at first light."

Without bothering to wait for her reaction, Gabriel brushed past her and disappeared down a long corridor.

An unexpected stab of misery managed to pierce the protective fog.

She felt...lost in the vast, imposing house. As if she was an imposter who was bound to be humiliated when she was at last exposed.

Which was, no doubt, exactly what her husband desired.

She was thankfully distracted as the housekeeper waved a plump hand toward the nearby stairs.

"This way, my lady."

My lady. Talia hid a sudden grimace.

She wished to heavens she was back in her father's library, forgotten among the dusty books.

Instead she forced a sad smile and headed for the stairs. "Thank you, Mrs. Manning."

She allowed herself to be escorted to a charming suite that was decorated with rich blue satin wallcovers that matched the curtains and upholstery on the rosewood furniture. Along one wall a series of windows overlooked the formal gardens and the distant mews, while through the doorway she could catch sight of an equally luxurious bedroom.

"It is not the largest apartment," Mrs. Manning said

kindly, "but I thought you might prefer a view of the garden."

"It is lovely," Talia murmured, her breath catching at the sight of the exquisite bouquets of roses that were set on the carved marble chimneypiece. Turning, she laid a hand on her companion's arm, well aware that her husband was not responsible for the considerate gesture. "I adore fresh flowers. Thank you."

The housekeeper cleared her throat, as if embarrassed by Talia's display of gratitude.

"It seemed appropriate for your wedding day."

Talia strolled toward the lovely view of the gardens, not surprised by the marble grotto that was larger than her aunt's cottage in Yorkshire.

"I am certain you are aware that I am not a typical bride. The earl has hardly made an effort to disguise the fact I am an unwanted intruder."

"It is no fault of your own, my lady," the servant surprisingly claimed. Was it possible Mrs. Manning felt a measure of sympathy for the earl's discarded bride? "His lordship is merely disappointed in Master Harry and his behavior toward you."

Talia was not so easily fooled, but she appreciated the woman's kind attempt.

"I was under the impression that Lord Ashcombe was equally averse to having me as a sister-in-law. I would have assumed that he was pleased to have me jilted." She grimaced. "At least until my father coerced him into honoring Mr. Richardson's promise."

"As to that, I suppose you shall soon enough discover that his lordship and Master Harry have a..." The housekeeper paused, searching for the appropriate word. "Thorny relationship."

Despite her earlier promise to treat her husband with

the same disdainful lack of interest as he had displayed toward her, Talia couldn't prevent her curiosity.

"I did suspect as much." She turned, watching as the servant fussed with the silver teapot set on a pier table. "It would not be easy to be a younger son."

"A good sight too easy, if you ask me," the woman muttered.

"I beg your pardon?"

For a moment the woman hesitated. Was she debating the wisdom of sharing family gossip? Then, obviously deciding that Talia was destined to discover the Ashcombe secrets, she straightened and squarely met Talia's curious gaze.

"The previous earl died near ten years ago, leaving his lordship to assume the title, as well as to take responsibility for his grieving mother and younger brother."

Ten years ago? Talia blinked in astonishment. She had no idea.

"He must have been very young."

"A week past his eighteenth birthday. Just a lad."

"Good heavens."

"Not that his lordship ever complained." Mrs. Manning heaved a sigh. "He returned from school and shouldered his father's duties while his mother remained in mourning and Master Harry began to fall into one scrape after another."

Against her will, Talia felt a stab of sympathy for the arrogant brute.

"There was no one to assist him?"

"The earl is not one to share his responsibility."

"Not particularly surprising," Talia said in dry tones.

Even before their farce of a wedding, Talia had sensed Gabriel's air of isolation.

At the time, she had imagined that his seeming need

to distance himself from others had given them something in common. Now, of course, she knew that it was merely an arrogant need to control those around him.

Just like her father.

Mrs. Manning heaved another soulful sigh. "A pity really."

"Why do you say that?"

"Perhaps if Master Harry had been expected to take his fair share of duties he would not have…"

"Left me at the altar?"

"Yes." The housekeeper's plump lips tightened with disapproval. "His lordship did attempt to put a halt to his brother's excesses, but Lady Ashcombe always was one to indulge him. If the earl refused to pay his brother's debts, then Master Harry would simply apply to his mother."

Talia frowned, rather taken back by the servant's revealing words. Even if she was now a member of the family, it was not often a servant was willing to openly gossip about her employers.

Not when the merest breach of confidence could see her tossed onto the streets.

Then Talia was struck by a sudden realization.

Mrs. Manning was clearly devoted to Gabriel. And while she might sincerely disapprove of his treatment of Talia, it was obvious she felt compelled to excuse his cruel manner.

Perhaps she was even ridiculous enough to hope that a truce between Gabriel and his new bride could eventually be called.

Talia swallowed a sigh.

A futile hope, but Talia did not have the heart to inform the kindly woman that her beloved Gabriel was a coldhearted bastard who believed his wife no better than a rank title-hunter who had used her father to bully him into marriage.

"That must have been frustrating for Lord Ashcombe," she instead agreed.

"Needless to say." The older woman frowned. "In fact, six months ago he at last…"

"Yes?"

"He insisted that her ladyship not interfere in his attempt to force Master Harry to live within his allowance."

"Ah." Talia's lips twisted. "That explains why he accepted my father's offer."

There was a brief hesitation. "Yes."

"And why Lord Ashcombe is so angry. He thought to teach his brother a lesson only to once again be the one to suffer the consequences." Talia pressed a hand to her aching heart. "It is no wonder he hates me."

Mrs. Manning shook her head. "He is angry for the moment, but once he has accepted that you are to be his countess, I am certain that all will be well."

Talia swallowed a hysterical urge to laugh. She was quite certain nothing would be well again.

"I wish I possessed your confidence," she said dryly.

Perhaps sensing Talia's disbelief, the housekeeper stepped forward, her expression troubled.

"His lordship can be a hard man in many ways," she admitted. "When he took the title at such a tender age there were any number of unscrupulous individuals who thought to take advantage of his inexperience, including several gentlemen who had claimed to be his friend. He had no choice but to learn how to protect himself and his family from those who would exploit his naïveté. But he has a good heart and he is fiercely loyal to those he considers his responsibility."

Talia shied from the temptation to pity the boy who

had lost his innocence at such a young age. The Earl of Ashcombe was determined to crush what little was left of her spirit. The moment she thought of him as anything but the enemy she would be lost.

"Responsibility?" She latched onto the revealing word. "What of those he loves?"

The housekeeper grimaced. "I fear he has become convinced that such an emotion is a weakness." She deliberately paused, meeting Talia's gaze. "A wise woman would remind him of the joy to be found in sharing his heart with another."

CHAPTER FOUR

GABRIEL HAD NO formal plans for his wedding day. Nothing beyond ensuring that his new bride understood she was an unwelcome intruder in his home.

Something he had achieved with admirable results if her stricken expression at his abrupt departure had been anything to go by.

But once away from his townhouse, he discovered himself turning his restless horse toward the outskirts of London, refusing to admit he was disturbed by the lingering image of Talia's pale face and wounded eyes.

What did it matter if she had looked like a forlorn waif as he had walked away from her? Or that she was spending her wedding day alone in an unfamiliar house? She was the one who had been willing to trade her soul for a title. She could damned well learn just how empty her victory was doomed to be.

Determined to dismiss Talia and the travesty of a wedding from his mind, he traveled through narrow lanes and at last into the countryside. He paused to watch a brilliantly painted wagon pass that was loaded with a bear locked in a cage and allowed himself to be distracted by the sight of two burly men wrestling in the middle of a village green.

But as he stopped in a small posting inn to slake his hunger with a simple meal of venison stew and freshly baked bread, his thoughts returned to his neglected bride.

Draining his third glass of ale, Gabriel shoved away from the small table set in the middle of the private parlor and strolled to glance out the window overlooking the stable yard. He barely noted the grooms bustling about their business or the stray dogs who skulked among the shadows, lured by the scents drifting from the kitchen. Instead his mind was filled with a pair of emerald green eyes and a tender, rosebud mouth.

Dammit.

He was in this godforsaken inn to forget the deceitful witch, not to be haunted by the vulnerability he had briefly glimpsed in her eyes or to dwell on the temptation of her lush curves. In a few hours she would be whisked off to Devonshire, and he could pretend that the wedding was nothing more than a horrid nightmare.

Draining yet another mug of ale, Gabriel found himself recalling precisely how the rose silk of Talia's gown had skimmed her curves and the way her string of pearls had gleamed against her ivory skin.

Was she seated in the formal dining room, savoring her new position as Countess of Ashcombe in isolated glory? Or was she hidden in her rooms, already regretting the choice to force him down the aisle?

Either image should have disgusted him.

Instead his blood heated at the thought of removing her soft rose gown and devoting the entire night to exploring the satin skin beneath.

And why should he not?

The question teased at his crumbling resolve.

It was his wedding night, was it not?

And since it was increasingly obvious that he couldn't rid her from his mind, why should he be driven from his home and forced to endure the dubious comforts of this damnable inn? He should be in his own chambers, en-

joying his own fire and fine brandy. And when he decided the time was ripe, he would enjoy the pleasure of
his warm, delectable wife.

After all, he would be a fool not to take advantage of
the one and only benefit of their unholy union.

And besides, the voice of the devil whispered in his
ear, *they weren't truly married until they consummated
their vows.*

He would not put it past the nasty Dobson to insist on
proof his daughter had been stripped of her innocence.

Watching the sun slide slowly toward the distant horizon, Gabriel at last slammed his empty mug on the table
and headed for the nearby door.

Enough, by God.

Talia would soon be on her way to Devonshire. Until
she was gone, there was no reason he should not sate the
unwelcome desire she had stirred to life.

Refusing to consider the knowledge that for the first
time since taking on the heavy duties of Earl of Ashcombe he was tossing aside his commonsense on a mere
whim, Gabriel left the posting inn and headed back to
London with fervid speed.

For all his haste, however, night had fully descended
by the time he reached the city. He cursed at the elegant
carriages that jammed the cobblestone streets and the
hordes of drunken bucks who spilled along the walk-
ways. It seemed that all of society had descended upon
Mayfair, making it all but impossible to reach his townhouse.

At last he entered the alley that led to his private mews
and, leaving his horse in the care of a uniformed groom,
Gabriel used the back entrance to enter his house and
make his way to the upper chambers.

He moved with a silence that ensured he would not

disturb the servants. He had no desire to announce his return. These few hours of madness would be forgotten the moment dawn arrived.

Reaching his rooms, he wrestled out of his clothing without the assistance of his valet and pulled on a richly embroidered robe over his already aroused body. Then, ignoring the fact he was behaving more like a common thief than the Earl of Ashcombe, he snuffed out the candles and glided through the dark corridors to the blue chambers.

Silently he pressed open Talia's door, a smile of anticipation curving his lips at the knowledge she hadn't turned the lock.

Resignation or invitation?

There was only one way to discover.

Stepping over the threshold, Gabriel closed the door and leaned against the wooden panels, covertly turning the key. At the same moment his gaze skimmed over the pretty rosewood furnishings, his heart slamming against his ribs as a slender form slowly rose from the window seat across the room.

He should have been amused. Or perhaps horrified.

At some point in the evening she had removed the wedding dress and replaced it with a ghastly monstrosity that he assumed was a nightgown. Christ. For a gentleman accustomed to females who understood a man enjoyed being teased and tantalized in the boudoir, he had never seen anything that resembled the yards and yards of white linen that swathed Talia from her chin to her toes. It looked like a funeral shroud. And to make matters worse, there were bows and ruffles and what looked to be a hundred buttons that ran from top to bottom.

How the devil any woman could sleep in the ridiculous garment defied his imagination.

But far from repulsed by her appearance, Gabriel's fingers twitched with the urge to slowly untangle her from the mounds of linen, slowly unveiling her voluptuous body.

What could be more enticing than unwrapping her as if she were a long-awaited gift?

He would lay her on the bed and explore every inch of her satin skin. First with his hands and then with his lips. And only when she was begging for release would he enter her and quench his aching need.

As if sensing his lecherous thoughts, Talia pressed a trembling hand to her throat. Her dark curls tumbled about her shoulders, and her emerald eyes were wide with shock.

Gabriel felt a momentary hesitation.

Hell, she looked so damned innocent.

"My lord," she breathed.

Annoyed by the brief stab of conscience, Gabriel grimly reminded himself that this female had been willing to become a sacrificial virgin to the highest title. He had held up his side of the bargain, it was time that she do the same.

A sardonic smile curved his lips as he pushed from the door and glided forward.

"Ah, my obedient bride."

Talia licked her lips. "What are you doing here?"

"Surely you cannot be surprised?" He circled around her stiff form, his hunter instinct fully aroused. "This is our wedding night."

"Yes, but..." She trembled as his fingers brushed her cheek. "I did not expect you."

"Obviously." He stopped directly before her and lowered his hand to tug at the ribbon of her hideous robe.

"Or did you choose this garment in the hopes it would send me fleeing in terror?"

"There is nothing wrong with my robe." Her husky voice brushed over his skin like a caress. "It is perfectly respectable."

Untangling the last of the ribbons, Gabriel turned his attention to the endless row of buttons.

"It at least answers one of my questions."

The sound of her jagged breath was the only indication that she was aware he was disrobing her, and Gabriel couldn't halt a renegade flare of admiration as she faced him with a fragile dignity.

"What question?"

His heart missed a beat as his fingers brushed the soft mound of her breast.

"Whether or not you are a virgin," he said, his voice oddly thick. "No female of experience would wear a garment that resembles a funeral shroud rather than a gown that enhances her natural…assets."

Her eyes flashed. "If you have come here to insult me…"

"You know why I am here."

Her brief display of temper faltered at his stark words. He felt her quiver beneath his hands, her pulse fluttering at the base of her throat.

"But you do not want me as your wife," she said huskily.

He swallowed his sharp laugh. She truly was naïve if she thought this night had anything to do with wanting her as a wife.

A biting need raced through him, and with a sharp motion he grasped the fabric of her robe and yanked it apart. He heard her gasp of shock as the remaining buttons scattered in a shower of impatience.

"And yet, here you are in my home, the Countess of Ashcombe," he rasped, his arousal heavy with desire as he parted the torn fabric to at last reveal the soft ivory curves.

Bloody hell. She was as perfect as he had imagined.

He tugged off the offensive robe, his hands lightly skimming over her narrow shoulders and down the delicate line of her collarbone. His blood sizzled as his gaze slid over the breasts that were full and tipped with nipples the color of ripe berries begging for his lips. Slowly, his attention lowered to her narrow waist that flared to feminine hips. Then, as his gaze reached the dark thatch of hair cradled between her legs, his fragile control snapped.

With a growl, he scooped her off her feet and headed across the room to the shadowed bedroom beyond.

"My lord," she breathed, her eyes wide with a combination of fear and an excitement she could not entirely disguise. "Why are you doing this?"

Gabriel felt a flare of triumph in the knowledge he was not alone in this ruthless awareness. Lowering his head, he claimed her mouth in a possessive kiss.

"I have no choice," he muttered against her lips.

She shivered beneath his touch, her hands grasping the lapels of his robe. "Have you been drinking?"

"Dutch courage."

She hissed, as if he'd slapped her. "If I am so repulsive that you need to become drunk to approach me, then why are you doing this?"

Repulsive? He was damn well enchanted.

His gut twisted as he lowered her on the bed. He was arrested by the sight of Talia stretched across the satin cover. In the silvery moonlight she appeared a creature of mist and magic. An elusive wood sprite that had strayed into London and might disappear in a puff of smoke.

He growled low in his throat, his savage hunger nearly overwhelming.

Not that he was about to admit as much to the woman. The thought of her holding power over him was enough to make his teeth clench.

"Because I will not be accused of not having consummated this absurd union," he growled. "No doubt Silas Dobson intends to arrive on my doorstep in the morning demanding to be shown proof of your deflowering."

She frowned in wary confusion. "Proof? I..." A sudden heat flooded her cheeks as she realized he was speaking of the ancient tradition of checking the marriage sheets for the spilled blood of her virginity. "Oh."

The bewildered innocence was all that was needed to complete her sensual spell, and with a muttered curse, Gabriel shrugged out of his robe and joined Talia on the bed, wrapping an arm around her shivering body before she could escape.

"Maidenly blushes," he whispered, his fingers stroking over her cheek. "Astonishing."

Her dark curls spread across the blue and ivory cover like a spill of ebony silk, her eyes shimmering like emeralds in the moonlight.

"I assure you that my father is satisfied we are wed," she said in a breathless rush, her hands fluttering to land against his chest. "He will not be demanding proof."

Gabriel buried his face in the curve of her neck, breathing deeply of her sweet scent. She smelled of soap and starch and purity.

A wondrously erotic combination.

"You expect me to take your word?" he demanded. "The word of a Dobson?"

"I am no longer a Dobson."

He jerked back, his commonsense telling him that he should be infuriated by her words, not…

Satisfied.

Crushing the disturbing sensation, Gabriel regarded his wife with a brooding intensity. His fingers outlined the trembling softness of her lips.

"It requires more than a signature on a piece of paper to become an Ashcombe."

Her breath rasped through the room. "My lord."

"Gabriel."

She blinked in confusion. "I beg your pardon?"

"You will call me Gabriel, not my lord," he commanded, uncertain why he was determined to hear his name on her lips.

"Gabriel," she murmured, her eyes wide. "I am not certain this is a sound notion."

With a groan he lowered his head to stroke his lips over her wide brow before trailing down the line of her delicate nose.

"Neither am I, but I will admit it grows more appealing by the moment."

She quivered. "Dear heavens."

"Talia." He used his thumb to part her lips, allowing himself a too-brief taste of her innocence. "An unusual name. Surely not your father's choice?"

Her nails dug into the bare skin of his chest but not in protest. Gabriel could feel the race of her heart and catch the scent of her arousal.

She might be inexperienced, but her body was already softening against him in silent invitation.

"I was named for my mother's mother," she said, the words distracted as his lips trailed over her cheek, pausing to nuzzle the corner of her mouth.

"A gypsy?"

She tensed at the question. "Does it matter?"

"Not at the moment." He allowed his hands to explore the smooth curve of her neck before at last moving to cup the glorious weight of one berry-tipped breast. He moaned deep in his throat. Hell, he was on the point of explosion from the mere feel of her. "You are so lush and yet so delicate. Like a Dresden figurine."

"I am…" Her words trailed away as he gently rolled the tip of her nipple between his fingers.

"Yes?" he prompted, kissing a path down her throat.

"I am uncertain what to do," she at last managed to confess.

Gabriel swallowed a curse. Trust Silas Dobson to send his daughter off to her wedding bed without giving her a hint what to expect.

Bastard.

"Leave matters to me," he growled against her silken skin, his hand skimming down her back to clutch the curve of her hip. "I am exactly certain what to do."

Her lips parted, but Gabriel was beyond coherent conversation.

Besides, he had no words to assuage her virginal unease. The only means to allay her fears was to demonstrate the marriage bed could offer more than sacrifice.

Dismissing the taunting voice that assured him his impatience had nothing to do with comforting his bride, and everything to do with the desire that had escalated to an unrelenting need, Gabriel claimed her mouth in a kiss that demanded utter surrender.

She briefly stiffened, floundering beneath his raw hunger. Hardly surprising, he instantly chastised himself. Hadn't he just told himself that Talia was a timid virgin in need of coaxing? Christ, in another moment he would be tumbling her like a two-bit whore.

The damned female might have trapped him into marriage, but, by God, he intended to have her begging for release before the night was over.

With grim determination he gentled his touch, his hand brushing down her naked thigh while his mouth teased at her lips until they slowly parted. Murmuring soft encouragement, he dipped his tongue into the moist heat of her mouth.

She again stiffened, and he swallowed a hiss of frustration. Surely she could not be frightened of a kiss?

Then, just when he was trying to convince himself to pull back, she gave a tiny sigh of pleasure, and her arms lifted to wrap around his neck.

Pure male satisfaction surged through him at her unspoken surrender.

He hadn't been deceiving himself. She wanted him.

Continuing to stroke his fingers in a lazy pattern along her thigh, Gabriel nipped at her full lower lip before blazing a path of kisses down her throat and over the curve of her breasts. She tasted of heat and sunshine that reminded him of lazy summer days at his childhood home in Devonshire.

Days before the heavy duties of his title had stolen his untroubled existence.

Her fingers clutched at his hair, her body arching with an unspoken plea.

His cock twitched in anticipation at the feel of her soft curves brushing against him. For all her inexperience she was a natural-born siren.

And for tonight she was his.

Sweeping his mouth downward, Gabriel captured the tip of her hardened nipple between his lips, savoring the sound of her soft gasps. The sweetest music.

"My lord," she rasped. "Gabriel."

"Shh," he whispered, subtly pressing a hand between her thighs. "Trust me."

She shivered, her hands shifting to run an impatient path down his back.

"You have given me little reason to trust…" Her breath caught as his finger dipped through the moist cleft between her legs. "Oh."

He laughed softly, circling the hard tip of her nipple with his tongue.

"Your first lesson as a wife is to accept your husband always knows best."

She muttered something beneath her breath at his smug words, but she was swift to cry out in wonderment as his finger slid with gentle insistence into her welcoming body. Gabriel pulled back to watch her delicate face flush with sensual heat, her thick tangle of lashes lowering and her lips parting as he stroked his finger in a slow, tantalizing tempo.

Christ, he had never seen anything so beautiful.

It was absurd.

He had been pleasured by the most talented courtesans in all of England. Hell, his last mistress had caused riots when she had first appeared on the stage.

So why then was this inexperienced wallflower making him tremble with savage hunger?

Refusing to contemplate the dangerous question, Gabriel instead reclaimed her lips in a kiss of fierce anticipation. A flare of triumph raced through him as she willingly met the thrust of his tongue with her own, her nails biting into his lower back as her body sought relief from her swelling tension.

He had done what he could to ease her maidenly fears. Now he was through with waiting. If he didn't have her soon, he was fairly certain he would go mad.

With one smooth motion he shifted on top of her body, settling between her legs with a groan of sheer relief. She gave a small gasp, but finding the tiny nub that made her squirm in bliss, Gabriel continued to pleasure her as he situated his cock into the opening of her body and entered her with one slow thrust.

A rasping moan tore from his throat. She was molten heat and exquisite tightness.

A perfect combination.

His heart forgot to beat as he drank deeply of the nectar of her mouth, waiting as Talia adjusted to his intimate invasion. Only when her muscles eased and he felt her hands running an impatient path up his back did he pull back his hips and plunge back into her slick warmth.

Brushing his lips down her cheek, Gabriel nipped at the lobe of her ear, relishing the crisp clean scent of her skin. Until this moment he did not realize how he disliked a female who drenched herself in perfume. Having his senses filled with the delectable woman in his arms, and not a choking cloud of flowers, only intensified his pleasure.

Lost in the urgency of his passion, he struggled to concentrate on the sounds of her soft moans and the rasp of her breath. He would not allow his searing need to overcome his determination for Talia to find her own release.

Burying his face in the curve of her neck, he kept his pace slow and steady, his hands shifting beneath her hips to angle them upward. Her nails bit into his flesh, her body arching as she neared her climax.

"Gabriel," she groaned. "I cannot…"

"Yes, you can," he coaxed in thick tones. "I will give you what you need."

Scattering kisses down her collarbone, he lowered his

head to suckle at the tip of her nipple, increasing his pace and urging her legs to wrap around his hips.

Gabriel heard Talia cry out in startled joy, the pulse of her release clutching at his cock. He clenched his teeth, his hips surging until he was buried deep inside her as a shattering climax slammed through him.

Time stopped as he rode out the storm of sensations that assaulted him. Then, with a low groan, he wrapped his arms around her quivering body and rolled to the side, pressing her against his chest.

A silence filled the room, broken only by their heavy breathing as they both struggled to recover from the explosive coupling.

It is time to walk away, a voice whispered in the back of his mind.

He had bedded his wife, ensuring their marriage was consummated and sating the unfathomable desire that had plagued him. Why would he linger?

But even as the thought of leaving passed through his mind, he dismissed it.

The uncomfortable truth was that he was not *sated.*

Despite the shockingly intense orgasm, he could already feel himself growing hard, and when she wiggled against him in an attempt to untangle herself from his arms, he instinctively tightened his grasp and growled in her ear.

"Do not move."

"My lord…Gabriel…" She tilted back her head, her eyes revealing her stunned bemusement at what had just occurred between them. "Surely we should discuss…"

"No discussion," he interrupted. Damnation, the last thing he desired was to discuss the cruel irony that the female who had so recently trapped him into marriage was capable of undermining ten years of self-discipline.

He wanted to drown in the sweet temptation of her body for the rest of the night and then forget this temporary bout of madness as if it had never happened. "There is only this…" He shoved his fingers into her satin hair, crushing her lips in a devouring kiss. "And this…" He slid his mouth down the line of her jaw and then along the curve of her neck. She whispered a soft moan, her eyes fluttering shut as he continued his downward exploration, using his teeth and tongue to rouse her untutored passion. "And this…" His lips closed around the tip of her nipple and all coherent thought ended.

CHAPTER FIVE

Carrick Park Estate in Devonshire, England

TALIA HAD NOT KNOWN what to expect when she'd left London to travel to Gabriel's remote estate in Devonshire.

In truth, she had barely given thought to her destination as the carriage had rattled over the cobblestones in the early-morning light. How could she when her thoughts were consumed with Gabriel and the hours she had spent in his arms?

It had all been so...extraordinary.

From the moment he had burst into her private chambers like a madman until he had disappeared without so much as a word just before dawn, it had all seemed like a strange dream that she might wake from at any moment.

He had been so coldly dismissive after the brief ceremony, she had never dreamed he would return with the expectation of sharing a marriage bed. And certainly she could never have anticipated his passion that had swept her away on a tidal wave of pleasure.

So why had he come to her?

Had it truly been out of fear that her father would demand proof of their consummation like some medieval villain? It seemed ridiculous. And besides, his seduction had not felt like a duty.

Even now, a month after arriving at her new home,

she still lay in bed at night, recalling each branding kiss and every skillful touch.

Not that his reasons truly mattered, she told herself for the hundredth time, giving a shake of her head as she strolled along the narrow dirt path that led from the thatched cottage to Carrick Park.

For all the hours he had devoted to pleasuring her into mindless abandon, he had been swift enough to walk away from her bed, not even bothering to make an appearance as she was loaded into the carriage and taken from his home.

His message was painfully clear.

She was still his frumpy, ill-bred, unwanted wife who he intended to bury in the country.

The knowledge might very well have been the last blow needed to crush what remained of her fragile spirit, but her arrival in Devonshire had proven to be more a blessing than a punishment.

From the moment she'd set foot at Carrick Park her heart had lightened, and her fear of the future had mysteriously eased.

Perhaps it was her first sight of the grand manor house.

Constructed near the limestone cliff overlooking the English Channel, the house had once been a monastery of pale brown stone. The newer additions blended nicely with the original structure with rows of Elizabethan windows and slanted roofs. Ivy climbed along the front bays, softening the angular lines and allowing the structure to meld with the untamed parkland that surrounded the estate. The same ivy could be found on the rambling stables and outbuildings that were spread beyond the gardens.

It was not as large or as tidily manicured as some country estates, but Talia found herself immediately drawn to the rugged, natural beauty.

It felt like…home.

Far more so than her father's gaudy house in Sloane Square. Or Gabriel's frigidly elegant townhouse.

But, more likely it was the unexpected realization that so far away from the incessant criticism of her father and the smoldering fury of her husband, she could breathe freely. She was finally given the opportunity to make decisions for herself, which filled her with a strength she never dreamed possible.

Over the past month she'd slowly managed to earn the trust of the wary servants and tenants who had clearly been leery of meeting the latest Countess of Ashcombe.

They did not care that she was the daughter of Silas Dobson or that her ancestors could not be traced back to the Garden of Eden. For them, all that mattered was her genuine interest in their lives and her willingness to do what was within her power to ease their troubles.

Passing by the small redbrick church with a slate roof and an enclosed porch that framed the entrance, Talia came to a halt at the sight of a slender, dark-haired gentleman. He stepped through the high hedge that separated the church from the vicarage.

A smile curved her lips. Vicar Jack Gerard did not resemble any man of God that Talia had ever met.

He was very young, not more than a few years older than Talia, and so exquisitely handsome that there was little wonder the pews were overflowing on Sunday morning. What woman could resist the perfect male features and velvet brown eyes that held a hint of devilish humor? And while he was careful to wear simple black coats and breeches with a modestly tied cravat, he possessed such an innate sense of style and grace that he made even the finest noblemen appear more like preening peacocks than gentlemen of fashion.

Of course, he would not cast Gabriel in the shade, a treacherous voice whispered in the back of her mind. For all his faults, her breathtakingly handsome husband possessed a dominating presence that commanded attention no matter where he might be.

It was a voice that Talia was swift to dismiss.

Gabriel clearly desired to pretend she did not exist. For her own peace of mind it would be wise for her to do the same.

Grimly turning her thoughts away from Gabriel, Talia studiously concentrated on the approaching vicar. Which allowed her to catch sight of his subtle change of expression when he realized he was not alone.

Was that…dismay?

There seemed no other word to describe his response.

But his momentary reaction was swiftly hidden behind a brilliant smile of welcome, and Talia assured herself that it was nothing more than a trick of the growing dusk.

As if to prove her point, the vicar took her hand and lifted her fingers to his lips, his kiss lingering just a hint too long.

"Good evening, my lady," he murmured, his low voice edged by an elusive accent.

It was rumored that his parents had fled the French revolution to settle in England, although Talia was painfully aware that gossip rarely held any truth. And so far as Talia was concerned his past did not matter.

From their first meeting he had treated her with a beguiling charm that she had greedily encouraged, allowing his flirtations to ease the wounds of Gabriel's sharp rejection.

Not to mention the icy lack of welcome from her more

aristocratic neighbors who had yet to issue an invitation to their exclusive gatherings.

She already considered him a dear friend.

"Vicar."

Lifting his head, he slowly inspected her apple-green walking dress edged with silver lace along the scooped bodice. A matching ribbon encircled her waist. Her bonnet was a jaunty yellow that had been dyed to match her half boots that peeked from beneath the hem of her gown.

Until arriving in Devonshire she would never have chosen a dress in such a vivid color, and certainly she would never have dared to reveal so much of her full bosom.

But with the vicar's gentle encouragement she had sought out the local dressmaker and ordered a complete new wardrobe. She had even started to wear her hair in a casual style that allowed several glossy strands to frame her face.

Now, the sight of the appreciation simmering in his eyes made each tedious hour spent being poked, prodded and measured worthwhile.

"I must say you are appearing particularly fine today," he said, continuing to hold her fingers in a gentle grip. "That gown suits you."

She shyly preened beneath the warmth of his gaze. "Do you think so?"

"I do. The shade brings out the emerald of your eyes." A wicked smile tugged at his lips. "May I indulge my vanity and tell myself that I can take a small measure of credit for your lovely ensemble?"

She chuckled. "You can take full credit, sir."

"Please, I really must insist that you call me Jack," he interrupted, giving her fingers a squeeze. "We are friends, are we not?"

She paused, a warning that her husband would not be pleased to discover his new bride speaking so intimately with another man. Even so, she tilted her chin in an unconscious gesture of pride.

Gabriel had given up his right to dictate her behavior when he had driven her from London.

"Jack," she breathed.

Satisfaction flared through his dark eyes. "Much better. Now, what were you saying?"

"I was admitting that I shall unfortunately never develop a talent for fashion. Which is why I am so thankful for your advice."

"A foolish business." He shrugged. "You have far more important talents."

"You are very kind."

"No, my dear, I speak with all sincerity," he assured her. "Your presence at Carrick Park has enriched the entire neighborhood."

"Jack…"

"Only this morning Mrs. Jordan was singing your praises for having so quickly acquired a suitable doctor." He overrode her embarrassed protest. "And Mr. Stone is convinced you are an angel for the meals you have provided for his family. And, of course, your plans for the new school have the entire countryside twittering with excitement."

With a laugh, Talia pressed her hands to her heated cheeks. Her entire life had been filled with criticism and the knowledge she was a disappointment to those who were supposed to love her.

She had no notion how to accept such admiration.

"Enough."

He took a step closer, releasing her hand so he could cup her chin in his palm.

"I simply wish you to know that your servants and tenants consider you to be one of the finest Countesses of Ashcombe in memory."

Genuine warmth filled her heart. The realization that she had the power to improve the lives of those who depended upon her had given a sense of purpose to her days. And more than that, it had offered a newfound confidence in herself.

Something she had never expected.

"It is pleasant to think that I am not an utter failure in my position."

His brows snapped into a frown. "Failure? Why would you say such a thing?"

"How can I not? As you are well aware, I have yet to be welcomed by my more noble neighbors. They are obviously not so pleased by my presence."

He studied her pale face. "Does that trouble you?"

She grimaced. "The thought of bringing shame to my husband's family troubles me."

Without warning Jack grasped her upper arms in a firm grip, his dark eyes blazing.

"Do not," he growled.

"Vicar…Jack."

"Forgive me, but I cannot allow you to talk such nonsense," he barked, not sounding the least apologetic.

Talia regarded him with a measure of surprise, taken off guard by the sudden vehemence in his tone.

"It is not nonsense to be concerned for my position as the Countess of Ashcombe."

"Surely your position means tending to those in need, which you have done with admirably, rather than wasting your time and resources on impressing those unworthy of your concern?"

Talia frowned, suddenly suspicious that Jack Gerard

hid dark depths behind his smooth charm. But she soon shrugged aside her brief moment of disquiet.

What was the matter with her? Jack was a handsome, excessively pleasant gentleman whom she counted a friend.

"I am not so certain my husband would agree with you," she said, returning her attention to their conversation.

"Then he is a fool."

"Jack," she gently chastised.

"My lady...Talia..." He paused, as if searching for the proper words. "I have only been here a short while, but the people tend to confide in me."

She laughed. It was rare that the church was not filled with eager females seeking a word alone with the handsome vicar.

"Yes, you do have a skill for earning the trust of others, especially if they happen to be the fairer sex," she teased.

His expression never eased. "Then you will believe me when I tell you that the locals had few kind words for the previous countess."

Her breath caught at his blunt confession. The sensible part of her knew she should gently turn the conversation in another direction. It was hardly polite to gossip about her mother-in-law with the local vicar. But a larger part of her was consumed with curiosity about the woman who had yet to acknowledge Talia as a member of her family.

"Why?"

"She is like far too many in society." His voice was edged with disgust. "She cares for nothing beyond her own comforts and her social standing. In less than a month you have managed to spend more time among the tenants than she has in the past thirty years. Certainly she has never taken the effort to learn their names or to discover their needs." He grimaced. "To be honest, I doubt she is even aware of them as more than additions to the barnyard animals."

Talia frowned. She had always thought the Countess of Ashcombe a conceited, overly proud woman when she had seen her in London, but it was disturbing to think she had no concern for the poor and vulnerable.

"I do not believe she could be entirely oblivious to those who depend upon her."

"No?" Jack pointed across the distant fields that provided a perfect view of Carrick Park. The sight was magnificent as the last rays of sunlight brushed the windows in pinks and violets, and the water cascading in the marble fountains sparkled like jewels. "Last winter she insisted that old Lucas be forced from the cottage that had been in his family for two hundred years because it spoiled her view of the church."

"Surely she did not realize…"

"The poor man begged on his knees to have his home spared, but he was tossed like so much rubbish into his daughter's care and his cottage was destroyed." He deliberately held her troubled gaze. "He died less than a fortnight later."

"I cannot accept she would be so cruel."

"It was more indifference than cruelty," he mused. "For aristocrats such as the countess, those without blue blood running through their veins are simply unworthy of their consideration."

She tugged from his lingering grip, licking her dry lips. She barely noticed that his dark gaze seemed fascinated by the small gesture.

"And what of my…" She still struggled with what to

call the man who had taken her as his bride, then stolen her innocence before shipping her off to the country. "Of the earl? The servants and tenants speak of him with great respect."

"As if they have a choice," he said dryly.

A sickness settled in the pit of her stomach. She could not explain why, but the thought of Gabriel as yet another worthless aristocrat living off the sweat of his tenants without offering them the assistance and appreciation they deserved made her heart ache with disappointment.

"Oh."

There was a brief hesitation, then without warning Jack heaved a harsh sigh.

"Forgive me, Talia. I am not being entirely fair."

She blinked in confusion. "I don't understand."

"From all I have heard your husband is a decent landlord who has done much to introduce the latest farming techniques to his tenants."

"But?" she prompted, sensing he was not revealing the full truth.

"I beg your pardon?"

"What are you not telling me?"

He gave a lift of his hands. "The earl tends to be an intimidating figure to most in the neighborhood. Few would dare approach him without invitation. Which means many have continued to suffer."

A portion of Talia's distress faded upon hearing Gabriel was merely aloof and not a callous brute. Surely with a bit of encouragement he could earn the trust of those in his care? Not that she intended to be the unfortunate individual making the suggestion, she acknowledged with a tiny shiver.

Nor would her companion. Not if his barely hidden sneer was any indication.

"You disapprove of my husband?" she demanded, wondering if the two men had ever crossed paths.

"I have little use for those who treat their power as a God-given right rather than a duty to others."

She narrowed her gaze at the intensity in his voice. "Are you a Jacobin?"

His charming smile returned in the blink of an eye. "I am a humble vicar who is devoted to his flock, not a revolutionary."

"Hmm." She tilted her head to the side. "Why do I sense there is much you keep hidden?"

Before she could realize his intent, Jack had reached to tug at a stray curl that rested against her cheek.

"I will admit that my estimation of the earl has risen considerably since your arrival at Carrick Park," he murmured, his dark gaze regarding her with blatant admiration. "I would never have suspected that he possessed the good sense to wed a lady of such value, rather than a typical debutante."

Talia blushed, vividly aware of the intimate touch of his hand against her cheek.

"You must know that I was not the bride of his choice," she said in flustered tones.

His thumb brushed her lower lip. "Are you so certain?"

"Of course." She regarded him in bewildered shock. He could not possibly mean that Gabriel was anything but horrified to be married to Silas Dobson's daughter. "He barely noted my existence until my father bullied him into marrying me."

"It is my experience that gentlemen such as Lord Ashcombe rarely allow themselves to be bullied into any situation, let alone into marriage."

She wrinkled her nose. "You have not yet had the untoward pleasure of meeting my father."

"I do not doubt he is a man of considerable…"

"Pigheaded stubbornness combined with a brute lack of morals?" she offered wryly.

"Whatever his power, he could never truly take on a wealthy peer of the realm," he smoothly continued. "He might have given Lord Ashcombe an excuse to take you as his bride, but the earl would never have wed you unless that was what he desired to do."

Talia's heart gave a strange leap of excitement before she hastily quelled the ridiculous reaction.

Jack clearly underestimated Gabriel's pride. He would have wed a savage from the colonies to avoid a nasty scandal. Now he hated her for the sacrifice he had been forced to make. And she did not blame him.

"You are quite mistaken."

His lips twisted. "Perhaps."

Giving a shake of her head, Talia parted her lips to continue her protests only to be distracted by the heavy tread of footsteps approaching from the cemetery behind the church.

With a frown she turned to watch two men dressed in rough woolen sailor coats and loose trousers come to an abrupt halt as they noticed her.

A strange chill inched down her spine at the sight of their heavily muscled bodies and their weathered faces that spoke of endless hours toiling in the sun. Still, it was not their rough appearances that made her consider the need to flee for safety, it was instead the unmistakable air of violence that hovered about them.

She took an instinctive step backward, not sure what to expect. Then surprisingly, she felt Jack move to stand protectively at her back, his hand circling her waist.

One of the two men glanced toward the vicar, and Talia tensed, terrified that they were about to be attacked.

Instead there was a taut moment of silence before they gave a respectful dip of their heads and turned to make their way into the church.

Talia gave a baffled shake of her head, not entirely certain what had just happened.

"Good heavens." She turned to meet Jack's wary gaze. "Who were those gentlemen?"

"No one who need concern you," he assured her.

Talia was far from comforted. "Are you certain? They look to be ruffians."

Jack shrugged. "Ruffians have as much need of spiritual guidance as any other. Even more so."

"But…"

"It grows late, Talia." Without warning, Jack leaned down to brush a soft kiss over her cheek. "Return to your home."

She ignored his forward manner, sensing that he was deliberately attempting to be rid of her.

Why?

Did he fear the men might still be a danger to her? Or was there some other reason for his desire to send her on her way?

"You do not wish me to call for the constable?"

"No." He gave her a small push down the narrow lane. "I will be fine. I will see you tomorrow."

Talia obediently headed up the pathway, waiting until she turned the sweeping corner that hid her from Jack's view before she darted into the nearby copse of trees and started to creep back toward the church.

There was something distinctly suspicious about the strangers. And while she admired Jack for his willingness to offer sanctuary to all who came to his church, she could not bear the thought that his kindness would leave him vulnerable to harm.

Or death.

Holding up her skirts to avoid becoming tangled in the thick undergrowth, Talia weaved her way through the trees, ignoring the odd sense of premonition that clutched at her heart. Who would not be unnerved at creeping through the gathering gloom?

Still, for the first time since she'd left London, she was conscious of the scurry of unseen animals among the bushes and the distant cry of an owl that filled the silence. And even more disturbing was the awareness of just how alone she was.

If something happened, who would hear her screams?

She gave a shake of her head. She would not allow Jack to be injured because she was frightened of shadows.

At last reaching the edge of the trees, Talia squared her shoulders and darted across the open yard to the back of the church. She pressed her back against the bricks, her heart lodged in her throat.

From inside the building she could hear the sound of voices, and before she lost her courage, she forced herself to inch toward the open window, sending up a silent prayer that no one would happen by.

How the devil would she explain the Countess of Ashcombe creeping through the dark and eavesdropping upon the local vicar?

She stopped at the edge of the window and tilted her head to peer into the room, easily recognizing the sacristy. How...odd. Why would the vicar take two strange men into a storage room for the church's most sacred possessions?

The most reasonable explanation would be that the men had forced Jack to the room in the hopes of discovering something of value. The church might be small, but there were several items made of silver as well as a few rare artifacts that a collector would pay a goodly sum to acquire. Which meant she should be dashing toward the nearest cottage to seek assistance.

But as her gaze shifted toward the three men who filled the room, she hesitated.

Jack did not look as if he were being held against his will. In fact, he appeared to be in charge of his companions as one of the men reached beneath his coat to toss a leather satchel at the vicar.

Jack eagerly tugged open the satchel and pulled out a stack of papers.

"These are the most recent maps?" he demanded, unfolding one of the papers and studying it with deep concentration.

The larger of the two men gave a grunt of agreement. "They were copied directly by a clerk at the Home Office."

Talia stilled. Dear lord. She might know very little of politics, but she was well aware that the Home Office was headquarters to the various leaders who plotted war against Napoleon.

Jack was nodding, his attention still on the map. "And this clerk is certain no one suspects that he duplicated them?"

"Aye." The stranger made a sound of annoyance. "Cost me a bloody fortune."

An icy sense of disbelief spread through Talia as she watched Jack shrug, vaguely recognizing this was not the kindly vicar she thought she knew.

The glimpse of ruthless authority she had so readily dismissed earlier was in full evidence as he carefully spread the papers across the narrow table in the center of the room. And his French accent was far more pronounced.

It was as if he had been playing in a masquerade, and now the true man beneath the disguise was exposed.

"Do not fear, you will be well rewarded once I can be certain these are genuine," Jack muttered.

The smaller stranger leaned over the table with a frown on his ruddy face.

"That ain't France, is it?"

"Very astute, Monsieur Henderson," Jack drawled, his tone mocking. "It happens to be Portugal."

"And why would the Frenchies be wanting a map of Portugal?"

A smile of satisfaction curved Jack's lips. "Because this tells us precisely where and when Sir Arthur Wellesley intends to land his army. And the battle strategy that he hopes to employ." He stroked a slender finger over the map. "Most informative."

Traitor...

The word whispered through her mind as Talia pressed a hand to her mouth. It was all so unbelievable. More like a plot from one of the thrilling novels she kept hidden in the privacy of her bedchamber than reality.

Who could ever suspect that the charming vicar in a remote village in Devonshire was attempting to destroy the British Empire?

The larger of the men folded his arms over his chest as he glared at the various maps spread across the table.

"Looks to me like a bumbling mess, but if you are satisfied, then so be it."

"I am." Jack offered a dip of his head. "And the emperor thanks you for your service."

The man snorted. "I ain't wantin' the thanks of bloody Napoleon. I want me money, nothing else."

"Of course, I..."

Jack came to an abrupt halt, then without warning his

head turned toward the window, almost as if he sensed Talia's presence. It was too late for Talia to duck away, and their shocked gazes locked before something that might have been regret flashed through his dark eyes.

"Mon Dieu," he breathed, shoving away from the table and heading toward the side door.

Talia gave a small shriek as she gathered her skirts and darted toward the nearby path. There was no thought to where she was headed, only a terrified need to escape.

Of course, it was a futile effort.

Even if she were not hampered by her layers of skirts and petticoats, she was no match for an athletic gentleman in his prime.

She was still in the churchyard when she felt strong arms circling her waist and hauling her squirming body against a hard chest. Then Jack leaned down his head to whisper directly in her ear.

"I truly wish you had heeded my advice, *ma petite.*"

CHAPTER SIX

THE GENTLEMEN'S CLUB on St. James's Street was filled with solid English furnishings and well-worn carpets that extended from the dining room to the discreet gaming rooms. On the white plaster walls were a series of oil paintings dedicated to the aristocracy's love for hunting, and overhead a heavy chandelier glistened in the early sunlight. The entire building smelled of mahogany, leather and tobacco smoke.

A familiar combination that usually soothed Gabriel.

This morning, however, he was on edge as he sat at a table near the front window of the morning room reading the *Times*. He was annoyingly aware of the servants in black knee-breeches as they scurried to and fro and the numerous gentlemen who were enjoying hushed conversations behind him.

He should have remained at the townhouse, a voice whispered in the back of his mind.

He had a perfectly lovely breakfast room that offered a view of his rose garden, rather than the narrow London street currently spread beneath him, and a cook eager to prepare whatever he desired. And of course, there was the decided benefit of being alone. The gawking gossips were currently studying him with an avid curiosity that made his teeth clench.

Unfortunately, he had devoted the past month to avoiding society. Unless he wished others to suspect he was

cowardly hiding from his supposed friends and acquaintances, he had no choice but to force himself to return to
his previous routine.

Which included an hour at his club, followed by a trip
to his tailor and then on to Tattersall's to have a look at
the horses to be auctioned.

Even if it meant he was to attract precisely the sort of
sordid attention he detested.

He tossed aside the unread paper and smoothed his
hand down the simply tied cravat that he had matched
with a pale blue jacket and ivory waistcoat, his brooding
gaze trained on the tip of his glossy boot.

Was it any wonder he was in a foul mood?

And he knew entirely where to lay the blame.

His aggravating wife.

His jaw tightened. Dammit. He had sent her to Devonshire to ensure she understood that she would never
again be allowed to manipulate him. He would be the
master of their relationship, and she would learn to be
an obedient wife or she would suffer the consequences.

But after waiting day after day for a message from his
suitably chastised bride, pleading to be allowed to return
to London, he found his temper fraying at her stubborn
lack of communication.

What the devil was the matter with the chit?

Surely she must be anxious to return to her precious
society so she could flaunt her newfound position as the
Countess of Ashcombe? For an ambitious female, being
trapped in the country should be a fate worse than death.

And yet, his housekeeper had written several letters revealing that Talia had swiftly become a favorite
among both his staff and tenants. Indeed, Mrs. Donaldson
had gushed with monotonous enthusiasm for the new-
est Countess of Ashcombe, assuring him that Talia had

settled nicely at the estate and revealed no desire what-soever to return to London.

Or to her husband.

So the question was—what game was his bride play-ing now?

The more cynical side of him insisted that Talia was merely biding her time in an effort to lure him into com-placency, and yet, he could not entirely believe such a simple explanation. His tenants might not be well edu-cated, but they were keen judges of character. They would have sensed if Talia were merely pretending to care.

And yet, she could not possibly be utterly innocent. Could she?

Tapping a slender finger on the side table situated next to his chair, Gabriel grimly admitted that the only means to discover the truth was to travel to Carrick Park. Be-neath his watchful gaze Talia would either reveal that she was truly her father's daughter or she would prove she was as much a victim as Gabriel was to Silas Dobson's ambitions.

Yes. His vague notion hardened to determination. He obviously had no choice but to leave London for Devon-shire. In fact, there was no reason he could not begin the journey today.

Without warning a savage flare of anticipation clutched his stomach. An anticipation that had nothing to do with discovering the truth and everything to do with returning his beautiful bride to his bed.

Christ, he ached for her.

It was ludicrous. He could have his pick of beautiful, willing women. All of them eager to offer him endless hours of pleasure.

But night after night he had slept alone, plagued by the memories of his dark-haired gypsy.

A prickle on the back of his neck shook Gabriel out of his delectable thoughts of Talia spread across his bed, his hands tangled in her dark hair as he thrust deep into her satin heat.

He turned his head, preparing to flay the unwelcome intruder with a few well-chosen words, only to have them die on his lip.

Damn.

His gaze skimmed over the tall gentleman with a large, muscular body who was currently attired in a cinnamon jacket and tan waistcoat, black breeches and glossy boots. The nobleman's light brown hair was cut shorter than the current fashion and his features were more forceful than handsome. And while his golden brown eyes often sim mered with amusement, they could also send any preening fop who hoped to garner his acquaintance fleeing in fear.

Hugo, Lord Rothwell.

And one of Gabriel's few friends.

"Is there a particular reason you are hovering behind me like a vulture, Hugo?" he demanded wryly, knowing it would be a futile effort to try to convince his friend that he preferred to be alone.

Hugo narrowed his golden gaze, absently toying with the signet ring on his little finger.

"I am attempting to decide if I have the nerve so early in the day to beard the lion in his den. Or shall I wait until I am in my cups and therefore impervious to your foul mood?"

Gabriel pointedly turned his attention toward the dunces clustered about the room casting covert glances in his direction.

"My mood would not be foul if I were not surrounded by idiots," he growled.

"Hmm." With the ease of a natural sportsman, Hugo lowered his large body into the leather chair opposite Gabriel. "That would not be my first guess as to why you have been snapping and snarling at every unwitting soul who has crossed your path over the past month."

"At least I have not yet taken to lodging bullets in those who annoy me," he smoothly pointed out, "although that might change at any moment."

Hugo smiled at the threat. "You do realize that you cannot keep society at bay forever? Eventually you will have to face their curiosity."

"Society's curiosity, or yours?"

"Both," Hugo admitted. "But considering we have been friends since I bloodied your nose our first day at Eton I surely deserve to be the first to be taken into your confidence?"

Gabriel snorted. "First of all, I was the one to bloody your nose after you attempted to pinch my favorite cricket bat. And I have never known you to take an interest in gossip."

"That is because the rumors have never before hinted that the proud and notoriously aloof Earl of Ashcombe has secretly wed the daughter of Silas Dobson."

Gabriel's jaw tightened at the mention of his offensive father-in-law.

"Obviously not so secretively."

"Is it true?"

There was a moment of silence before Gabriel gave a grudging nod of his head.

"Yes."

"Bloody hell," Hugo muttered.

"My sentiments exactly."

Hugo scowled at Gabriel's dry retort. "I suppose I need not ask how this particular disaster occurred," he

rasped. "Only Harry could force you into such an untenable situation."

Gabriel shrugged. Hugo had never bothered to hide
his disgust for Harry and his reckless extravagances.

"He certainly can take a share of the blame," he admitted.

"A share?" Hugo shook his head. "It is common knowledge that Harry jilted Miss Dobson after disappearing
with her dowry. Typical of him."

Gabriel ignored the stab of possessive outrage at the
mere thought of Talia wed to his brother.

"Quite typical," he agreed. "Which is why I should
have foreseen the looming danger. I was a fool."

Hugo breathed a low curse. "I will admit you were a
fool, but only for allowing your guilt at Harry's betrayal
to trap you into a vile marriage."

"Guilt?"

"Of course. Why else would you have wed the vulgar
wench?"

Gabriel parted his lips to inform his friend that it
hadn't been guilt but rather sordid blackmail that had
forced him into matrimony, but he swallowed the revealing words. It was not just embarrassment at having
to admit he had been bested by Silas Dobson, but a disturbing suspicion that he was not being entirely honest
with himself.

"My reasons do not concern you," he snapped.

There was a pause before Hugo reluctantly turned the
conversation.

"Have you managed to track down your brother?"

Gabriel shook his head. He had sent two of his most
trusted footmen in search of Harry the moment he'd realized he was missing, but thus far they had been unable

to discover anything more than the rumor his brother was seen heading toward Dover.

"Not yet."

"Bastard," Hugo hissed.

"He cannot elude me forever." Gabriel gave a sharp laugh. "Not that it truly matters now."

"No, the damage has been done." Hugo studied him for a long moment, seeming to consider his next words. "May I ask where you have stashed your blushing bride?"

Gabriel arched a brow. "Do you fear I've locked her in the wine cellar?"

"The rumor is that she has been whisked off to one of your estates, although I hold out hope that you had the good sense to drown her in the Thames." Hugo's lips twisted with a cruel humor. "Or at the very least had her transported to the colonies."

Gabriel's hand landed on the table with enough force to rattle his coffee cup and create a startled twitter of alarm that rippled through the room.

He ignored the disturbance, his gaze locked on his friend.

"This is my wife we are discussing."

Hugo frowned, his jaw jutted to a stubborn angle. "Yes, a grasping, overly ambitious harpy who does not even have the decency to possess a hint of grace or beauty."

Gabriel leaned forward, not giving a damn that his fury was entirely unreasonable.

"Not another word," he warned.

Glancing toward Gabriel's tightly clenched expression, Hugo jerkily settled back in his seat.

"Damn, Ashcombe," he growled. "What is the matter with you?"

It was a question that Gabriel had no answer for, nor did he particularly care at the moment. His only thought was ensuring his friend understood that Talia now belonged to him.

"I will not have anyone insulting the Countess of Ashcombe," he snarled. "Including you."

"Even if she forced you into marriage?"

"Talia…" Gabriel faltered, not certain he was prepared to share his doubts.

"What?"

"She claims she had no desire to wed either Harry or myself," he at last confessed.

Hugo waved his hand dismissively. "Of course she would deny trading her soul for a title. What woman would confess such a truth?"

"I am not completely convinced of her guilt."

His friend hissed, his eyes darkening with shock. "Have you taken leave of your senses?"

Gabriel narrowed his gaze. "Take care, Hugo."

"If she had no desire to wed, then all she had to do was say no. The days of buying and selling women as if they are cattle are long past," Hugo pressed. "She could not have been forced into marriage."

It was precisely what Gabriel had told himself, but now he glared at Hugo, barely resisting the urge to punch his closest friend in the nose.

"Have you had the misfortune to meet Silas Dobson?"

Hugo grimaced. "A nasty bit of goods, but a damned shrewd businessman. I have invested in his latest shipping venture."

"He is an uncouth brute who makes a habit of terrorizing those in his power."

"That does not mean Miss Dobson…"

"Lady Ashcombe."

Hugo's jaw tightened at Gabriel's interruption. "It does not necessarily follow that your wife is a victim. It is quite likely she was a willing conspirator with her father in plotting to claim the highest available title."

Gabriel impatiently shook his head. He would soon enough determine the truth for himself.

"Her guilt or innocence no longer matters."

Hugo's frustration was replaced by a flare of sympathy. "True enough," he murmured. "Harry made a deal with the devil and now you must pay."

Gabriel rolled his eyes. "Have you considered a career on the stage?"

"I…"

Hugo snapped his lips shut as a footman in the familiar blue-and-silver uniform of Ashcombe halted beside Gabriel and handed him a folded note.

"Pardon me, my lord," he apologized. "This has just arrived from Devonshire. The messenger said it is urgent."

"Thank you." Expecting information on his brother, Gabriel was unprepared for his housekeeper's plea for him to travel as fast as possible to Carrick Park. His blood ran cold as he shoved himself to his feet with enough violence to tumble his chair backward. "Damn. I must go."

"Go?" Hugo swiftly lifted himself upright. "Go where?"

"Your ill wishes for my wife have come to pass," he ground out, unfairly striking out at his friend as a fear he did not entirely understand clutched his heart.

Hugo flinched. "What the devil do you mean?"

"My wife has disappeared," Gabriel turned on his heel, headed for the door. "You had best pray I find her."

THE FRENCH CASTLE tucked in the countryside south of Paris retained much of its delicate charm despite the obvious ravages of war.

Built in a perfect square to frame the formal inner courtyard, the structure retained two towers from what Talia assumed to be a previous castle and vast wings that were constructed of a golden stone that shimmered in the sunlight. Along one wing a covered terrace was supported by a series of archways that led to the main residence that offered a striking double stone staircase and carved stones set above the large windows.

Among the surrounding gardens many of the statues and marble fountains had been destroyed by rioters, but inside, the endless procession of public chambers, salons and elegant galleries remained remarkably intact. And despite the fact she was being held captive, Talia could not prevent herself from appreciating the exquisite beauty that surrounded her.

Who could remain impervious to the priceless artwork that lined the walls, the massive tapestries, the inlaid wood floors and the breathtaking frescoes that graced the high ceilings?

Standing in one of the long galleries, Talia leaned against a fluted column that bracketed the high, arched window and gazed across the gardens to the distant road beyond.

Not for the first time since arriving at the palace three days ago she considered the possibility of simply walking out the front door and making her escape. She was alone, after all, and she did not doubt that she could travel a considerable distance before she was missed.

Unfortunately, she was not so stupid as to believe that she could actually make her way back to England.

Not only did she not speak French, but she had no money, no legal papers necessary to travel in France and no means to flee the estate beyond her own feet. At best she would be arrested before she reached the nearest village. At worst she would be taken captive by the numerous French soldiers who passed by the palace with unfortunate regularity.

She did not doubt they would be far less gentle toward her than Jack Gerard.

No…not Jack, but *Jacques,* she silently corrected with a deep sigh.

As furious as she was to have been kidnapped from her home, she could not deny that Jacques had done his best to keep her in comfort.

He had taken her from the church to a small boat kept among the local fishing vessels and had demanded his rough companions row them to a sleek yacht that had been hidden along a remote section of the coast. Thankfully he had sent the brutes back to London, and Talia had been put into the hands of his French crew, who had treated her as if she were a delicate treasure in constant need of coddling.

Once in France, the journey to the palace had been a mere blur as she had been placed alone in a carriage that had traveled for several hours at a bone-rattling speed through the countryside with only brief pauses so she could relieve herself among the bushes.

Since her arrival at the palace, she had been left to explore her surroundings in peace. She had been careful, though, to avoid the large outbuildings that had been given over to a great number of wounded soldiers and a dozen children that she had assumed were orphans.

This morning, however, she had sensed her solitude was about to come to an end. After emerging from her bath, she had discovered the gown she had been wearing since being kidnapped had mysteriously disappeared and was replaced by a lovely satin dress in a warm shade of ocher. There had also been matching slippers and expensive undergarments that had made her blush.

With no choice she had attired herself in the new clothing, although, without a maid, she had chosen to pull her hair into a simple braid that hung down her back. She would not be trapped in her chambers because she was too proud to take the unwanted clothing.

The footsteps she had been expecting for hours at last echoed through the gallery, and, accepting she could not avoid the inevitable, she turned to watch as Jacques Gerard strolled toward her.

A grudging smile tugged at her lips as she caught sight of his elegant charcoal-gray jacket that had been tailored to perfectly fit his lean body. His white cravat was tied in the latest style, and his black pantaloons clung with loving care to his muscular legs.

The humble vicar had been replaced by a gentleman with the sort of natural arrogance that was usually reserved to those born into power. And not for the first time Talia wondered just who this man truly was.

He was far too well-educated for a simple peasant, and yet, his hatred for the aristocracy was unmistakable.

A man of mystery.

Coming to a halt directly in front of her, Jacques reached for her hand, lifting her fingers to his mouth for a lingering kiss even as his gaze stroked with warm appreciation over her slender form.

"Bonsoir, ma petite," he murmured, his attention lingering on the scooped neckline trimmed with a pretty Brussels lace that lay like a promise against the full curve of her breasts. "I see that the *modiste* did not disappoint.

You look magnificent. Of course, you would appear even more magnificent if only I could coax a smile to those stubborn lips."

She blushed during his heated scrutiny, unaccustomed to such blatant admiration. But oddly, she did not shrink as was her custom beneath a male's attention, nor did she find herself plagued by the urge to stammer in embarrassment.

Perhaps it was being away from the constant badgering of her father that had stiffened her backbone. Or her growing confidence since becoming the Countess of Ashcombe.

Or perhaps it was Jacques who had never mocked her as a foolish wallflower but instead had treated her with a dignity and respect that she had never before experienced. At least until he had proven to be a traitor and kidnapped her, she wryly acknowledged.

Whatever the cause, she squarely met his steady gaze with a tilt of her chin.

"You are a fine one to call me stubborn." She brushed a hand down the exquisite material of her gown. "You know very well I would not have accepted your charity unless you had my own dress taken away."

He gave her fingers a light squeeze before allowing them to drop. "The clothes are a gift, not charity, and as a Frenchman renowned for his exquisite sense of fashion I had no choice but to rid the world of your tattered rags."

"Hardly a rag."

He waved aside her protest, his dark eyes shimmering with a wicked amusement that could tempt a saint.

"Besides, you are my guest. It is my duty, as well as my pleasure, to ensure you are provided with all the comforts you might desire."

"I am your prisoner, not your guest."

"Prisoner?" He lifted his brows in a pretense of innocence. "There are no bars on the windows and no shack-
les holding you against your will."

"It is beneath you to pretend that I am here of my own
free will," she chastised.

"Come, *ma petite,*" he coaxed, skimming a finger
down her cheek. "It has not been such a terrible adventure, has it?"

She jerked from his touch, her eyes narrowing at his
patronizing tone.

"I have been bullied and coerced and manipulated by
others my entire life, *Monsieur Gerard,*" she said between clenched teeth. "I had foolishly hoped I might have
found a place where I could control my own destiny, as
well as friends who appreciated my independence, when
I arrived at Carrick Park."

A brief flash of regret shot through his eyes before
he cupped her chin in his hand and regarded her with a
resolute expression.

"*Oui,* it was a foolish hope. You were never destined
to enjoy your independence for long."

She frowned. "There is no need to mock me."

"Talia, use that considerable intelligence of yours," he
commanded.

"What do you mean?"

"You could not have remained alone at Carrick Park."

"I do not comprehend why not," she protested. "It
seemed a satisfactory arrangement."

His lips twisted. "For you perhaps, but I can assure you
that your husband would soon have been joining you in
Devonshire. Or demanding that you return to London."

She stiffened at the mention of Gabriel. She had done
her best not to think of her husband since those first hours

after her kidnapping when she had ridiculously held on to a hope that he would come charging to her rescue. As if he would bother himself to chase after his unwanted wife even if he had known she was taken hostage. She was such a fool.

"Nonsense." Her voice held a bitter edge she could not entirely disguise. "He was quite happy to be rid of me."

Jacques regarded her as if she were impossibly naïve. "No, he wished to punish your father for having dared to threaten him," he said. "Once he is assured that he has established his dominance over you, and, more important, Silas Dobson, he will be anxious to claim his wife."

A treacherous memory of how Gabriel had already claimed her in the rumpled sheets of her bed briefly seared through her mind. Then, with a gasp, she hastily thrust aside the unwelcome image. What the devil was the matter with her?

"You know nothing of the situation." She took an awkward step away from her companion, thankful he could not read her thoughts. "Gabriel is eager to forget we were ever wed."

His eyes narrowed. "Even if such a ridiculous notion were true, he cannot forget you."

"Why not?"

"Because you are the Countess of Ashcombe, not some commoner's wife."

"I am aware of my title," she said tartly. Her wedding might have been a bleak affair, but she had no doubt that it had been perfectly legal. Had Gabriel not returned for the wedding night just to ensure…

No.

Not again.

"Then you should also be aware that, whatever Lord Ashcombe's personal opinion of you as his wife, his pride will not allow you to be a source of mockery among his peers." Jacques thankfully distracted her dangerous thoughts. "When he judges it to be the appropriate moment, he will use his considerable power to launch you into society."

Talia shuddered at the mere suggestion. She would as soon be left to rot in a French prison as be launched back into society.

"He cannot force them to accept me."

"Of course he can." Jacques's hand shifted to brush a stray curl from her cheek. "They will not dare to do anything but bow at your pretty feet."

Her humorless laugh floated eerily through the gallery. "Absurd."

He shrugged aside her disbelief. "Not that taking your place among society is your most important function as the new Countess of Ashcombe."

"I suppose you intend to tell me what it is?"

He stepped close enough to surround her in his male heat, his hands framing her face.

"I should not have to, no matter how innocent you might be."

Her heart skipped a beat. *"Mons..."*

"Jacques," he huskily insisted.

"Jacques," she impatiently muttered. "Just say what is upon your mind."

"Very well." His lips curved in a mocking smile. "The first and foremost duty of the Countess of Ashcombe is to produce the essential heir, *ma petite.*"

She sucked in a sharp breath, more disturbed by the brutal pang of need that clenched her stomach than by Jacques's audacity.

She wasn't stupid. In the days leading up to the wedding, there had lurked the knowledge that Gabriel would need an heir, but she had endured too many disappointments to willingly invite more. How could she have allowed herself to hope for a child when her husband might very well have decided he could not bear to bring himself to share her bed?

Even after their wedding night, she had refused to consider the possibility when it became evident she was not yet pregnant. Gabriel was obviously satisfied with his mistresses in town, leaving her alone in the country. The desperate desire to hold a baby in her arms might very well drive her mad if she allowed it to settle in her heart.

"I…"

Mistaking her unease for embarrassment, Jacques stroked his thumb over her heated cheek.

"You truly are an innocent."

"Not so innocent as you imagine," she said dryly.

"I find it charming." A dangerous emotion flared through his dark eyes. "I find *you* charming."

A stab of panic had Talia jerking away from his lingering touch. "I will not discuss this with you."

Jacques folded his arms over his chest, watching her nervous retreat with a narrowed gaze.

"What will you not discuss?" he asked. "The realization that your husband is not some mythical creature who you can pretend lives in some distant land and that eventually you will have to do your duty as his wife?"

"My relationship with Lord Ashcombe is none of your concern."

"I am merely attempting to reveal that your idyll would not have lasted beyond a few weeks," he persisted. "You should thank me for rescuing you from an existence that would never have made you happy."

"Rescuing me? I was kidnapped," she sharply reminded him. "And you know nothing of how to make me happy."

A smile of pure male confidence curled his lips. "I know you intimately, *ma petite.*"

Heat flared beneath her cheeks at his suggestive words. "Nonsense."

"I know you prefer to devote your days to helping others and that you would be miserable being forced back to the stifling ballrooms of London." His dark gaze skimmed over the exposed skin of her bosom. "I also suspect you are not eager to become a broodmare for a husband who has shown you nothing but contempt."

She abruptly whirled away, unwilling to reveal the awful truth that she would give anything to have a baby. A tiny child to whom she could offer all her love that had been rejected by others.

"Please, do not," she choked out.

Jacques bent his head to whisper in her ear, his gentle hands resting on her shoulders.

"Your talents would be respected here, *ma petite.* There is much need and few hands to offer assistance."

She shook her head. "I am no traitor."

"Come." Tightening his grip, Jacques steered her across the floor of the gallery to the arched windows that overlooked the inner courtyard. A reluctant smile curved her lips at the sight of a dozen children ranging in age from five to fifteen darting among the ruins of the statues and fountains, chasing a stray dog. "Do you see them, Talia?" Jacques demanded, his voice low and compelling. "They are not English or French, they are children. And all they know is that war has destroyed their homes and their families. Just think of the difference you could make in their lives."

Talia could not deny a tug of regret.

Her days in Devonshire had proved she possessed a talent for helping those in need, whether it was making certain a sickly tenant received meals from her kitchen or organizing the village to build a new school for the local children.

How much could she accomplish for those poor orphans?

She heaved a sigh. "You do not fight fair."

"I fight to win."

She thrust away his unexpectedly tempting offer and turned to meet his watchful gaze.

"Am I to be held here forever?"

He deliberately lifted his brow, glancing toward the beautiful Rubens's paintings displayed in gilt frames and the dangling chandeliers made from priceless Venetian glass.

"You disapprove of your lodgings?"

She thinned her lips, battling against his considerable charm.

"I simply wish to know what you intend for my future."

He reached to straighten the lace at her bosom. "Be at ease, Talia. Once the information I acquired has been used to defeat Wellesley, I will personally escort you back to Devonshire." He paused. "Although I have hopes that I will have convinced you to remain with me by that time."

She was far from comforted by his promise. "How can you speak so casually of what you have done? Do you not realize that hundreds, perhaps thousands, of British soldiers might die because of your treachery?"

"And hundreds, perhaps thousands, of French soldiers will be saved," he readily countered. "It is war, *ma petite*."

"A war started by your crazed emperor who will not be satisfied until he has conquered the world." Her scowl shifted toward the marble bust of Napoleon that had been placed on a teak-wood pedestal. "How can you give your loyalty to such a man?"

CHAPTER SEVEN

"I COULD ASK the same of you," Jacques countered, his jaw clenched. "How can you give your loyalty to a mad king and his *imbecile* son who devotes more attention to the gloss on his boots than to his people starving in the gutters?"

She lowered her eyes, unable to deny his condemnation. Not that she was prepared to admit the truth. Not to the man who was willing to betray those who had come to trust him, including herself.

"We shall never agree."

"You think not?" He waited until she lifted her head to meet his somber gaze. "We are not so different, you know."

She stilled. "What do you mean?"

He paused, as if not entirely certain he wished to explain himself. Then, with a tiny shrug, he turned his gaze toward the children still darting about the courtyard.

"My father was an artist who caught the attention of King Louis," he revealed in a soft, rigidly controlled voice. "He was commissioned to complete several sculptures for the *Tuileries* gardens."

She studied his profile, sensing his long-buried pain. "He must be very talented."

"He was."

"Oh." She cleared her throat. "He has passed?"

"When I was just a boy." A wistful smile curled his

lips. "Thankfully, I managed to salvage a few of his pieces."

Her annoyance with Jacques was forgotten as she stepped forward and laid a comforting hand on his arm. She had been devastated by the loss of her mother at a young age. No child should have to endure such pain.

"I would love to see them."

"Then you shall." He turned to meet her sympathetic expression. "He would have approved of you."

She shifted uneasily beneath his intent gaze. "What happened?"

He paused, clearly unaccustomed to sharing his past. Then he heaved a deep sigh.

"My mother had been an actress before wedding my father and she was..." His expression softened. "Exquisite."

"That I can well believe." His own beauty was potent.

He gave a dip of his head. "*Merci, ma petite.* Unfortunately, beauty can often be a curse for women."

"A curse?"

She blinked at his odd claim. Was beauty not an essential quality for a woman? God knew that she had suffered the consequences of daring to be less than lovely.

"My father was invited by the king to visit for several weeks at Versailles," Jacques explained. "He was, of course, delighted. An artist must depend upon the patronage of those with wealth. He hoped to acquire additional commissions."

"Did you travel with him?"

"No, I remained at our home in Paris with my tutor, but my mother joined him at the palace." His jaw clenched. "Within a few days she had caught the eye of the Comte de Rubell."

Talia bit her bottom lip, a sick sensation forming in the pit of her stomach.

"Oh."

"Being a member of nobility the Comte naturally assumed that my mother should be honored to warm his bed. He could not accept her rebuffs."

It was, unfortunately, a too familiar story.

Women without the protection of wealth or powerful connections would always be at the mercy of unscrupulous men.

Of course, even wealth did not necessarily protect a woman from being compelled to obey the demands of an overbearing male, she grimly acknowledged.

"Did he...force her?"

Pure hatred flared through Jacques's eyes. "That was his intention when my father arrived and stuck the bastard with his sword."

"Good for him," Talia said with staunch approval.

His lips twisted. "It was not a fairy tale with my father as the hero, *ma petite*. Although his attack caused no more than a flesh wound, he was taken to the Bastille and condemned to death."

She sucked in a harsh breath, horrified by the story. "Jacques, I am so sorry."

"As am I." He took a moment, raw emotion tightening his features before he struggled to regain command of his composure. "My father was a hardworking, decent man of honor who was killed as if he were no more than a stray dog."

"You loved him," she said softly.

"Oui." He managed a stiff smile. "And he adored me."

"Then you are fortunate, even if you only had him a short time." She felt a familiar tug at her heart. "The memory of my mother was often my only comfort after a particularly difficult evening among society."

He shrugged off her words of comfort. "Remarkably I do not feel fortunate."

She gave his arm a gentle squeeze. "What happened to your mother?"

"She returned to Paris only long enough to pack our belongings and to flee to England. Her cousin in London was willing to take us in."

"So that is why you speak English with such fluency."

"My mother married the youngest son of a baron who was willing to pay my tuition to Eton to keep me from being constantly underfoot." His tone was matter-of-fact, but Talia sensed that the rejection from his stepfather had only served to deepen his disgust for the aristocracy. "I was a well-polished Englishman until I came of age and was able to return to France."

"And yet you feel no loyalty at all to England?" she asked, unable to accept that he had made no friends during his years in school.

"I have no loyalty to a country that will allow the oppression of its people by a handful of bloated nobles who remain above the law."

"But…"

"Enough of this dreary talk of politics," he abruptly interrupted, pressing a slender finger to her lips. "I have come to request your companionship for dinner."

Talia rolled her eyes in wry resignation as Jacques retreated behind the practiced charm he used as a shield against the world.

"I should refuse," she muttered, ruefully aware she was unable to conjure the outrage she should be feeling at being held hostage by a French spy.

With a dramatic motion, Jacques pressed a hand to his heart. "You would not be so cruel."

"You are my enemy."

"Never." Without warning he leaned down to brush his lips over her cheek, then taking her hand he placed it on his arm and firmly led her down the gallery. "Come, *ma petite*. Allow me to prove just how...friendly I can be."

One week later

DUSK HAD FALLEN over the French countryside as Gabriel halted near the abandoned conservatory and studied the palace spread before him.

His gaze barely noted the imposing building that loomed over the countryside with rigid grandeur. He concentrated instead on the handful of soldiers lazily patrolling the grounds before shifting to the formal gardens where he could see the shadowy form of a lone woman walking through broken statues.

"Talia," he breathed, sinking to his knees as a violent sense of relief slammed through him.

The man at his side shifted forward, moving with surprising grace considering his large bulk.

"Are you certain?" Hugo demanded.

Gabriel turned to send his friend a sour glance.

It hadn't been his choice to have Hugo travel with him to France.

In fact, he had done everything but horsewhip the aggravating man to keep him from following him.

Unfortunately, Hugo was nothing if not tenacious and, ignoring Gabriel's commands, insults and threats of violence, he had stubbornly arrived at Carrick Park mere hours after Gabriel and then had refused to leave his side.

In the end, Gabriel had been too anxious to begin his search for Talia to battle with his friend. While Hugo made himself useful by carefully interviewing the servants to discover if they could offer any useful information, Gabriel had scoured the countryside.

Thank God the local tenants were devoted to the young Countess of Ashcombe. The moment the alarm had been raised at her failure to return for supper, they had spread throughout the neighborhood to find their beloved Talia. Within hours they had found two strangers who were staying at a local posting inn, each of them carrying far too much money for innocent travelers.

They had held the pair captive at the local gaol, where the magistrate had struggled to prevent the more bloodthirsty citizens from taking matters into their own hands.

Gabriel had found himself struggling to suppress his own bloodlust as he had questioned the insolent creatures, and it was Hugo who had prevented him from choking the life from the bastards when they had grudgingly revealed the truth of Jack Gerard and the fact he had taken Talia to his lair in France.

As it was, he'd managed to crack the ribs of one of the traitorous cowards and knocked the teeth from the other before Hugo had managed to pull him off.

By the next morning Gabriel had been on his private yacht, headed toward the coast of France with Hugo grimly at his side.

"It has been some time, but I am capable of recognizing my wife, Hugo," he assured his companion.

Hugo narrowed his golden eyes. "She does not appear to be a prisoner."

Gabriel swallowed a curse. This was precisely the reason that he had attempted to keep his friend from joining him on this quest, despite the knowledge he could have no more skilled or loyal companion.

"Looks can often be deceiving," he muttered.

"In that we are in perfect agreement." Hugo tensed as a soldier strolled along the flagstone path, passing close enough to the conservatory that they could catch the scent of his cigar. Hugo grabbed Gabriel's arm and tugged him toward the back of the building, his expression hard.

"Dammit, Ashcombe, we cannot linger here. The French soldiers might be as ignorant as they are incompetent, but they will eventually stumble across us. Besides, neither of us is as young as we used to be. Crouching in the bushes is damned uncomfortable."

Hugo grimaced as he glanced down at his ruined breeches covered in mud and his once glossy boots that were now scratched from the past hour of tromping through the thick forest surrounding the palace. Gabriel was equally rumpled, his jade coat ripped in several places and his cravat wrinkled from the late-summer heat. Even his hair was mussed and the stubble on his jaw revealed he was twelve hours past the need for a shave. A considerable change from the elegant image he was always careful to portray to society.

"I have no intention of leaving here without Talia," he growled.

Hugo shook his head. "Do not be a fool, Ashcombe."

"There is nothing foolish in rescuing my wife from the bastard who kidnapped her."

"You cannot simply charge into that nest of vipers," his friend persisted. "You would be shot before you ever reached the gardens."

Gabriel made a sound of impatience. He'd already accepted that he could not reach Talia.

Not yet.

"There will be no charging."

"Then what do you intend to do?"

"Once it grows darker I will be able to slip past the guards and find her."

Hugo's fingers dug into Gabriel's arm with a punishing grip. "No."

"This is not open to debate, Hugo."

"I will not allow you to commit suicide for a woman who is not worth—"

Gabriel barely realized he was moving before he had his friend pinned to the back of the conservatory. The savage fear that had haunted him since discovering Talia's absence was finally boiling over.

Christ. He'd been through hell imagining the various horrors that his bride might have endured. And now, being able to catch a glimpse of her in the distance, and yet knowing she was still out of reach, was torture.

"I warned you when you insisted on joining me that I would not endure insults to my wife," he seethed.

Predictably Hugo refused to give ground. The damnable man was one of the few whom Gabriel could not intimidate.

Which was no doubt the reason he was one of Gabriel's rare friends.

"And I will not willingly allow my friend to walk into danger," Hugo said between clenched teeth. "I have too few of them as it is."

With an effort, Gabriel regained command of his frayed temper, releasing Hugo and taking a jerky step backward.

"There will be little danger."

"Little danger?" Hugo scowled, waving a hand toward the distant gardens. "Perhaps you failed to notice the battalion of French soldiers milling about the palace?"

Gabriel shrugged, catching sight of two soldiers leaning against a broken fountain and flirting with a buxom maid.

"It is obvious that they are more interested in their entertainment than in keeping watch."

Hugo remained unimpressed. "That does not mean they will not eagerly shoot an intruder."

"Only if they realize there is an intruder," Gabriel countered, shrugging aside his friend's concern. He did not care if Napoleon and his entire army made a sudden appearance. Nothing was going to prevent him from retrieving his wife. "If you will recall, I managed to slip beneath the nose of our headmaster for years without being caught."

Sensing Gabriel's determination, Hugo muttered a vile curse. "I do not like this."

"Neither do I, but there is no choice."

"There is always a choice," Hugo argued. "As you have pointed out with revolting frequency, Talia is now the Countess of Ashcombe. All we need do is to locate the closest British troops and they will..."

"I have no intention of leaving my wife in the hands of the enemy another night and certainly not the days, or even weeks, it would take to gather an army," Gabriel ground out. "Besides, I will not risk Talia in the midst of a battle. We both know it is often the innocents who are injured in the heat of war."

"If she is innocent..."

"Enough," Gabriel snapped.

Hugo made a sound of impatience. "Would you listen to me, Ashcombe?" he rasped. "You have only the word of two traitors that she was taken against her will. What if you manage to approach her without being caught and she refuses to leave with you?" He paused. "Or worse, what if she reveals your presence to the French?"

Gabriel gritted his teeth, refusing to admit that Hugo's accusations struck a nerve.

In the back of his mind, however, a treacherous voice reminded him that he had sent a young, beautiful woman into the isolated countryside without so much as a companion to keep her occupied. Would it be so astonishing that she would turn to a handsome and charming vicar to ease her loneliness? Or even to fulfill the needs of her body that he had stirred to life on their wedding night?

Of course, it was the same voice that had convinced him that Talia had been as guilty as her father in trapping him in an unwanted marriage and was responsible for this mess to begin with.

For a gentleman who prided himself on his ability to confront any situation with a logic untainted by emotions, he behaved as if he were as witless as those dandies littering the London ballrooms.

The knowledge was as annoying as it was inexplicable.

"Return to the ship and ensure it is prepared to leave the moment I arrive with Talia," he commanded, his sharp tone warning he would endure no argument.

Hugo's jaw tightened, but he gave a reluctant nod.

"Very well."

"And, Hugo?"

His friend frowned. "Yes?"

"If I have not arrived by dawn tomorrow you are to return to England without me."

"No."

Gabriel narrowed his gaze. "You gave your word you would follow my orders when I allowed you to accompany me."

Hugo tossed his hands in the air, clearly at the end of his patience.

"I begin to wonder if marriage has softened your brain."

Gabriel's lips twisted. "I must admit that I wonder, as well."

Hugo headed toward the nearby trees. "Do not miss the ship."

"I shall do my best."

TALIA'S PRIVATE CHAMBERS were as magnificent as the rest of the palace.

The walls were covered by a pale green that matched the velvet curtains and the green-and-gold striped satin on the furnishings. A large fireplace made of white marble veined with black dominated one wall with a vast mirror framed in a profusion of gilt hanging over the mantel.

On the opposite wall a row of arched windows overlooked the sunken garden and the distant lake. While overhead a heavy crystal chandelier spilled a golden glow over the canopy bed set in the center of the room.

Still attired in her ruby satin dinner gown trimmed with French pearls at the plunging neckline and white roses along the cap sleeves, Talia sat in front of the satinwood dresser pulling a brush through her thick curls.

It had been over a week since her arrival at the palace, and while Jacques had been a charming companion when he was not meeting with the various guests who routinely traveled from Paris to speak with him, she was growing frustrated with her elegant prison.

As she should be, she acknowledged, tossing aside the brush and rising to her feet.

After accepting that she could not escape, she had in-

stead turned her thoughts to the looming disaster awaiting General Wellesley's troops.

But despite her efforts, she had yet to find the means
to send a warning to those poor men who were about to
march directly into an ambush. And she'd had even less
luck in discovering the sort of secret information that
might be used to England's advantage once Jacques returned her to Devonshire.

She was proving to be as much a failure at being a
daring adventuress as she was a society debutante.

Talia paced out the French doors that led to the balcony. She was leaning against the stone balustrade gazing at the moon-drenched garden when she caught the
unmistakable sound of a soft footfall behind her.

"Jacques?" she called, a frown marring her brow.
Until this moment she had never felt uneasy in these
private chambers, despite being a prisoner. The various
guards who roamed the palace and surrounding grounds
had treated her with a wary respect that assured her that
Jacques had left strict orders that she was not to be bothered. Now she realized just how vulnerable she truly was.
"Who is there?"

A large, distinctly male form stepped onto the balcony.

"It most certainly is not Jacques," a familiar voice
growled.

"Gabriel?" Talia gasped in shock, half suspecting
this must be a dream. It certainly would not be the first
time she'd imagined her husband magically appearing
to sweep her back to England. Of course, in her dreams
he had spoken sweet words of regret. His sharp retort
assured her that she was very much awake. "Dear God.
What are you doing here?"

He prowled forward, his golden hair shimmering in
the moonlight and his eyes a pure silver.

Talia shivered at the sudden danger that filled the air. How ironic that she felt perfectly comfortable with the man who had taken her captive, while her husband—the one man she should trust above all others—made her tremble with uncertainty.

"I should think that is obvious." His hooded gaze skimmed over her stiff form, lingering on her tumble of loose curls that spilled over her shoulders and down her back. "I have come to collect my wayward wife."

A breathless, aching sensation raced through Talia, making her acutely conscious of the vast amount of bare skin revealed by her gown and the manner in which it clung to her generous curves.

"How in heaven's name did you find me?" she rasped.

He halted a mere breath from her, the scent of his warm male skin teasing at her nose.

"I am not without skills."

"But…"

"Why did you assume another man would be entering your chambers?" he roughly interrupted.

Sudden fear that they would be overheard by the guards in the garden below jolted Talia out of her lingering sense of disbelief.

"Shh." She lifted a hand to press her fingers to his lips. "Someone will hear you."

He grabbed her wrist, his touch sending a sizzle of heat through her blood even as his eyes flashed with anger.

"Answer the question, Talia. Who is Jacques?"

She frowned in confusion. "He is…or *was* your vicar until he revealed himself as a traitor and kidnapped me."

"Jacques…Jack," he breathed in sudden comprehension. "Of course."

"Yes, Jack Gerard."

"And he is a frequent visitor?"

"I do not understand."

She furrowed her brow, wondering why on earth he appeared to be so preoccupied with her captor. Surely they should be concentrating on escaping before his presence was noticed?

Then realization struck like a slap to the face.

"Oh, my God." She jerked her hand from his grip. "Did you come here to rescue me or to discover if Jacques is my lover?"

His jaw clenched. "Is he?"

For a crazed moment Talia contemplated the pleasure of knocking the arrogant bastard over the edge of the balcony.

What sort of insufferable, selfish beast was more concerned with whether or not his wife might have strayed than her well-being after enduring the trauma of being kidnapped and held captive?

Then deciding his head was too thick to be harmed by a mere fall, Talia pushed her way past his large form to enter her bedchamber.

"You should leave before the guards discover you are here," she ordered between clenched teeth.

He was swiftly in pursuit. "You wish to remain?" he demanded.

"I wish..." She came to a sharp halt near the bed, recalling her ridiculous dreams of Gabriel's romantic charge to the rescue. "I am such an idiot."

He grabbed her shoulder, turning her to meet his fierce scowl.

"Talia."

"No." Instinctively she reached up to knock his hand away. "Do not touch me."

He froze, regarding her as if she had suddenly grown a second head.

"You are my wife."

Her humorless laugh echoed through the room. "A wife you insisted leave town mere hours after our wedding and to whom you haven't bothered to send so much as a note."

A flare of color crawled beneath his skin. Talia might have suspected he was embarrassed by her accusation if it weren't so absurd.

"And because I damaged your pride you turned your attentions to another man?" he snapped.

"I have never turned my attentions to another man."

"No?" His gaze swept over her expensive satin gown before shifting to the opulent splendor of her room. "It does not appear that way to me."

"Fine." Planting her hands on her hips, she shot Gabriel a fierce glare. Something she would never have dreamed possible only a few short weeks ago. "You desire the truth?"

His chin tilted to a haughty angle. "I will accept no less."

"Then I will admit that I found the Vicar Jack Gerard a kind and charming gentleman who treated me as if I were a true lady of quality and not a bit of rubbish that had to be buried out of sight."

"That was not…"

"But I have never considered him as more than a friend, and not even that since he forced me to accompany him to France," she continued without allowing him to defend the indefensible. "You may believe me or not. I do not particularly care."

CHAPTER EIGHT

GABRIEL CLENCHED HIS hands at his sides, regarding his wife with smoldering frustration.

What the devil had happened?

Everything had gone to plan as he had waited for the shadows to deepen before at last slipping through the gardens and finding an open window to enter the palace.

It had taken longer than he had expected to at last locate Talia's rooms, and he had been forced to hide more than once to avoid passing guards, but overall he had been pleased to reach Talia without alerting the numerous French swine of his presence.

Then he had heard his wife calling out the name of another man, and his determination to collect Talia and escape with all possible speed had been forgotten beneath a tidal wave of pure male fury.

He had risked his damned life to come to her rescue. How dare she be expecting another man in her private chambers. Especially attired in a slip of a gown that would make any man fantasize of sex?

Even if she spoke the truth and the bastard was not her lover.

And to make matters worse, she did not even possess the grace to apologize, instead attempting to paint him as the villain of the piece.

He shoved an impatient hand through his hair. "Tell

me how you came to be here," he commanded, attempting to regain command of the encounter.

"Why bother?" she mocked, her magnificent eyes flashing with a spirit that was at complete odds with the timid female who had stood at his side during their wedding. "You have obviously made your decision that I am not only a scheming peasant who forced you into marriage, but I am also so lacking in morals that I took a lover within days of becoming the Countess of Ashcombe and..." she sucked in a trembling breath that drew attention to the delectable swell of her breasts "...as the *coup de grace* I became a French spy."

The discomfort twisting his gut could not be guilt, he attempted to assure himself.

He was the Earl of Ashcombe. He had every right to question his wife.

"Tell me, Talia," he demanded.

Her eyes narrowed, but with a toss of her head she conceded to his demand.

"I happened to be passing by the church when I noticed two ruffians entering." She shrugged. "I was concerned they were up to some mischief, so I slipped to the back where I could see what they were doing."

His heart missed a painful beat at the mere thought of Talia confronting the two brutes currently being questioned by the Home Office in London.

"Damnation, woman. Have you no sense at all?" he chastised. "The Countess of Ashcombe does not walk country lanes without a servant and she most certainly does not confront...ruffians. If you have no concern for your pretty neck, then you should at least have a care for your reputation."

She should have been cowed by his censure. Instead she met him glare for glare.

"Just as you had a care for my reputation when you publicly shunned me?"

"Dammit," he snapped. "You should have returned to Carrick Park and sent a servant to investigate."

"I only intended to see if they meant harm before I decided whether or not to go in search of the magistrate."

"Instead you were captured."

She waved a hand, indicating the palatial room. "Obviously."

Gabriel's frustrated fury shifted toward the man who had dared to kidnap his wife. Although he had a vague memory of a new vicar being chosen for the local church, his visits to Devonshire had been consumed by his efforts to teach his reluctant tenants the latest farming techniques as well as restoring the manor house that had fallen into disrepair after his father's death. He had little time or interest in the spiritual welfare of his people.

Now he could only regret his failure to personally investigate Jack Gerard.

"I will kill him," Gabriel swore. "Were you injured?"

She rolled her eyes, appearing utterly unimpressed by his concern.

"Should that not have been your first question rather than accusing me of adultery?"

He growled in annoyance at her continued defiance. He was unaccustomed to anyone daring to lecture him, let alone his own wife.

"Bloody hell, when did my mouse become a shrew?"

"When I accepted my husband intended to treat me with the same disregard as my father."

He stiffened, deeply offended by the accusation. He had nothing in common with Silas Dobson.

He squashed the memory of standing at the window of his London townhouse, watching as Talia had entered the waiting carriage with an air of wounded defeat. At the time, he had done what he had thought was for the best.

That did not make him an uncouth, ill-bred bully, did it?

Of course it did not.

"If I intended to treat you with disregard then I would not be risking my life to rescue you," he pointed out in a harsh voice.

She shrugged aside his heroic deed, unconcerned that the Earl of Ashcombe would personally face hardship and peril when he could so easily have waited in London for the diplomats to attempt to gain her release.

"I am not sure why you bothered," she muttered.

"At the moment, neither am I," he barked before making yet another effort to regain control of his temper. Christ, this female would not be satisfied until he was fully unhinged. "Did the bastard attempt to take advantage of you?"

"No." She wrapped her arms around her waist. "Jacques has been a perfect gentleman."

He growled deep in his throat. "Perfect gentlemen do not betray their countrymen and kidnap vulnerable females," he ground out.

She sniffed. "How did you find me?"

Gabriel had endured enough. He was not certain what had happened to his shy, properly modest bride, but now was not the time for a marital spat.

Not when they were surrounded by the enemy.

"We can discuss my methods later." He crossed toward the door. "We must leave."

"Wait."

He halted to regard her with a flare of impatience. "Talia."

Turning her back on him, Talia stalked to the satin-wood armoire and began pulling out muslin gowns, petticoats and delicate stockings.

"I am not being hauled back to England without a toothbrush and a change of clothing," she said, her tone daring him to argue.

"Bring only the necessities." Gabriel crossed to spread one of the gowns over the mattress, then tucked her undergarments in the muslin folds before rolling it into a tidy bundle. "I have packed your belongings and have them waiting for you on my ship."

Talia's protest died on her lips as her eyes widened in disbelief.

"You packed a bag for me?"

He crossed to the washstand, collecting her toothbrush and tooth powder as well as the silver hairbrush and mirror, savagely promising to toss them in the rubbish the moment they reached his ship. No man would provide for Talia but himself.

She belonged to him.

Prickly temper and all.

"Actually I packed several bags since I have never before played lady's maid and was not entirely certain what you would need," he informed her.

"Why did you not have Mrs. Donaldson assist you?"

He snorted, recalling the wailing and handwringing that had filled his once peaceful home.

"Because the entire staff is prostrate with grief." He gave a shake of his head, still amazed by his servants' unashamed hysterics at Talia's disappearance. "I fear if I do not have you returned to their tender care soon the entire estate will collapse in despair."

Her lips tightened. "You needn't mock."

"I am not mocking, my dear." His gaze lingered on

the delicate beauty of her face, before skimming down to the body that was pure perfection. A dangerous sensation gripped his heart, forcing him to accept just how much he had missed this female. It was ludicrous. She had been little more than a stranger when he'd wed her. And yet the desire to have her near was a potent ache that refused to be dismissed. Dammit. "You have earned the loyalty of all those who depend upon Carrick Park for their livelihood. It is quite remarkable in such a short period of time."

"They are good people and I genuinely care about them," she said. "Unlike…"

A humorless smile twisted his lips as Talia hastily bit off her words.

"Yes?" he prompted.

"'Tis nothing."

"On the contrary. I would guess it was an insult." He watched the color flood her cheeks, ruefully acknowledging that for all of Talia's lack of blue blood she had already proven to be a better countess than a great many of his ancestors. Including the current dowager Countess of Ashcombe. "The only question is whether it was intended for me or my mother."

Her blush deepened and, grabbing a shawl from the armoire, Talia headed for the door.

"I am ready."

He hurried in her wake, catching her arm as she marched down the main corridor.

"This way," he said, tugging her into a small salon and through a narrow doorway hidden in the wall.

In silence they navigated the smothering darkness of the secret hallway that Gabriel had discovered during his search for Talia. The lack of dust and spiderwebs had warned him that the current occupants were familiar with the cramped corridor, but he doubted they actually patrolled the passageway.

Not that he was willing to lower his guard.

Pulling his loaded pistol from his pocket, he led Talia through the darkness until he at last slowed and pushed open the door to the vast library. He paused, ensuring that there was no one near before crossing the *Savonnerie* carpet to pull open the door leading to the terrace.

Earlier he had used the steps leading from the garden to the terrace to enter the palace. Now, however, he came to an abrupt halt as he caught faint sounds drifting from the nearby shadows.

"Damn."

Talia moved to his side. "Guards?" she whispered.

"Yes."

He attempted to pull her away, but she was already peering over the edge of the terrace.

"What are they—" She gasped as she caught sight of the soldier leaning against the fountain with a maid kneeling in front of him, his low moans of pleasure filling the air. "Oh."

He jerked her back into the library, annoyed that she had been exposed to such lewd behavior. Did Jacques have no control over his men?

Weaving a path through the gilt chairs covered in red velvet and the heavily scrolled desk, Gabriel pulled open the door to the connected room.

"Where does this lead?"

Talia shook her head. "I am not certain."

Gabriel cautiously entered what appeared to be an antechamber with a massive black marble fireplace and brocade chairs seated near a round table that held a jade and ivory chess set.

They had just crossed to the opposite door when the

sound of footsteps in the main corridor had them both
stiffening in alarm.

"Gabriel," Talia breathed.

"I hear them."

With long strides he crossed to yank aside the crimson curtains and pushed open the window sash.

Talia was swiftly at his side. "What are you doing?"

Gabriel leaned over the sill, surveying the garden two
stories below.

"It is not far to the garden."

"Are you mad?" Talia rasped.

"I will go first." Gabriel tossed the small bundle he
carried to the flower bed below the window before turning to grasp Talia's hand. "Once I'm certain no one is
near, I will whistle and you can join me."

Her eyes darkened with fear. "You want me to jump?"

"I will catch you."

"No." She wildly shook her head, her raven curls sliding sensuously over the bare skin of her shoulders. "I
cannot."

"Look at me, Talia." He slid a hand beneath her chin,
tilting her face up to meet his encouraging expression.
"You have already proven there is no challenge you cannot confront with courage. You can do this."

"But…"

Lowering his head, Gabriel ended her words of protest with a soft, lingering kiss that only hinted at the raw
need clawing deep inside him.

"Trust me," he whispered against her mouth.

TALIA WAS STILL reeling from her uncontrollable reaction
to Gabriel's branding kiss when he slung a leg over the
windowsill and leaped into the garden below. She gasped,

racing forward to peer into the darkness even as she told herself she was a fool to be concerned.

She had no notion why Gabriel had taken it upon himself to rush to her rescue, but it was certainly not because he had any finer feelings for her. Or even the most basic concern of a husband for his wife.

How could he when the aggravating man had done nothing but bully and accuse and insult her since his unexpected arrival on the terrace?

She could only presume that his pride could not bear the thought that the Countess of Ashcombe was being held captive by a French spy.

Much to her annoyance, however, she could not stop herself from breathlessly waiting for his whistle to assure her that all was well. Nor could she quell the flutter of panic when long minutes passed with nothing but the distant cry of an owl to break the silence.

Gripping the edge of the window she leaned forward, her fear for Gabriel overcoming her intense dislike for heights.

"Gabriel?" she cried. "Are you hurt?"

There was a rustle from the nearby hedges, then her heart froze at the sight of Gabriel stepping into the moonlight with Jacques on one side and a French soldier on the other with a gun pointed directly at Gabriel's head.

"Stay where you are, *ma petite*," Jacques commanded, casting Gabriel a mocking smile. "It would be a sin to break your lovely neck just when you are about to be rid of your unwanted husband."

"Jacques, no." She shook her head in horror. "Please."

"Ah, how sweetly she pleads for the husband who has treated her with less respect than he would show a stray dog," Jacques drawled. "Do you know what I think, my lord?"

Gabriel held himself with arrogant indifference, as if he were standing in the middle of a ballroom rather than being held captive by his enemies.

"I do not give a damn."

Jacques's smile widened. "I think she would be far happier as a widow," he taunted. "I know I will be."

Even from a distance Talia could feel the tangible fury that filled the air as Gabriel glared toward the smirking Frenchman.

"She is mine," he rasped.

"Non." Jacques shook his head. "She might legally be the Countess of Ashcombe, but you have yet to earn her as a wife."

A chilling expression hardened Gabriel's face. "You are no doubt right, but I can assure you that I will see you in hell before you lay a hand upon her."

"I intend to lay more than a hand—"

"Jacques," Talia interrupted in sharp tones, knowing the Frenchman was simply attempting to goad Gabriel.

"Forgive me, *ma petite,*" Jacques apologized, glancing over her shoulder as the sound of approaching footsteps echoed behind her. "André will escort you to your room."

Talia did not bother to glance at the man at her side. She was familiar with the slender young soldier who had often paused to speak with her during her walks through the gardens. He had always been gracious, but Talia had never doubted his utter loyalty to Jacques.

"What do you intend to do with my husband?"

Jacques shrugged. "For now he will enjoy the delights of my cellar."

She chewed her bottom lip. "You swear he will not be hurt?"

"There will be no injuries that will not heal." Jacques

regarded Gabriel with blatant disgust. "At least for now. I make no promises for the future." Lifting a slender hand, he motioned toward the hovering soldier. "André, ensure our guest is made comfortable."

"No...wait..."

Talia's words of protest went unheeded as André grabbed her around the waist and with one smooth motion yanked her out of the window and slung her over his shoulder.

Her last sight was that of Gabriel struggling against the soldier and Jacques, who had wrapped his arms behind him, his face twisted in lethal rage.

"Get your hands off my wife," he shouted. "Talia!"

BLINDED BY his violent fury at seeing Talia manhandled by the damned soldier, Gabriel struggled against the arms that held him captive, refusing to calm until he felt a gun pressed to his temple.

"Do not be an idiot, Ashcombe," Jacques rasped. "She is beyond your reach."

With an effort Gabriel leashed his primitive compulsion to battle his way to Talia. Damnation, how could he rescue his wife if he were dead?

Ending his struggles, he stood rigid as Jacques and the soldier warily released him, shifting the gun to aim it at his heart.

For the moment the damned Frenchman held the upper hand, but soon...soon he would find the means to reverse the situation. And then he would take vicious delight in destroying Jacques Gerard before collecting his wife and returning her to Carrick Park.

And his bed.

"If she is harmed..."

"Thus far I am the only gentleman of her acquaintance that hasn't offered her harm," Jacques pointed out in silky tones, waving his hand toward the nearby path. "This way."

Gabriel clenched his teeth, unable to deny the charge, damn the bastard.

Even when he had come to rescue his wife from the clutches of the evil French he had managed to insult her with his accusations.

And why?

Because she stirred feelings inside him that were as incomprehensible as they were unwelcome?

Forcing himself to follow at the Frenchman's side, he wrenched his tangled thoughts from his wife, concentrating on the dangers at hand.

"A charming home for a vicar," he drawled.

"Oui." A smile of bleak satisfaction curved Jacques's mouth. "It once belonged to the gentleman who condemned my father to death. Ironic, is it not?"

"There is nothing ironic in countrymen slaughtering one another."

"So speaks the pampered nobleman," Jacques said and sneered. "You would not be so smug if you were forced to watch your children starving in the gutters."

Gabriel arched a brow, deliberately allowing his gaze to skim the vast gardens and sprawling palace that surrounded them.

"Instead you drown your citizens in blood while you take comfort in the luxury you profess to detest. How many have died since your grand revolution?"

With the typical conceit of a zealot, the man shrugged aside the thousands of deaths suffered since the assault on the Bastille. Deaths that only continued beneath the rule of Napoleon with his insatiable lust for power.

"Freedom is not without cost."

Gabriel snorted in disgust. "Is that what you tell your orphans?"

"They will understand that sacrifices were necessary when Napoleon is victorious."

"More likely they will return to starving in the gutters when the Corsican monster is destroyed and his allies scurry away like the pathetic cowards they are."

Gabriel enjoyed a stab of satisfaction as Jacques's expression tightened, but with admirable control the Frenchman smoothed his features.

"Time will tell which of us is correct." Altering his course, Jacques led Gabriel through a low archway. He paused to retrieve a lit torch from a bracket on the stone wall before he pulled open a door that led to a stone staircase cut deep into the ground. Behind them the French soldier held his gun at the ready, preventing Gabriel from any foolish hope of a swift escape. "Although it is questionable whether or not you will live long enough to enjoy France's inevitable triumph," Jacques continued in smug tones.

Gabriel refused to be goaded, instead distracting himself by memorizing the path through the narrow tunnels that had been chiseled beneath the palace.

"You might be an arrogant bastard who is willing to sacrifice his honor for a futile war, but not even you would be foolish enough to murder the Earl of Ashcombe," he challenged.

"Who would know?" Jacques waved a hand to indicate the damp passageway. "I possess a convenient talent for making bodies disappear."

Gabriel forced a stubborn smile, as his companion pushed open a heavy wooden door and waved him inside the cavernous room that had obviously been a wine cellar before being emptied of its shelves of bottles. Now there was nothing more than a few narrow cots and a meager washstand to fill the emptiness.

"You do not think I traveled here alone, do you?" he demanded, stepping into the room and turning to regard his captor with a nonchalance he could only hope would fool the Frenchman.

He refused to consider what would happen if it were discovered that his only ally was already headed back to his ship.

"We shall soon discover. I have my soldiers searching the area."

"My men are wise enough to avoid capture," Gabriel drawled.

Jacques chuckled. "A pity their master was not so wise, eh Ashcombe?"

Gabriel fisted his hands, battling back the desire to throttle the conceited fop.

Patience, he sternly reminded himself.

Soon enough he would manage to escape, and then Jacques Gerard would learn the meaning of regret.

For now he had to content himself with banishing that annoying smirk from his overly handsome face.

"I was wise enough to outwit you," he said, folding his arms over his chest.

The taunting edge in his voice had the desired effect as Jacques slowly narrowed his gaze.

"An odd boast considering you are the one being locked in the cellars."

"Perhaps, but I have the pleasure of knowing that I have ruined your attempts to lead Wellesley's men into an ambush."

A thick, explosive fury trembled through the air.

"How very clever of you," Jacques snarled. "Do you mind sharing how you managed to discover…" He bit off his words with a sudden hiss. "Ah, Henderson and his brother."

Gabriel savored the man's biting disappointment. "Yes, your partners were quite forthcoming with a bit of encouragement."

It took long moments before the Frenchman heaved out a sigh, his ire replaced with derisive resignation.

"A pity, but I always knew they were immoral wretches who would betray their own mother if they could make a profit," he admitted. "I trust they will be suitably punished for their treachery?"

"Of course." Gabriel twisted the knife. "As will their accomplice in the Home Office who has also been captured."

A muscle knotted in Jacques's jaw as he considered the various repercussions at the discovery of his conspirators.

"I presume Henderson also gave you the necessary information to find me?"

"Yes."

"Merde." Jacques shook his head. "It was a risk to reveal my destination, but they had promised to continue our rather profitable arrangement."

Gabriel growled low in his throat at the man's casual words. The *profitable arrangement* had no doubt cost the lives of dozens, perhaps even hundreds, of British soldiers over the past year.

"I assure you that your arrangement is at an end," he snapped.

The mocking amusement returned to Jacques's face. "True, but thankfully they were not my only associates and I do have Talia to offer me comfort." His smile widened. "And speaking of your beautiful wife, I truly should ensure that she has not been unduly disturbed by your unwelcome arrival. *Bonsoir,* Ashcombe."

Gabriel rushed forward just as the door was slammed in his face. With a curse he pounded his fist against the thick wood.

"Touch her and I will kill you, you bastard."

CHAPTER NINE

IT SEEMED AN ETERNITY had passed before Talia heard the sound of approaching footsteps, although she knew it had been less than an hour since André had returned her to her luxurious chambers and firmly locked the door.

Anxiously pacing from one end of the room to the other, Talia came to an abrupt halt as the key was turned in the lock, and the door was pressed open.

"Jacques," she breathed, pressing a hand to her quivering stomach as the Frenchman strolled to the center of the carpet with his usual grace. "What have you done to my..." As always she stumbled over the unfamiliar word. "Gabriel?" she instead muttered.

A hint of satisfaction touched Jacques's handsome features.

"You cannot even bear to claim him as your husband, can you, *ma petite?*"

Her chin tilted. She was tired, frustrated and terrified that Gabriel might be seriously harmed or worse, all because of his impetuous urge to rescue her.

"Do not presume that you comprehend my feelings for Gabriel," she warned. "The truth is that I do not understand them myself."

"He does not deserve your loyalty."

Talia's lips twisted. Jacques did have a point.

Gabriel had hardly been a doting husband. Not even

when he had arrived to heroically sweep her back to England.

But the mere thought of the irksome fiend being hurt was enough to make her stomach heave and her heart ache.

"That is for me to decide."

Jacques shook his head ruefully. "So forgiving."

She planted her hands on her hips. "You are avoiding my question."

"His lordship is comfortably settled in the cellars." Jacques looked as if he had just bitten into a lemon. "For now at least."

"What do you intend to do with him?"

With a restless motion Jacques moved toward the mantel to arrange the delicate porcelain figurines.

"I will admit I am greatly tempted to tie him to the nearest tree and use him as target practice for my soldiers."

"Dear God...no."

He turned back to meet her horrified gaze. "Fortunately for your husband, I am not a self-indulgent aristocrat who thinks of nothing beyond his own pleasure."

"What do you mean?"

Jacques shrugged. "The Earl of Ashcombe is an arrogant *cretin,* but I do not doubt his mother will be willing to offer a tidy sum of money for his return. I intend to send a demand for his ransom tonight."

Talia bit her lower lip, torn between relief that Gabriel was to be spared and dismay at the thought of his mother being subjected to the terrifying ordeal of knowing her son was being held captive by French spies.

"You cannot be so cruel."

"It is what must be done." Jacques did not even bother

to appear apologetic. "I have hungry mouths to feed and dangerously empty coffers."

"Tell me how much you will request for Gabriel's release and I will ensure that it is delivered to you," she countered. "There is no need to bully an old woman."

His brows snapped together. "Have you forgotten that old woman has publicly shunned you since your marriage?"

Talia flinched. Of course she had not forgotten. Nor was she naïve enough to imagine that the dowager countess would ever consider her as anything other than an embarrassment that should be hidden from society.

But, while the Ashcombes might not consider her worthy, Talia was now a member of the family, and she would do whatever was necessary to protect them.

"What does it matter so long as you have the money to feed your children?"

"You…" Jacques gave a shake of his head, regarding her with an odd expression.

"What?"

"I have forgotten there are still truly good people in this world." He stepped forward, gently brushing her heavy curls from her cheek. "You terrify me."

She shifted with unease beneath the intensity of his stare.

"Now you are taunting me."

"Non." His fingers brushed down the line of her jaw. "You are one of those women who tempt a man to reform his sinful ways. Dangerous."

Talia frowned at the absurdity of his claim.

She had been at the mercy of men since the day she'd been born. Her father. Harry. Gabriel. And now even Jacques. All of them had forced their will upon her.

"Very charming, but if I have discovered nothing else

it is that no man is willing to reform his sinful ways for a mere woman. Or at least, not for me." She scowled as Jacques's laughter rang through the room. "What is so amusing?"

His eyes shimmered with a rueful humor. "I have devoted my entire life to gaining freedom for the French people, even when it meant returning to England and deceiving those neighbors who trusted me. And yet I have risked everything to bring you with me rather than disposing of you as I should have."

"You could never kill an innocent," she protested.

"I have done far worse, *ma petite*." A wistful smile curved his lips. "But when you look at me with those beautifully trusting eyes, I long to be the man that you see."

"Jacques."

"And what you have done to me pales in comparison to the destruction that you have wrought in your poor husband," he continued.

"That is not amusing."

Jacques clicked his tongue. "Surely you must be aware that before your marriage the Earl of Ashcombe was notorious for being an arrogant, overly proud gentleman who remained aloof from all but a few privileged friends?"

"I suppose he was considered aloof," she grudgingly conceded.

"He was a coldhearted bastard," Jacques corrected in dry tones, "but within a few weeks you have reduced him to a possessive barbarian who recklessly charged into danger the moment he realized that you were missing."

"That is..." She sucked in a deep breath. "You are being absurd."

"The poor man is currently roaring like a demented madman in my cellars." His smile held an edge of satisfaction. He was evidently pleased by the thought of Gabriel suffering. "What further proof do you desire?"

For a moment of utter madness, Talia allowed herself to believe Gabriel had come to consider her as more than a burden that must be suffered for the sake of his family pride. But she hastily squashed the ridiculous notion.

This was not the time or place for absurdities.

"All I desire is to be allowed to return to England with my husband." She pulled from his lingering touch. "How much money do you require?"

He folded his arms over his chest, regarding her with a brooding gaze.

"I said that I would be willing to trade the Earl of Ashcombe for a sizeable donation to my orphans. I did not include you in the bargain."

A chill settled in the pit of Talia's stomach. "You promised to release me once the battle with Wellesley had begun."

"Perhaps I find that I cannot."

"Jacques."

"You are weary, *ma petite,*" he muttered, moving to brush a light kiss over her lips before crossing firmly toward the door. "Go to bed and we will discuss this in the morning."

Talia watched him leave the room, closing and locking the door behind his slender form.

Surely he must be teasing her?

For all of his charming flirtations, he could not truly desire to keep her in France.

Could he?

Chewing her bottom lip, Talia paced the floor, shifting through her limited options.

For once she did not intend to sit idly by and wait to discover what new disaster fate had concocted for her.

On this occasion she intended to take command of her own destiny.

SOPHIA REYNARD moved through the sleepy palace with a proud grace that had once made her the toast of the Parisian stage and had captured the adoration of her vast audience.

Although some would claim it was the beauty of her pale ivory features contrasted with her auburn curls that had earned her fame. Or her expressive eyes that were closer to black than brown. Or even her tall, willowy form that appeared elegant whether in rags or, as it was now, draped in a sapphire silk dressing gown with black velvet bows begging to be undone.

Sophia, however, had always known it was her acting skills that had catapulted her from her mother's fetid rooms in *Halles,* near the old Cemetery of the Innocents to the finest mansions in *Chaussée d'Antin* and the *Faubourg Saint-Germain.*

Onstage she could capture the humor of Molière or the tragedy of Racine. And offstage...well, that was where her genuine talent was revealed.

With the skill that only the finest courtesans were able to acquire, she was capable of becoming any gentleman's deepest desire.

She could be shy or naughty. Timid or daring. Sweet or vulgar. She could converse with the most celebrated intellectuals or tell jokes that would make a sailor blush. And most important of all, she could make a man feel as if he were without equal when he pulled her into his arms.

It was those talents that had allowed her to survive the

revolution even when her aristocratic lovers were being
slaughtered. And eventually to capture the interest of
Napoleon for several months after his rise to power.

She was a born survivor.

Unfortunately, she was not always wise.

She had met Jacques Gerard in Paris five years before
and for the first time in her thirty years she had been immediately bewitched.

It went beyond a predictable attraction to his handsome face and fine form, although she was not yet so
jaded she could not appreciate the flutters of excitement
that raced through her when he glanced in her direction. Indeed, she had suddenly been transported back to
the long-ago days when she'd still been young and naïve
enough to believe in love.

But it was more his restless intelligence and the ardent
intensity that simmered about him.

He was radiant, incandescent.

Whether he was plotting war strategies with Napoleon
or seducing her into his bed, he was driven by passions
that set her body and her heart—her very soul—on fire.

Within a few days she had fallen deeply in love with
the elusive man, remaining faithful to him despite their
long times apart, as Jacques spent months and sometimes
years in England.

Not that she was foolish enough to assume he was
equally celibate. He was a man, after all. Who of them
was not swift enough to expect loyalty from a woman
while they happily bedded every maiden willing to lift
her skirts?

Still, Jacques had never displayed any affection or lingering interest for any other female.

Until now...

Pausing to smooth her expression into one of pleasant anticipation, Sophia stepped into Jacques's private chambers, her heart missing a painful beat at the sight of him leaning against the windowsill, a half-empty glass of brandy in his slender hands.

He appeared remarkably suited to the lavish gold-and-ivory room with his elegant beauty and his slender body attired in a brocade robe. In truth, she had always wondered if he had more noble blood running through him than he wished to admit. He looked far more like an aristocrat than a peasant.

It was a suspicion she was careful to keep to herself. He would find nothing amusing in the notion there was blue blood running through his veins.

Especially tonight, she ruefully acknowledged, noting the tense set of his shoulders and his grim expression.

She faltered momentarily. She had sought out Jacques to demand explanations.

But did she truly desire to hear what he might say?

The cowardly part of her was not at all certain she was prepared to discover the truth. Not if it were destined to crush her stupid heart.

But she had not survived for thirty years by being a coward. Sucking in a deep breath, she forced herself to cross past the gilt beechwood chairs and the oval parquetry table inset with Sevres porcelain that was placed near the white marble fireplace. She had nearly reached the scrolled rosewood desk that groaned beneath the maps, stacks of waiting messages, journals and scribbled notes when Jacques sensed her presence and whirled to regard her with a scowl.

Sophia kept her smile intact as she came to a smooth halt. "Am I intruding?"

Just for a heartbeat an emotion perilously close to regret touched his handsome face, as if she had reminded him of something he preferred to forget. Then, with his usual charm, he stepped forward to lift her fingers to his lips.

"Sophia, you are a vision of loveliness as always," he murmured, speaking in French with a hint of an English accent that always sent a tingle of pleasure down her spine. "Is that a new dressing gown?"

"*Oui*. I discovered a very talented *modiste* in Paris while I counted the days until your return to France." She deliberately lowered her voice to a sensuous invitation. "I have been anxiously awaiting an opportunity to reveal my treasures."

"The treasure is not to be found in silks or satins. It is you, *ma belle*." His dark gaze ran an appreciative survey down her body. "You would be breathtaking in a sackcloth."

"A treasure that is easily forgotten, it would seem."

She instantly regretted her impetuous words as he released her hand and took a step backward, his expression guarded.

Sacré bleu. What was the matter with her? She had once been a master of such games.

"Ah, you have come to chastise me for having neglected you," he accused.

"I would hope I am not so foolish as to chastise my lover. There is no more certain means to tarnish a man's affection." She sought to keep her tone teasing. "I will admit, however, that I am curious as to what has kept you so occupied that you cannot spare so much as an hour to spend in my company."

"Forgive me, *ma belle*." He waved a hand toward the nearby desk. "I fear that I had no notion that organizing a handful of spies could be so time-consuming."

"So your distraction has nothing to do with your English guests?"

A surge of anger hardened his features. "Of course it does. The black plague—"

"Black plague?" she interrupted in confusion.

"More properly known as the Earl of Ashcombe," he grimly clarified, "has not only had the audacity to trespass into my home, but he has ruined a perfect opportunity for our soldiers to strike a mortal blow against our enemies." He clenched his hands. "To make matters worse, he has exposed my associate in the Home Office who was providing a vital source of information. It will take me months to undo the damage he has wrought."

"Ah, I see. A black plague, indeed," she readily agreed, her gaze lingering on the tight line of his jaw. Was his resentment caused by the Earl's destruction of his secret arrangements or Ashcombe's attempt to rescue his young bride? "What will you do with him?"

Jacques shrugged. "I am in the process of composing a letter to the dowager countess demanding a ransom for the return of her son. I do not doubt that she will be eager to share a large portion of her vast fortune to ensure the earl's safety."

She stroked a dark curl that she had deliberately left to lay against the swell of her ivory bosom.

"What of his wife?"

Jacques visibly stiffened. "Talia?"

"Oui."

"I fear the dowager has no love for the current countess," he said dryly, his thoughts unreadable. "She would be more likely to pay for me to keep Talia as to have her returned."

"And will you?"

"Will I what?"

"Keep her."

A keen pain sliced through Sophia's heart as Jacques abruptly turned to pace toward the fireplace. So her suspicions were not mere fancies.

Not entirely surprising.

According to the rumors, the Countess of Ashcombe had managed to bewitch every male from the most seasoned soldier to the youngest orphan with her ready friendliness and kind heart.

And, of course, what man could possibly resist the thought of a young and beautiful woman who was alone and so terribly vulnerable?

"It is a decision to which I will have to give some thought," he muttered.

Sophia was too intelligent to press for an answer. Instead she carefully eased her way past his instinctive need to play hero to the more prosaic side of his nature.

"Her father is very wealthy, is he not?" she asked softly.

He shrugged. "As rich as Croesus, if the gossips are to be believed."

"Then surely he would be willing to pay a ransom for his only child?"

His scowl returned. "It is difficult to know with men such as Silas Dobson. He was willing to sell Talia to the highest title, so it is obvious he has little affection for her." His voice was edged with disgust. Jacques found social climbers as repugnant as nobles. "He might very well decide his daughter is no longer his responsibility."

"There is only one means to discover if he is willing to pay," she gently urged. "I shall be happy to assist you in writing the ransom note…"

"Non."

"Jacques?"

His eyes blazed with a warning that could not be ignored. "The Countess of Ashcombe is my responsibility and I will decide her future without interference. Is that understood?"

Sophia bit back her words of protest. *Mon Dieu.* Had she not caused enough harm for one night?

She had intended to be subtle. She was, after all, a woman who had been beguiling men since the tender age of thirteen. It should have been a simple matter to discover the depth of Jacques's feelings for Talia and from there to covertly begin the process of eroding his regard for the unwelcome bitch.

She had done it a dozen times before.

Perhaps a hundred.

But never for a man she loved, her battered heart whispered.

And now her blundering had only made Jacques more stubbornly determined to protect the poor, sadly abused Lady Ashcombe.

"Of course," she managed to murmur.

With jerky motions, Jacques pulled out the chair near the desk. "I should return to my correspondence."

"As you wish." Forcing herself to cross the room, Sophia paused at the door. "Do not work too hard, *chéri.* You must remain strong for all of us."

He did not bother to glance in her direction. *"Bonsoir, ma belle."*

"Bonsoir."

Sophia walked down the vast hallway, the rustle of her silk gown the only sound to break the heavy silence. She paid no heed, however, to the empty grandeur of her surroundings as she traveled grimly back toward her chambers.

Her disturbing encounter with Jacques had convinced

her that she had no choice. The Countess of Ashcombe had to leave France.

The sooner the better.

And there was only one certain means of accomplishing her goal.

With her decision made, Sophia entered her rooms to collect a blanket. Then dismissing the voice that whispered she was taking the greatest risk of her life, she silently made her way to Jacques's private office. Her heart was thundering in her chest as she snuck into the darkened room. But she refused to give in to fear as she searched until she at last discovered what she was seeking in a locked desk drawer.

Slipping the small piece of jewelry in one pocket of her dressing gown and a sealed letter in the other pocket, she headed back into the hallway and toward the nearest staircase with an air of purpose.

She continued her swift pace ever downward, sweeping past the curious guards until she reached the cellars and the soldier who stood directly before the locked door.

Summoning her most charming smile, Sophia gestured toward the blanket in her hand and assured the wary guard that Jacques had sent her to make certain their guest was made comfortable. The man hesitated, then with a faint shrug he turned the key in the lock and pulled open the heavy oak door.

Sophia stepped past him, waiting for the door to be shut behind her before moving into the shadowed room, her breath squeezed from her lungs as the tall gentleman lifted his graceful form off the narrow cot and prowled toward her.

Even for a woman jaded by a lifetime of men, Sophia had to admit this one was a magnificent specimen.

In the torchlight his hair shimmered like the finest

gold, and his perfectly chiseled features looked more fitted for an angel than a mere man. But for all his astonishing beauty, Sophia felt a chill of premonition inching
down her spine.

Unlike most of the nobles she had entertained over the
years, the Earl of Ashcombe was no primping dandy, nor
was he a debauched lecher. *Non.* This gentleman was a
sleek, dangerous predator who regarded her with a cold,
silver gaze that seemed to pierce through her hard-earned
defenses.

"Well, well," he drawled. "Jacques might be a ghastly
host, but he does possess an exquisite taste in guards."
He ran a blatant gaze down the length of her body. "Or
are you here in the guise of a maid?"

She tossed aside the blanket, offering him the famed
smile that had seduced men, from chimney sweeps to
royalty.

"How can you be so certain I am not a genuine maid?"
she said huskily.

His eyes narrowed, but thankfully he seemed as susceptible as every other gentleman to her allure, and stepping forward, he captured her hands in a light grip.

"Few servants can afford a gown made of pure silk.
And these hands…" His thumb brushed her inner wrist
with a touch that spoke of his vast experience in pleasing women. "Soft and smooth. They have never known
hard labor."

"While your hands are finely crafted like those of
an artist and yet, strong enough for a warrior. An enticing combination." Her throaty words were cut off as she
found herself being roughly shoved against the brick wall
of the cellar, her captor using his large body to restrain
her instinctive attempt to escape. Sophia froze, her lips
twisting with the rueful acceptance that it was Ashcombe

who had lured her into a false sense of security rather than the other way around. She did not know whether to be insulted or impressed. "My lord. Should we not at least be introduced before you attempt such intimacies?" she quipped.

His expression was set in cruel lines. "Does Jacques think me a fool?"

"Actually he refers to you as the black plague."

"Tell me why he sent you."

Sophia shivered beneath the impact of his icy gaze. Up close the Earl of Ashcombe was even more intimidating than at a distance.

She felt very much as if she had poked a sleeping lion, and now she was about to suffer the consequences.

"He does not know I am here," she responded.

His jaw tightened. "I have no patience for such tedious games."

With an effort, Sophia stiffened her spine and forced a teasing smile to her lips. This was too important to lose her courage now.

"I assure you, my lord, my games are never tedious."

His gaze flicked with chilling indifference down her slender body, seemingly disinterested in the perfection of her curves.

"You are either here in the hopes of seducing information from me or in an effort to lure me from my wife." His gaze snapped back to her face. "Both of which are doomed to failure."

She couldn't curb the stab of bitterness. "*Non,* I could never hope to lure a gentleman from the bewitching allure of the Countess of Ashcombe."

"What do you know of my wife?" he growled.

"I know that she cannot be allowed to remain here."

He frowned, caught off guard by her simple words. "Who the devil are you?"

"Sophia Reynard."

"Sophia." He slowly tested her name on his lips. "Why is that so familiar?"

Her chin tilted with pride. "Before my retirement I was considered one of the finest actresses in Paris."

"Ah, yes." Frigid recognition flared through his eyes. "You were a companion to Napoleon."

Sophia rolled her eyes. No matter what her success upon the stage had been she would always be renowned for her powerful lovers, never for her considerable skill as an actress.

Such a pity men were allowed to rule the world.

"That is all in the past," she informed him.

"Then why are you at this palace?"

"I should think that would be rather obvious to such a worldly gentleman," she said dryly.

"Good God." He grimaced. "Jacques Gerard?"

"*Oui*. He is handsome and charming and a *magnifique* lover. More important, he is a skillful leader who is destined for greatness."

Lord Ashcombe shrugged. "Only if Napoleon succeeds."

"Which he must do," she said, her voice thick with sincerity. "And to accomplish his victory he has need of Jacques."

He studied her for a long, unnerving moment. Then slowly he stepped back, although Sophia was not foolish enough to believe he would allow her to escape, even if she desired to.

"Why did you seek me out?"

She smoothed a nervous hand down the silk of her

gown. "Since Jacques's return to France I find myself growing concerned."

"So you should," he taunted. "He is a treacherous bastard who should be delivered to the guillotine with all possible haste."

"My concern is that he is being distracted from his responsibility."

"If you have no desire for him to be distracted then perhaps you should consider leaving the palace."

Her lips twisted in a smile of self-derision. "Much to my dismay I find that I am not the distraction, my lord." She met his gaze squarely. "It is your wife."

CHAPTER TEN

STANDING SO HE COULD keep an eye on both his unexpected intruder and the door, Gabriel narrowed his gaze and resisted the urge to throttle Sophia Reynard.

There was no doubt the female was a stunning beauty.

Her silky hair and dark eyes set against the pale alabaster of her skin gave her an exotic air that would make any man think of warm nights and satin sheets.

But Gabriel had never been a gentleman who allowed himself to be led by his cock.

So far the female had attempted to distract him with a peek of her bosom and a few seductive smiles. Now obviously she had turned her tactics to insulting his wife and attempting to make him question her honor.

"Be very careful what you imply, Sophia," he rasped.

Her mouth tightened with something that might have been resentment.

"I merely speak the truth."

"My wife is above reproach and if you think to say otherwise you will regret—"

"My lord," she interrupted with brittle impatience. "I would never be so mad as to question the Countess of Ashcombe's honor, but you must realize that she is precisely the sort of female to stir Jacques's most protective instincts."

Against his will, Gabriel found himself hesitating. He wanted to dismiss her words as a trick, but how could

he? There was only one reason that the Frenchman had
brought Talia to this palace and treated her as a welcome
guest rather than a prisoner.

He wanted her for himself.

White-hot fury exploded through him.

"She belongs to me."

"You have an odd means of claiming her," Sophia said,
her voice edged with annoyance. "I am not entirely certain why you chose to abandon your young and beautiful
bride in the countryside. It was highly irresponsible and
destined to rouse the primitive desires of every man the
neighborhood over to rush to her rescue."

He scowled, ignoring the unpleasant realization that
she had a point.

"I did not abandon her."

"She was alone and vulnerable, an irresistible target
for a man who worships the memory of his father."

He feverishly paced across the cellar, his heart giving
a strange lurch at the thought of his wife feeling alone
and vulnerable while he had been in London, pompously
wallowing in his self-righteousness.

"What does his father have to do with Talia?"

"The previous Monsieur Gerard was willing to die to
protect his wife from the cruelty of a villainous nobleman. How could Jacques not be eager to charge to the
rescue of a damsel in distress?"

Gabriel snorted. "The bastard did not charge to the
rescue. He kidnapped her and now is holding her prisoner."

"In his mind he is the hero rescuing her from you, the
evil blackguard threatening to destroy her life," Sophia
ruthlessly pressed.

Male possession clawed through him. Talia was his.
And he would kill any man who thought otherwise.

"I assume that you have a purpose in seeking me out?" he seethed.

Her dark eyes smoldered with barely suppressed emotion as she stepped from the wall.

"I wish your wife to disappear from France and I believe you are the gentleman to accomplish the delicate task."

"I would, of course, be delighted to return my wife to our home in England, but perhaps you might have noticed I am currently being held captive." He waved a hand toward the door. "Unless you have magically made the guards disappear?"

"*Non,* but I am willing to distract them while you escape."

He studied her with blatant suspicion. "Why?"

Her brow wrinkled in confusion. *"Pardon?"*

"Why would you assist me?"

"I have told you, I desire the countess to be taken far away from France."

"Mere jealousy would not compel you to betray your lover, and certainly not your country."

A tragic smile curved her lips as she stood proudly beneath his accusing gaze. "You understand nothing of women if you are unaware that we will sacrifice everything for love."

A pang of envy—or was it longing?—briefly pierced his heart before he angrily dismissed the sensation.

Love was nothing more than a pretty illusion that females used to disguise their primitive passions. Couples were drawn together by lust, by power or by wealth. It had nothing to do with rosebuds and moonbeams.

"Actually I understand enough of women to be suspicious when a beautiful female simply appears, offering precisely what I most desire," he said and sneered.

"There is always a price to be paid. Usually one I have no wish to pay."

She made a sound of impatience. "What could I hope to gain by assisting you to escape?"

"It is not something I intend to discover." He regarded her stubbornly. "Frankly, I do not trust you, Sophia Reynard."

There was a long silence, as if the woman were pondering some deep problem, then at last she heaved a sigh.

"A pity," she muttered. "I had hoped to avoid this."

"Avoid what?"

She visibly squared her shoulder. "I will prove that I am willing to sacrifice all to reclaim my lover."

His brow arched. "A charming offer, but one that does not interest me."

Her expression hardened with annoyance. "I do not intend to share my body."

"Then what?"

"I..."

"Yes?"

"I can reveal the English traitor who is Jacques's partner."

Hardly an earth-shattering offer considering they had already dealt with the immoral bastards.

"We have captured his partners."

"*Non,* you captured a few trifling employees."

He stiffened at her derisive tone. "A clerk in the Home Office is hardly trifling."

"Perhaps not, but he is easily replaced." She paused. "So long as one is acquainted with a gentleman who is in the proper position to replace him."

"Jacques?" he asked, baffled by her vague hints.

She gave a vehement shake of her head. "Jacques avoids London like the plague. It is essential that he main-tain a discreet presence in England so as not to attract unwanted attention."

"Why?"

"His mother resides in London. She has no notion of his…"

Gabriel was not entirely surprised that the Frenchman would have family in England. His English had been far too polished for him not to have spent several years in England.

"Treachery?" he suggested.

"Of his daring crusade," she corrected sharply. "And of course, the ruffians he employs to transport the information from London could never cultivate the necessary contacts within the government and military." She stepped forward, holding his gaze. "*Non,* only a gentleman of noble birth could provide the access that Jacques needs."

His lips parted to deny the mere thought that a noble gentleman could ever be involved in such a sordid scheme, but he stopped short. He, better than anyone, understood that some of the greatest thieves, murderers and cutthroats were not in the stews, but traveled the hallowed streets of Mayfair.

Besides, she had a point. Jacques had to have a powerful patron to have become such a successful spy.

"Very well, I accept that there must be a gentleman of considerable social standing to have connections within the Home Office," he grudgingly conceded.

"And if I offer you the identity of the traitor you will leave France with your wife?" she demanded. "Your word?"

Gabriel hesitated. He had assumed from the moment the beautiful woman had entered the cellar that this was a trap. He would be a fool not to.

But could he in all conscience ignore any opportunity to discover a traitor to the crown?

Who knew how many British soldiers had been lost because of the mysterious bastard? And how many more would be put at risk in the future?

He had no choice but to allow her to take the lead in the farce they were playing.

At least for now.

"My word."

"The traitor is…"

She allowed her words to dangle, feigning a reluctance that was no doubt intended to whet his appetite. Instead it just annoyed him.

"Yes?" he snapped.

"Mr. Harry Richardson."

Silence filled the cellar as Gabriel struggled to accept she had dared accuse his brother. Then, with a murderous fury he grasped her arms and hauled her forward to glare down at her treacherous beauty.

"You bitch," he rasped. "I knew this was a trick."

Her face paled to a sickly shade of ash, but she grimly refused to admit the truth.

"*Non.* You must listen to me."

"Listen to the filthy lies that drip with such ease from those lovely lips?" He shifted his hand to wrap his fingers around her neck, his grip just hard enough to reveal how easily he could put an end to her lies. "I have a better notion. Why do I not choke the truth from you?"

He felt her swallow convulsively, her eyes darkening in genuine fear.

"My pocket," she managed to squeeze out.

"What?"

"Reach into my pocket."

"Why?" he mocked. "Do you have a viper hidden?"

"I have proof."

Gabriel gave a sharp laugh, not certain why he was surprised that his enemies would sink to accusing his own brother of such treachery.

Was there not a saying that "the rules of fair play do not apply in love and war?"

Keeping one hand wrapped around her throat, Gabriel used the other to slip into the pocket of her dressing gown.

"I had already planned to kill Jacques Gerard, now I intend to make certain that the process is as slow and painful as..." He forgot how to speak as he pulled out the small, round object he found in her pocket and glanced at the antique gold ring carved with a familiar signet. "What the hell?"

"You recognize the ring?" she asked softly.

Recognize it? Of course he damned well recognized the thing. Hadn't he personally put it on his brother's finger after his father's funeral? He had worn it himself until he had been forced to accept the ring bearing the Ashcombe crest.

He barely dared to breathe as he fought back the deluge of emotions that threatened to drown him.

Shock. Disbelief. Rage.

Insufferable regret.

"Where did you find it?"

"Jacques demanded it of your brother when Harry agreed to become a spy for France."

He was shaking his head in denial before she ever finished her vile accusation.

"No."

"Jacques sensed that Harry might prove to be an unreliable ally so he desired a token to ensure your brother would not decide to betray his new employer," she pressed.

His gut twisted, his blood running cold even as he told himself that it was a cruel trick.

Whatever Harry's numerous sins, he would never betray his country.

Never.

He clenched his fingers around the ring. "Why this?"

Sophia shrugged. "The ring would expose Harry's own sins should he ever decide to be...indiscreet."

"It proves nothing," he forced himself to mutter. "The ring could easily have been stolen from Carrick Park. No doubt *Vicar*—" he mockingly stressed the title "—Gerard was often welcomed into my home."

She regarded him with something perilously close to pity as she reached into her other pocket and pulled out a folded piece of parchment.

"And this?"

With a curse he snatched the paper from her hand, still attempting to convince himself that this was a deception. It only took a glance, however, for harsh reality to slam into him with agonizing force.

It was not just Harry's signature or the stamped wax seal next to it that convinced him the note confessing his brother's willing pledge to the Emperor Napoleon Bonaparte and his agreement to offer Jacques Gerard any assistance he might require that convinced him that it was not a forgery. It was the careless, nearly illegible penmanship that was distinctly his brother's. It would be near impossible to duplicate.

Damnation.

His mind reeled as the appalling implications of his brother's treachery bit deep into his heart.

Soldiers had died. He shuddered to think how many.

The Corsican monster had been allowed to continue his rampage across Europe and now the Peninsula, because England and her allies had been constantly one step behind. And masses had been driven from their homes to flee from the raging battles.

Was there any worse crime that could be committed?

Unwelcome memories of Harry seared through Gabriel's mind. Images of Harry arriving home in the early morning hours appearing drunk and disheveled with the stench of cheap perfume on his clothing. Of the young man badgering his mother for yet another loan to pay for a flamboyant carriage or box at the theater. Of the burly men who arrived on the doorstep demanding payment from one gambling hell or another.

Weak and self-indulgent.

Two faults that had proven more dangerous than any murderous madman.

Unable to stand still, Gabriel paced across the dirt floor, his mind in turmoil.

Was it possible his brother had been forced into becoming a spy? Had he been blackmailed into writing the damned note?

As unlikely as it might seem, it was the slim thread he could grasp at.

"Tell me from the beginning."

Sophia cleared her throat, no doubt relieved that Gabriel had not chosen to kill the messenger.

"From what Jacques has revealed, he and Harry attended school together."

Gabriel frowned, unable to believe that the intensely driven Jacques could ever have chosen a shallow gamester who considered nothing beyond his own pleasures as a companion.

"They were friends?"

"I do not know the entire story, but they were at least acquainted closely enough for your brother to be aware of Jacques's sympathies for the revolution, as well as his return to France and loyalty to Napoleon."

Gabriel glanced toward his companion. "How can you be certain?"

"Because he made a most surprising visit to this palace over a year ago."

Harry had traveled to France?

"Exactly when?" he demanded.

Sophia took a moment to consider her answer. "Two years ago this past April," she at last revealed. "I cannot give you the precise day."

It was Gabriel's turn to hesitate as he shifted through his memories, wanting to be able to prove that Harry had been safely in London when this woman claimed he was here bartering away his soul.

Unfortunately he had a vague recollection of his mother pouting for weeks because her beloved Harry had refused to accompany her to London for the beginning of the season. Gabriel had been equally surprised by his brother's insistence to remain at Carrick Park, considering his intense dislike for the countryside.

If he'd had any notion the evil that his brother had been plotting…

With a hiss he shoved aside his worthless regrets.

Later he could wallow in guilt and self-recriminations. For now he needed to discover how this nightmare had started and where it was headed.

"He arrived without invitation?"

"He traveled with Madame Martine, who was his current lover," Sophia said, watching his restless movements with a wary gaze. "I believe she was the one to suggest that Harry could ease his financial difficulties by forming an alliance with Jacques. Your brother is a gentleman with a love for the extravagant."

Gabriel snorted. "I am painfully aware of my brother's expensive habits, but I find it difficult to believe that he would ever reach the level of depravity necessary to betray one's own country. Not unless he was being forced."

"There was no force necessary, as you must know, my lord," she said with a hint of sympathy. "There are those men whose souls are barren. They seek to fill the emptiness with ever more exotic pleasures, but nothing can offer them peace."

His hands clenched as her words sliced through his heart with painful precision.

"You know nothing of my brother," he argued, even knowing he could no longer deny the truth.

"I would suspect that I know him better than you, my lord." A sad smile curved her lips. "I, at least, can see him for who he is."

"I do not doubt you have vast experience in knowing a great number of men," he snidely retorted.

Her lips thinned at his insult, but she refused to be silenced.

"Have you considered the notion that your brother not only betrayed his country, but his family, as well?"

"And what is that supposed to mean?"

"How do you believe Jacques acquired his position as vicar upon your estate?"

Gabriel had assumed that there was nothing left to shock him when it came to his brother's lack of morals. A foolish presumption that left him unprepared for the accusation that Harry would not only abuse his position in Gabriel's family, but that he would expose his mother and their tenants to the dangers of ruthless spies and immoral traitors on his land.

Sickening pain shifted to lethal fury.

When he got his hands on his brother he intended to… what?

Hand him over to the authorities and submit his mother to watching her child hanged as a traitor and then endure the shame of being shunned by society?

Allow him to once again walk away with no repercussions?

God almighty. What a mess.

"Damnation," he breathed.

Sophia stepped toward him. "Do you accept that I speak the truth?"

"It would seem I have no choice." With a motion devoid of his usual grace, Gabriel shoved the ring and note into the pocket of his breeches. "I can, however, ensure that your lover release my brother from the threat of exposure."

She shrugged. "You can take them if you wish, but it will not protect Harry."

His brows snapped together. "There are other items?"

"If there are none now, there soon will be."

"An empty bluff," he growled.

"Poor Lord Ashcombe." Sophia regarded him with a pity that set his teeth on edge. "Only this morning Jacques received word from your brother demanding money and a place to remain hidden from the *'devils his brother had sent in pursuit of him.'*"

A humorless smile stretched Gabriel's lips at the irony of the situation. He had sent his servants to find his brother so he could punish him for having forced Gabriel into an unwanted wedding.

Who could have guessed that jilting Talia would prove to be the least of his sins?

"And Jacques agreed to assist Harry?"

"Of course. As the brother of the Earl of Ashcombe, Harry is a priceless associate."

"Where did the letter come from?"

"Here."

Gabriel went rigid at the unexpected word. "In the palace?"

"*Non.* The letter was delivered from Calais." They both froze as the muffled sound of voices floated through the door. "My lord, someone approaches. We can delay no longer."

With a low curse, Gabriel yanked his thoughts from his brother and concentrated on the dangers at hand. He would not have to worry about Harry if he ended up in an unmarked French grave.

"Fine."

Still unwilling to fully trust Sophia, he moved to wrap an imprisoning arm around her shoulders as he led her toward the door. He did not intend to have an enemy follow him.

He had been stabbed in the back enough for one day.

Besides, she would make a handy hostage if the need arose.

He had nearly reached the opposite side of the cellar when there was a squeak of the hinges, and the heavy door was being pushed open.

Cursing his lack of a weapon, Gabriel had no choice but to helplessly watch as the door swung slowly inward.

Prepared for one of the guards or even Jacques, Gabriel was stunned into immobility at the sight of the familiar female with a mass of untamed curls and emerald green eyes clutching a small bundle in her arms.

"God almighty..." he breathed. "Talia?"

CHAPTER ELEVEN

AFTER RECOVERING FROM the considerable drop from her window, Talia had hastily searched for her belongings that Gabriel had left in the garden after being captured. It had taken only a few moments before she was sneaking through the darkness in search of the cellars.

Along the way she had dodged and darted past the various guards while inwardly preparing herself to accept that Gabriel might very well be in dire condition.

Who knew what Jacques might have done to him?

He could be chained to the walls. Or recovering from a brutal beating. Or maimed from some hideous torture.

Her imagination had conjured any number of terrible fates, but she had never once considered the possibility that he would be passing his time with a beautiful, near-naked woman wrapped in his arms.

Worthless pig.

Coming to an awkward halt, she regarded her husband with a proud tilt of her chin.

"Forgive me," she uttered through gritted teeth. "I had the most ridiculous notion that you might desire to be rescued." Her gaze shifted to the woman at his side, not at all comforted by the realization that she was a good ten years her senior. What did it matter? The woman was the sort of sensual siren who would be tempting men until the day she died. "It did not occur that you might be occupied."

The unknown woman ran a dark, scrutinizing gaze over Talia, a mysterious smile curving her lips.

"You must be the Countess of Ashcombe."

"I am," Talia admitted. "And you are?"

"Sophia Reynard."

Even her name was temptingly exotic, Talia acknowledged, pettily wishing the woman at least possessed a wart to mar her perfection.

Having the decency to remove his arms from his lover, Gabriel stepped toward her with a forbidding frown.

"Talia, how the devil did you escape your rooms?"

"I crawled out the window."

He sucked in a harsh breath. "Dammit, you could have broken you neck."

Well, so much for gratitude. Unappreciative sod.

"You were the one urging me to leap from the window not three hours ago."

"Yes, when I was there to catch you," he growled, looking as if he could not quite believe her lack of intelligence.

She sniffed. "Obviously you were too busy to be of assistance, so I had little choice but to risk my neck."

"What of the guards?" Sophia interrupted.

Talia returned her attention to Gabriel's companion with a shrug.

"It was easy enough to slip past most of them."

The female lifted her brows. "And the soldier at the door?"

Talia bit her lip at the stab of regret that pierced her heart.

"Yes, well, I do feel rather badly about poor Pierre," she admitted. "He has been so kind to me."

At her words both Gabriel and Sophia skirted past her. Talia turned to watch Gabriel fully yank open the door, while Sophia gazed down at the large soldier who lay crumpled on the ground.

"Sacré bleu," she muttered. "Is he dead?"

Talia stiffened in outrage. "Certainly not. He will soon awaken." She grimaced as she considered what awaited him. "Although I fear he might have a dreadfully thick head. I do hope his wife knows to brew him a tincture of lavender."

"Christ." Gabriel glanced back at Talia with an expression of disbelief. "I am not certain I could have floored the brute. How the hell did you do it?"

She reached into the folds of the dress that was wrapped around her belongings and pulled out the small, smoothly carved wooden cudgel.

"I am not proud of myself, but I pretended that I had something in my slipper and when he bent down to assist me I hit him with this."

"What is it?" Sophia demanded.

"When I was younger I spent time with my father upon the docks. I was befriended by a Portuguese sailor who carved this for me and taught me the best means of striking a man." Talia smiled at the memory of Santos, who'd been endlessly patient with a lonely girl in desperate need of affection. "My father always insisted that I carry it with me for protection."

Gabriel studied the tiny weapon with an unreadable expression. "You had that hidden on your person at our wedding?"

"It was in my reticule." She frowned at the strange question. "Why?"

He grimaced. "Good God."

Without warning Sophia's throaty chuckle filled the air. "Do you know, my lady, I was quite prepared to detest you, but I discover myself as helplessly enchanted as everyone else." She turned her head to toss Gabriel a mocking glance. "I trust you to take her far away from France and do not allow her to return."

"I—"

Talia's angry retort was interrupted as Gabriel moved to take her arm.

"Can you distract the guards?" he asked of Sophia.

The older woman smiled. "Actually, I think I can do better than that." She tugged the torch from the wall bracket and stepped through the door. "This way."

With little choice, Talia allowed Gabriel to tug her from the room and down the low passageway.

No one spoke as they turned off the main pathway into a narrow tunnel that was filled with cobwebs and goodness knew what nasty creatures. Talia instinctively pressed closer to Gabriel, for the moment more afraid of the small furry rats scurrying around her feet than the one walking at her side.

After what seemed to be an eternity, Sophia led them out of the tunnel into an abandoned garden that was situated behind the kitchens. Pausing long enough to make certain there were no guards near, Sophia led them through the overgrown pathway, pushing open an ivy-covered gate and scurrying toward the nearby woods.

Shifting the bundle in her arms, Talia lifted her skirts to keep pace as they wove their way through the thick trees, only coming to a halt when they were well out of sight of the palace.

Sophia turned, shoving the torch into Gabriel's hand. "I will leave you here."

"You will say nothing of our conversation to anyone," Gabriel commanded, sharing a glance with the older woman that spoke of mutual understanding and hidden meanings.

"I have no more desire than you to share our secrets." With a glance toward the stewing Talia, Sophia leaned forward to place a lingering kiss on Gabriel's cheek. *"Bon voyage,* my lord."

With a last smug smile toward Talia, the aggravating witch slid smoothly into the shadows and disappeared. At the same moment Gabriel hurried Talia in the opposite direction, ignoring her protests as her skirts were shredded to tatters from the underbrush.

He continued the punishing pace for the next two hours, battling a path for them with sheer brute force. Talia might have been impressed with his prowess if she had not been plagued by the memory of Sophia.

Had the two of them just risen from the narrow cot when she'd entered the cellar, or had she intruded before they could become intimate?

And why did either option make her desire to blacken his eye?

She had known when they'd wed that Gabriel was bound to have dozens of mistresses. Fidelity was considered a puritanical concept among society, and nothing could be more bourgeoisie than to display affection for one's own wife or husband.

Besides, Gabriel had made it clear when he'd visited her with that damnable marriage contract that, while he was capable of demanding her loyalty, he had no desire to promise his own.

Of course he was bound to fill his bed with one beautiful woman after another.

Unfortunately, logic did not ease her simmering anger, and when he at last paused to offer her a rest, she was in no humor for his stern disapproval.

"You look like a ragamuffin," he growled, pulling a

handkerchief from his pocket to scrub at the dirt marring her cheek.

"Perhaps you would have preferred to be running through the woods with the lovely Sophia? She would never dare look like a ragamuffin," she snapped.

He scowled, but his fingers were gentle as he moved the handkerchief to a spot near her lips.

"I would prefer that you discontinue your habit of rushing headlong into danger."

"Habit?" She glared into the predatory beauty of his face, unable to believe even Gabriel could hold her to blame for being kidnapped. "Have you taken leave of your senses?"

The silver eyes shimmered in the stray shaft of moonlight, the light breeze weaving through the thick trees to stir his golden hair. Perhaps it was their untamed surroundings or the danger of their situation, but the icily aloof Earl of Ashcombe had suddenly been replaced by a menacing stranger.

"Obviously I have or I would never have let you out of my sight after our wedding. A mistake I intend to correct from this moment on."

She shivered at the husky threat. Not with fear, but with a wholly feminine reaction to his blatant claim of ownership.

Angered by her ridiculous response, she narrowed her gaze. "I should have left you to rot with your pretty French tart."

The tension quivering in the air remained, but something that might have been satisfaction flared through his eyes.

"I had no notion that you would prove to be such a jealous wife."

She flinched at the disturbing accusation, refusing to admit the sensations churning through her.

"I am not jealous."

"No?"

"Certainly not. You, after all, made no promise of fidelity."

He regarded her as if he were offended by her words. "I am your husband."

"That has no meaning among nobles. Society treats marriage as nothing more than empty vows and—" She gasped as Gabriel hauled her against his rigid body, his arms lashing around her to hold her in place. "What are you doing?"

"I assure you that our vows were not empty. You are mine and I will not endure you taking a lover." His eyes blazed with a perilous fire. "Not ever."

Again she felt that thrill of excitement at his primitive claim, and again she was swift to squash it.

"While you are allowed to do as you please, as I recall," she instead muttered.

His gaze lowered to linger on her lips. "What I please is to have my wife in my bed where she belongs."

Talia trembled, acutely aware of his warm body pressed so intimately against her own.

This had to be some new punishment, she told herself. He could not possibly want her with the raw hunger that tightened his face and hardened his body.

"Ah, yes, which explains why you so eagerly banished me to the country," she reminded him.

His head lowered until his breath brushed her cheek in the promise of a kiss.

"I was angry and not thinking clearly."

She dared not allow herself to be swayed. "And why

I just discovered you with a near-naked woman in your arms."

He shifted to nibble at the edge of her lips. "She was not in my arms."

Renegade excitement tingled through her, making her knees weak and her heart flutter.

"But she had been, had she not?" She had to know the truth. It was like a nagging thorn in the center of her heart.

He teased her lips with slow, melting kisses. "I have no interest in women such as Sophia," he whispered, his hands tracing the delicate curve of her spine. "Not so long as I have my sweet, biddable bride returned to me."

It was her sharp, urgent response to his touch that had Talia abruptly turning her head to escape the delectable kisses. She did not want to remember the breathtaking pleasure of being skillfully ravished by her husband. Or the aching satisfaction of being held tenderly in his arms as she slept.

It had only made the inevitable rejection more painful to endure.

"That sweet biddable bride no longer exists," she snapped.

He nuzzled at the pulse pounding at the base of her throat, his tongue tasting of the fluttering beat.

"I could demand her return."

She grasped the lapels of his jacket as warm bliss poured like honey through her body. Oh, heavens, she wanted to press even closer to his hard muscles. To feel those clever fingers stroking over her bare skin and his lips exploring her in the same intimate manner he had used during their wedding night.

Instead she held herself rigid.

She had her pride, did she not?

"You could demand that the sun rise in the west, but it is likely you would be disappointed."

He chuckled at her stubbornness, obviously aware that she was far from indifferent to his touch.

"There are husbands who would beat you into submission," he said, his mouth finding a vulnerable spot just below her ear.

She quivered, swallowing her moan of pleasure. "I am not helpless."

"So you have proven." His lips feathered against her skin, sending another rash of pleasure through her. "And in truth, only the weak and lazy must resort to violence to earn the cooperation of a beautiful woman." His hands cupped the curve of her buttocks, pressing her against the thrust of his arousal. "There are far more pleasant means to tame her."

She forced her hands against his chest, perturbed by the aching need that pulsed deep inside her.

"No."

He pulled back to regard her with a brooding intensity. "Frightened I might speak the truth?"

Yes. She was terrified.

After years of her father's bullying, followed by Gabriel's brutal humiliation, Talia had at last settled into a comfortable existence. It was unnerving to think that he had only to kiss her to have her toss aside all she had gained over the past weeks just to fulfill a physical desire.

"This is hardly the time or place for such nonsense," she said huskily.

Gabriel lifted his head with obvious reluctance, his eyes dark with frustration.

"Soon, my dear," he said, his voice a low warning. "Very soon."

THE NEXT FEW HOURS proved to be distinctly unpleasant for Gabriel.

It was bad enough to be forced to clear a path through the thick underbrush while he was fully aroused and aching with unfulfilled need. Hell, each step was a misery, making him wonder why he had been stupid enough to take her in his arms.

But it was the biting fear that they might stumble into even worse danger as they haphazardly fled from Jacques Gerard that haunted his every move.

He needed to find shelter where they could rest and wait for daylight. Once he could determine their exact position, he was confident he could lead them to his waiting yacht with little difficulty.

Of course, finding a shelter in the middle of enemy territory was easier said than done.

It was nearing dawn when they at last stepped from the trees, and he caught sight of a farmhouse set near a wide stream.

Even from a distance he could determine that the house had been recently burned, leaving little more than a charred shell of bricks. Thankfully, a large barn across the stable yard appeared to be reasonably intact.

Coming to a halt, he placed his hands lightly on Talia's shoulders, his heart lurching as the brush of pink sunlight revealed the weariness that shadowed her eyes and slumped her shoulders. Her hair had long since become a mass of tangled curls, while her dress was ruined beyond repair.

She was on the edge of utter collapse, but not once had she complained or demanded that he carry her through the rough countryside. Of course, he could hardly be surprised. This was the same woman who had leaped from her window and attacked a hulking French soldier to rescue him from the cellars.

He knew of no other woman who possessed her unflinching bravery. Certainly no ladies of society.

He shuddered at the mere thought of his mother or any other female he had known over the years being in Talia's situation. Gods, there would have been nothing but shrieking and swooning and hysterical demands that he somehow whisk them magically back to the comforts of their home.

A wry smile twisted his lips at the pride that surged through him. The irony of the situation was not lost on him.

Mere weeks ago he had condemned her for not being worthy to become his bride. And now he had to accept that she was far superior to any other female who had the blood of nobility running through her veins.

A female of genuine worth, not just shallow polish.

"Wait here," he commanded in soft tones.

She frowned. "Where are you going?"

He nodded toward the farmhouse. "You can barely keep yourself upright. We must find a place to rest."

"Jacques will soon discover we have escaped," she protested. "The guards will be searching for us."

He tucked a curl behind her ear, his thumb brushing the bruises beneath her eyes.

"There is a vast amount of land between Jacques's lair and England," he assured her. "So long as we do not collapse in the middle of the road from exhaustion, we should be safe enough."

She rolled her eyes. "Must you always have your own way?"

"Of course, I am an earl," he said with a playful arrogance that brought a welcome flush of color to her cheeks. "It is my destiny to have my own way. Besides which, I am always right, so why should I not insist on others bowing to my—"

She slapped a hand across his mouth, her eyes narrowed. "If you continue on I fear I will be vilely ill."

Grasping her hand, he pressed her fingers to his lips before stepping back.

"Rest here. I will return in a moment."

She bit her lip, obvious concern shimmering in her eyes. "Gabriel."

"Be at ease," he soothed, "I only intend to make sure there is no one near. I will soon return."

"Unless you are shot."

"You will not be rid of me that easily, my dear." His faint smile faded as he regarded her somberly. "Do not move from this spot, do you understand?"

She waved a limp hand. "I am too weary to disobey you, my lord."

"Good. Perhaps God does answer prayers," he muttered, turning on his heel to head across the damp meadow.

Giving the burnt cottage a cursory inspection, Gabriel shifted his attention to the detached stone barn with a red tile roof that had received only minimum damage from the fire. He pulled open the wide wooden door, cautiously searching through the two-storied structure before moving on to the remaining outbuildings and the surrounding grounds.

Only when he was certain there were no hidden dangers did he return to Talia, his lips thinning at the sight of her seated on the ground, her head bowed in weariness.

Dammit, he was her husband.

She should never have been exposed to such danger. Or have been forced to endure such harsh conditions.

It was untenable.

In the future he would make certain she did not take a step outside the door unless he was firmly at her side.

Dismissing Talia's inevitable outrage at his restriction, Gabriel leaned down to scoop her into his arms, his determination hardening at the feel of her tiny body cradled against his chest. Despite her delectable curves, she was as light as a feather.

Clearly he would also have to supervise her meals from now on, he decided. He would not have it said he refused to feed his own wife.

Her eyes fluttered open as he carried her across the field.

"What are you doing?"

"It is time you were tucked in bed."

"Oh, it is evil of you to tease me," she complained, her voice thick with exhaustion. "I would give anything to be in the comfort of my bed."

His lips twisted, knowing whatever she would be willing to give was nothing in comparison to what he would sacrifice for the opportunity to join her in the comforts of her bed.

He had wanted her for so long it had become a perpetual ache.

With an effort, he managed a strained smile. "A proper wife would claim she was content so long as she was at her husband's side."

"Well, bully for the proper wife," she countered, although she readily nestled her head against his shoulder. "I want a soft mattress and a feather pillow and linen sheets."

He shook his head at her continued defiance. "What am I to do with you?"

"What do you want to do with me?"

"A dangerous question."

Their gazes clashed with a sudden flare of heat and delayed promise. He felt Talia tense before she lowered her lashes, shielding the emotions she did not wish to share.

But it was too late.

Talia might have transformed from a shy mouse to a prickly shrew, but she wanted him with the same blinding need that held him captive.

Satisfaction coursed through him, easing his frustration as they entered the barn, and he crossed the plank floor to the far corner that was piled with loose hay.

The air was musty with only a hint of rosy dawn penetrating through the shuttered windows. From the loft above there was the unmistakable scratch of scurrying mice. Still, it was reasonably clean with a tidy row of farm equipment along one wall that had been left behind, as well as a few household items that had been rescued from the farmhouse. No doubt the owners hoped to return once the war had run its predictable course.

"Here," he murmured, bending to lay Talia on the hay. "Not the most comfortable of beds, but it is better than the ground. Give me your bundle."

Taking her rolled up dress, he tucked it beneath her head. Then, struggling out of his tight jacket, he gently laid it across her shoulders. Only when he was certain she was as comfortable as possible, did he lie down beside her and tuck her against his body.

She stiffened. "Gabriel?"

"Shh." He laid a finger across her lips. "We will have only a few hours to rest. Close your eyes and go to sleep."

Braced for an argument, Gabriel was unprepared when she instead snuggled into his embrace and, with a soft sigh, allowed her eyes to close. Within moments, she was deeply asleep.

Barely daring to breathe, he brushed the dark curls from her cheek and skimmed his lips over her forehead, savoring her sweet lilac scent. For long, timeless moments he simply gazed at the pale beauty of her face, allowing the sight of her to ease the savage fear that had been gnawing at him since her disappearance.

Then, feeling ridiculously content, he pressed his lips to her throat and gave in to his own weariness.

IT WAS MIDMORNING when Gabriel awoke with a stiff neck and empty stomach to discover the rosy dawn had been replaced with threatening clouds.

Careful not to disturb his slumbering wife, he left the barn, needing to stretch his cramped muscles. And of course, there was the necessity of making a thorough search of the area. The barn was remote, but they were still in the middle of France. He would not lower his guard until they were safely returned to Devonshire.

It took a half hour to be certain there were no lurking dangers, then another half hour to bathe in the local stream before he was filling two pails with water and using a third to gather apples from a nearby orchard.

The raindrops were just beginning to fall when he stepped back into the barn. He kicked the door closed behind him, blocking out the damp as well as the distant rumble of thunder, leaving the barn shrouded in hay-scented shadows.

Not that he minded the barren surroundings, he realized with a start of surprise.

Odd for a man who had spent his entire life pampered by luxury.

Perhaps it was the knowledge that for the first time since becoming the earl there was no secretary badgering him with reports from his various estates. Or awaiting correspondence from his Man of Business. Or the endless bills that arrived each morning. Not to mention his responsibilities to his position in the House of Lords. There were no servants hovering just out of sight. No mother with her constant complaints and no brother with his selfish demands.

He was utterly alone with Talia.

And that was nothing less than paradise.

Kneeling at Talia's side, Gabriel put the ladle he had cleaned into one of the buckets of water and set out the apples on his handkerchief. Not the finest breakfast, but it would serve for now.

He turned his head as Talia stirred, a smile curving his lips as she instinctively reached for him. She stiffened when she found nothing but empty boards, her eyes snapping open.

"Gabriel?"

"I am here, little shrew," he murmured in soothing tones. "And I come bearing gifts."

With a blink, she struggled to a seated position, her eyes widening at the sight of apples.

"Where did you get them?"

"The apples came from the nearby orchard and the water from the stream just beyond the cottage."

She turned her head, allowing her gaze to slide over his disheveled appearance. He smiled wryly, knowing precisely what she was seeing. His hair was still wet from the stream and finger-combed to curl against his forehead. His jaw was unshaven and his thin linen shirt hung open at the neck to reveal a shocking amount of his chest.

No doubt he possessed all the elegance of a pirate, but he did not miss the manner in which her eyes darkened and breath quickened.

An answering surge of awareness thundered through him with shocking speed. Lord. How had this delicate gypsy managed to ensnare him with such ease? Certainly no other female had ever consumed him to the point where he thought he might go mad if he did not have her.

Now.

Obviously sensing the prickles of heat in the air, Talia nervously cleared her throat.

"Did you fall in?"

His laughter rumbled through the air as he shifted to settle behind her, his fingers nimbly dealing with the tiny ivory buttons.

"I thought we could both use a good scrub, although I assumed you would prefer privacy for your bath."

He heard her sharply drawn breath as her bodice was pulled relentlessly downward.

"Gabriel, what are you doing?"

"Assisting my wife with her morning ablutions." Bending his head, Gabriel planted hungry kisses down the side of her neck. "It is the duty of a devoted husband, is it not?"

"Certainly not. It is the duty of the husband to stand guard at the door and make certain—"

Her words were lost in a low moan of pleasure as he unlaced her corset and tossed it aside to cup her breasts through the sheer fabric of her chemise.

"Do you enjoy that?" he whispered, brushing his thumbs over the tight peaks of her nipples. "Perhaps you would prefer this?" He plucked the ribbons holding up her undergarment and pushed it aside to cup the satin weight of her breasts in his hands.

She fell back against his chest, her entire body shivering in reaction to his bold caresses.

"Gabriel, we are in a barn," she started to protest.

His tongue tasted the pulse that beat at a frantic pace at the base of her throat before he trailed a line of kisses down her shoulder.

"Yes, I know."

"In full daylight."

With a subtle motion he stroked his hands down her body, removing the female clothing that stood in his path.

"So it is."

Her lips parted on a small gasp as he turned her to the side and laid her back on the hay, clearly becoming aware for the first time that she was completely naked.

"With heaven knows how many French soldiers searching for us," she rasped.

Gabriel wrenched off his boots before yanking his shirt over his head and tossing it aside.

"But it has started to rain," he informed her, ridding himself of his breeches before he stretched out next to her, his fingers threading through the glorious satin of her hair. "It would be foolish to risk the rising streams or becoming stuck in the mud."

"The soldiers…"

He brought an end to her argument, covering her mouth with his own.

Excitement exploded through him at the first taste of her honey lips, his hands greedily exploring her luscious curves.

"We are well hidden, Talia. Let us forget the world," he whispered. "At least for now."

In answer, she tentatively lifted her slender arms to

wrap them around his neck, and Gabriel growled in approval, dipping his head to lick a rose-tipped breast. She arched upward in pleasure, her fingers tunneling into his hair.

"Yes," she whispered.

Tugging the nipple between his lips, Gabriel skimmed his hand down the length of her spine, lingering on the curve of her buttocks. His erection twitched at the sensation of her soft, feminine flesh beneath his hand. He could spend the entire day exploring her from the top of her tousled curls to the tips of her tiny toes.

Or perhaps not, he conceded as she shifted to brush against his aching cock.

Such a delectable exploration might have to wait until he had sated his burning lust.

More than once.

"Touch me," he pleaded softly, allowing his hand to continue down the back of her thigh, urging her legs to part.

She hesitated only a moment before he felt the shy brush of her fingers down his back. He growled, stunned by the raw pleasure at her timid caress. He did not know how it was possible for an untutored innocent to set him on fire, but there was no denying her power.

Returning to claim her in a kiss of masculine demand, he used his tongue to urge her lips apart, bliss clenching his muscles as he at last gained access to the sweet warmth of her mouth.

She tasted of all the things in life that were good and decent. He wanted to capture that goodness, as if it could heal his jaded soul.

He trembled, his breathing ragged as her hand slid over his ribs to search the tense muscles of his chest. Distantly he was aware of the rain pelting against the roof tiles and the occasional streaks of lightning that outlined the shutters, but wrapped in the warm cocoon of the barn he allowed himself to become lost in the sensations searing through him.

Taking care not to startle Talia, Gabriel smoothed his fingers up the inner flesh of her thigh, tracing aimless patterns as she threatened to stiffen at the intimate contact.

"Trust me, Talia," he murmured, scattering hot kisses over her face.

"Yes."

Something shifted inside Gabriel at the soft word. Something so significant that he did not dare examine it too closely.

With a shake of his head at his ridiculous fancy, he set about stirring her to a fever pitch of desire.

His kisses became more heated as he followed a path over her cheek and down her throat. He paused to lick and suckle her straining breasts before he moved down her quivering stomach.

Gabriel lifted his head, capturing her darkened gaze as he settled between her legs, his fingers sliding delicately through her feminine heat.

"Oh," she gasped, a flush of pleasure staining her cheeks.

He chuckled, slowly replacing his fingers with his tongue. She gave a small shriek that settled into a groan of ecstasy as her eyes slid shut.

And it was ecstasy.

Paradise.

Over and over he teased at her tiny bud of pleasure before dipping his tongue into her body, bringing her to the edge of completion before pulling back.

Her eyes flew open, her gaze laced with need. "Please...Gabriel."

"Yes," he choked out, unable to wait another moment.

Gathering her in his arms, he rolled onto his back, shifting until she was perched atop him. Her eyes widened at the unfamiliar position and, pressing her hands against his chest, she regarded him in puzzlement.

"This will be more comfortable for you," he muttered, barely able to speak as her legs naturally draped on either side of his hips, her pelvis pressed perfectly against his arousal.

She bit her bottom lip. "I am not certain what to do."

His heart squeezed. She was so beautiful with her hair tumbled over her bare shoulders and her body flushed with need.

"I will show you," he assured her, reaching to guide her hand to his straining erection.

The breath was slammed from his body as she gingerly curled her fingers around him, nearly unmanning him. Gods. He was supposed to be a sophisticated lover, not a randy schoolboy.

"Like this?" she asked.

"Precisely like that," he groaned. "Now guide me inside you."

She fumbled awkwardly as she attempted to adjust him at the entrance to her body, but gritting his teeth Gabriel managed to avoid embarrassing himself. Then with a low groan he was at last pushing his way into her moist channel.

"Gabriel," she moaned, her nails scoring his chest as Gabriel grasped her hips and lifted her upward before plunging back into her with a slow, exquisite tempo.

"Talia," he echoed, the savage pleasure already tightening his lower stomach. "My sweet shrew."

Her lips parted as she found his rhythm, her head tilted back as she rode him with an enthusiasm that all too swiftly had him rushing toward his release. With a muttered curse, he angled his hips upward, pressing ever deeper as his pace increased.

Incoherent words tumbled from Talia's lips as she squeezed her eyes shut, her beautiful body arching as she was overtaken by her climax. Gabriel watched in fascination as she surrendered to the pleasure he had given her, but the sensation of her body clasping his cock in tiny ripples all too soon had him giving one last thrust before he was shouting out with a bliss he felt to his very soul.

Feeling Talia collapse against his chest, Gabriel wrapped his arms around her trembling body, struggling to recall how to breathe.

Just for those few moments, the world truly had disappeared.

CHAPTER TWELVE

SOPHIA WAS SEATED at the vanity, lazily pulling a brush through her damp curls, when the door to her private bedchamber was thrust open, banging with loud emphasis against the wall.

She barely flinched.

Despite the apprehension that had plagued her since leaving her bed, she had forced herself to follow her usual routine. She had enjoyed a cup of coffee while skimming through a letter from an acquaintance in Paris. She had chosen the gown she desired to be ironed by her maid, then there had been a hot bath before she had pulled on a gossamer dressing gown and began preparing for the day.

All the while she had been bracing herself for this confrontation.

Which was why she was able to calmly set aside her brush as Jacques stormed into the room, his face tight with fury.

"Did you think I would not discover your betrayal?" he accused.

Sophia rose to her feet with elegant composure. Absently she noted her companion's black jacket and the dove-gray waistcoat that was fitted with tailored perfection to his lean body. His black pantaloons clung to his thighs before being hidden beneath his tall boots that held the gloss of the finest leather. He was, as always, breathtakingly beautiful.

"Non," she answered, her husky voice the only indication of her unease. "I was fully aware you would learn of my visit to the Earl of Ashcombe."

"More than a visit." He stepped close enough for her to catch the light scent of bay water that clung to his skin. "You assisted him in escaping."

Her sharp, humorless laugh filled the vast room. "Unfortunately I can take little credit for his release. It was your precious Talia who proved to be the true heroine."

He stilled, regarding her with a hint of surprise. "You are jealous of her?"

Stupid man. Did he truly not realize the torture he was forcing her to endure?

"Naturellement."

With a jerky movement, Sophia crossed the *Savonnerie* carpet that matched the pale lavender satin wall panels and the cream curtains that framed the tall windows. There was a large walnut bed set in the center of the room with a scrolled armoire and vanity along one wall. Sophia halted near the oval table that held a collection of tiny miniatures and aimlessly studied one of a cherubic child with wide blue eyes and an innocent smile. Her hand instinctively lifted to her empty womb.

"She is young, beautiful, courageous and yet tragically vulnerable," she explained. "She is the sort of woman who men die for."

"A pity her husband will not be so obliging," Jacques muttered.

"His death will not give you what you desire, you know."

"You are wrong. I desire very much for Talia to be a widow."

She pressed a hand to her aching heart, turning to meet his stubborn glare.

"I witnessed the earl and his countess together, Jacques."

He shrugged. "And?"

"She is desperately in love with him."

His eyes flashed with annoyance. "Impossible. The bastard abandoned her mere hours after their wedding. She would never be so foolish as to offer such an arrogant pig her affection."

A derisive smile tugged at her lips. "Women are renowned for offering unworthy men their affection."

"He considers her beneath him. How could he possibly make her happy?"

"You could not be more mistaken," she said softly. "I have seen the manner Lord Ashcombe stares at his wife. He is enchanted by her." An unwelcome stab of envy made her shiver. "Just as every other man appears to be."

A silence greeted her bitter words, then with slow, deliberate steps, Jacques prowled toward her.

"Why did you allow the prisoners to escape?"

Sophia's heart fluttered. *Merde.* Why had she ever been foolish enough to allow her emotions to become entangled? Until Jacques, she had managed to walk away from her various affairs unscathed.

Now...

Now she felt as raw and vulnerable as if her soul had been stripped bare.

"They were dangerous," she murmured.

He grasped her shoulders, his expression hard. "They were worth a large fortune that we desperately need."

"There was no certainty you would have received a ransom for the earl," she argued, refusing to apologize. "He is, after all, a favorite of the prince. It is more likely we would have discovered an alarming number of British soldiers laying siege to the Palace."

His eyes narrowed. "And Talia?"

"She distracted you from what is important."

"From you?

"From your pledge to Napoleon."

Disbelieving fury darkened his eyes. "You dare to speak to me of loyalty to our emperor after your betrayal?"

"I do not consider avoiding an unnecessary skirmish with the British army a betrayal."

"And do you consider the theft of the small tokens that have ensured the loyalty of Mr. Richardson as betrayal?"

She flinched, abruptly lowering her head to hide her guilty flush. She had not expected him to realize the extent of her treachery so swiftly.

"What do you wish me to say?"

His hand shifted to cup her chin, gently forcing her face upward to meet his searching gaze.

"The truth."

"The truth is that I desired Lady Ashcombe to disappear from France, and releasing her husband seemed the most efficient means of accomplishing my goal," she answered with a blunt honesty that caught them both off guard. "Are you satisfied?"

For the briefest of moments Jacques's expression seemed to soften, and a fragile hope swelled in her heart. There was surely a hint of the affection he had once showered upon her lurking in the back of his beautiful eyes? Even perhaps a guilt for having hurt her.

Then, just as swiftly, his anger returned, and he stepped back with a sharp motion.

"*Non,*" he said harshly. "I am far from satisfied. Your selfishness has threatened to expose our greatest treasure in battling the British. I cannot allow Ashcombe to reach England."

Disappointment lodged like a lead ball in the pit of her stomach.

"Harry Richardson cannot be a treasure if he is hiding in France." Her voice was dull as she struggled against the horrid realization that she had taken a risk and lost it all. "Indeed, he is nothing more than a liability."

He shrugged. "Once I have captured Ashcombe, then his brother can return to London and seek out a new spy in the Home Office."

"The British government is already aware they have traitors in their midst." She wrapped her arms around her waist, feeling chilled despite the warm summer breeze blowing through the open window. "If Harry makes a sudden reappearance in London without his distinguished brother, do you not think it will be suspicious?"

"We will devise a believable story that will divert attention long enough to acquire the information we need so France will be victorious."

She shook her head. "No, it is too late. Lord Ashcombe escaped hours ago." She did not say the name that hung between the two of them—Talia—or the fact that Jacques's determination to capture the prisoners had more to do with his frantic need to rescue Lady Ashcombe than to return Harry to London. It was like a barrier that rose between them. "You cannot possibly catch him now."

"I will not have to catch him. I intend to be waiting for him." His gaze flicked over her tense expression. "And you made it possible, *ma belle.*"

Sophia frowned in wary confusion. *"Comment?"*

"I am willing to wager that beyond revealing young

Harry's role as my cohort, you also shared the fact that he is currently residing in Calais," he drawled.

She forced herself to meet his gaze with a proud indifference that masked her churning emotions.

"So what if I did?"

"The honorable Earl of Ashcombe will not be able to resist the compulsion to track down his brother and attempt to salvage his soul from the evil French," he said and sneered.

"Lord Ashcombe is not stupid," she protested. "I believe we all know that Harry Richardson is beyond salvation."

"Then he will wish to wring his worthless neck," Jacques said, offering her a shallow bow before heading toward the door. "In either event he will not leave France without finding his brother. When he does, he shall once again be my prisoner."

Standing in the center of her bedchamber, Sophia allowed scalding tears to track down her cheeks for the first time in thirty years.

TALIA WAS UNCERTAIN how long she lay entangled in Gabriel's arms, and in truth she did not try to keep track. It was enough to float in the sweet glow of contentment as the storm overhead faded in fury and at last passed.

She should perhaps regret giving herself with such eagerness to Gabriel, she acknowledged with a sigh. He had, after all, proven to be a miserable husband who had insulted her, abandoned her and overall treated her with a shocking lack of respect.

And she was far from forgiving him.

But in truth, she was too content to stir up the necessary remorse.

It was not the fact he had rushed to France in an attempt to save her, she hastily assured herself. Or that he had done everything in his power to see to her comfort despite their rough surroundings.

She was not so weak as to be swayed into believing this man had genuine concern for her. Such thoughts could only lead to disappointment. And God knew, she had endured enough disappointment for a lifetime.

But she was female enough to appreciate the touch of a skilled lover. And since she was expected to share the bed of her husband regardless of her own feelings, why not enjoy what he offered?

All very logical until his clever fingers brushed along the curve of her waist, sending a jolt of anticipation shivering through her body.

Meeting his silver gaze, Talia felt more than mere desire stirring deep within her. The dangerous warmth spoke of emotions that were best destroyed before they could break her heart.

"The rain has stopped," she struggled to choke out.

He chuckled softly, his hand boldly cupping her breast and allowing his thumb to tease at her sensitive nipple.

"Has it?"

She shifted her gaze to the shuttered windows, attempting to ignore the pleasure coiling through the pit of her stomach at each stroke of his thumb.

"Yes." She swallowed a low moan, lowering her eyes to meet his smoldering gaze. "Should we not be leaving?"

A stark, haunting pain rippled over his beautiful features before he was determinedly lowering his head to nuzzle a line of kisses along her collarbone.

"No doubt we should," he murmured, his breath sending prickles of pleasure over the upper curve of her breast.

Talia threaded her fingers through his hair and attempted to bring a halt to his caresses before she became utterly lost in his exquisite seduction.

There was something Gabriel was attempting to hide from her. Something that was clearly causing him great distress.

"Gabriel," she said when he ignored her tugs on his hair.

"Hmm?"

"What is troubling you?"

He traced the tip of her breast with his tongue. "At the moment, nothing."

"But…" Talia bit off her words, grimly accepting the unpalatable truth that while Gabriel might be willing to share his passion, he obviously still found her an unworthy confidante. And why should he? He had, after all, made it quite clear that their marriage was nothing more than a necessary evil. She swallowed the stupid lump that was lodged in her throat. "Never mind."

Lifting his head, Gabriel gazed down at her with a sudden frown.

"A typical female response that is intended to ensure that I do mind."

She stiffened, offended by his unfair accusation. "I do not play such games. If you do not wish to share your thoughts, then so be it."

A hint of color flared along his cheekbones, but braced for a scathing response, Talia was unprepared as Gabriel surged to his feet, roughly shoving his fingers through his hair.

"Have you considered the notion that I might wish to escape from my thoughts for a while?"

His voice was low, but she did not miss the edge of raw distress. Thrusting aside her ingrained modesty, Talia ignored the fact they were both stark naked and lifted herself off the wooden floor to stand directly before him.

Lightly she touched his arm. "Is it possible to escape from your thoughts?"

Without warning he wrapped his arms around her waist, hauling her against his body with a tormented urgency.

"It depends upon the distraction," he rasped, his lips moving in a tender caress over her temple and down her cheek, until he reached the corner of her mouth. It was then that he realized she remained stiff in his arms, her hands pressed against his chest, not in denial but not in welcome. Yanking back his head, he regarded her with a simmering frustration. "Damnation. Why do I feel as if I am being managed?"

She tilted her chin. "I told you, I do not—"

"For a female who does not play games you are remarkably good at them," he interrupted in sharp tones, then sensing how easily he had wounded her, he heaved a sigh and pressed his forehead to hers. "Forgive me, Talia. You are right, I am troubled."

Talia carefully considered her words, unwilling to destroy this fragile moment.

"Do you fear that we will not be able to escape the French?" she at last inquired.

A brief flare of amusement shimmered in his eyes. "Are you attempting to be insulting?"

"Of course not."

"Good. You may be assured I shall have you safely aboard my ship by nightfall," he drawled.

"Then what is it?"

There was a tense silence as he fought against his inbred instinct to deal with his troubles on his own. He had devoted a lifetime to shouldering responsibilities and protecting others. It would never be easy for him to share.

Wisely, Talia forced herself to wait, knowing he would only retreat if she pressed him.

Eventually he lifted his head, although he kept his arms wrapped around her, as if he needed the warmth of her body snuggled close.

"I discovered information concerning my brother that I have not yet managed to accept," he confessed, his voice hoarse.

Her mouth went dry with horror. "Dear lord, he is not—"

"No," he hastily interrupted, his expression impossible to read. "He enjoys the unjust health of most sinners, so far as I know." His jaw clenched. "Indeed, I have learned he is currently residing in Calais."

"Calais?" Talia blinked in confusion. "Calais, France?"

He gave a sharp nod. "Yes."

"That's absurd. What would he be doing in Calais?"

"Avoiding the men whom I sent in pursuit of him, for one thing. And for another..." He grimaced in disgust.

Talia lifted a hand to lightly touch his cheek. "Gabriel?"

A bleak emotion darkened his silver eyes, sending a chill of foreboding down Talia's spine.

"For another he is attempting to fleece Jacques Gerard for the funds necessary to continue his extravagant lifestyle in France."

Harry and Jacques were acquainted? It would be natural when they were in Devonshire, although Talia could not imagine Harry ever wishing to become friendly with a vicar, even if he did reside on his family's estate. But they were in France, and if Harry knew that Jacques was here, then he must also know that he was a spy.

Which would mean…she cut off the thought before it could fully form.

"I do not understand."

"I wish to hell I did not," Gabriel muttered. "Harry is a traitor."

Even with a suspicion of what was coming, Talia reeled from the shocking announcement.

"No." She pulled away, shaking her head in denial. "It cannot be."

As if predicting her disbelief, Gabriel was already moving to pull out a folded note from his jacket, shoving it into her hand.

"Here."

It took only a moment to skim through the signed confession, her heart sinking with every word. Dear lord, she had always thought Harry weak, but this…

She handed the note back to Gabriel with a dreary expression. "How could he do such a thing?"

"I have no answer," Gabriel said bleakly. "Harry has always been spoiled by my mother, but so are any number of noblemen and they do not become spies."

"Not you," she said before she could halt the words.

He lifted his brows. "I beg your pardon?"

She wrapped her arms over her breasts, feeling oddly exposed.

"You were not overindulged," she reluctantly clarified.

Gabriel gently draped his jacket around her shoulders, tucking it around her body.

"No, when I was not at school I was expected to spend my days with my father to learn the duties of an earl," he agreed without a hint of regret at having been denied a childhood. Indeed, his expression softened with obvious fondness at the mention of his father. "My earliest memories are leading a team of mules through a field while my father helped the tenants toss hay onto the cart they pulled."

She studied him. Truly studied him. The fallen-angel beauty of his face. The elegance of his body. The power he carried with such ease. And the confidence of a man who had been adored his entire life.

The sight reminded her of her earlier belief that Harry had lived his entire life in Gabriel's shadow.

"Harry never joined you?"

Gabriel gave a lift of one shoulder. "He had no interest in the estates, only in the luxury they provided for him."

"Or perhaps he resented your close relationship with your father," she cautiously suggested. "It would explain why your mother was so eager to overindulge him."

He instantly bristled. "My father was not to blame for Harry's treachery."

"Of course not," she soothed. "But Harry's resentment might have begun at an early age and been encouraged by your remarkable popularity among society." She smiled wryly. "You do, after all, put most gentlemen in the shade."

"And so now it is my fault?" he demanded, his expression caught between annoyance and pure male vanity.

"No." She shook her head. "We all have burdens to bear from our childhood. For some, it makes them stronger, for others..." She clutched the jacket tighter, trying to disguise her horror at the evil that must infect Harry to allow him to betray his own country. Gabriel was suffering enough without her making him feel worse. "They use their past as an excuse to remain weak."

He gave a restless shrug. "It no longer matters why he has chosen his path."

"I suppose that is true." She regarded him with concern. "The question is…"

"What I intend to do with him."

"Yes."

The pain returned to his face as he folded her back into his arms, laying his cheek on top of her head.

"I do not know," he admitted. "There is no good solution."

Well, that was certainly an understatement.

Wrapping her arms around his waist, she laid her head over the steady beat of his heart, wishing she had the words to offer him comfort.

"I am sorry, Gabriel."

His fingers threaded through her hair in an absent caress. "If he is tried and found guilty, the scandal will not only tarnish the Ashcombe name for generations to come, but it will destroy my mother."

"Must his guilt be revealed?" she demanded softly.

She felt him shudder, his hands slipping beneath the jacket, seeking the warmth of her skin.

"Even if I could live with the shame of protecting my family at the cost of my country, such things have a way of being exposed," he said harshly. "Indeed, I am shocked that Harry was capable of keeping his sins hidden for so long. He has never been discreet."

An icy sense of premonition lodged in the pit of her stomach, although she had no need of foresight to know that having to expose his brother as a traitor would break something vital within Gabriel.

"Then allow fate to take its course," she coaxed. "You need not be the one responsible to decide which it will be."

His chest expanded beneath her head as he drew in a deep breath.

"I have always been responsible for my brother."

She pulled back her head to regard him with a strained smile, not forgetting that she was yet another burden he had been forced to shoulder for his brother.

"Yes, I am well aware of the sacrifices you are willing to make for Harry."

Braced for his ready agreement, Talia's heart leaped as his eyes instead darkened to smoke, sending a breathless thrill singing through her.

"Some are not so burdensome as others," he said lowly.

This time she made no protest as his mouth lightly teased over her cheek before settling on her lips.

Perhaps she could not ease his troubles or prevent the looming disaster, but for the moment she could give Gabriel a few moments of distraction.

Closing her mind to the bittersweet emotions tugging at her heart, Talia shrugged off the jacket, allowing it to slide to the ground as she wound her arms around his neck.

Even knowing that every moment spent with Gabriel was destined to entangle her stupid heart ever more tightly, she could not deny his need that she could feel with every burning kiss and every stroke of his hand.

In return she offered an eager response that made him groan with approval, gathering her close as he lowered her onto the hay-strewn floor.

"Talia..." he whispered, gazing down at her with a vulnerability that seared away any lingering barriers she tried to place between them. "My beautiful gypsy."

She smiled wryly at his husky words. "You call me such charming names," she said. "Mouse...shrew... gypsy..."

"Wife," he added softly, bending down to claim her lips in a kiss of raw need.

The simple word made something shift deep inside her, and, desperate to divert her mind from the dangerous emotions, she focused on the sensation of his hands gliding down her back. Arching closer to the heat of his body, she explored the hard planes of his chest, smiling as she felt the vibrations of his groan beneath her palms.

She might never have Gabriel's heart, but his body was eager to belong to her.

Refusing to consider how many other women had known him just as intimately in the past and how many were yet to know him in the future, Talia tilted back her head as he nibbled a path of kisses down the sensitive line of her throat.

For the moment he was hers. Completely and utterly.

His mouth traced the curve of her breast before he captured the tip of her nipple between his lips, making her gasp in sharp pleasure.

"Yes," she muttered in approval.

Continuing to pleasure her, Gabriel reached to grasp her hand, guiding it down to his straining erection.

Talia paused, feeling oddly shy. Then, curiosity overcame her modesty, and with a hesitant touch she curled her fingers around his hard length.

Gabriel muttered a low curse as she stroked from the tip to the wider base, taking time to discover the soft pouch beneath his erection before stroking upward.

"Christ," he breathed, his hand shifting to part her legs. "You have only to touch me and I am lost."

He was not the only one lost, she acknowledged as his hand sought the heart of her femininity that was already damp with her aching need. A moan wrenched from her throat as a slender finger dipped into the heat of her body, her hips instinctively lifting in silent invitation.

Oh, yes. Her eyes fluttered shut. Already she could

feel the delectable pressure beginning to build in the center of her womb, and her fingers tightened on his arousal making him moan in pleasure.

"Wait, Talia," he pleaded, covering her hand.

She frowned. "Wait?"

"My control is not as impervious as I had so arrogantly assumed," he murmured, his lips teasing along the line of her shoulder as he gently turned her to lie on her side.

"Gabriel?" she breathed in confusion.

"I promise to please you," he said, his lips brushing her ear as he molded himself against her back.

Talia did not doubt Gabriel's skill. How could she when her entire body trembled on the precipice of bliss? But she found herself floundering as he gently tugged her leg up and over his hip.

Surely this could not be right?

Of course, the feel of his lips nuzzling at the curve of her neck was delectable, and his hands were expertly exploring her full breasts, tugging her nipples into full arousal before they were sliding down her body with wicked intent.

She swallowed a gasp as his fingers slid between her legs, parting her most intimate flesh. Then with exquisite slowness he pressed his erection deep into her moist channel.

"Oh...lord."

She struggled to form her words only to have them evaporate entirely when his fingers discovered the center of her pleasure, and he stroked her in tempo with his shallow thrusts.

"Do you want more, Talia?"

More? She whimpered, not certain she could bear more without shattering into a thousand pieces. Then he shifted the angle of his thrusts, plunging deeper, and she reached backward to dig her nails into the muscles of his hip.

"Yes, please, yes."

The rasp of their heavy breaths filled the air along with the scent of hay and passion. Talia squeezed her eyes shut, her body moving to meet his thrusts with increasing urgency.

"Talia," he groaned, his hips slamming upward as his seed poured into her, triggering her own release.

She cried out in ecstasy, indifferent to their rough surroundings or the dangers that waited just outside the door.

For now nothing mattered beyond the feel of Gabriel's arms wrapped around her and the wild beat of his heart against her back.

Keeping her eyes closed, Talia oddly thought of her grandmother, and how she would have assured Talia to live in the moment.

They were, after all, two people alone in the world, brought together by a quirk of fate and yet, somehow destined to have arrived at this precise place.

Why try to deny what was meant to be?

CHAPTER THIRTEEN

LEAVING TALIA TO wash and change into her clean gown, Gabriel crept through the countryside, not returning until he had managed to steal a horse from a small village not far from the main road.

Not that the plodding farm animal offered the speed he would have wished for, but the beast was sure-footed, and even with the burden of both Gabriel and Talia, he managed a steady pace that had them arriving at the coast just south of Calais well before dusk.

Halting long enough to vault to the ground, Gabriel took the reins and led the animal along the narrow path that led to the water.

"Are you certain your ship will be waiting?" Talia demanded, her face pale with weariness, although her spine remained stiff with the determination that made him smile.

His beautiful, courageous gypsy.

Of course, her newly exposed spirit was not entirely a blessing.

One might expect that after their breathtaking intimacy she would prove to be far more compliant and eager to please him. It was, after all, the behavior he had become accustomed to in his mistresses.

Talia, however, had spent the first of the journey chastising him for stealing a horse from a poor French family who were no doubt deeply suffering the loss and the second half sunk in her own thoughts, her manner so distant it made him long to drag her from the horse and crush her in his arms until she was once again moaning in eager anticipation of his touch.

He could not explain why, but it annoyed him that she was capable of putting a distance between them. She was his wife. She should belong to him completely.

Aggravated by his ridiculous thoughts, Gabriel forced himself to concentrate on far more important matters.

"Yes, it will be waiting," he assured her. "Despite my commands that my crew return to England should I be captured, I am quite certain they will have refused to leave without me."

"You should be honored by such loyalty," she murmured.

He grimaced, not for the first time considering Hugo's reaction to their arrival.

"I am, under most circumstances." He grimaced. "But I fear I should warn you that one of my companions might not be entirely welcoming."

She swayed in the saddle, so tired she could barely sit upright.

"Which companion?"

He protectively moved to catch her should she fall. "Hugo, Lord Rothwell."

"He is your associate?"

"We have been friends since our days at school." His gaze scanned the thickening trees that lined the path, his steps slowing. They were too close to escape to walk into a trap now. "Actually Hugo has always been more a brother to me than Harry."

"No doubt you both had more in common."

"True." He sent her a startled glance. Few people understood his close relationship with Hugo. Certainly not his mother, who constantly complained that he should be devoting his time and attention to his brother. "We were both our father's heirs and expected to behave in a manner befitting our stations. Not always an easy task for two high-spirited boys who wished to join in the antics of the other students."

"Yes." A sudden bitterness edged her voice. "Fathers can often have unreasonable expectations of their children."

His hand reached to touch her leg, meeting her gaze with a silent promise.

"Silas Dobson will never be allowed to bully you again," he swore, already having planned to speak with Dobson the moment they returned to England. The man would understand that he was not to go near Talia unless Gabriel was at her side. "I can assure you of that."

An unexpected blush touched her cheeks at his low words, her lashes lowering to hide her expressive eyes.

"Why do you believe Lord Rothwell will not be welcoming?" she demanded. "Does he disapprove of my lack of noble blood?"

Gabriel swallowed a sigh, wishing that he could trust his friend to behave himself so he did not have to have this uncomfortable conversation. It was bound to remind her of his own prejudices when they wed.

Unfortunately, he did not doubt for a moment that Hugo would make very clear that Talia was aware of his disapproval.

"He was offended by our hasty wedding," he reluctantly admitted.

He felt her stiffen beneath his hand. "And by the fact my father blackmailed you into taking me as your bride?"

"It did not improve his opinion."

There was a moment of silence before she heaved a

sigh. "I do not hold him to blame. It is an opinion shared by most of society, no doubt."

"Do not fear." He lifted a shoulder. "Once Hugo comes to know you, he will swiftly conclude that you are far too good for me."

She shook her head at his deliberately light words. "Highly unlikely."

"Trust me."

"And the rest of society?" she asked.

"It is quite possible my choice of bride will be the last concern of society," he reminded her, his senses suddenly tingling with alarm.

He ground to a halt, hurriedly studying their surroundings. A hint of dusk was just beginning to brush the sky, adding violet hues to the fog steadily creeping through the trees. In the distance the sound of small animals could be heard scampering through the thick vegetation, but closer to hand there was nothing but silence.

Something or someone was near.

"Talia, do not move," he warned, fiercely regretting he had not taken the time to find a weapon to replace those taken by Jacques Gerard.

"What is it?" she whispered.

He deliberately stepped in front of the horse, prepared to send the beast bolting if necessary.

"Show yourself," he commanded in loud tones.

There was a rustle behind a nearby tree, then with a smooth motion an impressively large man with ruffled brown hair and a mocking smile stepped onto the path.

"Your instincts are growing slow with your old age, Ashcombe." Hugo made a show of returning his dueling pistol to the pocket of his dark cloak he had pulled over his pale green jacket and gray breeches. "I could have used you for target practice."

Gabriel felt a flood of relief at the sight of his friend, although his expression was chiding as he met the steady golden gaze.

"And your advanced years have utterly destroyed your hearing," he countered. "I commanded you to return to England."

Hugo shrugged. "I never doubted you would outwit a handful of French coxcombs."

"Actually it was Talia who managed our escape," he corrected, turning back toward his silent companion and plucking her out of the saddle. He barely allowed her feet to touch the muddy path before he had her tucked against his side. "She has proven to be amazingly resourceful."

Hugo's eyes narrowed as he watched Gabriel's protective manner. "Yes, I can imagine."

Gabriel's expression hardened with warning. "Hugo."

Talia cleared her throat as the two men glared at one another.

"Is the yacht nearby?"

"Just beyond the trees," Hugo answered grudgingly, his gaze never leaving Gabriel.

"Thank God," she murmured. Then as the silence returned she heaved a deep sigh. "What about the horse? We cannot just abandon him."

Giving the horse a pat on his flank, Gabriel watched as the beast slowly turned and plodded back down the trail.

"He will find his way home," he assured his tender-hearted companion.

"You are certain?"

"Who else would want the spiritless creature?"

She smiled, no doubt sensing his amusement at her concern.

"It is just that I do not like to think about him wandering through the countryside alone."

Hugo snorted. Gabriel sent him an annoyed scowl, aware his friend was watching their exchange with pronounced disapproval.

"Hugo, return to the yacht and ensure that a hot bath is waiting for my wife."

Hugo's hands clenched at his sides, but, unwilling to argue in the midst of enemy territory, he gave a stiff nod of his head.

"As you wish."

Waiting until his friend had disappeared around a bend in the road, Gabriel grasped Talia's elbow and followed in Hugo's wake.

"Do not allow him to trouble you."

She smiled wryly. "Simple for you to say. He is rather...intimidating."

Intimidating was not precisely the description that Gabriel would have used at the moment.

Obnoxious jackass came to mind.

"I will speak with him."

"No." She adamantly declined his offer. "I would rather you did not."

"Why?"

"He is your friend and he is concerned for your happiness." Her expression was impossible to read. "I do not fault him for that."

"I will not allow him—"

She pressed a finger to his lips. "I would prefer to think of the hot bath awaiting me than dwell on Lord Rothwell's disapproval. That is a problem for another day."

Gabriel swallowed his words of argument. What was

the use in upsetting his wife? He would deal with Hugo in private.

They traveled in silence, at last stepping out of the trees to discover the rocky coastline directly before them.

Talia grimaced at the sight of the steep cliff, but with her typical habit of facing the difficulties in her life without complaint, she firmly grasped his arm and allowed him to lead her down the narrow trail.

The footing was loose, and a shower of pebbles greeted every treacherous step, but slowly they managed to wind their way to the bottom of the cliff.

Gabriel allowed Talia only a few moments to catch her breath before steering her around a large boulder that jutted nearly to the edge of the water. As he had suspected, a small rowboat awaited them along with a burly sailor who silently assisted Talia into the boat. Once Gabriel was settled beside her, the man rowed them toward the nearby yacht with swift efficiency.

Turning his head, Gabriel watched as Talia caught sight of the sleek vessel that had been made by the finest craftsmen in England.

Her eyes widened in suitable wonder, taking in the teardrop-shaped hull and the huge mast that could withstand the most fearsome storm. It was not, perhaps, as large as many crafts, but it was built for speed and comfort, not to impress others.

His brows drew together as he realized the crew was bustling along the decks, preparing to return the earl and his countess back to England. Calculating his next move, his features hardened briefly before he was able to smooth his expression. Talia was too perceptive not to suspect his plans if he did not take care.

There was a bustle of activity as they reached the yacht as a dozen sailors all rushed to help them climb aboard, their wide grins revealing their pride in his ability to sneak beneath the very noses of the French and return unscathed.

Of course, they did not yet know the full tale, he acknowledged wryly, leading Talia away from the curious sailors to the cabins below.

They passed through the galley and then the front saloon that was decorated in pale shades of blue and gray before reaching his private cabin. Pressing open the door, he allowed Talia to enter first, his lips twitching as she sucked in a startled breath.

"Good heavens."

He stepped next to her, his gaze skimming over the polished walnut paneling and cleverly built-in furniture that was constructed on the same sleek, elegant lines of the actual yacht. Only the brass fittings and the moss-green blanket on the bed offered a hint of color, allowing the beauty of the wood to command attention.

"Does it please you?" he asked.

She moved forward, her hand stroking over the writing desk inlaid with teak.

"Very much."

"It was built by my design."

She sent him a startled glance. "Yours?"

His lips twisted, more at his ridiculous urge to boast than by her astonishment.

"Why does that surprise you?"

"It is remarkably..."

"What?"

"Comfortable."

He nodded, his blood heating at the sight of her slender fingers caressing the glossy wood. The same fingers that had touched him with such eager passion just hours ago.

The image of her poised above him, her face flushed with pleasure, seared through his mind. He cursed, shifting as he hardened with a painful arousal. It was surely indecent to desire his own wife with such ferocity, but only the knowledge that his servants were even now preparing her bath kept him from slamming shut the door and tossing her on the bed.

Instead, he forced himself to lead her through the connecting door to the attached cabin that was designed along the same lines as his own.

"Being the Earl of Ashcombe means a burdensome amount of formality," he said tightly. "This is one of my few means of escape."

She lifted her brows, as if caught off guard by his response.

"I never considered that you would find it burdensome."

His lips twisted. Did she truly think he enjoyed being surrounded by cold marble and simpering sycophants? That he truly desired a horde of servants constantly underfoot who were deeply offended by his slightest attempt to decrease the pomp and ceremony?

"The title comes with great gifts along with a great duty," he informed her. "I do not take either for granted."

She shifted, touching his jaw with the tips of her fingers in a gentle gesture of understanding. His chest tightened with a dangerous emotion as he lifted his hand to press her fingers against his cheek.

He was uncertain how long they stood there, silently lost in one another, but the fragile moment was interrupted by the large sailors who set the copper tub into the center of the cabin followed by two more who carried the buckets of hot water.

Scowling at the curious gazes from his crew, he

stepped back, waving a hand toward the shelves cut into the paneling.

"You will find your belongings next to the bunk." His hand shifted toward the rope hanging near the small window. "If there is anything else you need, just pull the bell and a servant will answer."

She frowned. "Where are you going?"

"I must speak with my captain."

"We'll be leaving soon?"

"Quite soon."

She shivered. "Thank God."

He was wasting precious time, but unable to resist temptation, Gabriel reached to grasp her shoulders, jerking her forward to claim her lips in a swift, branding kiss before he was setting her away and turning toward the door.

"Enjoy your bath and then have a rest," he ordered on his way out of the cabin. "I will have a tray delivered once we have set sail."

TALIA FINISHED her bath and pulled on an ivory muslin gown with jade ribbons edging cap sleeves and a frilled hem. The unease that had been stewing in the pit of her stomach became unbearable.

Swiftly braiding her damp hair, she tugged on a pair of calfskin boots and went in search of her missing husband.

No doubt she was being ridiculous.

It was perfectly reasonable that Gabriel was still speaking with the captain. Or even overseeing the crew that she could hear scurrying overhead. Or maybe he had been caught by Lord Rothwell, who was attempting to convince him of all the fine reasons to leave the current Countess of Ashcombe in France.

But she could not forget his thinly veiled agitation that had remained even after they were safely aboard and the fierce kiss that had felt like...goodbye.

He had been hiding something from her, and she had a horrible suspicion she knew precisely what it was.

Finding the connecting cabin empty, Talia moved through the saloon and the galley before making her way up to the deck that bustled with activity. She was not particularly surprised to discover that the sky was painted with shades of deepening plum as dusk spread across the countryside, but her heart lurched at the feel of movement beneath her feet.

God, no. They were slipping away from shore.

For a moment she stood still, her gaze desperately searching for the sight of Gabriel's familiar profile, her blood running cold as she was forced to accept he was not among the sailors.

Now what did she do?

"You should be belowdecks, my lady." The large form of Lord Rothwell appeared at her side, his expression hard. "We are preparing to cast off."

Ignoring the near tangible judgment in the air, Talia stabbed him with an impatient frown.

"Where is Gabriel?"

The large man shrugged. "In his cabin. He said he was in dire need of a bath and I agreed."

She pressed a hand to her quivering stomach. Oh, lord, she was too late.

"You must stop the boat."

Not surprisingly Lord Rothwell regarded her as if she had taken leave of her senses.

"It is a yacht," he corrected in icy tones, "and it cannot simply be stopped."

Only a few weeks ago, Talia would have wilted beneath the barely hidden contempt. She would have gone to any lengths to avoid a disturbing confrontation.

Now she squared her shoulders and pointed a finger directly in Lord Rothwell's handsome face. Gabriel needed her. She would face down the devil himself if necessary.

"I do not care what it is called or what you need do to bar us from leaving, just do it," she spat out. "I must return to the shore."

His brows jerked together, obviously shocked by her fierce response. "Why?"

"Because Gabriel is not in his cabin."

"Then he is no doubt with the captain."

Talia clenched her hands at her sides, her gaze trained on the distant cliffs that appeared like a forbidding barrier in the gathering gloom.

Did she dare?

Gabriel had offered her his trust when he had shared the truth of Harry's treachery. It had been a rare gift that he offered to few in his life, and she knew beyond a shadow of a doubt if she betrayed that trust their relationship would be destroyed beyond repair.

But could she allow herself to be meekly hauled back to England with the knowledge that Gabriel was confronting his brother alone? Or worse, walking into a trap carefully laid by Jacques?

She shivered, an unbearable dread swelling in her heart.

No. No matter what the cost, she could not abandon Gabriel. She would deal with the consequences when he was safely returned to the yacht.

Slowly turning, she met Lord Rothwell's golden gaze. "No, Gabriel is not with the captain." She paused to gather her shaky courage. "He is on his way to Calais."

A thunderous silence greeted her words, then grasping her elbow, Lord Rothwell tugged her away from the curious sailors, his voice pitched low to ensure it would not travel.

"Why the devil would he be going to Calais?"

She licked her dry lips. "Because his brother is hiding there."

"Harry?" He shook his head. "Harry is in Calais?"

The yacht swayed as the sails were unfurled, and Talia desperately glanced toward the shore.

"I will explain later." She pressed a hand to her racing heart, her expression pleading. "For now you must tell them to stop."

She sensed him tense, his entire body poised for battle. Just as Gabriel would have been, she thought with a wistful pang. The two men clearly shared more in common than their titles.

There was the same ruthless, driving power that Gabriel possessed. Not to mention the air of arrogant authority that came as naturally as breathing.

He did not, however, shout for the sailors to halt their business, or command the captain to drop the anchor as she had hoped.

Instead he studied her in grim silence before sucking in a deep breath.

"No."

"No?" What the devil was the matter with the man? "Did you hear me? Gabriel is not aboard."

"He obviously gave the command to cast off, which means he understood the yacht would leave without him."

She shook her head in confusion. "What does it matter?"

"He desires you to be safe."

She ignored the edge in his voice that revealed he

would rather toss her to the wolves and go in search of his friend. What did she care what he thought of her so long as he assisted her in finding Gabriel?

"He is not thinking clearly at the moment."

"Granted, but I cannot go against his wishes."

"But you already have," she boldly reminded him. "Gabriel told me that he ordered you to return to England and yet you remained."

His jaw jutted in a stubborn motion. "I am at liberty to risk my own life, but I sense that Gabriel would never forgive me if I risked yours."

Tossing her hands in the air, she turned away from the aggravating brute.

"This is absurd."

She had barely taken a step when Lord Rothwell clamped a hand on her upper arm and whirled her about.

"Where are you going?"

"If you will not order the captain to stop this nonsense, then I will."

"He will not listen."

She stiffened her spine. "I am the Countess of Ashcombe, I will make him listen."

His brow furrowed as he regarded her with an odd intensity. Almost as if he had never seen her before.

"You may be the countess, but the servants will not disobey Gabriel."

Her lips thinned at the absolute certainty in his voice. She did not doubt for a moment that he spoke the truth. After all, he was obviously well acquainted with the crew.

"Typical," she snapped. "I knew a title would prove to be as worthless as it was pretentious."

"If that was true you would never have trapped my friend into marriage."

"I had nothing to do with—" She bit off her words in

frustration, slapping away his hand so she could bend down to tug off her boots. "Believe what you will. There is no time."

She heard him mutter a curse as she tossed aside the boots and reached beneath her skirt to pull off her stockings. Her father had insisted that she learn to swim at an early age. She was certain she had not forgotten how.

What she intended to do after she reached the shore without shoes or stockings was something she would decide once she was there.

"Wait," Lord Rothwell growled. "Have you taken leave of your senses?"

Lifting her head she allowed him to see the staunch determination etched on her face.

"I will not allow Gabriel to travel to Calais alone," she stormed.

He swore, glancing toward the shore that was becoming ever more distant.

"Is he in danger?"

"Perhaps not physical danger," she admitted, "but he will have need of me."

He returned his attention to her, his golden gaze sweeping over her pale face.

"You intend to swim back to shore?"

"If necessary."

He stood utterly motionless, clearly torn between his pledge to Gabriel and his instincts to rush to the rescue.

At last, he gave a shake of his head and swept past Talia with a fierce sense of purpose.

"Captain…"

CHAPTER FOURTEEN

LIKE MANY HARBOR TOWNS Calais had endured its share of invasions.

Julius Caesar had occupied the city to launch his invasion of England. The British King Edward III had laid siege for nearly a year in 1346, starving the city into surrender. And the Spanish had claimed ownership in the late 1500s. But while each conquest had left its mark, the city remained a simple fishing village at heart, with its own unique charm.

Confined within its yellowed walls, the town faced the waiting sea with a vast pier lined with fishing boats and a heavy fortress complete with a drawbridge.

Gabriel moved through the narrow streets, past the *Place d'Armes* in the center of town, barely noting the black watchtower, or the old town hall as he studied the small houses with their white shutters and the occasional *cafés* that were filled with French soldiers. The night air was filled with distant chimes and the sound of laughter, the moonlight illuminating the stone archway as he turned onto the *Rue de Guise*.

It was all very quaint, but hardly the sort of peaceful setting to attract his brother. He needed to discover the less savory part of town.

Almost on cue a ragged street urchin darted from the shadows, clearly intent on picking his pocket. With ease, Gabriel grabbed the boy, who could not have been more than twelve, by the collar of his woolen coat, lifting him off his feet so they were eye to eye.

"Your name," he growled in French, taking an inventory of the too-thin body and filthy, though intelligent little face. "And do not even consider lying unless you wish me to turn you over to the authorities."

There was a pause as the boy studied him with a shrewd gaze that was far too knowing for his tender age. Then, clearly accepting that Gabriel was not a pervert with a taste for young boys, he regarded him with a defiant expression.

"Armand."

"Armand, I have a small task for you."

He narrowed his pale brown eyes.

"What sort of task?"

Within moments Gabriel had described his brother in detail as well as his usual preference of entertainment. Then, pulling several coins from his pocket as a promised reward, he sent Armand dashing through the streets. The boy was obviously well acquainted with the seedier sections of Calais and would be capable of tracking down Harry far more easily than Gabriel.

Standing in the shadows as he waited for Armand's return, Gabriel briefly allowed his thoughts to stray to Talia.

By now she should be well on her way to England. Had she realized yet he was not aboard the yacht? And if she had, was she anxious at his absence? Or was she secretly pleased to be rid of her bully of a husband?

The thought made him frown, even as he told himself he was being an idiot.

Had Talia not risked her own life to rescue him from Jacques Gerard's cellars? And had she not responded with a ready urgency to his touch?

She might not have forgiven or forgotten the less than favorable beginning of their marriage, but she had obviously accepted him as her husband.

What more did he desire?

Dismissing the odd ache in the center of his heart, Gabriel returned his attention to his dark surroundings. He would deal with his wife when he returned to England, for tonight he had enough to occupy his mind.

Prepared when the French lad abruptly darted from a nearby alley, Gabriel stepped from the shadows.

"You have found him?"

The boy gave a sharp nod. "Follow me."

Gabriel grasped Armand's arm before he could dart away, his expression grim with warning.

"Take care, Armand. I am not a pigeon ripe for plucking."

"Non, monsieur." The boy's expression of innocence was obviously rehearsed, but there was no mistaking the hint of genuine alarm in his brown eyes. "You have my word of honor."

Releasing his grip, Gabriel gave a nod of his head. "Then let us be on our way."

Armand led him past the old church where King Richard II had wed Isabelle of Valois and beyond the spacious steeply roofed *Hotel Dessein* with its elegant facade that catered to the more respectable visitors.

The farther from the center of town they traveled the narrower the streets and the shabbier the buildings until at last Armand slowed his rapid pace and Gabriel caught sight of the English-style building with hexagonal turrets and an inner courtyard where a number of drunken coxcombs mingled among the brightly lit gaming tables. Beyond the courtyard the open doors revealed a gaudily decorated salon. A number of females were temptingly posed to entice the gentlemen who had grown tired of the cards and dice and preferred a more intimate entertainment.

Cautiously, Gabriel inched toward the opening to the courtyard. He remained hidden in the shadows as Armand pointed toward the familiar young gentleman with tousled brown hair and pale eyes that were already glazed by drink.

Harry.

"Voilà," Armand breathed, a cocky smile curving his lips.

Gabriel briefly studied his brother who was elegantly attired in a gold jacket and a black waistcoat embroidered with golden thread, his blood running cold at Harry's nonchalant comfort among the French dandies.

Did he have no shame whatsoever?

Bridling his urge to rush into the courtyard and drag his brother from the *bordel,* he instead forced himself to turn toward the lad at his side.

"Is there another entrance?"

"This way."

With a familiarity that made Gabriel wonder how much time Armand spent with the local whores, the boy led him along the stone wall that surrounded the property, pausing at a narrow wooden door.

Waiting for Gabriel's nod, Armand pushed open the door and led him into a private garden with a perfect view of the courtyard.

"Will this do?" he asked.

"It will do very well." Gabriel pulled out a fistful of coins and pressed them into the boy's hand. "It is late, return to your home, Armand."

"Merci, monsieur," Armand breathed, his expression stunned at the small fortune. *"Merci."*

"Straight home," he commanded, shaking his head as the boy offered a cheeky grin and dashed through the door.

Accepting that there was nothing he could do for Armand, he turned to study his brother through the trellis.

He had managed to track down Harry, but now what? No matter what his fury, he was not stupid enough to create a scene when there were a few thousand French soldiers camped just outside the walls of the city.

Then again, he had no desire to stand in a damp garden for the entire night, waiting for his brother to grow weary of his entertainments and return to his lodgings.

Brooding on a possible means to lure his brother from the newly introduced *La Roulette,* Gabriel was slow to react when a slender form appeared from the stone steps behind him.

"Ah, *bonjour,*" a husky female voice murmured.

Gabriel reached beneath his jacket for his loaded pistol, and smoothly turned to confront the vixen behind him. Her curls were the color of summer wheat tumbling over her shoulders left bare by a sheer robe. Her features were delicately drawn and her hazel eyes charming, if one ignored the calculating manner they slid over the strange man standing in her garden. With one glance Gabriel was confident that she knew the precise worth of his wine jacket and ivory waistcoat that had been perfectly sculpted to his body and the small fortune needed to purchase the ruby sparkling in the folds of his cravat.

"You are in need of companionship?" A smile curved her lips as she ran a finger along her plunging neckline, drawing attention to the tempting curve of her breasts. "I am Monique."

"Non," he impatiently declined, only to realize the

lovely female was precisely the bait he needed to attract his prey. "Wait, Monique."

Turning back, the woman approached him with a smile of pure invitation.

"You have changed your mind?" she purred, her hands skimming over his jacket. "You will not regret your purchase."

He lightly grasped her wrists, preventing her skillful touch from heading ever lower.

"I have a small task I wish you to perform."

Her chuckle was perfectly pitched to stir a man's deepest fantasies.

Or at least most men, he ruefully corrected.

He had already discovered that his interest in women, no matter how lovely or talented they might be, had been restricted to dark-haired gypsies with emerald eyes.

"I shall be pleased to perform any tasks you desire."

"That will not be necessary," he said, firmly putting her at a distance.

Her smile never faltered as her hands shifted to the velvet ribbon that held her nearly transparent gown together.

"You prefer that I…"

"No," he hastily reached to grasp her hand before she was standing stark naked.

She frowned. "Then what do you desire?"

With a tug on her hand, he positioned her near the trellis, pointing his finger at his brother.

"Do you see the young gentleman standing near the roulette table?"

"Monsieur Richardson?"

His jaw clenched at her ready recognition. Obviously Harry was a regular customer.

"Yes."

"Of course." She tossed him a smug smile. "He has often wished to spend time in my company, but he must content himself with the less expensive companions."

"Then it would appear that tonight his luck is about to turn," Gabriel murmured. "Do you have a room near?"

Monique waved a hand toward the stone staircase. "On the top floor, the third door on the left." Her eyes narrowed. "But if there are to be two gentlemen then I will demand double the price."

Gabriel shrugged. "I will happily double the price, but all I ask of you is your assistance in luring the gentleman upstairs without revealing my presence and then the opportunity to speak with him in private."

"And what of me?" she asked with obvious suspicion.

"You will have the luxury of enjoying an hour or so of peace." His gaze studied the perfect oval of her face, noticing the fine lines that were just beginning to frame her eyes. "Surely a preferable means of spending your evening?"

Surprisingly the woman stepped close enough to brush her full breasts against his chest.

"It would be preferable on most evenings. However, tonight I believe I would rather have company, so long as it is you."

He shook his head, once again pushing her firmly away. "A charming notion, but I have pressing business with Monsieur Richardson."

Monique pouted at Gabriel's discreet rejection. "If he owes you money, then I fear you are to be disappointed," she warned. "He is heavily in debt to Francois."

"Francois?"

Her lips twisted with disgust. "The owner of this charming establishment."

"Of course." He shook his head at Harry's dismal predictability, even as he grimly reminded himself that yet another gambling debt was the least of his concerns. "It is a personal matter."

Perhaps sensing his smoldering fury, the whore gave a lift of her brows.

"You do not intend to kill him, do you?"

"If I do, I promise to remove the body." Reaching into the inner pocket of his jacket, he removed several bank notes and held them in the light that spilled from the brightly lit torches. "Can you convince him to join you?"

Greed flared through her eyes before she was flashing Gabriel a smile of pure feminine conceit.

"*Chérie,* I could convince a saint to join me, and I assure you Monsieur Richardson is no saint."

"Truer words were never spoken," he muttered. "I will be waiting in your room."

She gave a toss of her golden curls, plucking the notes from his fingers and tucking them into the bodice of her robe.

"And when you have finished your business, perhaps we can discover a means to enjoy the remainder of the night, eh?"

With a noncommittal smile, Gabriel waited for Monique to slip out of the garden and stroll across the courtyard before making his way up the spiral staircase and entering the top floor of the turret.

He made a cautious inventory of the low velvet sofas and tapestries that hung on the stone walls in a poor imitation of a sultan's harem. Then stepping into the corridor, he made his way to Monique's room, not surprised to discover it was simply yet elegantly decorated.

She was obviously the most expensive of the house whores, and the gold and ivory furnishings had been perfectly designed to set off her pale beauty.

Ignoring the wide bed draped in satin and the intimate tools of punishment that some gentlemen preferred, Gabriel paced the polished wood floor, a heavy dread tightening his chest and making it difficult to breathe.

He had been so intent on locating Harry and getting him alone, that he had not actually considered what was to come next.

Why hadn't he simply returned to England with his wife? Even now they would be tucked in his narrow bunk, Talia's lush body wrapped around him and his dark thoughts lost in the drowning pleasure of her touch.

He could have left Harry to travel his path to hell and concentrated on his own future.

Unfortunately, he was not naïve enough to believe that ignoring his brother would be an end to the matter. How could he build a future with Talia when he was always waiting for the looming disaster to strike?

Besides, his conscience would never allow him to forget the damage Harry had caused, and the danger he posed so long as he remained a secret traitor to England.

He continued his pacing until at last he heard the sound of approaching footsteps and his brother's familiar chuckle echoing through the hallway.

"Come, wench, just a taste."

"Enough, monsieur," Monique protested, "wait until we have reached my room."

"A modest whore?" Harry mocked.

"Intimacy is always best savored in privacy."

"Not always. I do not mind a public performance with a beautiful woman." There was another chuckle. "Or two."

Gabriel heard what sounded like Monique slapping away his brother's hand, then the door to the bedchamber was being shoved open.

"Just through here, monsieur."

"I hope you have more than an hour, I—"

Strolling into the room, Harry came to an abrupt halt
at the sight of Gabriel. For one timeless moment, the
two brothers stared at one another, Harry flushing with
guilt in the same manner he'd exhibited when Gabriel
had caught him in some misdemeanor as a child.

It lasted less than a heartbeat before Harry was retreating behind a brittle pretense of indifference.

"Well, well. I did not expect you to join in our fun,
Gabriel."

Gabriel's gaze shifted to Monique, stupidly disappointed by his brother's response to his sudden appearance. But then, what had he expected?

Overwhelming shame? A plea for forgiveness?

"That will be all, my dear," he assured the female.

The woman sent him a lingering smile. "I shall be in
the private salon at the end of the hall if you wish to find
me when you have concluded your business."

Gabriel dipped his head. *"Merci."*

They waited in silence for Monique to leave the room
closing the door behind her. Then, with a derisive snort,
Harry crossed to the side table to grasp a bottle of whis-
key, yanking out the cork and taking a deep drink.

"Yet another victim of the irresistible Ashcombe
charm?" he rasped.

"Merely a female seeking to earn a living," Gabriel
countered, his eyes narrowing as the light from the candles played over his brother's face, revealing his sallow
complexion and lines of dissipation beside his pale eyes.

Christ, he appeared twice his age.

"You have no need to remind me you are not only
blessed with overwhelming attraction, but with bottomless coffers, as well," Harry muttered.

"Hardly bottomless and you have had more than your fair share of my coffers," Gabriel reminded him. "All of which you have tossed away on selfish pursuits of pleasure."

"And what else is the purpose of a younger son other than to pursue his pleasure?" he demanded. "It is not as if I was ever wanted or needed as more than a spare in the ghastly event something should happen to the glorious heir."

"Very poetic." Gabriel's lips thinned. "Did you rehearse this little speech?"

Harry took another swig. "Bastard."

Gabriel's hands twitched as he battled back the urge to grab his brother and shake some sense into him.

"I have attempted more than once to include you in the management of the estates, but you claimed to have no interest in such tedious business."

"And devote my days to bowing and scraping to the Lord of the Manor like your other servants?" Harry drawled. "No, I thank you."

"If it was my presence that was so abhorrent then there was nothing to prevent you from using your allowance to purchase your own estate."

Harry snorted, bitterness hardening his expression as he recklessly tossed the whisky bottle into the fireplace.

"A tiny fiefdom of my very own while you rule half of England?"

"Christ." Gabriel shook his head, recalling Talia's perceptive speculation that Harry had resented Gabriel's close relationship with their father. A sick sense of resignation settled in the pit of his gut. It was disturbing to realize that his brother's antipathy had started at such an early age. "How did I not see this?"

"See what?"

"The childish jealousy that you have allowed to rot your soul."

Harry hunched his shoulders, petulantly refusing to acknowledge his own culpability.

"How did you find me?" His lips twisted in a mocking taunt. "I know it could not have been those buffoons you sent after me. I managed to divert them before I ever reached Dover."

"Jacques Gerard."

Harry faltered at Gabriel's smooth response. "Impossible, he would never…"

Gabriel stepped forward. Any hope that the Frenchwoman had lied about his brother's connection died a swift death at Harry's stumbling words.

"He would never reveal that he is a French spy and that you are a traitor who betrayed your king and country for no other reason than pathetic greed?" Gabriel growled, pain ripping through him with stunning force.

Even prepared, he reeled from the impact of his brother's betrayal.

"Absurd," Harry blustered. "I do not know what the man has told you, but it is obvious he is attempting to turn you against me."

Gabriel lifted a weary hand. "No. No more lies, Harry. I know the entire sordid story."

Harry licked his lips, his expression guarded. No doubt his clever mind was already seeking the best means to slither out of trouble. Just as he had been doing his entire life.

"And of course, you would believe the word of a French scoundrel over your own brother?"

"Unfortunately you have proven you are no longer worthy of my trust." Gabriel deliberately caught and held his brother's gaze. "Or my respect."

Something flickered deep in his brother's eyes, but before Gabriel could fool himself into believing that it was regret, Harry was turning away with a shrug.

"I have survived without both for most of my life, I will no doubt continue to do just fine without them in the future."

Gabriel studied his brother's tense back. "Which begs the question of precisely how you do intend to survive? Jacques Gerard will not continue to support you now that your treachery has been exposed."

"Perhaps I shall follow in your footsteps and wed an obscenely wealthy chit who has just climbed out of the gutter—" Harry's words were cut off as Gabriel shoved him face-first into the wall. The younger man glared over his shoulder, unable to move with Gabriel pressed against his back. "What the hell?"

"You will never speak of my wife again, do you hear me?" Gabriel hissed.

Harry's shock faded to smug amusement as he mistakenly assumed that Gabriel's fury was at having been forced into wedding his younger brother's cast-off fiancée.

"Do you know how I laughed when I heard you had been bullied into taking Dowdy Dobson as the Countess of Ashcombe?" he taunted. "For once my perfect brother has become the laughingstock of society."

Gabriel muttered a curse, as disturbed by the hideous thought that Talia might even now have been wed to his brother as by the thought of Harry's treachery.

Christ, he could not have endured having her so near and yet forever out of his reach.

"You know nothing," he said.

"Tell me, Gabriel, do you often have Silas join you and mother for dinner at that mausoleum of a townhouse?

Or has he been condemned to the country with your ri-diculous wife?" Harry laughed at his own joke. "Fitting if you had lodged him in the barn. He is a pig of a man who isn't fit to polish the boots of a true gentleman."

Gabriel made a sound of distaste. "And yet you were willing to steal his hard-earned money."

"It is what he deserves for daring to believe he could force his nasty presence among his betters."

The very fact that Gabriel had been equally condemn-ing of Silas Dobson only increased his annoyance. With a low hiss, Gabriel stepped away from his brother, watch-ing with a jaundiced gaze as Harry slowly turned to face him.

"You are not only a coward, Harry, but you are a fool," he snapped.

The younger man lifted a hand to straighten his cra-vat, his expression sardonic.

"No, on this occasion it is you who are the fool. Not even your lofty position can bear the shame of possessing an awkward lump of a wife who—" This time Gabriel made no effort to restrain his temper. With one smooth motion his fist connected with Harry's jaw, smacking him back against the wall with a satisfying force. Spit-ting out a mouthful of blood, Harry pressed a hand to his bruised jaw, staring at Gabriel in disbelief. "Damn you. You knocked a tooth loose."

Gabriel narrowed his gaze. "The next occasion you speak of my wife I will break your damned neck."

There was a startled pause before Harry lowered his hand and studied Gabriel with an incredulous expression.

"My God. You have feelings for the wench." He gave a short, humorless laugh. "What a joke. The Earl of Ash-combe in love with his own wife."

Gabriel shrugged, refusing to rise to the bait. He might

not be prepared to label his feelings for Talia, but he had no desire to deny she had become a necessary part of his life.

"It is no joke. She is quite remarkable." He smiled at the unexpected irony of their situation. "In fact, if your only sin was having jilted Talia and forcing me to wed her, I should be in your debt." His smile faded to leave a bleak expression. "But we both know that what you have done puts you beyond redemption."

Harry paced toward the window that overlooked the dark street below, his hands fisted at his sides.

"I do not need one of your sanctimonious lectures, brother. Unless you intend to offer me a means to pay off my debts, then I suggest that you return to your remarkable wife and your perfect existence."

"You believe I can return to England and simply forget my brother has betrayed his country?"

"Why not?" Harry gave a casual lift of his shoulder. "Your precious conscience remains pure."

Gabriel was stunned by his brother's sheer indifference. Was he truly so far corrupted that he felt no shame whatsoever for his sins?

"Christ, do you have no concept of the damage you have wrought?" he thundered. "How many British soldiers have died because of you? How many families have been destroyed?"

"And what choice did I have?" Harry asked in sulky tones. "You refused to pay my debts and the bill collectors were becoming…troublesome."

"Your allowance has always been more than generous, not to mention the money you were constantly demanding from mother."

"I had a run of bad luck. It is bound to change eventually."

Gabriel shook his head, realizing it was too late.

Too late for all of them.

His brother was beyond redemption, fully believing he had the right to do whatever he pleased, indifferent to the pain he caused others. He had no regrets at having betrayed his country and would no doubt do so again if there was money to be earned.

Which meant that Gabriel had no choice but to stop this madness.

"No, there will be no opportunity for your luck to change," he said, a heavy sadness replacing his anger.

Perhaps sensing Gabriel's sudden resolve, Harry pushed away from the window, a frown marring his brow.

"And what is that supposed to mean?"

"Too often I have excused your excesses and allowed you to avoid the unpleasant repercussions of your mistakes." Gabriel heaved a sigh. "Perhaps if I had forced you to accept responsibility you would not be so lacking in principles."

Harry tilted his chin in typical defiance. "What do you intend to do, Gabriel? Have me drawn and quartered?"

"I intend to return you to England where you will stand trial for your crimes."

His words were greeted with shocked silence, then Harry's brittle laugh rang through the room.

"That is hardly amusing, brother."

"No," Gabriel readily agreed, "there is nothing amusing in this hellish situation."

"You would never expose me as a traitor. It would besmirch the Ashcombe name beyond repair."

Gabriel clenched his hands. "Since when have you given a damn about our name?"

Something perilously close to hatred darkened Harry's eyes before he forced a callous sneer to his lips.

"I don't, but you do."

Gabriel could not deny the truth of his words. The thought of knowing he was even partially responsible for tarnishing the Ashcombe title would haunt him forever. But the knowledge paled in comparison to the damage his brother had caused.

"There are some duties more important than protecting our family's reputation. You cannot be allowed to threaten the war against Napoleon, no matter what the cost."

Harry paled, as if slowly realizing that this was not yet another scrape he could walk away from unscathed.

"And what about mother?" he challenged, attempting a ridiculous outrage at Gabriel's threat. "She will never survive the shame of having her beloved son condemned as a spy."

Gabriel did not allow himself to think of his mother or her reaction to the humiliation she would suffer. No doubt she would hold Gabriel entirely to blame for not having allowed Harry to escape and the scandal to be swept beneath the carpet.

Yet another burden to bear.

"It will be difficult for all of us, but you have left me no options."

"I do not believe you." Harry shifted uneasily. "This... this is a bluff."

"No." Gabriel shook his head. "No bluff."

"You would never risk your pride to punish me."

Gabriel folded his arms over his chest, his expression revealing his unwavering determination.

"We will leave for England in the morning."

Intent on his brother, Gabriel barely paid heed to the sound of the door being thrust open, not until Harry's eyes widened with surprise. He glanced to the side, expecting to discover Monique or even a drunken patron in search of a whore stepping into the room.

Instead his hand was instinctively reaching for the pistol he'd tucked beneath his jacket at the sight of the all-too familiar Frenchman, his own pistol already pointed at Gabriel's heart.

"I will agree that Harry will be returning to England as soon as possible," Jacques Gerard drawled. "You, my lord, on the other hand, will be remaining in France as my very special guest."

CHAPTER FIFTEEN

HALTING JUST WITHIN the gates of Calais, Lord Rothwell tugged Talia into the shadows of a slumbering church, his expression set in obstinate lines as he repeated the same lecture she had endured since leaving the yacht and making their way along the rugged coastline.

"No," she at last interrupted. She could not bear to listen any longer to Lord Rothwells's tedious list of reasons why she must remain hidden near the gates while he explored the streets in search of Gabriel. "I will not be left behind."

Dressed entirely in black, Hugo heaved a resigned sigh even as he studied her with odd fascination. Almost as if he did not quite know what to make of her.

"Dammit, are you always so stubborn?"

Talia squared her shoulders, prepared for battle. "I am not being stubborn, this is simply something I must do."

"Because you care for Gabriel."

It was a statement of fact, not a question, and Talia shrugged in embarrassment at the realization that he had so easily read her aching need to reach Gabriel.

"He is my husband."

The nobleman shrugged, his handsome face shrouded in shadows.

"That has little meaning in society."

There was no arguing with his logic. Marriages among

the *ton* were made to consolidate power or wealth or social standing. Usually a combination of all three.

The unions had nothing to do with something so foolish as love.

"It has meaning to me," she muttered. So what if she was revealing emotions she preferred to keep hidden? Her pride was not nearly so important as rescuing her husband. "I cannot wait here doing nothing when Gabriel is in danger."

Lord Rothwell gave a slow shake of his head. "He did warn me that you are unique."

Talia flinched. Unique, of course, was just another means of branding her as peculiar. An insult she had endured since her arrival in London.

"I will not apologize for being concerned for my husband's welfare," she hissed.

Catching her by surprise, Rothwell abruptly reached out to give her hand a gentle squeeze.

"No, it is I who owe you an apology."

"Why would you owe me an apology?" she demanded warily.

"Because I know the folly of society's habit of judging others upon nothing more substantial than rumors and innuendoes." He heaved another sigh. "And yet that is precisely what I did to you."

Was the arrogant brute actually apologizing? She would have wagered her mother's pearl necklace that such a man had never admitted to being wrong in his entire life.

Bemused, she met the steady golden gaze. "You were concerned for your friend."

He dipped his head in agreement. "I was, but even after I realized he was far from unhappy with his marriage I continued to allow my prejudice to sway me." He offered her a rueful smile. "It is not a mistake I will make again."

Her answering smile was wistful. After his unexpected honesty, how could she be any less truthful?

"No, it was not a mistake," she assured him softly, her gaze absently straying over the dark silhouette of the *Place d'Armes* that had once been the center of Calais with its medieval watchtower and tidy square that was lined with shops. "I will never be a suitable Countess of Ashcombe."

"You are wrong." He hooked a finger beneath her chin and tugged her face back to meet his somber expression. "I love Gabriel, but there is no ignoring that over the past few years he has become...lost."

"Lost?"

Rothwell carefully considered his words. "He was always conscious of his responsibilities as heir apparent, but with the unexpected death of his father at such a young age he has become increasingly isolated and inclined to distrust others."

It was precisely what his housekeeper had revealed to her the day of her wedding to Gabriel. At the time she'd had no notion that it would be her husband's hidden vulnerabilities that would be her undoing.

"He was alone," she whispered.

"Precisely," Rothwell agreed. "And I suspect that the typical society marriage would only have ensured his continued loneliness. He did not need the frigid perfection of a society maiden. He needed the warmth of a woman." His fingers briefly squeezed her chin before he was pulling away. "Your warmth."

His soft words touched the place deep inside her that feared she would never be more than a shameful burden Gabriel would have to bear for the sake of his family.

The thought she could offer her husband a gift that a flawless young debutant could not was a belief she desperately wished to cling to.

"Thank you," she murmured.

"I speak nothing but the truth." His expression hardened. "Which is why I cannot allow you to put yourself in danger. I do not know what would become of Gabriel if he lost you."

Realizing that she had been subtly outmaneuvered, Talia narrowed her gaze.

"You are very clever, Lord Rothwell," she chided. "I pity the female you decide to wed. She will have to be on constant guard to avoid being manipulated by your charm."

He arched a brow. "There will be no need for manipulation. I intend to make certain my bride is delighted to obey my every command."

Talia snorted at the imperious certainty in his tone. How typical of a nobleman to speak of his mythical wife as if she were a well-trained hound rather than a flesh-and-blood woman with her own needs.

And how pathetic so many females allowed themselves to be treated in such a fashion.

Thankfully, she was no longer hampered by the expectations of society.

She would do whatever it might take to find and rescue Gabriel, but she would never again be his meek, subservient bride.

"Now I truly do pity her, but Gabriel was not so fortunate," she informed her companion. "I intend to go with you and that is the end of the matter."

With a shake of his head, Rothwell grasped her arm in a firm grip and tugged her toward the nearby street, his mouth thin with frustration.

"Stubborn female."

It was becoming a familiar accusation, and Talia merely smiled as she was hauled through the darkness, content with her small victory. Eventually Lord Rothwell would decide that the danger was too great, and he would put down his foot. She was certain at that point no amount of pleading would alter his mind.

They remained silent as they traveled away from the city walls, traveling through increasingly elegant neighborhoods as they left the busy docks and coffee shops behind. The large nobleman walked with a purpose, as if he had a particular destination in mind that was not among the terraced townhouses with their red-tiled roofs and high arched windows that allowed light to spill onto the streets.

Talia followed in his wake, absently searching every shadowed alcove and alley as they hurried through the darkness. She did not expect to actually stumble over Gabriel. Their luck could not possibly be that good. But that did not keep her heart from leaping each time she caught sight of a large gentleman strolling down the street or stepping from a house.

They turned a corner, on the point of heading out of the neighborhood, when Talia came to a shocked halt, her hand reaching to grasp her companion's arm.

"Wait."

Standing at her side, Lord Rothwell regarded her with an impatient scowl.

"What is it?"

She pointed toward a large house on the corner that was built of pale sandstone with a wide balcony on the second floor and a steeply pitched roof. There was a small garden that separated it from the surrounding homes and a narrow path that led to the mews behind the establishment.

"Jacques Gerard is here."

His scowl only deepened. "How can you be so certain?"

"I recognize the carriage." She pointed toward the lavish maroon-and-gold vehicle that she had last seen in Jacques's stables at the palace. It was impossible to believe that there were a large number of similar carriages in France. "Besides, his need to avenge himself against the French aristocracy would demand that he take command of the finest home in Calais."

Rothwell stilled, almost as if he were a hunter on the sudden scent of his prey. The image made Talia shiver, for the first time realizing just how dangerous an enemy this man would be.

"His presence in town does not necessarily have anything to do with Gabriel," the nobleman pointed out.

Talia shrugged. "Do you believe in coincidences?"

"No."

"Neither do I." Talia made no protest as Rothwell tugged her into the bushes planted along the fence surrounding the house, her thoughts consumed with fear for her husband. Had Jacques already found Gabriel? Was he holding him captive inside or had he…

As if sensing her swelling panic, Hugo placed a comforting arm around her shoulder, bending his head to whisper directly in her ears.

"Talia, do not leap to conclusions," he murmured. "We do not know for certain that Gabriel is within."

"Perhaps not, but we both know that Harry was more than likely sent here as a trap." She tensed as a figure suddenly moved near the front door, his rigid stance suggesting he was a trained soldier. A guard. Her gaze shifted upward, belatedly realizing there was yet another soldier on the upper balcony, as well as two more by the carriage.

Any doubt that Jacques Gerard was within was banished by the sight of the soldiers. No ordinary citizen would have need of armed guards. "Lord Rothwell, we must find a means to get inside one way or another."

"Not an easy task. Maybe even an impossible task," he muttered, his attention on the guards who surrounded the house. "There appear to be men at every entrance."

She unconsciously bit her lower lip, considering the best means of sneaking past the lurking soldiers.

"Not impossible."

With a frown, Rothwell turned her so he could study her resolute expression.

"Why do I sense I am not going to like what you are plotting?"

"We need a distraction."

His lips flattened. "And you intend to be that distraction?"

She shrugged. "It makes the most sense. Jacques will not harm me…"

"No."

His tone warned that he would not compromise, but still Talia had to try. It was, after all, the best solution to slipping past the guards. With her sudden appearance, there would be enough of a stir that her companion could find a door or window that was untended.

"But…"

"No."

She heaved a frustrated sigh. "Do you have a better plan?"

The golden eyes glittered with an unmistakable warning. "Yes, you will remain here and I will sneak through the servants' entrance. Once I discover whether or not Gabriel is within I will return and we will decide what we are to do next."

"Fine," she growled, acknowledging defeat with ill grace.

Why could men never accept that they might on occasion need the assistance of a woman?

Easily reading her rebellious thoughts, the nobleman grasped her chin and glared down at her pale face.

"Talia?"

"What?"

"If you move so much as a muscle from this spot I will put you over my knee and beat you soundly. Do you comprehend?"

He refused to loosen his grip until she'd given a grudging nod, then pausing long enough to withdraw a pistol he had tucked beneath his jacket, he was slipping along the line of bushes toward the back of the house.

"Men," she muttered in resignation, shivering despite the warm summer breeze.

She wanted to be confident that Lord Rothwell would manage to slip into the house undetected and return with the assurance that Gabriel was nowhere to be found in the townhouse, but even as the nobleman disappeared she felt a chill of dread inch down her spine.

Barely daring to breathe, she remained hidden in the bushes, her attention locked on the house as an odd sense of menace crawled over her skin.

Or perhaps not so odd, she was forced to accept as a pistol being cocked sounded directly behind her.

"Oh…damn," she grumbled, slowly turning to meet the velvet brown gaze of Jacques Gerard.

A charming smile curved his lips as he reached out to tuck a stray curl behind her ear.

"*Bonsoir, ma belle.* I thought I might find you lurking in the dark."

THE LIBRARY WAS TYPICAL of aristocrats who were more concerned with impressing others than offering a comfortable room to enjoy the collection of leather-bound tomes.

Bookshelves towered two stories up to the frescoes of Greek muses painted on the ceiling. Delicate satinwood furnishings, upholstered in a pale green satin and carved by the finest French craftsmen, were formally arranged across the floral carpet. And a white marble banister lined the second-floor walkway before framing the wide steps that led down to the main room.

Even the crystal figurines on the scrolled marble chimneypiece glowed with a cold, untouchable beauty in the light from the Venetian chandelier.

Of course, Gabriel might have been a bit more appreciative of his surroundings if he were not currently seated on the floor with his arms tied around a fluted column at his back. His dark mood was not improved when one of the double doors was pressed open and Jacques Gerard arrogantly strolled into the room.

The bastard.

It had been less than three hours since the Frenchman had managed to capture him and forced him to this townhouse. But it seemed like an eternity since he had been roughly bound to the column by two French soldiers while Jacques had disappeared along with Harry, who'd refused to even glance in his direction.

During that time Gabriel had been left to stew in his frustrated fury, wavering between outrage at his brother's utter lack of conscience and his own stupidity in being caught off guard.

Again.

"I trust you are comfortable?" Jacques taunted.

Gabriel hid his savage emotions behind a mocking smile.

"Is this not rather excessive?" He glanced at his bound hands. "I am a mere nobleman, not a rabid tiger."

Jacques smiled, taking obvious pleasure in Gabriel's humiliation.

"I try to learn from my mistakes, my lord. You will not be offered the opportunity to escape again."

"So I am to remain shackled in your library until the end of the war? Or do you intend to return me to your cellars?"

Jacques folded his arms over his chest, his smile slowly fading.

"Neither, I fear."

Gabriel frowned, attempting to read the man's indecipherable expression. There was a sudden tension about the Frenchman that boded ill for someone, and Gabriel very much feared that someone was going to be him.

"Dare I ask what your intentions are?"

"You will be pleased to know that I took your words of warning to heart."

"I am flattered, of course," Gabriel said cautiously, not comforted by Jacques's brittle tone. "But you will forgive me if I find that difficult to believe. If you had listened to me, then I would not be shackled like an animal."

"I speak of returning Harry to London."

Gabriel clenched his teeth against the stab of pain at the mention of his brother. Where was the younger man? Was he still at the townhouse or had he already forgotten that his brother was tied like an animal in the library and gone in search of entertainment?

"You can return him whenever you desire, but the word of his treachery will soon be common knowledge throughout England. He is no longer of use to you."

Jacques gave a sharp laugh. "Do not be so hasty, Ash-combe. Harry may yet prove valuable."

"Indeed?"

Glancing over his shoulder, Jacques gave a sharp command. With a faint shuffle, two soldiers entered the room carrying a large, unconscious man.

Jacques waved a hand. "Place him on the sofa."

Grunting beneath the strain, the soldiers lowered the motionless body of Lord Rothwell on the green-and-gold striped sofa, the delicate piece of furniture groaning beneath Hugo's heavy frame.

Rage blasted through Gabriel at the sight of the blood that dripped down Hugo's face from an obvious blow to his temple.

"Damn you," he rasped, indifferent to the ropes that were rubbing his wrists raw as he struggled to reach his friend.

"There is no need to behave as a madman," Jacques chastised. "Your friend lives. At least for now."

Gabriel sagged back against the marble column as he allowed the knowledge that Hugo was alive to ease his grief.

Christ, he would never have forgiven himself if his friend had been killed because of his stupidity.

Then, as the terror receded, his mind cleared, and he realized the implications of Hugo's presence in Calais.

What the hell was his friend doing here?

He was supposed to be on the yacht with Talia, ensuring that she was safely returned to England.

"Where did you capture him?" he growled.

"Lord Rothwell was kind enough to drop into my hands like a ripe plum. Much like yourself," Jacques said, sneering. "So you see, the word of Harry's fine efforts for France remain a secret."

"No." Gabriel refused to accept defeat. "Lady Ashcombe and my crew are out of your reach. She will not allow Harry to continue his betrayal."

Jacques snorted at Gabriel's bravado. "You forget that I know Talia better than you, Ashcombe."

The Frenchman was fortunate that Gabriel was bound to the column. Otherwise he would surely be dead.

Talia belonged to him.

And the fact that this man would dare to believe he could take her away was like a match being tossed onto a powder keg.

"You know nothing of my wife, you bastard."

Jacques's secretive smile was a deliberate reminder that Talia had turned to the Frenchman for much-needed comfort after her husband had discarded her.

"I know she felt compelled to ensure that a poor country vicar was not being harmed by a pair of ruffians despite the obvious danger to herself," he smoothly pointed out. "And that she risked her own neck to rescue a husband who is utterly unworthy of her concern. She would never have left France if she feared you were in danger."

A cold premonition stabbed through his heart. He knew Talia would never leave him in jeopardy. Hell, that was the reason he had not told her of his plans.

But even if she had discovered his absence before the ship had set sail, he could not believe his crew or his friend would have been so excessively stupid as to allow her to come in search of him.

"Whatever her preference, Hugo would have insisted that Talia return to England."

"He could have insisted all he desired, but she would not have left you behind."

The smug assurance in the Frenchman's voice sliced

through Gabriel, his vague sense of unease becoming a hard knot of dread.

"You have captured her."

Jacques offered a mocking dip of his head. *"Oui."*

Gabriel growled low in his throat, his fear for Talia a tangible force that threatened to choke him.

Bloody hell. He should never have left the yacht. Pride and his ever-present sense of duty might have demanded that he capture his brother and return him to England so he could face his punishment, but his heart had warned him to remain with Talia.

Unfortunately, he had forgotten how to listen to his heart the day he'd buried his father.

Now his wife was once again paying for his inability to be the husband she needed.

"Where is she?"

"Safely tucked in my private suite." There was a taunting pause. "Where she belongs."

Gabriel silently contemplated the pleasure of smashing the smug grin off Jacques Gerard's too-handsome face. Or maybe he would wrap his hands around the bastard's neck and squeeze the life from him.

Yes, that was precisely what he needed to soothe his gnawing frustration.

Instead he forced himself to thrust aside the maddening thought of his wife once again in this man's clutches and attempted to concentrate on his limited options.

He could do nothing to help Talia until he managed to escape. Or better yet, to convince Jacques to release him.

"Even without our return to England, you cannot hope to return Harry to London as your spy," he said with the unwavering confidence that he used when arguing a bill before the House of Lords.

It was amazing what could be accomplished with sheer audacity.

Jacques shrugged. "They have no reason to suspect your brother as anything more than a cad who left his bride at the altar and then disappeared with her dowry." Jacques squared his shoulders, a disturbingly grim expression replacing his mocking smile. "Still, his current state of disgrace might impede his ability to move without restraint among society, which is why I intend to ensure that no door will be closed to him."

"And how do you intend to accomplish such a feat?"

A prickling tension filled the vast library before Jacques met Gabriel's searching gaze with a defiant tilt of his chin.

"I intend to make him the Earl of Ashcombe," he said. "No one will dare snub him once he stands in your shoes."

Gabriel tensed, disbelief slamming into him.

Holy hell, he was an idiot.

He had been prepared for Jacques to hold him hostage. And even for the predictable demands for money to ensure his release. It was what any nobleman could expect after being captured by the enemy.

But he had never truly considered he would be sacrificed so Harry could return to London as the Earl of Ashcombe.

Now he struggled to accept Jacques's bloodthirsty plot.

"You intend to murder me?"

"War is a brutal affair. Sacrifices must be made." Jacques glanced toward Hugo, who remained unconscious on the sofa. "A pity really. The two of you would have brought a fine ransom."

Gabriel's disbelief was forgotten as a flare of panic

seared through him. It was one thing for his life to be threatened, it was quite another to watch in frustration as his friend lay helpless and unable to protect himself.

"And Talia?" he rasped. "Will she be a brutal sacrifice as well?"

"Non," Jacques snapped, appearing ridiculously offended by the question. "She will not be harmed, although she will not be allowed to leave France." Regaining command of his composure, the Frenchman managed a faint smile. "In time she will not wish to."

His fury remained potent at the knowledge Talia was being held captive, but Jacques's taunt went wide of the mark.

The tantalizing memory of Talia wrapped in his arms, her sweet cries of pleasure filling the air as she'd responded to him without reservation assured him that she had given him more than the pleasure of her body.

She had given him her trust and her loyalty.

Two gifts that were more precious than any amount of treasure.

"Your conceit is as bloated as it is misplaced," he warned in cold derision. "No matter how undeserving I might be of Talia, she is a woman of utter devotion. She will never forgive the man who murdered her husband."

Jacques smoothed a hand over his elegantly tied cravat, a large diamond glittering from the ring on his slender finger.

"I can be quite persuasive when I choose." He spoke with the confidence of a man accustomed to success among the opposite sex. "And surely you would wish her to be happy?"

Gabriel curled his upper lip in disgust. "What I wish is for you to rot in hell."

Jacques waved a dismissive hand. "My inevitable fate,

no doubt, but not before I have led France into her glorious future."

"Using my brother as your pawn?"

"Precisely." The Frenchman dipped his head in agreement. "He shall make quite a dashing Earl of Ashcombe, do you not think? And with his position in the House of Lords, he will have access to the most closely guarded secrets of the British Empire. I predict our partnership will be excessively profitable for both of us."

Gabriel's blood ran cold.

Jacques was right, damn his black heart. Although Harry's position as the younger brother to the Earl of Ashcombe had always ensured him a place among the *ton,* his habit of spending his evenings in a drunken haze, not to mention his preference for gambling dens and whorehouses to polite society, had kept his name off the guest list of many hostesses.

And of course, there would be no gentleman who would willingly discuss confidential information with a scandal-seeking gamester who was notoriously in need of funds.

But as the Earl of Ashcombe...

Harry would suddenly find himself in demand at the most elite gatherings where political conversations often turned to the ongoing war. And, as Jacques had so smugly pointed out, he would be a member of parliament with the ability to mingle among those in command of the British troops.

Hell, he could request an audience with the prince without causing undue curiosity.

And all it would take would be one indiscreet conversation, or a set of maps left carelessly on a table, and disaster would strike.

Gabriel shook his head. Jacques's plan promised a

spiderweb of horrifying possibilities, but his thoughts refused to consider the future.

Not when he had yet to accept the dastardly plot was more than just a product of the Frenchman's deluded imagination.

"Have you discussed this latest scheme with my brother?" he demanded, his voice oddly harsh.

Jacques arched a brow. "Do you nurture the hope that Harry will balk at stepping into your shoes?" he taunted. "I assure you that you could not be more mistaken. I believe he would pull the trigger if necessary to gain the title he has always coveted."

Gabriel gave a sharp shake of his head. He refused to consider his last ugly encounter with his brother. Or the barely concealed bitterness that had marred their relationship for far too long.

Whatever their differences, they were family. In the end, Harry would do what was right.

How could he believe otherwise?

"You are a fool." He tugged against the ropes that bound his wrists, indifferent to the raw, weeping wounds that marred his skin. "Whatever Harry's sins, he would never wish for my death."

A humorless smile curved Jacques's lips as he turned to head for the door.

"Then it would appear that you know as little about your brother as you do your wife."

CHAPTER SIXTEEN

GABRIEL MUTTERED a vile curse as the Frenchman disappeared from the library.

He was a man who had become accustomed to being in utter command of his world and those around him. He gave an order, and it was obeyed without question and without fuss. And while Harry's antics were a constant source of annoyance, he had been confident that his younger brother would eventually mature and put aside his reckless need to shock society.

Now, trussed up like a pig for slaughter, with his wife being held captive by a French Lothario, and his brother cast in the role of Cain, he had never felt so utterly impotent in his life.

As if his brooding frustration had managed to penetrate Hugo's unconsciousness, the large nobleman stirred on the sofa.

"Well this is a damned fine muddle you have gotten us into," Hugo muttered, forcing open his eyes with a pained groan.

A sharp relief pierced through Gabriel's black mood as he watched Hugo cautiously press himself into a seated position, lifting his hand to his wounded temple.

"I can see the blow to your head did not addle what few wits you possess," Gabriel teased.

"Not for lack of effort." Hugo's gaze skimmed over the vast library before taking a slow inventory of Gabriel's awkward position on the floor. "You have the most charming acquaintances, old friend."

Gabriel gritted his teeth. "Charming is not precisely how I would describe Jacques Gerard."

Hugo grimaced, his face pale and his eyes shadowed with a lingering pain.

"No, me, neither." He paused to study Gabriel with concern. "Are you harmed?"

"Nothing beyond my pride."

"Did you locate Harry?"

A humorless smile twisted Gabriel's lips. "Ah, I see my wife has revealed the dismal tale of my brother's betrayal."

"I gave her little choice," Hugo admitted. "We had quite a battle of wills when it came time to sail to England."

Gabriel sent his friend a disapproving frown. "A battle she obviously won despite my attempts to ensure her safe return to England."

Hugo reached beneath his jacket to withdraw a starched handkerchief, absently wiping the blood from his face. Gabriel sent up a silent prayer of thanks that the wound seemed to have stopped bleeding, although it was swollen and bruised.

Not that his companion would be in any condition to toss himself into battle anytime soon.

Gabriel doubted his friend would be able to stand upright at the moment.

"Yes, well, you should not have wed such a stubborn minx," Hugo accused. "She threatened to leap overboard if we did not return her to shore."

Gabriel smiled with rueful resignation.

Only a few weeks ago he would have claimed there was nothing less desirable than a stubborn female. A

proper maiden understood that it was her duty to be led
by a gentleman, especially if that gentleman also happened to be her husband.

And in truth, his life would no doubt be far less complicated if Talia were the sort of woman who were content to remain quietly secluded at Carrick Park instead
of tossing herself headfirst into danger.

But Gabriel felt nothing but pride at the thought of
Talia's staunch courage.

"You should have tied her to the mast," he said, not
entirely jesting.

Hugo snorted. "I doubt even that would have stopped
her."

"True."

Silence descended before Hugo was tossing aside the
soiled handkerchief and clearing his throat.

"I was mistaken."

Gabriel lifted his brows at the abrupt statement. "You
are often mistaken, Hugo. You shall have to be more specific."

"I misjudged your wife." His expression was somber.
"She is not the shallow title hunter that I thought her to
be."

"No, she is not."

"And she cares for you a great deal," he continued,
heaving a sigh. "Foolish woman."

It was foolish, of course. She deserved a gentleman
who would have wooed her with the pretty words and
thoughtful gestures every maiden desired. Not an arrogant oaf who had ruined her wedding day and then insisted on taking her innocence before banishing her to
the country.

But unfortunately for Talia, it did not matter to him
how worthy or unworthy he might be. She was bound

irrevocably to him. And he would never, ever allow her to escape his grasp.

"Not only foolish, but impulsive and reckless," he said with a shake of his head.

Hugo did not bother to disagree, his gaze darting toward the doorway to ensure the guards in the hallway were not yet aware he was awake before he leaned forward and spoke in a low whisper.

"She was hidden across the street when I was captured. Perhaps she will have the sense to return to the yacht—"

"Too late," Gabriel interrupted, his voice tight with barely restrained fury. "Jacques has her imprisoned upstairs."

"Damn." Hugo's face reflected his stark regret. "Forgive me, Gabriel. I have failed you."

"No, Talia is mine to protect," Gabriel protested, unwilling to allow his friend to shoulder the burden that was his to bear. "I should have ensured she was safely installed at Carrick Park before returning to track down Harry."

Hugo dipped his head in agreement, his previous distrust of Talia obviously replaced by a newfound respect. Nothing less than a miracle, considering the nobleman was notorious for his disdain toward most females.

"You did not tell me if you managed to track down your brother," Hugo reminded him.

"I did." Gabriel sucked in a harsh breath. "Unfortunately."

Hugo narrowed his gaze. "He was the bait for the damned Frenchman's trap?"

Gabriel hesitated, torn between the cynical voice in the back of his mind that whispered Harry was proving to be capable of any sin, and the fierce need to believe he would never deliberately lure Gabriel into the hands of his enemies.

"I do not think that he realized what Jacques intended."

Hugo made a sound of disgust. "You still defend him?"

Gabriel shrugged. "No, but his surprise was as great as my own when Jacques made his appearance at the *bordel*."

"You were at a whorehouse?"

"Where else would I find my brother?"

A hint of amusement simmered in Hugo's golden eyes. "You might wish to avoid mentioning your precise location when you discuss this with Talia."

Gabriel gave an impatient shrug, even as he tucked away the sage warning. Hugo was right. It probably would be best to keep that bit of information to himself.

"My point is that I do not believe he even realized I was in France until I cornered him."

Hugo appeared far from convinced. "If Harry was not a part of the plot, then where is he?"

Gabriel leaned his aching head against the column, the thought of his brother a raw, aching wound in the center of his heart.

"I am not entirely certain."

"But he is aware that you are being held captive?"

Gabriel shifted his gaze toward the massive globe made of ivory and gold that was situated beneath a bay window.

"Yes."

"Gabriel, what are you hiding?"

For a long moment Gabriel found himself reluctant to reveal Jacques Gerard's ruthless plot.

Why?

Did he hope that by ignoring the hideous threat it

would make it less of a possibility? Rather like warding off the evil eye, he wryly admitted, inanely wondering if Talia's gypsy grandmother would approve.

Or was it simple shame?

After all, no gentleman of honor wished to admit their own brother was not only a despicable spy, but that he might very well be plotting his death.

In either case, he owed his friend the truth.

Hugo had been willing to risk his neck to rescue his friend. He deserved to know the danger they both faced.

With an effort, Gabriel forced his gaze back to his friend.

"Jacques Gerard just left the room after informing me that Harry is about to become the next Earl of Ashcombe."

"Impossible—" Hugo began, only to suck in a sharp breath as he realized that there was one means to make it possible. "Damnation."

"Precisely," Gabriel agreed in clipped tones. "And I fear you are to be sacrificed along with me to elevate my brother to the title."

Hugo breathed a few choice curses, his contempt for Harry etched into his expression.

"And Harry has agreed to this plan?"

Gabriel wearily shrugged. "I pray he has not, but in truth...I do not know."

As if sensing Gabriel's reluctance to discuss Harry's potential for fratricide, Hugo narrowed his gaze with a sudden surge of determination.

"Well, it does not matter," he announced firmly. "Neither of us is going to be sacrificed."

Gabriel smiled wryly. "Agreed."

The golden gaze shifted toward the doorway where two soldiers were standing guard.

"Now we just need to discover the means to avoid our imminent death."

JACQUES DID NOT allow himself the opportunity to consider his bold decision as he headed to the private study at the back of the townhouse.

It was his favorite room in the house that had once belonged to the Comte de Devanne.

Although not as large as the library, it was a spacious chamber. Gilt-wood armchairs with teal velvet covers matched the curtains covering the windows overlooking the back garden. A pair of lacquer cabinets framed a Brussels tapestry along the far wall while the heavy oak desk was set to face the white marble fireplace veined with gold.

He had removed the ornate figurines and porcelain plates that had littered the room before he had claimed it as his own, replacing them with the precious sculptures his father had completed before his untimely death.

It was his private domain that no one dared enter without his specific invitation.

Or at least no one with any amount of sense, he corrected, anger flaring through him as the door to the study was thrust open and Harry Richardson strolled in as if he were a welcome guest rather than a necessary pest.

"Harry." Carefully sealing the letter he had just completed, Jacques rose from the desk and crossed toward the side door that opened into the connected antechamber. "I do not recall issuing an invitation for you to join me."

An all too familiar sullen expression marred the younger man's face.

"I need to speak with you."

Gesturing to the soldier who stood guard in the ante-chamber, Jacques handed him the folded note. Despite the lateness of the hour, he wanted his emperor to be fully aware of his change in plans.

Not that he doubted Napoleon would protest his scheme. He was ruthless in his quest to conquer Europe. And perhaps the world.

There were no sacrifices too great to fulfill his ambitions.

"See that this is delivered to the emperor without delay," he commanded.

"*Oui.*"

With military precision the guard turned on his heel and rushed from the room. The letter would be in Napoleon's hands within a few days.

Strolling back to his desk, he settled on the corner as he sent his companion a mocking gaze.

"You see how a good soldier is capable of obeying orders?"

A flush crawled beneath Harry's pale skin. "I am not one of your damned soldiers."

Jacques flicked a dismissive glance over the man's rumpled clothing that had no doubt cost a small fortune. The conceited peacock was precisely the sort of hedonistic aristocrat that Jacques had always detested.

"*Non,* I would never depend upon you to protect me in the midst of battle. You would be fleeing in terror from the first shot."

The dandy stiffened in ridiculous outrage. "Are you calling me a coward?"

Jacques shrugged. "Do you deny the claim?"

"Would a coward risk death to become a spy?"

"There is no honor in what you have done," Jacques

said, sneering, readily turning his vile temper on the fool before him. He had known from the moment he had tossed his lot with Napoleon that there would be difficult decisions to be made. War was not the noble business of a young man's fancy. Too often victory demanded that a man make sacrifices that he would never willingly choose. And certainly it forced unsavory alliances. But that did not mean he had to be pleased with the loss of his conscience. "You became a spy because you are a self-indulgent coxcomb who was willing to betray everyone and everything you supposedly held dear for money."

Not surprisingly Harry blinked in astonishment at Jacques's brutal honesty. For years Jacques had courted and wooed the insolent pup, encouraging his reckless dissipation even as he whispered constant reminders of how unfair life was to have blessed Gabriel with so many riches while Harry was forced to live on a beggar's allowance.

It had all been so terribly simple.

"You were not so disdainful when you suggested that we become allies," Harry said, pouting. "In fact, you implied I was a hero for my daring."

Jacques gave a lift of his shoulder. "I had need of you."

Harry frowned. "And now?"

"Now you have need of me," he said, folding his arms over his chest, his pitiless gaze never shifting from the younger's man's face. "Or more precisely you have need of what I can offer you."

Although not nearly so intelligent as his elder brother, Harry was not entirely stupid. He was forced to accept that his brief fantasy as a dashing adventurer was coming to a painful end.

"I have requested nothing more than a place to remain

hidden from our mutual enemies," he muttered. "You owe me that much."

"I owe you nothing." Jacques smiled. "But fortunately for you, I intend to offer you your deepest desire."

Harry licked his dry lips, his hands clenched at his sides. "And what would you know of my deepest desire?"

"It is obvious to anyone who knows you, *mon ami,* that you are consumed with lust for your brother's position."

He paled, shaking his head in pointless denial. "That is absurd."

"I agree," Jacques mocked, sickened by the thought of placing this cowardly ass in a position of power. "You are a nasty toad who is unworthy of the title. Unfortunately, the current Earl of Ashcombe is a formidable gentleman of honor and ruthless integrity who I might have admired if he had not been standing in the path of what I most desire." He shrugged, refusing to contemplate the fact he was about to order the cold-blooded murder of a nobleman. "You, on the other hand, are without pesky morals, which suits my needs perfectly."

If possible, Harry lost even more color, leaving his skin ashen.

"Even if I was fool enough to want the title, it is not a damned bauble that can be passed from one person to another," he rasped.

Jacques's lips flattened at the bitter memories of his childhood spent on the fringes of French aristocracy. There had been no need to explain that as a son of a mere artist, no matter how talented Jean-Luc Gerard might have been, he would always be considered inferior to the prissy dandies who sashayed the streets of Paris.

"I am well aware of the laws of heredity," he snarled. "Laws that I intend to ensure are destroyed in France."

Harry waved an impatient hand. "You may do whatever you bloody well want in France, but in England there are very precise rituals that must be observed to inherit a title."

"And?"

"I cannot simply appear among the House of Lords and demand the Lord Chancellor proclaim me the next Earl of Ashcombe just because my brother has disappeared." Growing agitated, Harry paced across the room, a thin sheen of sweat on his forehead. "It will take years before they will agree to declare Gabriel dead. You know damned well how they all dote on him. No doubt the entire nation will be expected to go into mourning. And it will be years more before the Letters Patent would ever be offered to me."

"There will be no need to have your brother declared dead," Jacques assured him.

Coming to a halt, Harry regarded him with an insolent expression that made Jacques long to thrash him.

"You believe they will take my word for his untimely demise?"

Jacques straightened from the desk, his expression grim. "They will so long as you have his lifeless corpse to show them."

"A corpse?" Harry blinked, his mouth hanging open as the implication of Jacques's words sank through his thick skull. "You cannot…"

"Oh, come, Harry, there is no need to pretend such outraged shock," Jacques drawled.

Snapping his lips together, Harry glared at him with impotent fury.

"It is no pretense, you bastard."

"Of course it is." Jacques arched a brow. "You must have known from the moment your brother discovered that you had bartered your soul to Napoleon that he would have to die." He deliberately paused. "If you did not, then you are an idiot."

"You have him captured. He is no threat."

"I have already discovered not to underestimate your brother. So long as he lives, he will be a threat," Jacques muttered with a grimace. "Besides, did you not just assure me that it would be impossible for you to take his place without a proper funeral for the current earl?"

Harry hunched his shoulders, as usual unwilling to accept that his choices had a cost that must be paid.

"There is no need for me to be the Earl of Ashcombe to discover another contact within the Home Office. I shall return to London…"

"*Non.*"

"What?"

Jacques heaved an impatient sigh. "Have you forgotten you are currently embroiled in a nasty scandal after having abandoned your bride at the altar and taken off with her dowry?"

He did not even possess the grace to appear guilty as he waved a dismissive hand.

"It will have passed now that my brother has wed Talia."

Jacques rolled his eyes. Harry truly believed his sins had once again been swept beneath the carpet by his brother.

"And how do you intend to explain their mysterious disappearance?"

Harry was momentarily stumped by the perfectly reasonable question. But with the skill of a born prevaricator, he offered a ready lie.

"It must be known by Gabriel's servants that Talia was kidnapped by you and that he traveled to France to rescue her," he pointed out. "It will be assumed that he is still searching for her or he is captured."

"Which will ensure that I am hunted by every British soldier in France." Jacques shook his head. "*Non,* I thank you."

The younger man scowled, predictably indifferent to the notion of Jacques being pursued by the entire British army.

"Then I will say that they have returned and have traveled to my brother's estate in Scotland to recuperate from their ordeal."

"And they took Lord Rothwell along as a chaperone?" Jacques scoffed.

Harry hissed with impatience, his face drawn with believable tension. Had Jacques not been so sadly familiar with the selfish cad, he might have been convinced Harry truly cared whether his brother lived or died.

"We can conjure some tale that will satisfy society."

"I am not willing to risk our profitable arrangement on the hope you can deceive those who are already inclined to distrust you." His lips twisted into a humorless smile. "And you cannot deny that your position as the Earl of Ashcombe would be worth a great deal more to me than a scapegrace younger son."

Harry returned to his furied pacing, his jaw clenched and the sweat dripping down his narrow face.

"Dammit, I do not want the title," he growled.

"Is that a jest?" Jacques demanded, watching the nobleman's restless motions with a narrowed gaze. "You have spent your entire life consumed with jealousy."

"I will admit that I have resented being forever found inferior to my perfect brother, but that does not mean I wish to step into his shoes," Harry muttered. "And I most certainly do not wish to have him murdered."

Jacques made a sound of disgust. "I could almost believe you if I had not spent hours listening to your drunken boast."

His accusation brought Harry to an abrupt halt, his expression suddenly wary. And for good reason. Who had not been in Harry's company and not had to endure his tedious complaints of the injustice of the world in general and his elder brother in particular?

"What drunken boast?"

"That the title of Earl of Ashcombe was wasted on a humorless prig who should have been drowned at birth," he reminded his companion in sardonic tones. "That you would have been a far superior heir had fate not been so cruel."

"A man will say anything when he is in his cups," Harry said with a peevish frown.

"*Oui,* and almost always it is the truth."

"No. I do not want this." Harry tugged at his rumpled cravat, as if it was choking him. "You ask too much."

"I do not *ask,* Harry," Jacques corrected in soft, lethal tones. "I am informing you what is to occur."

Harry's throat convulsed as he struggled to swallow his swelling panic.

"You cannot force me to take the title," he blustered. "If you kill my brother I will refuse to return to England."

Jacques gave a grunt of disgust. "I notice you do not threaten to expose yourself as a traitor to your country. That, of course, would put any end to my hope of using you as a spy, but then you would have to face the consequences of your sins, would you not?" He watched the fear darken Harry's eyes, sensing that he had the fool precisely where he desired. "Something you have never been willing to do."

"Say what you will, I refuse to become the Earl of

Ashcombe," Harry warned, but his swagger had been reduced to a childish whine.

Jacques stepped close enough to grasp the lapels of Harry's tailored coat, his expression merciless.

"Careful, *mon ami,* the moment you cease to be of use to me is the moment I lodge a bullet in your heart." He smiled at the sound of Harry's tortured struggle to breathe. "And make no mistake the pleasure it will give me to rid the world of your worthless presence."

The pale eyes glittered with hatred. "Damn you."

Jacques thrust Harry toward the door, weary of the sordid business.

"Return to your foolish entertainments while the men tend to business, Harry," he commanded. "I shall let you know when I have need of you." He waited until the Englishman had stumbled across the room. "Oh, and Harry," he drawled.

Grasping the doorjamb, Harry glared over his shoulder. "What?"

"Do not stray far."

He jerked as if he had been slapped. "I am a prisoner?"

"Calais is surrounded by French soldiers who are eager to spill English blood." Jacques grinned. "Only a fool would willingly become their target."

CHAPTER SEVENTEEN

WAITING UNTIL HE heard the sounds of Harry slamming the front door of the townhouse, Jacques heaved a sigh and headed out of the study.

He intended to return to the library and finish the nasty duty awaiting him there. After all, Lord Rothwell would soon awaken. It was imperative that he had them quietly...exterminated...before they could cause more trouble.

The sooner he was finished with the task, the sooner he could have Harry returned to London and the sooner they could discover what the British military was planning.

His feet, however, refused to obey, and rather than leading him downstairs, he found himself headed for his private chambers.

Perhaps he should ensure Talia was still locked in his bedchamber, he argued with the voice of reason in the back of his mind. The last thing he desired was for her to sneak out of the room and witness the death of her husband.

It was bound to be difficult enough for her to accept becoming a widow.

Refusing to contemplate Talia's reaction once she realized Gabriel was dead, Jacques was distracted by the slam of drawers coming from the bedchamber directly across the hall.

With a frown he pushed open the door to watch as Sophia stormed from the cherrywood armoire to shove a satin gown into a case lying open on the canopied bed.

Wise enough not to enter a room with a furious woman who had an artillery of crystal perfume bottles and heavy silver candlesticks at her disposal, Jacques instead leaned a shoulder against the doorjamb.

"You are displeased with your chambers?" he demanded.

With a small gasp, Sophia whirled to confront him, her midnight eyes flashing fire.

"I could hardly admit to being displeased when it was I who insisted it be refurbished to suit my taste," she muttered, casting a glower about the room dramatically decorated in black and gold to emphasize Sophia's own exotic beauty. Even the fireplace was made of black marble to contrast with the bed that was draped in a shimmering gold satin.

He briefly recalled Sophia's pleasure as the last of the workmen had left, and they had christened the wide bed in a storm of passion. By the time they had finished, his cravat had been dangling from the gilt chandelier and trousers tossed on the window seat.

He swallowed a sudden sigh. *Sacré bleu.* It all seemed a very long time ago, and not for the first time he questioned his decision to bring Sophia to Calais.

After her betrayal, he had been determined to pack her off to Paris. How could he possibly trust she would not allow her emotions to overcome her common sense? Especially now that Talia was once again his prisoner.

But in the end, he'd found himself commanding her to pack her bags and join him on the short journey. He'd claimed that he desired to keep her close at hand where he could ensure her good behavior, but the truth of the matter was his motives were not so easy to comprehend.

All he knew for certain was that the thought of her walking away was unacceptable.

"Then why are you packing your bags?" he asked.

She tossed her head as she moved to the lacquered dresser and pulled out a handful of lacy undergarments.

"I should think it obvious."

"Perhaps to you, but I will admit to being baffled." His gaze followed her path back to the bed, her hands unsteady as she dropped her belongings on the growing pile. "Explain yourself."

The dark gaze lifted to stab him with a smoldering glare. "You have the woman you want, do you not?"

It was a question he had not allowed himself to consider. After all, Talia was perfect for him. She possessed precisely the sort of qualities that he desired in a female. She was spirited and courageous and yet, so sweetly vulnerable that he longed to wrap her in his arms and keep her safe. And of course, only a dead man would not find her curvaceous body a source of constant enticement.

But that did not lessen his desire for Sophia. Or his fury at the thought of her packing her bags and leaving him.

"I assume that you refer to Lady Ashcombe?"

"I do," she snapped. "Unless you have yet another female hidden in your rooms?"

He shrugged. "For the moment she is my prisoner."

She folded her arms beneath her lovely bosom that was emphasized by the low cut of her rose-and-silver striped gown.

"Please do not treat me as if I am an idiot, Jacques."

A delectable hunger shivered through him, making him wonder if she would spit and scratch if he tumbled her onto the wide bed or welcome him with the raw passion that always shimmered between them.

He ruefully squashed the urge to discover which she might choose, instead moving forward to block her path to the dresser.

"I was not aware that was what I was doing," he murmured, grasping her arms and pressing her back toward the bed. "Cease this nonsense and sit down."

Perching stiffly on the edge of the mattress, Sophia regarded him in defiance.

"Now what?"

"How did you discover that Talia was here?"

She shrugged. "The entire household is whispering that you have not only captured Lord Ashcombe but his wife and friend, Lord Rothwell, as well."

Jacques snapped his teeth together, damning loose tongues that could spread gossip faster than wildfire.

It was not that he was idiotic enough to believe he could keep his prisoners a secret, but he had hoped to be rid of Ashcombe and Rothwell before the word of their presence began to spread through the streets of Calais.

Not only was it going to be a difficult enough task to haul two corpses and a petulant Harry Richardson onto a ship that he had commanded be docked just north of the town without attracting undue attention, but he had not lied to Harry when he'd said there were several hundred French soldiers outside the city walls. It would take very little to provoke them into a frenzied thirst for English blood.

Especially if that blood happened to be that of an English aristocrat.

"My household should concentrate on their duties and not on gossiping about matters that do not concern them," he growled.

"You cannot fault them for their interest," she sniffed, her eyes flashing fury. "It is, after all, believed that you intend to slay Lord Ashcombe in order to make the lovely Talia a widow and mistress of your household."

He dropped her hands, his spine stiffening at the implication in her low words.

Certainly he had taken pleasure in taunting Ashcombe with the threat of making Talia a widow, but he would never murder a man simply to acquire a wife. No matter how much he might desire her.

"My decision regarding Lord Ashcombe has nothing to do with Talia," he said in harsh denial.

Her brows rose in disbelief. *"Non?"*

"Non. I am doing what is best for France." He frowned with impatience. "Even you must admit that having the Earl of Ashcombe as my spy rather than a mere younger brother is preferable."

She stubbornly refused to admit the truth of his words. "You were not so eager to be rid of the current earl until you were bewitched by his beautiful bride."

He muttered a curse, the temptation to press Sophia back onto the mattress and drown his troubled heart in the pleasure of her soft, satin skin nearly overwhelming.

What would it matter if he pushed aside his unpleasant duties for a few hours and indulged himself in the sensuous delight Sophia offered?

Then, with an effort, he pulled back, hoping the space would return his fading sanity even if his body was hard and restless with unfulfilled need.

"Harry was a suitable partner until our tidy arrangement was exposed. Now the government will be even more vigilant and it will take more than a bribe in the proper hand to receive the information we need." He shook his head in disgust. It was infuriating to have lost his contact in the Home Office. The information he had been receiving might very well have made the difference in winning or losing the war. "Besides, it was too risky to attempt to kill Lord Ashcombe while he was in England. A nobleman of his wealth and status is forever surrounded by servants and sycophants." He shrugged. "Now, however, there is no one to protect him."

A strange expression fluttered over her lovely face. Something that might have been regret.

But why?

She did not know the Earl of Ashcombe well enough to mourn his death. Could it be she feared what the toll would be on Jacques's soul for commanding the death of an aristocrat?

"What of his brother?" she asked.

"As always, Monsieur Richardson's only concern is for his own selfish needs," Jacques muttered in disgust. "I truly believe he would barter his mother if he thought it necessary."

"And Lord Rothwell?"

Jacques did not allow himself to hesitate. "He will share his companion's unfortunate fate."

"But not Lady Ashcombe," she pressed.

His brows snapped together at her ridiculous question. Did she truly believe he had become the sort of man who would slay a vulnerable maiden?

"There is no need for her death."

"Of course not." There was a long, uncomfortable silence before she tilted her chin and regarded him sternly. "Do you intend to make her your wife?"

He shifted in sudden discomfort. *Mon Dieu.* Surely a man was not expected to discuss his future wife with his current mistress?

It was...unsavory.

"Is that not rather presumptuous?" he hedged. "I have not yet made her a widow."

"But that is your wish?"

"Who can say?" With a burst of impatience he paced across the floor, uncertain when his life had become so complicated. He almost wished he could turn back the clock to when he was still the idealistic young man who had first returned to France, determined to dedicate his life to his country. "It is enough to concentrate on each day as it unfolds, is it not?"

A wistful smile curved her full lips. "That was what I once told myself."

Jacques ignored the sensation, perilously close to guilt, that tugged at his heart.

"And now?"

"Now, I must consider my future." Her gaze shifted toward the bag lying open on the bed. "I am no longer a young maiden, after all."

"What do you intend to do?"

"For now I shall return to Paris."

"Will you resume your career on the stage?"

"Perhaps."

He came to an abrupt halt, a scowl marring his brow. "Do you have a gentleman awaiting you?"

Sophia was gracefully on her feet again, moving to the armoire to take out the last of her gowns.

"There are always gentlemen."

Sheer fury at the thought of her going from his arms to another man seared through him.

It did not matter that she was a courtesan. Or that he had barely acknowledged her presence since bringing Talia to France. She was…a part of his life. And she had no right to leave him.

"Sophia, quit this foolishness," he snapped as she dumped the dresses atop the pile in her bag.

"What foolishness?" She refused to glance in his direction. "Leaving you?"

He waved aside the blunt question. "It is too late to travel to Paris tonight."

"Then I will leave at first light."

"Non."

Now she did lift her head to look at him, her expression hard as she met his frustrated gaze.

"The decision is not yours to make, Jacques."

With three long strides he had his hands clenched around her upper arms.

"You are mine to protect."

Her dark eyes flashed a brazen challenge at his possessive tone.

"Protect me from what?"

"Napoleon has attempted to bring order to the masses, but we both know that his efforts are not always successful." He latched onto the first thought that came to mind. "With so many soldiers roaming the streets a woman on her own is always at risk."

She appeared unimpressed with his logic. "The streets of Paris have never been safe, *chérie,* which I discovered at a very young age." The edge in her voice hinted at the high cost of her survival. "Thankfully, I am no fragile flower. Unlike your precious Talia, I have learned how to depend upon my own wits."

Jacques was wise enough not to inform his mistress that Talia had proven she was more than capable of depending upon her wits. Instead he shifted his hand to cup her cheek, his thumb brushing the sensuous curve of her bottom lip.

"I do not doubt your ability to fend for yourself, Sophia, only the need to do so," he gently corrected. "You will always have a place in my home."

"As your mistress?"

"As my..." He hesitated, irritated by her refusal to simply accept his offer of protection. What did she want from him? "As my friend."

Without warning she yanked herself from his grip, the candlelight shimmering off the hint of fire in her dark curls.

"You might wish to discuss my position in your household with Talia," she retorted in biting tones. "There are few women who would desire a previous lover beneath her roof."

"I have more than one home. You may choose to live wherever you please."

His reasonable suggestion was met with a furious hiss as Sophia turned to slam down the lid of her case.

"Ah, a female for every establishment," she taunted. "How terribly convenient for you."

His own temper flared. Was he not doing everything in his power to ensure she was kept in luxury when any other gentleman would have tossed her into the street after he'd finished with her? She should be showering him with gratitude, not hissing at him like a wounded cat.

"You are deliberately attempting to misunderstand me," he charged.

"*Non,* I understand perfectly. You no longer desire me, but you cannot bear the thought I might find another gentleman who does. Admit the truth, Jacques."

He stiffened, refusing to consider the accuracy of her words.

If she desired to play the role of the martyr, then who was he to thwart her tragic exit?

"Very well. You have obviously made your decision." He offered a stiff bow before heading toward the door. "I will have a carriage at your disposal."

GABRIEL DID NOT attempt to smother his groan of relief as Hugo at last managed to loosen the ropes that had cut deep furrows into his wrists.

"Damn," Hugo breathed, frowning as Gabriel pulled out his handkerchief to wipe away the crusted blood. "Those wounds will be infected if they are not properly cleaned."

"A worry for later." He tossed aside the soiled handkerchief, turning his attention to his companion's ashen face. "How is your head?"

"Aching." Hugo grimaced, straightening before he headed directly for the brandy bottle set on a walnut sideboard. "Although I believe this should help ease the pain."

"Shh," Gabriel murmured. "We do not want to alert the guards that you are awake and that I am free."

"What does it matter?" Hugo took a swig of the spirits directly from the bottle, his features tight with pain. "Without a weapon we have no hope of getting past the soldiers."

Gabriel struggled to his feet, stretching his cramped muscles even as he sent his companion a warning glare.

"I have no intention of leaving without Talia."

Hugo lifted a slender hand. "Be at ease, Ashcombe, it never occurred to me that we would leave without your wife."

"Forgive me." Gabriel pressed the heel of his hand to his throbbing temple. "It has been a trying few days."

Hugo took another swig of the brandy. "I should say it has been a trying few months."

"True." Gabriel heaved a rueful sigh, moving to cast a cautious glance out the window. He counted two guards on the front balcony and another near the gate that opened onto the public street before returning his attention to his companion. "My life has not been the same since Silas Dobson blackmailed me into marrying his daughter."

Setting aside the bottle, Hugo leaned against the side table, obviously still weak from the blow he had taken to his head.

"I am not certain whether to envy you or thank God I have no infuriated father forcing me down the aisle."

Gabriel sympathized with his confusion.

It was not that he regretted having Talia as his bride. Hell, she was nothing less than a miracle. Who could ever have imagined that she could fill his life with a joy he had never expected, let alone deserved?

But he knew deep in his heart that a part of her would never forgive or forget his boorish behavior during the days leading to their farce of a wedding and the manner in which he had neglected her for weeks after they had become man and wife.

And that no matter how readily she might respond to his touch or how loyal she might be to him and their relationship, she would always keep her heart protected. How could she not when he had destroyed her trust?

"Only a fool would envy either of us at the moment," he said wryly.

"In that we agree." Hugo paused, folding his arms over his chest. "Of course, if you would be reasonable, then there might be a solution to our current dilemma."

Gabriel was shaking his head before his friend even finished speaking.

"No."

Hugo pushed away from the side table, his brows lowered with irritation.

"You have not even heard my suggestion."

"There is no need," Gabriel assured his companion. "I am well enough acquainted with you to know you are about to make some ridiculous offer to distract the guards while I rescue Talia and escape to my yacht."

Hugo squared his shoulders, preparing for a fight. "It is the only logical plan."

Knowing it would be pointless to convince the man it was too risky, Gabriel instead heaved a deep sigh.

"Really, Hugo, martyrs are so tediously boring."

"Not a martyr, a gambler," he argued, his chin set to an aggressive angle. "Once you have escaped, the odds are in my favor that the soldiers will charge in pursuit of you and I shall be able to stroll away unnoticed. In truth, I will be in less danger than you."

"No." Gabriel once again shook his head. "If anyone is to offer the distraction, it will be me. It is my fault you were captured."

"I make my own decisions, Ashcombe," Hugo growled. "And if anyone is to be held to blame it is your brother."

"You would, of course, assume I am guilty," an unexpected male voice drawled from behind them. "You never did like me, did you, Rothwell?"

Gabriel whirled on his heel. His brother was standing in a hidden doorway revealed by a narrow portion of the bookshelf that had just swung inward.

For an explosive moment Gabriel stared at Harry in disbelief, half expecting the sight of the slender young man with tousled brown hair and pugnacious expression to be a figment of his imagination.

Hugo charged past Gabriel in a gust of fury, clearly

intent on pummeling the man he held fully responsible for their current troubles.

"You bastard."

Not allowing himself the opportunity to consider the insanity of stepping in front of the large nobleman intent on murder, Gabriel wrapped his arms around his friend's chest and struggled to bring him to a halt.

"Wait, Hugo," he ground out, his muscles straining at the effort of keeping the man from escaping.

"Why?" Hugo demanded between clenched teeth. "He deserves to be skinned alive, like those damned natives do in the colonies."

"I need to speak with him before you do any permanent harm."

"Fine."

Muttering his opinion of craven rats who should be shot on sight, Hugo stepped back, although the tension in his large body warned it would take little provocation to shatter his control.

Gabriel turned back toward Harry, grimly hoping he was not making a mistake in bringing a swift end to the reunion.

"What the hell are you doing sneaking up on us?"

Harry shrugged. "I would think that it was obvious. I did not want Jacques or his guards to know I have returned to the house."

Gabriel narrowed his gaze. "How did you know about the hidden doorway?"

"I have had a fortnight to explore the house while waiting to hear from Jacques." Harry glanced over his shoulder at the dark emptiness that stretched behind him. "I stumbled across the secret tunnel a few days ago. I assume the previous owner dabbled in smuggling."

It was a reasonable assumption. Calais had long been

the primary port for smuggled goods from England. There was, no doubt, any number of homes built with hidden tunnels.

Hugo snorted. "Why am I not surprised you would have found a means to sneak about?"

Harry stepped out of the tunnel, regarding Hugo with a mocking smile.

"Should I be like you, Rothwell?" he demanded. "Strutting about as if I own the damned world and expecting the lesser folk to worship at my feet?"

"Can we finish this squabble later?" Gabriel interrupted, his attention never wavering from his brother. "Where does the passageway lead?"

"To the cellars."

Gabriel nodded, the faintest hope stirring in the pit of his stomach.

Was it possible they might slip past the guards unnoticed?

"Is there a way out of the house?"

"Yes, there is a coal chute that opens in the back garden." Harry grimaced as he glanced down at his expensive jacket that was marred with black streaks. "Which explains why my once pristine coat is now ruined beyond repair."

"Is it guarded?"

"No." Harry brushed a clinging cobweb from his arm. "So far as I can determine no one has been in the passageway for years. I doubt Jacques is aware that they even exist."

"Does one of the passages lead upstairs?"

Harry frowned at the abrupt question. "I have not inspected them that far."

Without warning, Hugo had moved to grasp Gabriel's arm, his expression rigid with disbelief.

"Have you taken leave of your senses?" he barked. "You cannot mean to trust him."

Gabriel scowled. "You believe this to be a trap?"

Hugo growled in disgust. "I think Harry would happily lead both of us to the slaughter if it meant him becoming the next Earl of Ashcombe," he cruelly reminded Gabriel. "It is what he has always desired."

"Dammit," Harry burst out, appearing unbearably harassed. "Why would anyone believe that I would want your stupid title?" He waved his arms in a motion that nearly sent a carved crystal chess set tumbling from the pier table to the ground. "It is nothing but tedious duty and responsibility that I have sought to avoid my entire life, not to mention an endless parade of folks constantly demanding one thing or another. I should rather toss myself in the sea than be burdened with your position."

Hugo's laugh cut sharply through the library. "I could assist you into the sea..."

"Hugo," Gabriel wearily muttered.

His friend had always taken great delight in antagonizing Harry, but now there was an added edge of violence he could barely constrain.

Harry, of course, did nothing to ease the tension. Indeed, the sardonic curl of his lips was a deliberate attempt to goad the large nobleman.

"Well, Gabriel," he prodded. "Do you believe I am here to lead you into a trap?"

Gabriel's lips twisted. "You have not made it easy to trust you, Harry."

A flush crawled over Harry's narrow face, making him appear young and oddly vulnerable.

"I may be a debauched scoundrel who has betrayed his country, but I have never wished you harm, brother," he insisted, his voice harsh with sincerity. "Never, ever that."

The two brothers stared at one another, the years briefly falling away to when they had been just two care-free lads running about the massive estate and causing mischief whenever they could slip away from the nurs-ery. That had been before the old earl had determined it was time for Gabriel to begin his training as the heir ap-parent and Harry had been left in the hands of his overly indulgent mother.

When they had been…brothers.

The fragile connection was broken as Hugo's fingers dug into Gabriel's arm with obvious irritation.

"He may not have wished your death, but you may be certain that if Jacques gave him the choice between his life or yours, he would choose his own every time," he gritted.

"I was already given the choice, you arrogant ass," Harry snapped. "I was told to turn a blind eye and allow you to be sacrificed or Jacques will put a bullet in my heart." He squared his shoulders. "I am risking as much as you by being here."

Gabriel turned a deaf ear to the squabbling, instead concentrating on the vague plans that were formulating in the back of his mind.

He understood Hugo's reluctance to trust Harry. Christ, *he* didn't trust his brother. But for the moment their only hope of escape lay in the hidden passageways, and he was not going to allow his doubt to prevent him from grasping the unexpected opportunity.

What the devil did they have to lose?

"Harry, I wish you to lead Hugo to the cellars."

His brother frowned at the abrupt command. "What of you?"

Hugo shook his head, already suspecting Gabriel's plan. "Dammit, no."

Harry stepped forward in puzzlement. "What the devil is happening?"

Gabriel did not allow his attention to stray from Hugo. If his friend refused to cooperate, then his hasty scheme would be ruined before it could be given an opportunity to succeed.

"I have already warned you I will not leave without Talia," he reminded the nobleman.

Hugo shrugged. "Then we will all go together to rescue her."

"No, I will not argue." Gabriel stubbornly refused to consider the offer. "You will accompany Harry to the cellars and wait for us there. If we do not arrive within half an hour, then the two of you will escape to the yacht." He pointed a finger in Hugo's face. "And this time, old friend, you will ensure that it sails."

Hugo stiffened in outrage. "I most certainly will not."

"Oh, for God's sake," Harry snapped. "We are all going to end up dead if we stand here like a gaggle of fishwives."

"You would be eager to save your own neck," Hugo muttered.

Harry stabbed him with an exasperated glare. "As any man of intelligence would be, but it is my familiarity with my brother's arrogant belief he was born for the sole purpose of ordering others about that resigns me to the inevitable." He pointedly glanced toward Gabriel, who made no effort to hide his stubborn determination. "Our choices would seem to be standing here and arguing or heading to the cellars so Gabriel can go in pursuit of his wife."

"He is right," Gabriel said, pushing his friend toward

the opening in the bookcase. "Go with Harry and I will join you as swiftly as I can."

"Fine." Hugo reluctantly headed toward the passageway, glancing over his shoulder to reveal his disgruntled expression. "But, I make no promises that I will not have strangled your charming brother by the time you arrive."

Gabriel paused long enough to snatch a candle from the nearby candelabra before following Hugo and his brother into the musty tunnel.

"Just so long as you do not alert the guards."

CHAPTER EIGHTEEN

TALIA FELT no guilt as she pressed her ear to the door and eavesdropped on the heated argument between Jacques and Sophia.

Her numerous governesses had never trained her in the proper manners of being held prisoner by a French spy, but her rare afternoons among the dockhands had taught her that a young female must be willing to toss aside polite manners when necessary.

Besides, she continued to hold on to the hope that the Frenchwoman could convince Jacques to release his prisoners and return to his palace. It did not matter to Talia why Sophia was desperate to be rid of her, only that she managed to convince Jacques he was better served by leaving them behind in Calais while he returned to his duties elsewhere.

It was a hope that died a swift death as she heard Jacques storm from the room and cross the corridor. He was headed directly toward the door where she was leaning.

Scrambling to tug the small cudgel from her reticule, Talia pressed herself against the wall, once again thinking back to those dockhands who had tutored her in defending herself. She would have only one opportunity to overcome a larger opponent. Once she lost the element of surprise, she was defeated.

Barely daring to breathe, she lifted her arm as the

door was thrust open. Then, forcing herself to wait until Jacques had stepped fully into the room, she lunged forward, swinging the cudgel downward.

It would have been a successful attack if not for the full skirts that wrapped about her ankles at precisely the wrong time. A risk that the men who had taught her that particular attack never had to take into account.

Tripped off balance, her swing went wide, and with a muffled curse Jacques was turning to wrap her tightly in his arms, her weapon dropping to the carpet.

"Sacré bleu," he breathed, his eyes glittering with irritation. "Is that any way to treat a gentleman who has treated you as an honored guest?"

She stood stiffly, meeting his chiding gaze without apology. Perhaps Jacques had been charmingly polite as he had escorted her into the townhouse and directly to these private chambers. But that had not deterred him from locking the door when he had left, nor from threatening to kill her husband and Lord Rothwell.

"An honored guest is not locked in her rooms."

His brows lifted. "Would you have preferred that I tied you to the bed?"

"I would have preferred that you had allowed me to bash you in the head," she retorted.

With an exasperated shake of his head, Jacques dropped his arms and stepped back.

"What have I done to be plagued with such troublesome females?"

Talia snorted at the genuine irritation in his voice. Only a male could degrade one woman while holding another captive and blame them both for being troublesome.

Such arrogance would never fail to astonish her.

"You do not deserve her, you know," she accused.

"Pardon?"

"Sophia," she clarified. "She adores you, but you treat her as if she is no more than a courtesan to be dismissed on a whim."

He arched a brow. "I hesitate to shock you, *ma petite,* but that is precisely what she is."

Talia was well beyond shock after the past weeks. "If you consider her as nothing more than a harlot, then you should not have made her fall in love with you."

Jacques's eyes widened in disbelief. "You hold me to blame?"

"Of course." Talia gave a lift of her shoulder. "You obviously encouraged her affections."

"Is that not what a gentleman is expected to do with a courtesan?"

"I do not mean…" She struggled for a delicate means to express her argument. "Physically."

With a sharp laugh, he turned to pace across the Oriental carpet, choosing an enamel snuff box from the scrolled mantel and flicking open the lid.

"Thank goodness, since that is a customary part of the relationship," he said, taking a delicate sniff of the scented tobacco.

She glanced toward the cudgel on the floor, regretting the lost opportunity to bang his thick skull. Not only because she had missed a chance to escape, but simply because he obviously needed a good smack to the head.

"I meant that you no doubt confided in her and shared far more than just your bed," she accused.

He stiffened, his expression defensive. "And how would you know that?"

"Women can be quite foolish when it comes to men, but Sophia is too sophisticated to have risked her heart if she did not believe you considered her as more than a bed partner."

"It no longer matters." He abruptly set aside the enamel box, restlessly pacing toward the window that offered a view of the street shrouded in the heavy silence that came just before dawn. "She is returning to Paris in a few hours."

She studied his tense profile. "Not if you ask her to stay."

"I did." He turned to meet her steady gaze. "She does not appreciate your presence in my home."

Talia made a strangled sound, wondering if he were being deliberately obtuse.

"Of course she does not." Talia planted her hands on her hips. "Do you have no feelings for her whatsoever?"

He stiffened, almost as if he were offended by her question. Ridiculous man. Then, narrowing his eyes, he smiled in cold amusement.

"Ah, very clever."

"Clever?"

He folded his arms over his chest. "You hope that if you can rouse my loyalty to Sophia that I will agree to release you and appease her jealousy."

It was, of course, precisely what she desired, but Talia was not stupid enough to admit as much. Jacques was not certain his desire for Sophia was greater than his overpowering need to avenge his father's death.

"Am I not allowed to feel sympathy for a woman who is being abandoned by the man she was silly enough to trust?" she asked instead. "I do, after all, have some experience with that kind of disappointment."

A surprising fury darkened his eyes. "Do not compare me to Harry Richardson."

"Then be a better man than he."

Her challenging words rang through the air as he studied her with an odd expression.

"You are not the wounded child who first set foot in Devonshire."

A faint smile curved her lips as she recalled her arrival at Carrick Park. She had truly felt like a child who was being unfairly punished. She had been lost and alone and unable to contemplate a future that promised any happiness.

Now she could only be thankful that she was no longer that timid girl who allowed others to determine her worth. She had discovered a strength within herself.

A strength that did not depend on others' opinions.

"No. That child has thankfully matured into a woman," she agreed. "And a wife."

His lips tightened. "The Countess of Ashcombe?"

"That is merely a title." She shrugged. "I shall always be Talia."

"Thank God," he growled. "You are too fine a female to be wasted upon the aristocracy."

About to inform him that when she spoke of becoming Gabriel's wife that it had nothing to do with her rise to nobility, Talia bit off her words as she caught sight of a wooden panel sliding open across the room.

At first she thought it must have been a trick of the flickering firelight, but she realized the paneling had truly shifted to reveal a passageway beyond. And that there was the outline of a male form in the shadowed darkness.

A scream rose to her throat. God almighty, was there a soldier attempting to sneak into her private rooms? Or was it some savage off the streets?

Thankfully the scream remained lodged in her throat as the intruder shifted just enough that she could recognize the elegant features and golden hair. Gabriel? Good...lord.

Her mouth snapped shut as he lifted a slender finger to his lips and silently slid the paneling closed, hiding him and the passageway from prying eyes.

Not that his arrival had gone entirely unnoticed, she realized as she checked her startled reaction.

Returning her attention to Jacques, her heart missed a terrified beat at the sight of his suspicious expression.

"Talia?" He frowned down at her pale face. "What is wrong?"

Sensing he would not be satisfied by a simple denial of her startled reaction, she deliberately swayed, pressing a hand to her head.

"Oh."

"Tell me, *ma petite*. Has something frightened you?"

"No. I...I suddenly feel dizzy."

Her ploy appeared to be successful as Jacques swiftly grasped her arms and steered her toward the bed with tender care.

"Sit down," he murmured, pressing her arms until she was perched on the edge of the mattress. His hand shifted to brush against her forehead. "You have no fever."

She managed a stiff smile, wondering if she were imagining the lingering suspicion beneath his display of concern.

"I am not ill, only hungry," she assured him. "I have had only an apple to eat today."

"Why did you not tell me?"

"I assumed that you starve all your prisoners."

Her words had been teasing, but Jacques scowled, clearly offended by her implication she had been abused. Of course, he was a gentleman who took his need to protect women very much to heart, she reminded herself, feeling a stab of unwelcome sympathy.

"I have offered you nothing but my protection, *ma petite.*"

She grimaced, attempting to appear wan and defenseless without overplaying her role.

"Perhaps, but the situation is...difficult."

"Oui." He studied her upturned face with an unnerving intensity. "I understand."

She licked her dry lips. "Could I have a tray?"

His hesitation was so fleeting, Talia managed to convince herself that she had imagined it.

"Of course." He brushed his fingers down her cheek before offering a shallow bow. "I will return in a few moments."

"Thank you."

Watching as he left the room and closed the door, Talia gingerly rose and crossed the room to listen to his retreating footsteps that echoed down the hall. Only when she was certain he was truly gone did she turn and hurry toward the panel, giving it a light tap to indicate that Jacques was gone.

With a faint whisper the panel slid open, and Gabriel stepped into the room, catching her off guard as he muttered a curse and wrapped her in his arms, his grip so tight that it became a challenge to breathe.

Not that she protested. Pressing her face against the solid wall of his chest, she ran her hands down his back, anxious to assure herself he was unharmed.

"Dear God. I was so worried," she breathed. "How did you escape?"

His lips brushed her temple before he pulled back, revealing his tense expression.

"That is something we can discuss once we are out of here."

"Yes."

He glanced around the elegant room, his lips thinning at the unmistakable sight of Jacques's clothing hanging in the wardrobe and his boots standing beside the fireplace.

"Is there anything that you need?" he rasped.

She reached up to press her lips to the hard line of his jaw.

"Nothing but you."

His silver eyes flashed with an emotion that made her heart leap.

"Talia…"

The flicker of the candles was the only warning as the door to the room was abruptly shoved open, and Jacques stepped over the threshold. Talia silently cursed her stupidity as the Frenchman's gaze fell upon Gabriel with a resignation that proved he had not been deceived by her pretense of hunger for even a moment.

So foolish. She had sensed his wariness, had she not? But she had allowed her eagerness to be rid of his unwelcome presence to dismiss her fears. And in doing so, she had all but invited Gabriel into the waiting trap.

Shutting the door, Jacques pulled a pistol from a pocket of his jacket, pointing it toward Gabriel.

"What a touching reunion."

GABRIEL'S ARMS instinctively tightened around Talia as the Frenchman moved to the center of the room, resisting the urge to yank her into the tunnel and attempt to escape before the Frenchman could call for his guards. He would not risk Talia being hit by a stray bullet intended for him.

"I truly am growing weary of you, Jacques Gerard."

"The feeling is quite mutual, Lord Ashcombe." Jacques gave a small wave of the pistol. "Release Talia and step away from her."

Talia made a small sound of distress, clinging tightly to his arm.

"No."

"Talia, do not fear," he murmured, placing a gentle kiss on her cheek before untangling her fingers from his jacket and pushing her out of the line of fire. "Everything will be fine."

Fearless as always, she turned to send their captor a fierce glare.

"Please do not hurt him."

"He has left me little option, *ma petite.*"

Gabriel's hands clenched at Jacques's intimate glance toward Talia. By God, when would the bastard accept that Talia was his wife and that she would never willingly belong to another man?

"Do not blame me for your murderous tendencies," he snarled. "And keep your endearments for your mistress. You will refer to my wife as Lady Ashcombe."

Jacques smiled, clearly amused by Gabriel's fierce jealousy.

"How did you discover the passageway?"

With a mocking smile Gabriel gave a smooth lift of his shoulder.

"Hugo is a remarkably stubborn gentleman who refused to accept we were trapped." The words were not entirely a lie. "He searched until he found the entrance to the passageway in the library."

Jacques considered a long moment before giving a sharp shake of his head.

"*Non.* It is too much a coincidence that you should

simply stumble across a hidden passageway when you have need of one. Only someone who has spent time exploring the house could have known of it." His eyes narrowed. "So who is the traitor? A guard? A servant? Ah…" A disdainful smile twisted his lips. "Harry."

"Harry?" Gabriel lifted his brows. "He has made his decision to offer you his loyalty. I no longer consider him my brother."

Jacques shook his head, too clever to be so easily fooled.

"So I believed, but then I have discovered never to place my faith in the cowardly sod," he drawled. "He would betray me as easily as he betrayed you. Where is he?"

Gabriel gave a lift of his hands, futilely hoping that Hugo and his brother would obey his command to return to his yacht.

"If you speak of Harry I have no notion." He smiled, his expression bland. "Hugo, on the other hand, has escaped and is currently on his way back to England to warn them of my brother's treachery."

Jacques heaved a patronizing sigh. "Must we play this tedious game?"

Gabriel managed to keep his smile in place even as he comforted himself with the thought of his fist smashing into the man's arrogant face.

"It would appear we must."

"No matter." Jacques shrugged. "My guards will swiftly hunt down my missing guests."

Gabriel could not deny the truth of his words. Even if Harry had managed to convince Hugo to escape from the cellars, they could not be more than a block or two away. What he needed was a distraction.

Not giving himself time to consider the danger, he paced forward, his expression taunting.

"As I have told you, Hugo has already escaped," he said. "Any hope you might have to return Harry to England as a spy is ruined."

"Stop right there," Jacques warned, the pistol aimed directly at Gabriel's heart. "I have delayed this long enough."

Intent on the Frenchman, Gabriel briefly forgot his impulsive wife. A mistake he soon regretted as she darted toward Jacques, ignoring the pistol in his hand with a lack of fear that made Gabriel's blood run cold.

Dammit. She was surely going to put him in his grave.

"No, Jacques," she pleaded, reaching to place a hand on his arm. "Please, I beg of you."

Gabriel came to a rigid halt, terrified he might accidently startle the Frenchman who had already turned his attention toward Talia. Christ, it would take no more than a stray sneeze to cause the twitchy man to pull the trigger.

"Forgive me, Talia," Jacques murmured.

"Never." She shook her head in vehement denial. "I will never forgive you."

Jacques pulled his arm from her grasp, shifting to the side and unwittingly jostling a pier table. The small movement was enough to send a Chinese vase toppling to the floor. Gabriel swore as the sound of splintering pottery filled the air, making Talia give a startled scream and Jacques wave the gun in a dangerous arch.

His gaze remained trained on the pistol even when he heard the door to the chamber being thrust open and the sound of an unmistakable female gasp.

"Jacques, are you—"

Gabriel did not hesitate. As Jacques jerked toward the

door he launched himself forward, using his superior bulk to knock the pistol from the bastard's hands and ram him into the floor.

There was a satisfying grunt of pain as Jacques smacked his head against the floor, but before he could get his arms wrapped around the man, he was caught off guard by an infuriated Sophia Reynard who charged forward to pummel his back with surprising force.

Trying to shrug aside the madwoman, Gabriel lost his grip on Jacques who promptly pulled a dagger from beneath his jacket and pressed it to Gabriel's neck.

"Move and I will slice open your throat."

TALIA WATCHED in frozen fear as Gabriel knocked Jacques to the ground. Was he demented? For God's sake, Jacques was holding a loaded gun. He could have been killed.

Clearly the Earl of Ashcombe was in need of a stern lecture on how a proper husband was supposed to behave.

And it certainly did not include risking his fool neck.

Braced for the explosive sound of a gunshot, her knees went weak when instead she watched the pistol fly from Jacques's hand to land near the bed. Oh, thank God. She pressed a hand to her thundering heart.

Miraculously, Gabriel had survived his reckless attack, and as she turned her attention back to the two men wrestling on the carpet she realized that he appeared to actually have gained the upper hand as he pressed Jacques to the floor with his larger form.

Her relief, however, was short-lived. Only distantly aware of Sophia entering the room, Talia was unprepared when the woman abruptly rushed across the room to smack Gabriel in the middle of his back.

"No," she breathed, already moving forward to launch

her own attack when Jacques pressed the dagger to Gabriel's neck and threatened to slit his throat.

Time seemed to stop as Talia skidded to a halt.

What should she do? Barely daring to breathe, she hastily reviewed her limited options.

She could not possibly overpower Jacques, even if she were willing to put Gabriel in harm's way. Which she most certainly was not. And while she might be able to use the passageway to find Lord Rothwell, she would never be able to return in time to prevent Jacques from...

She shuddered, refusing to admit she was helpless.

She glanced about the room, briefly considering her small cudgel that lay forgotten near the doorway. She was skilled in knocking a man senseless with the weapon, but only when she could strike without warning. Besides, she dare not attack Jacques while he held the knife to Gabriel's throat.

Desperate, her attention shifted to the gun that was nearly hidden beneath the bed.

She was no experienced duelist, but she had been taught the basics of shooting a pistol. It was not a particularly difficult task, considering the weapon was already primed and ready to be fired. However, not even the finest marksman could be certain of hitting Jacques without putting Gabriel at serious risk.

But then, she did not need to shoot Jacques, she abruptly realized. There was a far easier method of forcing him to release Gabriel.

Or at least, she hoped it would be easier.

Keeping her gaze locked on the three who had seemingly forgotten her presence, Talia covertly shifted until she was standing next to the bed. Only then did she cautiously bend down to grasp the gun, hiding it in the folds of her skirt as she straightened.

She forced herself to count to ten, ensuring that no one was taking notice of her before she inched her way along the edge of the room. Then, refusing to contemplate her battered conscience, she darted forward and pressed the gun directly to Sophia's temple.

"Release him, Jacques, or I will shoot her," she warned in harsh tones.

She sensed Sophia tense in alarm, but she dared not allow her gaze to stray from Jacques who kept the dagger firmly pressed to Gabriel's throat.

Silence filled the room, broken only by the tick of the ormolu clock on the mantel.

Talia swallowed the lump in her throat, noting Gabriel's furious glare and Sophia's faint tremors as she waited for Jacques to accept he had been bested.

"You wouldn't," he rasped at last.

"Do not be so certain," she warned. "I am desperate."

There was another silence before Sophia released an unsteady laugh.

"You are wasting your time, my lady," she said, her own gaze lingering on the man she loved. "Jacques cares far more for his glorious dreams than a flesh-and-blood female who cannot compete with a fantasy."

Talia shook her head, not missing the fear that had briefly flared through Jacques's eyes. He was far more anxious at the thought of Sophia being in danger than he cared to admit.

Perhaps even to himself.

"I think you underestimate his attachment to you," she murmured. "Is that not true, Jacques?"

With an effort he managed to curl his lips into a stiff smile.

"Do not be a fool, *ma petite*. You will never forgive yourself if you hurt an innocent."

Talia deliberately shifted her gaze to the very large
dagger that was currently pressed to Gabriel's throat.

"I will never forgive myself if I stand aside and allow
you to murder my husband," she countered, the sincerity in her voice unmistakable. "Put down the knife."

Jacques's lips flattened as his narrowed gaze searched
her bleak expression.

"You know I cannot do that."

Sophia jerked, clearly wounded by Jacques's words.
"I did warn you," she breathed.

"Jacques, do not test my resolve," Talia warned. "I am
the daughter of Silas Dobson. I have been taught from
the cradle that only the ruthless survive."

Jacques shook his head in denial. "You are not ruthless."

Gabriel snorted, his burning gaze never wavering from
Talia's pale face.

"And you claimed to know my wife," he mocked.

Talia glanced toward the pistol she held to Sophia's
temple, praying Jacques could not detect her pulse that
raced in pure terror or the revulsion that clenched her
stomach.

"Make your choice."

"Wait," the Frenchman commanded, his gaze shifting
toward the silent Sophia. "Let us not be hasty."

"Jacques," she pressed, sensing his faltering resolu-
tion.

Jacques frowned in frustration. "You swear to release
her?"

"I swear."

"Mon Dieu." Jacques slowly pulled the dagger away
from Gabriel's throat, his expression grim as Gabriel
surged to his feet and snatched the knife from his unre-
sisting fingers. "Talia, you gave your word."

"Of course."

Talia lowered the pistol and stepped away from the Frenchwoman, her entire body wobbling with relief as Gabriel stepped next to her and placed a comforting arm around her shoulders. The tense confrontation had lasted only a few minutes, but it felt as if an eternity had passed since she had picked up the horrid gun.

Pushing himself to his feet, Jacques angrily adjusted his cuffs before he waved a hand toward the door.

"Leave us, Sophia."

"No," Gabriel snapped. "She remains."

Jacques hissed his opinion of arrogant English noblemen through clenched teeth.

"You will hold a helpless female as a hostage?" he demanded.

"We both know that females are rarely helpless and I will not allow her to alert the guards," Gabriel countered. "She will not be harmed so long as you do as I say."

"And precisely what do you intend to do with us?"

A cold, lethal smile curved Gabriel's lips. "That entirely depends on you, Monsieur Gerard."

CHAPTER NINETEEN

TALIA FROWNED AS Gabriel removed his arm from her shoulders and gently tugged the pistol from her grip, tucking the large dagger beneath his jacket. All she desired was to escape from the townhouse and return to the waiting yacht, but she sensed that it would not be as simple as walking out the door.

"Gabriel?" she murmured, not doubting for a moment he already had a plan to escape.

As expected, he offered a confident smile. "We will need a candle, my dear."

"Yes."

She grabbed a burning candle from the mantel, relieved that her shivering was beginning to lessen and that her knees were no longer threatening to buckle.

Gabriel dipped a head toward the silent Frenchwoman who held herself proudly.

"Now if you will kindly lead Sophia into the passageway, Jacques and I will be close behind you."

Without prompting, Sophia moved to enter the dark tunnel, and Talia hurried to walk at her side. She was in no mood to have to chase down the unpredictable woman if she decided to bolt.

Behind her, Talia heard the sound of male footsteps and she paused, the flicker of the candlelight dancing over the stone walls that were shrouded in dust and the low wooden-beamed ceiling.

"Which way?" she demanded.

"To the right," Gabriel directed. "You will see a set of stairs just beyond the corner. They lead to the cellars."

Following his directions, Talia walked beside Sophia, pretending she did not hear the faint scuttle of mice. Surely a few small rodents were the least of her concerns?

"I am sorry, but I could not allow him to kill Gabriel," she said as they reached the stairs, needing to distract herself from her raw nerves.

The older woman lifted the hem of her thin robe as she cautiously navigated the narrow steps.

"Would you have pulled the trigger?"

Talia grimaced. Although she refused to regret doing what was necessary to keep Gabriel alive, it was not a question she desired to ponder.

Not when it made her wonder if she had inherited more of her father's merciless nature than she had realized.

"In all honesty, I do not know," she muttered.

There was an awkward pause before Sophia gently cleared her throat.

"I suppose I should be offering you my appreciation."

"Appreciation?"

The Frenchwoman smiled wryly. "I would never have dared to believe Jacques would choose me over his loyalty to France." She sliced a glance toward Talia. "Or his desire for you."

Talia shook her head, unable to believe a woman of Sophia's sophistication was not readily aware of Jacques's devotion. She was precisely the sort of woman that must have had dozens of men worshipping her pretty feet over the years.

But perhaps even beautiful women could be insecure

when their heart was involved, she realized with a flare of surprise.

Odd to consider after all the years she had assumed those annoyingly fashionable debutantes were never plagued by painful doubts.

"He loves you if only he were not too stubborn to accept his feelings," she assured her companion.

Unexpectedly Sophia sucked in a sharp breath. "Do not say such a thing, *s'il vous plait.*"

Talia blinked in confusion at the woman's fierce response. "Why not? You have just pointed out that he proved that he cares for you."

The woman pitched her voice low enough to ensure it would not carry through the shadowed tunnel.

"I will agree he holds an affection for me," she grudgingly confessed. "And, of course, the thought that I was in danger would have stirred his protective instincts, but I would never be idiotic enough to believe he could offer more."

Talia reached to give the woman's arm a comforting squeeze, recalling her own misery when Gabriel had sent her to Carrick Park. She had been quite convinced at the time that she was destined to spend her life alone and unloved.

Now...

She swallowed a sigh. Now she was not quite so certain of her future.

"It is not idiotic to hope," she murmured softly.

"Almost you tempt me," Sophia said with a sigh. Then, turning her head, she studied Talia with a somber expression. "Talia."

"Yes?"

"Do not doubt that had our positions been reversed, I should not hesitate to pull the trigger."

Talia nearly stumbled over the bottom step at the blunt confession.

"I shall keep that in mind."

KEEPING THE PISTOL aimed at the Frenchman walking at his side, Gabriel kept a close watch on the two females a few steps ahead of them. They whispered together as if they were old friends, but he was not as trusting as Talia. Sophia was not the typical society maiden content to demurely depend upon a gentleman's offer of protection. He did not doubt that beneath her fragile beauty she was as dangerous as any cutthroat.

Thankfully she made no effort to attack Talia, and as they reached the end of the passageway, Gabriel shifted his concern to the closed door that blocked their path. He was not going to charge into the cellars without being assured there were no nasty surprises awaiting them.

With his current streak of luck, he might very well discover Napoleon and the entire French army filling the cellars.

Shoving Jacques forward to overtake the two females, he reached out to grasp Talia's arm and tugged her to a halt.

"Wait, Talia," he commanded, blowing out her candle to plunge them in blackness.

She readily stepped aside as he slowly pushed open the door, his pistol pointed into the darkness beyond.

"Hugo?" he called softly, the musty scent of aged barrels and damp stone wafting through the air.

There was a faint scrape and then light bloomed in the darkness as Hugo lit a candle and crossed to peer out the door. His golden gaze narrowed at the sight of Jacques and Sophia standing in the tunnel.

"You did not warn me you intended to bring guests."

Harry stepped forward, his expression sulky as he regarded the Frenchman who had once been his partner.

"Gabriel, what the devil are you doing with this bastard? We need to get away from here."

Jacques laughed with mocking amusement at the younger man's obvious discomfort.

"Turning traitor yet again, eh, Harry?"

"I am merely attempting to right a wrong," Harry said in sullen tones. "Or at least to right one of many wrongs. I can never fully repay the damage I have caused."

"I would be impressed if I did not know you are a weak-willed worm who was willing to sell your soul to the highest bidder," Jacques retorted.

Harry stiffened, his eyes dark with guilt. "It is your fault I ever became involved in the nasty business," he accused. "If you had not offered to pay my debts I should never have been tempted."

Jacques snorted. "Pathetic."

Hugo shouldered aside the younger man, regarding Gabriel with impatience.

"Well?"

Gabriel nodded. "There is no longer a need to sneak through the dark when Monsieur Gerard has a fine carriage to return us to the yacht."

Hugo frowned. "What of the soldiers? They are surrounding the house."

Gabriel glanced toward his surly captive. "We will use Monsieur Gerard to ensure our safe passage."

"Are you certain that is wise?" Hugo demanded. "There is no guarantee that an ambitious guard will not be willing to sacrifice his leader for an opportunity to prevent our escape. Napoleon might very well be impressed enough by his initiative to earn a promotion."

It was a reasonable concern. Even if the guards were

unquestionably loyal to Jacques Gerard, there was always the danger that one might inadvertently discharge his weapon at the sight of his leader being kidnapped by the enemy. And once the first shot had been fired, then there would be no derailing the attack.

"You should pay heed to your friend, Ashcombe," Jacques said, interrupting Gabriel's inner debate. "My guards will never allow you to escape."

Gabriel grimaced. There were no safe choices, but one thing was for certain—they could not hide in the house forever. And the longer they waited, the more opportunity for the guards to seek the assistance of the numerous soldiers camped outside the city walls.

"It is a risk, but with a carriage we will be better protected than if we attempt to flee on foot, and certainly we shall be able to travel at a greater speed," he said.

Talia moved to his side, her face pale but resolute. His tiny warrior.

"There was a carriage waiting at the side of the house when we arrived," she announced.

It had to be the carriage that Jacques had used to haul them to the townhouse, Gabriel decided.

"Harry, you lead the way."

"But..." The younger man bit off his protest and glared at Gabriel. "I suppose that you assume I deserve to be shot like a stray dog?"

Gabriel heaved an exasperated sigh. "What I assume is that you know the shortest route out of the cellars and to a side door."

"Oh." With an awkward shrug, Harry turned to cross the stone floor, heading past the towering shelves of dusty wine bottles. "This way."

Gabriel shifted to press the pistol to Jacques's back even as he glanced at his friend.

"Hugo, if you would escort Mademoiselle Reynard?"

Hugo nodded, reaching to grasp Sophia's arm. "Of course."

"Non," Jacques growled. "She remains here."

Gabriel shook his head. "I will release her once we have reached the yacht. Until then I intend to keep her close at hand."

"So much for the famed chivalry of English noblemen."

"Perhaps I would have more chivalry if you had not kidnapped my wife."

With a nod toward Talia he watched as she quickly crossed the floor and climbed the narrow flight of stairs closely followed by Hugo and Sophia. Then, giving the Frenchman a shove forward, they made their way out of the cellars and into the kitchens.

Casting a swift glance about the silent room to make certain there were no lurking servants hidden among the worn tables and piles of firewood, Gabriel walked to where his companions were clustered about the entrance to the side alley.

"Stand aside," he requested in a low voice, pulling open the door and jerking Jacques through the opening and onto the narrow porch. There was a shuffle of movement as several uniformed guards stepped into the light of the flickering torches, their curious expressions hardening to anger as Gabriel lifted the pistol to press it to Jacques's temple in an unspoken threat. "Tell them to place their weapons on the ground and to step away from the carriage," he ordered the Frenchman, the edge in his voice warning that he would pull the trigger if necessary.

Jacques stiffened, as if considering a ridiculous act of heroism. Then, sanity returned, and he spoke in rapid

French, commanding the guards to lower their weapons and to retreat to the back garden.

Reluctantly, the men bent down to place their pistols on the ground, although Gabriel was not stupid enough to believe they did not have several weapons still hidden beneath their uniforms. Straightening, they hesitated until Jacques offered a faint nod. Only then did they back toward the gate leading to the garden.

"Harry, if you would be so good as to gather the weapons?" he said, leading Jacques down the steps.

His brother brushed past him, collecting the pistols off the ground. Keeping one, he handed another to Hugo and dumped the others in a nearby rain barrel.

Hugo joined Gabriel with his hand still clenched around Sophia's arm.

"Do you want her inside the carriage?" he demanded.

Gabriel glanced toward the shiny vehicle that was still hitched to the pair of restless bays.

"Yes, I will need you and Harry up top to make certain there are no unpleasant surprises."

Moving forward Hugo pulled open the door to the carriage and lifted a stoic Sophia onto the leather bench seat before turning to assist Talia. Once the women were settled, Hugo stood aside as Jacques crawled into the carriage muttering his desire to see the entire British Empire fall into the sea.

Gabriel moved forward to join the others as Harry climbed into the seat on top of the carriage.

"I will handle the ribbons," he announced.

"No," Hugo growled, moving to untangle the reins from the hitching post and swinging easily onto the carriage, his large form knocking the slender Harry to the side. "I was witness to your spectacular race down St. James's Street where you injured a dozen pedestrians before overturning and destroying your carriage along with Sir Barclay's."

Harry glared at Hugo. "I was drunk."

"No doubt, but more important you are a cow-handed greenhorn who is a danger to himself and others," Hugo informed him dryly.

Harry shifted his gaze to his brother. "Gabriel."

"I should have let the two of you kill one another in the cellars," Gabriel muttered. "Hugo, get us out of here."

"Aye, sir."

Barely waiting for Gabriel to climb into the carriage and close the door, Hugo urged the horses down the alley. Once they reached the main street, he swerved to take them directly south, the swift pace making the vehicle sway and the clatter of horseshoes echo through the sleepy streets.

Inside the carriage the passengers maintained a grim silence. The two women sat stiffly on the seat, clearly unnerved by the air of violence that threatened to explode at any moment. Across from them, Gabriel kept the pistol aimed at the dangerous Frenchman even as he shifted so he could keep watch on the street behind them. It would be difficult to attack a moving carriage but not impossible, and he did not intend to be caught off guard.

Still traveling at breakneck speed, they charged through the city gates to the countryside beyond, but Gabriel remained on alert. Despite the lingering gloom, he had not been blind to the silhouettes of men on horseback that had been barely visible in the distance. It was near enough dawn that the forms might have been servants or merchants going about their business. Hell, they could be drunken noblemen attempting to stumble their way home from the various gambling dens and whorehouses.

But with his current streak of luck, he would bet his last quid that they were Jacques's guards in pursuit.

They had traveled several miles before Hugo was forced to slow the pace of the carriage as he turned onto the narrow path leading toward the shore. The side-to-side swaying of the vehicle settled into a jolting rattle that nearly sent the four of them out of their seats as Hugo steered them over the rocks and fallen logs that threatened to impede their retreat. Gabriel tensed his jaw, casting a worried glance toward Talia who had grasped the leather strap that dangled from the roof. She was so tiny she was being bounced around like a rag doll.

At last they came to a blessed halt, and Gabriel bent forward to shove open the door.

"Jacques, if you will be so good as to descend first?" he drawled. "I would not desire any ambitious guards that might have followed us to become overeager."

"Coward," the Frenchman muttered.

"Cautious," Gabriel amended, deliberately glancing at the women who sat in weary silence on the opposite seat. "And, Jacques, do not forget that it is not only your life that hangs in the balance."

In the midst of crawling out of the carriage, Jacques paused to glare at Gabriel.

"Threaten Sophia again and I will—"

"Yes?"

An icy fury tightened the man's features. "Do not tempt me."

"It grows late, or rather early, and I desire a hot bath and a warm bed." Gabriel pressed the pistol to the man's forehead. "Now move or I will decide you are not worth the trouble of keeping alive."

"Vermine."

Gabriel waited for Jacques to step out of the carriage,

shifting to the side so he could keep a watch on the small clearing. Beyond the barren emptiness he could see a thick line of trees on one side and on the other the sheer cliff that overlooked the sea.

There was no movement, but that did not mean that there were not dangers skulking in the shadows.

After several minutes passed with no shots being fired, Gabriel turned his attention toward Sophia huddled in the far corner of the carriage.

"Mademoiselle Reynard." He waved a hand toward the door.

She sent him a dark glare as she climbed over his long legs and out the door, clearly displeased with the turn of events. He ignored her antagonism, his hand reaching out to halt his wife from following in Sophia's wake.

"A moment, my dear."

She wrinkled her nose as she met his warning frown. "Yes, I know, Gabriel. I am not to do anything stupid."

His heart squeezed with an unfamiliar emotion as he gazed down at the pale beauty of her face. When had he memorized every line and sweep of her features? Had it just been since the ceremony? Or had he been secretly treasuring her image long before they were forced down the aisle?

"I do not suppose you would actually offer such a promise?" he asked in rueful tones.

Her magnificent emerald eyes darkened with stoic courage.

"I cannot."

"You realize that if anything was to happen to you…"

She pressed her fingers to his mouth, silencing his concerns.

"Nothing will happen," she assured him. "We are within sight of your boat."

"Yacht, my lady," he corrected, grasping her wrist and lightly kissing the tips of her fingers. Then his lips were seeking the rapid pulse beneath the delicate skin of her inner wrist. "And we are not yet aboard. Until we are, I refuse to allow you out of my sight."

A delicate blush stole beneath her cheeks. "And once we are aboard?"

Heat exploded as he leaned forward to steal a swift, devouring kiss.

"I intend to devote the entire voyage to having my wicked way with you," he whispered against her lips.

For a mindless moment Gabriel was aware of nothing beyond the softness of Talia's mouth and the shiver of excitement that raced through his body. Then, the unwelcome intrusion of approaching footsteps wrenched him back to reality.

"Gabriel, do you intend to linger the entire night?" his brother called with obvious impatience.

"Damn." Pulling back, he reluctantly loosened his grip on Talia's hand and allowed her to climb out of the carriage.

He followed swiftly behind her, stepping onto the rocky path before turning to remove the glass lantern from the side of the carriage. The flame was weak, but it remained dark enough that it should be easily spotted by his crew upon the yacht.

"Hugo, if you will keep an eye upon our prisoners, I will signal my captain."

He moved toward the edge of the cliff, holding the lamp above his head to swing it in a slow pattern that would alert the captain to send a rowboat to shore.

"Hopefully there will be no need to wait," Hugo said as he moved to Gabriel's side. "I left a boat hidden just beyond the rocks. I will make certain it is still there."

Gabriel paused before giving a reluctant nod. He disliked the thought of Hugo being alone, but then again, the sooner they could be off the cliff the better. It felt very much like a trap at the moment.

"Take care," he muttered. "I am certain we were followed."

"I will." Hugo shifted his gaze toward Harry who stood only a few feet away. "But I am more concerned for you. Do not forget that there is more than one enemy you must guard against."

Harry took an angry step forward. "Just go check on the damned boat, Rothwell."

With a last glare at the young man, Hugo turned to make his way down the treacherous path of the cliff, abruptly disappearing from view.

Trusting his friend had not taken a tumble and broken his neck, Gabriel turned back to his companions. Jacques and Sophia remained in the center of the small clearing, but he noted in approval that Talia had shifted to stand near the carriage, wise enough to remain out of the line of fire should the lurking soldiers attack.

How the devil had he ever thought he would be satisfied with a missish society female who would have spent the past few days in screeching hysterics?

With a last lingering glance at the woman who had become a vital part of his life, Gabriel turned back to meet Jacques's scowl of frustration.

"You promised to release Sophia," he reminded Gabriel in fiery tones.

"She will be allowed to return to Calais once we are away from the shore."

Jacques was not appeased. "You will abandon a vulnerable female in the midst of this godforsaken countryside?" His lips twisted as he glanced toward Talia, intentionally reminding Gabriel of his decision to send his young bride to Carrick Park alone. "Ah, of course you will. It does seem to be a habit of yours."

Annoying ass.

With an effort Gabriel dismissed the taunt. "I do not doubt your soldiers will be delighted to protect her."

The Frenchman shrugged, not bothering to try to convince Gabriel they were alone.

"If you are so certain they are nearby, then why not allow Sophia to join them now?"

"I would not wish to encourage you to do something stupid." Gabriel waved his pistol toward the nearby trees. "Her presence ensures your good behavior until we reach my yacht."

Jacques stretched his lips into a humorless smile. "So I am to be taken to England?"

"You were pleased enough to visit before," Gabriel mocked.

"So I was," Jacques admitted. He ignored the fuming female at his side, her countenance warning she would not be left behind. "I presume that I am to be exposed as a French spy?"

"That is a decision to be made by a higher authority than me."

"And your brother?"

Gabriel tensed, refusing to be distracted by the agonizing choices that awaited him once they returned to England.

"Harry is no longer your concern," he snarled.

"Are you so certain?" Jacques arched a sardonic brow. "I would say his fate is very much in my hands."

There was no mistaking the threat in his tone, and narrowing his gaze, Gabriel marched forward to grasp the man by his arm, yanking him across the uneven ground.

He came to a halt on the opposite side of the carriage, far enough from the others to prevent their conversation from being overheard.

"What are you implying?"

Pulling from his grasp, Jacques smoothed a hand down his wrinkled jacket and tugged a lace cuff back into place. Gabriel clenched his teeth, barely preventing himself from smashing a fist into the sneering face.

"Once I have been turned over to the English authorities I am bound to be put to the Inquisition," Jacques said smoothly.

"And?"

"And I can scarcely be expected to keep your brother's priceless assistance in stealing information from the Home Office a secret. The poor boy will be forever ruined, if not put to death as a traitor."

Jacques merely repeated what had been going through Gabriel's mind since learning of Harry's betrayal. But hearing it announced so bluntly was like a physical blow.

Christ, he would rather take a beating than imagine what was to come.

"Harry chose his fate when he agreed to your devil's bargain," he forced himself to mutter, his voice harsh.

"Fates can be altered." Jacques nodded his head toward the faint outline of the distant yacht that was just becoming visible in the faint brush of dawn. "Return to England without me and no one need ever know that Harry is a traitor."

"I would know."

Jacques snorted. "I am aware you have always taken pride in being a pompous prig who considers himself superior to mere mortals, but I would have thought you have learned something from your wife."

Gabriel flinched. Why? It was not the first occasion

he'd been called a pompous prig. His preference for maintaining a dignified presence among society rather than prancing about like a silly fop did not endear him to his peers.

But the Frenchman's well-played mention of Talia was a painful reminder that he had all too recently allowed his pride to rule in a decision he would regret for all eternity.

"What does my marriage have to do with Harry?" he demanded before he could put back the question.

"You nearly destroyed a fine woman with your desire to punish her."

Gabriel's brows snapped together. He needed no reminders of the damage he had caused his young bride.

"It was never my desire to punish Talia."

"Non?" Jacques shifted his gaze back to Gabriel, his expression knowing. "You blamed her for having brought shame to the precious Ashcombe family, did you not? And you were anxious to prove to Silas Dobson and society you would not tolerate being embarrassed." He gave a disgusted shake of his head. "Talia would have been crushed by your need for revenge if not for her considerable courage."

He growled beneath his breath, once again fighting the urge to pummel the aggravating bastard.

"You know nothing of the matter."

"I know you are threatening to toss your brother to the wolves to salvage your pride, just as you did with Talia."

He knew Jacques was attempting to manipulate him, but the accusation sliced through Gabriel with silky ease.

"Talia was an innocent," Gabriel muttered, as much to remind himself as his companion. "Harry betrayed his country for profit. If I truly desired to protect myself, I would hide his sins rather than expose them to the world."

"What of your pride? The Earl of Ascombe stripped of his pride has nothing," Jacques taunted, lifting his hand as Gabriel's lips parted to offer a scathing retort. "Oh, the polite world will pretend to be aghast over Harry's treachery, but then they will all realize they predicted that he would come to a bad end. Then, of course, they will rush to sympathize with the poor Earl of Ashcombe who has been forced to endure the terrible antics of his younger brother for so many years and who has now so bravely stepped forward to renounce the boy as a spy." He paused, watching Gabriel like a viper assessing its prey. An accurate description for a man who spewed his words like poison. "You shall be nothing less than a national hero."

Gabriel tightened his fingers on the pistol, wishing to God he had never heard the name Jacques Gerard.

"You would say anything to avoid the hangman."

Jacques shrugged. "Certainly, but that does not make my words any less true."

CHAPTER TWENTY

JACQUES HAD DEVOTED his years in England to becoming the polished gentleman that his mother had always wanted him to be, even as he had secretly prepared for his return to France as a skilled soldier.

Oh, not as a traditional warrior who could wave around a pointy sword or shoot a man at twenty paces. There were always fools who could be taught to march in line and use a weapon without killing himself. But instead he had honed his talent in manipulating people, discovering that those about him could be used like pawns upon a chessboard with the proper incentives. It was only a matter of finding each individual weakness and exploiting it.

The world might condemn his sly scheming as beneath a true gentleman, but he had been indifferent to the censure. It was a supposedly honorable gentleman who had attempted to rape his mother and sent his father to his death.

And there was no arguing with the success of his efforts. By the time he had arrived in Paris he had mastered his talent in coercion, with a dozen high-ranking Englishmen dangling on his strings to show for it.

Including Mr. Harry Richardson.

Much to his annoyance, however, he found the Earl of Ashcombe was impervious to his attempts at manipulation. The arrogant bastard was too stubborn to be so easily led.

Not that he intended to concede defeat. He shifted his attention to the loaded pistol trained at his chest. Gabriel's glare silently dared him to attempt an escape so he could have reason to shoot.

For all of Gabriel's conceit, he was not nearly so certain of his decision to expose Harry as a traitor as he desired Jacques to believe. With the proper prodding, even this pigheaded man could be convinced to change his mind.

Unfortunately, his subtle assault was suddenly interrupted by the sound of a high whistle that came from the shore below the cliff.

Gabriel squared his shoulders, his expression one of bleak intent.

"Hugo has arrived with the boat."

He gave a small wave of the pistol, and Jacques grudgingly moved back into the clearing. His gaze instinctively sought out Sophia who remained standing with rigid fear several feet from the others.

An answering fear clenched Jacques's heart.

A tense promise of violence vibrated through the air as he came to a halt, and he cast a covert glance toward the nearby trees. He could not see his guards, but he could sense their increasingly restless presence. What would happen when Gabriel attempted to force him down the cliff?

He shivered at the looming potential for chaos.

Perhaps echoing his thoughts, Gabriel backed toward the edge of the cliff, briefly turning his attention toward his wife.

"Talia, you go down first." When there was no re-

sponse to his command, Gabriel swallowed his pride and
sent her a desperate glance. "Please."

Talia hesitated, clearly torn between an instinctual
urge to protect her husband and the knowledge that he
could not give his full attention to the lurking soldiers
so long as she was near.

"Fine."

Talia stiffly turned to make her way slowly down the
cliff. There was an uncomfortable silence until they at
last heard Hugo's whistle to indicate Lady Ashcombe
had reached the boat. Then Gabriel glanced toward his
brother who was nervously aiming his pistol toward the
nearby trees. Jacques held his breath, knowing it would
take very little for the twitchy dandy to be startled into
firing his weapon.

"Harry, you will be next."

The younger man scowled at the sharp command. "We
are not alone."

"I see them," Gabriel assured his brother. "Get to the
boat."

Harry shook his head. "No. You take Jacques and I
will keep them at bay."

Jacques gave a startled laugh. "*Sacré bleu.* Is it possible that the worm has at last acquired a spine?"

The two brothers ignored him as they glared at one
another in growing frustration.

"Harry, do as I say," Gabriel snapped.

Harry jutted his chin, looking strangely older in the
faint wash of dawn.

"Not on this occasion," Harry said, his expression set
in stubborn lines.

"Dammit…" Gabriel gave a frustrated shake of his
head before turning his attention to Jacques. "Come."

A prickle of unease raced over Jacques's skin as he

glanced toward Sophia. It felt as if they were standing on top of a powder keg, and that the slightest move might set off a fatal explosion.

He did not fear for himself. God knew that he had been courting an early grave since he'd tossed his lot in with Napoleon. He had long ago made peace with the notion he might never live long enough to witness the end of the war.

But the torturous thought of Sophia being put at risk tightened his chest until it was impossible to breathe.

He held up a warning hand as she took a hesitant step in his direction.

"Sophia, remain where you are," he rasped. "You will be safe."

Her dark eyes flashed with the passion he had taken for granted far too long.

"I do not want to be safe, I want to be with you."

"*Non,* Sophia do not—"

As if her movement had triggered the brewing storm, there was a sharp staccato of weapons being fired from behind the nearest trees.

Panic slammed through Jacques as he launched himself forward and knocked Sophia to the ground, covering her slender body with his own.

"*Arrêtez,*" he shouted, hearing the sound of Gabriel and Harry returning fire. Then as a bullet flew past his face close enough to singe his ear, he waved an arm in the air. "*Mon dieu.* Cease your fire, you idiots."

A thick silence abruptly descended, the air filled with the acrid stench of gunpowder. Jacques risked a quick glance over his shoulder to watch as Harry clutched his chest and sank to the ground, Gabriel falling to his knees beside his wounded brother.

It was now or never, Jacques realized as he rose to his feet and grasped Sophia's hand to pull her upright.

"This way," a French soldier called from the distance.

Jacques took a step forward but faltered as Sophia stumbled and nearly fell.

"Sophia," he breathed in fear, wrapping protective arms around her. "Were you hit?"

"It is only my ankle," she breathed, pressing her hands against his chest. "Go ahead, the Englishmen will not harm me."

"Foolish female," he muttered as he scooped her off her feet.

"Jacques," Sophia protested, attempting to wiggle out of his arms.

"*Non,* do not struggle," he commanded as he charged toward the trees, half expecting a bullet to pierce his back with every step.

"But…"

"Shh."

He refused to acknowledge her frustrated glare, keeping his gaze trained straight ahead. Did the silly fool truly believe he would leave her behind?

Reaching the edge of the small clearing, Jacques waded through the thicket of underbrush that ripped at his pantaloons and ruined the gloss of his boots. At last he entered the narrow band of trees, and one of the soldiers stepped forward to offer a shallow bow.

"I will need your horse," he informed the young soldier who looked barely old enough to be out of the nursery.

"Of course."

Obeying with admirable eagerness, the soldier darted deeper into the trees before he reappeared, leading a chestnut mare by the reins. Two mounted soldiers followed behind them, both as young as the first.

"Do you wish us to capture the English swine?" a dark-haired soldier demanded, his avid expression revealing his innocence. A man who had killed another was never eager to repeat the experience.

"*Non.* We could not reach them without casualties, and we shall soon be outmanned by Ashcombe's crew." With one smooth motion, he lifted Sophia into the saddle of the waiting horse, then sliding one foot into the stirrup, he grasped the horn and pulled himself up to swing his leg over the horse and settle behind her. The mare skittered to one side, but with a firm hold on the reins he swiftly brought her back under control. "We will return to Calais and alert the soldiers. They can send a warship in pursuit."

"As you command."

The dark-haired soldier did not bother to hide his disappointment, but trained to obey his superiors, he gave a nod of his head and turned to urge his horse toward the path leading back to Calais.

Jacques waited as the second mounted soldier paused to allow his compatriot to leap onto the saddle behind him and disappeared into the trees before he urged his own horse into a steady trot.

"Hold on tight, *ma belle,*" he murmured, not bothering to glance behind him.

To hell with the Earl of Ashcombe and his damnable brother. If there was any justice the pair of them would drown on their journey back to England.

"Forgive me, Jacques." A soft female voice broke into his pleasant imaginings of Gabriel sinking to the bottom of the Channel.

With a frown he glanced down, studying the regret that darkened Sophia's eyes.

"Forgive you?"

"This entire…" she searched for the proper word "…debacle is my fault."

Debacle was an apt description, Jacques had to ruefully agree, but there was no one to blame but himself.

"What is your fault?"

"I should never have assisted Lord and Lady Ashcombe in escaping from the palace."

With gentle care he cradled her against his chest, savoring the beauty of her pale face in the cresting dawn.

"That is in the past," he assured her. "We will not speak of it again."

"And tonight?" she persisted, almost as if she needed to punish herself. "If I had not intruded, they would not have been allowed to escape yet again."

The path led them beyond the trees and between the rolling fields that were bathed in a glistening dew.

"You were concerned for me."

"Only in part." She heaved a sigh. "I knew you were in your private chambers with Talia and when I heard the sound of crashing glass I used it as an excuse to interrupt. I was afraid…"

"And you were afraid of what?" he prompted as her words faltered.

"I was afraid that you intended to take her to your bed."

"And you thought you could prevent the seduction?"

"I was not thinking," she professed huskily. "I was following my poor heart that could not bear the thought of you with another."

He slowed the pace of his mount at her unexpected confession. The beautiful actress had always been successful in keeping her feelings hidden even as she pandered to his needs. Now he found himself instinctively shying from the emotions that smoldered in her dark eyes.

"Sophia."

She averted her face to stare at the passing fields, effectively hiding her expression.

"I know you do not wish to be burdened with my unwanted affections, Jacques." The words were so low he could barely catch them. "But I very nearly lost you this evening and I could not bear the thought of you dying without knowing that I love you."

"I…" He shifted in the saddle, shying from her blunt confession. "We will discuss this later," he muttered.

He felt her stiffen in his arms. "There is no need for discussion, *chérie*."

But Jacques found himself annoyed by the stark resignation that hardened her profile. A preference to discuss such a…delicate subject in the comfort of his home rather than on the back of a horse when they were both so weary was considerably different than hoping to ignore it altogether.

"Are you so certain?"

"Oui." She turned back to meet his gaze, understandably confused by his unpredictable reactions. "I comprehend that I have overstepped the boundaries of our liaison."

"I was not aware our liaison had boundaries."

Her brows jerked together. "Do not mock me, Jacques."

"That was not my intent—"

"A courtesan's first lesson is never to allow her emotions to become entangled," she interrupted, a faint color staining her cheeks. "Gentlemen seek our companionship for pleasure, not duty."

Duty? His blood heated at the mere thought of their time together.

Both in and out of bed.

"Well, it is certainly true that I have never considered you a duty, *ma belle*," he said wryly.

Her expression remained bleak. "And you never shall." She tilted her chin. "It was not my place to interfere in your relationship with Talia. She is obviously a lady of quality and if you desire to claim her as your own then I shall wish you happiness."

"Will you? You do not sound particularly happy," he teased softly.

Her eyes filled with tears. "Please, Jacques."

"No tears, Sophia," he commanded gruffly, startled by her vulnerable state.

Over the years he had become accustomed to females who sought to sway him with tears and tantrums, but never, ever Sophia.

"There are no tears," she ridiculously denied. "I never cry."

Tenderness surged through him as he studied the female who snuggled against his chest, her dark hair spilling over his arm that he had circled around her shoulders. She appeared oddly fragile.

"Another lesson of courtesans?"

She blinked, giving a delicate sniff. *"Oui."*

"I have no desire to claim Talia, *ma belle*," he said, realizing as he said the words that they were true. He had enjoyed the thought of rescuing Talia from the cruel hands of her neglectful husband. And savoring the knowledge that he was striking a painful blow at the English nobles by stealing a countess from beneath their arrogant noses. But his heart had already been stolen by another. "I have no desire to claim any woman but you."

She flinched, almost as if he had slapped her. "Do not say such a thing."

He barely noticed as they trailed ever farther behind his guards, the steady hoofbeats the only sound to stir the early-morning air.

Was the female being deliberately difficult?

She had just professed her love for him, had she not?

Now that he had admitted to his own desire, she was behaving as if he had threatened to drown her in the nearest well.

"Even if it is the truth?" he growled.

"It cannot be." Her lips flattened as she battled to conceal the emotions that smoldered in her dark eyes. "You wish for a proper female who you will be proud to have standing at your side. Not an aging actress who was born in the gutters."

He lifted a brow. "You seem to forget that my mother was an actress."

"And you were forced to suffer because of her," she reminded him in raw tones.

He lifted his head sharply, his gaze shifting toward the distant silhouette of Calais.

As difficult as it was to admit, even to himself, there had always been a treacherous part of him that held his mother to blame for his father's death. Insanity, of course. His mother was not responsible for her haunting beauty. Or his father's volatile reaction that had ended with him locked within the Bastille.

But as a young man forced to mature without his beloved *papa,* he had been unable to keep from wondering how his life might have been different had his mother not captured the roaming eye of a lecher.

Was it possible that he had held Sophia at a distance precisely because she reminded him of his mother?

The thought was enough to send a jolt of shame through his heart.

"Non," he roughly denied. "I suffered because of a depraved scoundrel devoid of morals or honor. A nobleman who is now as dead as my father."

"But not forgotten," she said softly.

"He will never be forgotten. And I will never halt my efforts to be rid of men like him," Jacques swore, returning his gaze to meet her guarded expression. "Will you fight at my side, Sophia Reynard?"

She paused, clearly sensing that he was asking for more than just another ally in the war against the tyrannous ruling class.

"I will be at your side so long as you desire me, but—"

He bent his head to crush her lips in a passionate kiss.

"That is all I need." He pulled back to peer deep into her wide eyes. "You are all that I need, *ma belle.*"

"Jacques," she breathed in surrender.

Hunger speared through him, and tightening his grip around her slender body, he urged his horse into a faster pace.

"It is time we were home."

IN SOME DISTANT part of his mind Gabriel was aware of Jacques escaping along with Sophia and his guards. Even more distantly he could hear the fading sound of Hugo rowing Talia toward the yacht, his mate obviously having the good sense to cast off the moment he heard the gunshot.

His concentration, however, was utterly absorbed in his foolish brother.

Christ.

What the devil was the matter with Harry? He should have scurried behind the protection of the carriage the moment the bullets had started to fly. Instead, the impulsive idiot had launched himself forward, taking a bullet that surely would have killed Gabriel.

"Dammit, Harry," he muttered, arranging his brother flat on his back so he could run his hands down his limp body. "What were you thinking?"

With a grimace, Harry lifted his lashes to reveal pain-glazed eyes.

"Clearly I was not thinking at all," he muttered.

Unable to find any obvious injuries, Gabriel attempted to tug aside Harry's tightly fitted jacket.

"Where were you hit?"

"Leave it be, Gabriel." Harry weakly knocked aside Gabriel's hand, pulling the jacket over the blood that was already staining the white linen shirt beneath. "There is nothing you can do for me here."

Gabriel settled back on his heels, conceding Harry's point. He had no supplies that would assist in tending to a wound, even if he possessed the skills to do so. His only comfort was the hope that the bullet had caught Harry closer to his shoulder than his heart.

"Hugo has taken Talia to the yacht, but the captain will have sent a boat when we first arrived," he said, attempting to comfort his brother. "It should arrive at any moment."

"What of Jacques?"

Gabriel glanced across the clearing, realizing that dawn had well arrived, spreading a rosy light across the landscape.

"He has bolted."

Harry attempted to lift his head, as if not trusting Gabriel's word.

"You are certain?"

"Hold still, you foolish cub," Gabriel commanded urgently, a fear clenching his heart at the ashen pallor of his brother's face. Bloody hell. Just hours ago he had been determined to turn his brother over as a traitor to his country. Now he would give his own life to make certain Harry lived. "Jacques and his men are gone," he rasped. "Although I do not doubt they will send soldiers to search for us."

Accepting they were out of danger for the moment, Harry lowered his head back to the ground with a heavy sigh.

"I do not suppose you managed to wound the bastard?"

Gabriel shook his head in regret. He had managed a shot in the direction of the Frenchman, but before he could even consider reloading his pistol Harry had been hit, and he had forgotten everything but carrying his brother out of the line of fire.

"Not to my knowledge."

"A pity."

It was, of course, but not as great a pity as witnessing his brother stretched on the ground with a bullet lodged in his flesh.

"Why did you do it, Harry?" he demanded.

"Do what?"

Gabriel hissed out a painful breath. Never so long as he lived would he forget the sight of Harry leaping in front of him.

"Take a bullet that was intended for me?"

Harry turned his head, remaining silent for so long Gabriel thought he might ignore the question. At last he heaved a sigh and turned back to meet Gabriel's worried gaze.

"Do you remember the Christmas morning that I slipped away from my nurse so I could show father I was old enough for the new pair of skates you had given to me?"

Gabriel shuddered. It had been a Christmas he had never forgotten. He had purchased the ice skates from a local craftsman, never considering the notion his father might consider Harry too irresponsible to own a pair. Of course, the moment the earl had forbidden his youngest son to keep them, Harry had taken off with the intent to prove his father wrong.

Gabriel had followed him, but he'd only arrived just as Harry skated toward the center of the lake where the ice was the weakest.

"You fell through the ice," he said, vividly recalling the terror that had seared through him as his brother disappeared from sight.

"And you pulled me out." Harry managed a tight smile. "You saved my life that day. Tonight I repaid my debt."

"There was no debt." Gabriel frowned. "You are my brother. It is my duty to protect you."

"You have always done your best." Harry's smile became oddly wistful. "But, you could never protect me from my own demons, Gabriel. They are mine to battle."

Gabriel tensed. God almighty, how many endless, miserable years had he waited for his brother to take responsibility for his failures? To at last realize that his troubles were of his own making? And yet, now that Harry had spoken the words he had waited to hear, he felt none of the satisfaction he had anticipated.

Hell, they only managed to make him feel more guilty.

"I should have done more," he muttered.

"The fault was not yours." Harry reached to squeeze Gabriel's hand, genuine regret adding a hint of maturity to his slender face. "It has never been yours."

Gabriel shook his head, refusing to debate the issue.

Not when his brother was wounded, perhaps even dying, and they were trapped in enemy territory.

"Now is not the time for this discussion," he said gruffly, a surge of relief racing through him at the soft call from the distant shore. Obviously his captain had indeed seen his signal and sent a boat. "Thank God. We shall soon be safe."

Harry grimaced, his hand lifting to press against his injured shoulder.

"I will never make it down the cliff."

"There is no need to worry. I will return in a moment with one of my crew to carry you down to the shore."

As Gabriel began to straighten, Harry's grip tightened on his arm with surprising strength.

"Wait, Gabriel."

"Harry, we must not delay," he growled, his brows drawn together with impatient concern. His captain was not a trained surgeon, but he was capable of tending to most wounds. "Your injury…"

"No, this must be said now."

Gabriel sank back to his knees, unwilling to struggle with his brother and risk further injury.

"What?"

"I am sorry."

Gabriel's heart twisted at the raw guilt that shone in his brother's eyes.

"I know, Harry, but we can finish this once we are aboard the yacht."

"No, it must be now."

Gabriel nodded reluctantly. "Very well. What do you wish to tell me?"

"My relationship with Jacques all began so innocently," Harry said, his voice thick with self-disgust.

"Somehow I do not associate Jacques with innocence."

"True, but it seemed so at the time. Jacques and I were schoolmates."

"So he said," Gabriel confessed, condemning to hell whatever ill fate had crossed Harry's path with the damned Frenchman. "I cannot imagine the two of you having had much in common."

Harry snorted, his hand lifting to impatiently brush back the brown curls that had tumbled onto his forehead.

"No, he was far too somber and studious for my taste, and of course, he did little to disguise his revolutionary tendencies." Harry's expression was distant as he became lost in his memories. "But he came upon me one evening while I was in the midst of a nasty disagreement with several upperclassmen. They were under the impression I owed them a great deal of money." He gave a short, humorless laugh. "No doubt because I did."

Gabriel was not surprised that his brother had started his career of living in dun territory at such a tender age. Or that he had incurred the wrath of his fellow students with his blithe disregard in accepting responsibility.

"What did he do?"

"He not only paid my debt, but he carried me back to my rooms and tended to my numerous bruises." Harry's lips twisted. "I thought he must be my guardian angel."

"A clever means to earn your loyalty."

"Jacques was never stupid."

Gabriel had to agree. The Frenchman was cunning and ruthless, with the instincts of Machiavelli.

"What did he demand in return?"

"Nothing until I was preparing to leave school and take my place in society. Then he requested that I carry a packet of letters to London."

"What letters?"

"I do not know," Harry admitted in a dismissive voice. "And I doubt they were of any importance."

Gabriel frowned at his flippant tone. Had his brother learned nothing? Jacques clearly had a well-practiced routine of using dupes to transport vital information.

"How can you be certain?"

"Because his true purpose was to ensure that I was introduced to Juliette," Harry said bitterly.

It took a moment for Gabriel to realize that his brother was referring to the voluptuous French widow of an English diplomat. Gabriel had been dimly aware that the golden-haired beauty had drifted in and out of his brother's bed over the years, but he had always assumed it had been nothing more than a casual affair.

At least until he had discovered that the woman had traveled with Harry to France.

"Madame Martine," he spat in disgust.

"I was such an idiot." Harry closed his eyes, visibly pained by his memories. "Jacques was well aware that I was ripe to be seduced by such a beautiful woman who could easily manipulate me."

"Not an uncommon failing among young men."

Harry snorted. "Not you."

"Do not be so certain," Gabriel argued. "My first mistress managed to coax me into buying her several pieces of fine jewelry as well as a new carriage and matching horses to pull it before I realized she was sharing her favors with several other gentlemen at the same time."

"Juliette cost me more than my yearly allowance." Harry lifted his lashes to reveal the torment in his eyes. "It was with her urging that I became such a reckless fool. I was desperate to impress her with my daring deeds and my boundless wealth." His jaw tightened. "And of course, she was clever enough to be forever prodding my jealousy toward you. I would have done anything to prove I was as worthy as you in her eyes."

Gabriel heaved a rough sigh, shoving aside his stab of guilt as he considered the implications of his brother's confession.

"Including an offer to establish Jacques as the local vicar of Carrick Park?" he asked.

"Yes." Harry shook his head, then bit off a curse as the movement jostled his wound. "A difficult task, I might add," he seethed.

It should have been an impossible task, Gabriel silently acknowledged, detesting the thought that church officials might have been bribed or bullied into turning a blind eye to *Vicar Gerard* of Carrick Park.

"Someday I wish to hear how you accomplished such a feat," he warned.

"Someday."

Gabriel allowed his brother to remain evasive. He would eventually discover the truth of the matter. But he was suddenly struck by a more pressing question.

"I do not comprehend why you agreed to wed Talia if you were being supported by Jacques."

Harry flushed, revealing a genuine embarrassment for his heartless behavior.

"I had a brief moment of conscience," he said, smiling wryly at Gabriel's sudden scowl. "It is true, although I do not blame you if you find it difficult to believe. I thought that once I had my hands on Dobson's money I could cut my ties to Jacques and walk away unscathed."

"You thought he could be bribed?"

"Absurd, of course." His sharp laugh cut through the hushed silence. "I was assured that there was no means to end my...partnership with the damned Frenchman."

"And that is when you fled to Calais?"

"Yes, once again forcing you to pay for my sins," Harry acknowledged, his expression hardening. "But no more. I have learned my lesson, I swear. Things will be different in the future."

Gabriel shied from his brother's heartfelt promise. He desperately wanted to believe that Harry had truly changed, but how often had he been disappointed in the past?

"Enough of this, you must conserve your strength while I fetch some help," he said brusquely.

Once again Harry's fingers dug into Gabriel's arm, keeping him from rising.

"First I must give you this," Harry said, wincing as he fumbled beneath his jacket and at last pulled out a folded piece of parchment that he shoved into Gabriel's hand.

Shifting to catch the faint light cresting the horizon, Gabriel unfolded the paper and scanned the list of names that were written in a neat column.

He frowned as he recognized several of the gentlemen. "What is it?"

"The names of those Englishmen hired by Jacques."

Even suspecting the truth, Gabriel felt an icy dread settle in his heart. Christ, just how deeply had the rot penetrated?

The men on the list were gentlemen of society, some of them members of parliament. Gentlemen of power and influence who could cause untold damage if they truly had sold their loyalty to Napoleon.

The question was how Jacques Gerard managed to lure, or perhaps even force, them into becoming traitors and how willing they had been to betray their country.

"How did you get your hands on this?" he rasped.

Harry returned his hand to cover his wound, his breath hissing between his teeth in pain.

"I made a search of the vicarage at Carrick Park after I became engaged to Talia," he said, a fine sheen of sweat visible on his brow. "I knew I must destroy the letter that I had written to confess my guilt if I hoped to be rid of Jacques. Unfortunately I was unable to find my letter, but I did discover the names tucked in a prayer book."

"Does he know that you have this?"

"No." There was a hint of satisfaction in his tone. "I made a copy and returned the original to the book. I intended to use this as a bargaining chip when I felt the time was right."

It was a powerful bargaining chip, indeed. Gabriel did not doubt that Jacques would be willing to barter a great deal to ensure the list did not fall into the hands of British officials.

And the fact that Harry had handed it over to Gabriel rather than keeping it to use for his own benefit was almost as shocking as the names on the list.

"And now?" he demanded, wondering if this was to be a trap.

"Now it is yours." Harry regarded him with a wry smile before being racked by a deep cough that chilled Gabriel's blood. "You will do what is right," he at last gasped. "You always do."

"No, Harry—"

"That was not an insult, Gabriel," his brother interrupted hoarsely. "I have always admired your unwavering integrity, even when it infuriated me. I only hope someday you will be as proud of me as I have always been of you."

An excruciating pain sliced through his heart.

Did his brother fear he was dying? Was that why he had demanded the opportunity to confess his sin and hand over the secret list?

No. Gabriel gave an unconscious shake of his head. He would not allow it.

His brother was going to live, by God. Even if he had to follow him to hell and haul him back.

"Remain still."

Gabriel rose to his feet, moving to retrieve the loaded pistol his brother had dropped when he was shot and returned to press it into Harry's hand before he headed toward the edge of the cliff.

"Gabriel…"

"I will return as swiftly as I am able."

Not giving Harry an opportunity to argue, Gabriel angled along the edge of the steep precipice, at last stumbling across the path that led down to the muddy shore. His boots were ruined and his jacket torn from the rocks protruding from the side of the cliff, but at last he slid to a halt near the rowboat that was waiting in the shallow water.

"You." He pointed at one of the two crewmen who were seated in the boat. "Come with me."

"Aye, my lord."

With stoic movements that helped to leash the sickening dread spreading through his heart, Gabriel retraced his steps up the path of the cliff, occasionally glancing over his shoulder to ensure the sailor was close behind.

Everything would be fine, he assured himself. He would collect Harry and they would return to the yacht where the captain would clean and bind his wound. The fool might have a scar to display to his friends, but it would be a small price to pay.

Keeping the thought forefront in his mind, Gabriel reached the top of the cliff and jogged back toward the carriage. The entire trip had taken less than a quarter of an hour, but he was anxious to return to his brother.

He became even more anxious when he arrived at the precise spot where he had left Harry only to discover the carriage, along with his brother, was gone.

What the hell?

"Search the woods for Master Harry," he directed the puzzled sailor with a wave of his hand.

"Master Harry?"

"I left him here. He was injured."

"Oh. Aye."

The young man hurried to obey the sharp command, while Gabriel bent down to inspect the dirt path that led away from the clearing.

He found a faint trace of blood as well as several separate footprints, but there was nothing to indicate a struggle. Not that he had expected to find evidence of a battle.

No. If his brother had been attacked while Gabriel was going for assistance he would have called out. Or at least fired the pistol that Gabriel had left with him.

The most logical explanation for Harry's disappearance was that he had waited for Gabriel to go for help and then used the carriage to escape.

He had been expertly deceived.

Again.

CHAPTER TWENTY-ONE

TALIA PACED THE cramped floor of her cabin, avoiding the narrow bunk bed despite her relentless fatigue that urged her to crawl beneath the covers.

Over the past hour she had allowed Lord Rothwell to bully her into eating a light supper followed by a hot bath. She had even changed into a linen night gown, but she stubbornly refused to go to bed until Gabriel had returned to the yacht.

Why bother? She would never be able to sleep. Not when she was consumed with fear for her husband.

Turning on her heel, she tossed back her loose curls and cursed herself for having allowed Gabriel to convince her to join Lord Rothwell in the tiny boat.

At the time, of course, she had assumed the others were following directly behind her. But, she had barely managed to settle on the wooden bench when the first shot had echoed through the air. Dismissing her protests, Rothwell had thrust the oars into the water and rowed them toward the distant yacht with firm strokes.

Worse, the overbearing wretch had threatened her with physical violence if she dared to attempt a return to shore.

Now she was trapped on the boat, or yacht, or whatever the blazes Gabriel insisted that the ship be called, with no knowledge of what was happening on the cliffs that were barely visible through the porthole.

She had lost track of time, although she was aware

that morning sunlight was spilling into the cabin. The sound of her door opening had her spinning around with a startled gasp.

Gabriel.

Her heart stopped as her frantic gaze skimmed over his ruffled golden hair. His lean face was shadowed with the hint of his unshaved whiskers, and his muscular form was covered in a blue satin robe.

He looked weary and rumpled, but blessedly unharmed.

"Oh, thank God," she breathed, taking several steps forward before coming to an awkward halt. Despite the past few days, she had not entirely forgotten the forbidding Earl of Ashcombe who would have been horrified to have his undignified wife tossing herself in his arms. She cleared the lump from her throat. "You are well?"

Perhaps sensing her unease, Gabriel surged forward, pulling her against his chest and burying his face in her thick curls.

"Yes, I am well," he said in gruff tones.

For a long moment Talia simply savored the feel of his arms wrapped around her and the hard press of his muscles against her soft curves. Sucking in a deep breath, she allowed his warm, male scent to ease away her fear.

Lord almighty, she had been so terrified that he had been shot or captured or…with a shudder she yanked her thoughts away from the wrenching image of this man lying dead on the hard ground. It was unbearable.

Eventually he lifted his head, although he kept her tucked close to his body. She regarded him with a haunted gaze.

"When we heard the gunshots, Lord Rothwell insisted that we return to the yacht." Her jaw tightened with re-

membered annoyance. "He gave me no choice but to accompany him."

A glint of amusement shimmered in his eyes. "Hugo
did mention you were reluctant to leave until he convinced you that it would be best to have you safely away
from the danger."

"He did not *convince* me. He threatened to knock me
over the head with the oar if I attempted to escape from
the boat."

Gabriel chuckled. "While I deplore his crude methods, I have to admit I applaud his good sense."

Her glare was as sharp as a dagger. As delighted as
she was to have him alive and well, she did not appreciate being treated as if she were a helpless ninny.

"Indeed?"

"I could not possibly have concentrated on Jacques
or his overeager soldiers if I was worried for you." His
smile abruptly faded, and she felt his body tense. "As it
was…"

"Gabriel?"

He glanced toward the porthole, his expression bleak
in the faint light.

"My brother was injured."

"Oh, no." Genuine regret pierced Talia's heart. No matter what her own feelings toward the young man who had
jilted her, she knew how much Gabriel loved his scapegrace of a brother. He would be devastated if he were
mortally wounded. "How badly has he been hurt?"

"I am not entirely certain."

She laid a hand on his cheek, gently turning his face
back to meet her sympathetic gaze.

"You should be with him."

A muscle knotted in his jaw at her soft words. "He is
not here."

She blinked in confusion. "I do not understand."

"He is not aboard the yacht."

"But..." She was struck by an agonizing thought. "Good heavens he is not..."

"No." Gabriel swiftly alleviated her alarm. "His wound was not fatal."

She released a relieved breath, but her wariness remained. Gabriel was clearly troubled, and she was certain that it was due to his brother.

"Tell me what happened," she urged.

With a sigh he lowered his arms and took a step backward. Talia shivered at the loss of his warmth, unnerved by just how desperately she missed the pleasure of being snuggled against his chest.

When had she allowed herself to become dependent upon his touch?

Thankfully oblivious to her dangerous thoughts, Gabriel shoved a hand through his hair, his silver eyes shimmering with a savage emotion that smoldered just beneath his brittle composure.

"When the soldiers attacked, Harry leaped in front of me."

"Harry?" Caught by surprise, Talia was unable to disguise her shock. "He leaped in front of you?"

His lips twisted. "You are no more shocked than I was by his sudden display of courage. He has never before considered anyone beyond himself."

"Perhaps he has truly matured," Talia suggested, more hopeful than convinced. Harry Richardson had been a selfish scoundrel for so long it was difficult to imagine he was capable of changing. Still, miracles occurred every day. "He did, after all, help us to escape."

Gabriel grimaced. "Perhaps, but his sudden maturity could not have occurred at a worse moment."

She frowned in confusion. Surely Gabriel wished for his brother to mature into an honorable man? Then she realized the source of his distress.

"When he leaped in front of you he was injured?"

"Yes." His voice was tight with guilt. "That bullet was intended for me."

"Do not say that," she said, horrified.

"It is the truth, but Harry was moving before I could stop him." His hands clenched at his sides, and Talia was certain that he was already attempting to punish himself for Harry's injury. "Before I knew what was happening I heard a shot and he was falling to the ground bleeding."

Talia parted her lips to assure her husband that it was not his fault, only to bite back the words. Why bother? Gabriel could no more alter his habit of assuming responsibility for those he cared about than she could curb her need to reassure him.

"Where was he hit?" she instead demanded.

He shrugged. "I assumed his upper chest, although he refused to allow me to inspect the wound."

"Refused?" It was difficult to imagine Harry not taking full advantage of his role as the wounded hero. "Why would he refuse?"

"My hope is that he wished to disguise the fact that he was not injured as severely as I feared."

"Surely not." Her brows snapped together. "He must have known you were frantic with worry. Not even Harry could be so cruel."

He smiled at her outrage. "I do not believe he was attempting to be cruel on this occasion, but if I had known he was capable of walking I would have insisted that he accompany me down the cliff rather than leave him alone while I went for assistance."

"Oh." She pressed a hand to her heart. "Jacques?"

"No, the Frenchman and his guards had already fled before my crew arrived," he said in soothing tones, although his expression remained hard with frustration. "Which was why I did not hesitate to leave Harry on his own. It never occurred to me that he would use the opportunity to escape."

She barely noted the sensation of the yacht's swaying motion as they gathered speed and headed toward England. Indeed, she was impervious to everything beyond Gabriel's pale face and the shadows beneath his eyes.

"You are saying that Harry is gone?"

"Yes."

She hesitated. His expression was neutral, clearly struggling against his instinctive resistance to share his thoughts and feelings with another. He had been trained to appear invulnerable, no matter how he might long to lean on another.

Then, gathering her courage, she moved to lay a comforting hand upon his arm.

Whether Gabriel knew it or not, he needed her. Especially now.

"Do you believe he intends to return to Calais?" she asked.

He shook his head. "He could not possibly be that much a fool. Jacques would have him shot on sight."

She had to agree with his reasoning. Jacques had not been pleased to discover his English lackey had betrayed him.

"Then where would he go?"

"I cannot say."

"Do you intend to send someone in search of him?"

There was a long silence as he brooded on the question, an unmistakable concern darkening his eyes before he heaved a deep sigh.

"Maybe after we have returned to England. Then again, it is perhaps best he disappears for the time being."

He shook his head, as if attempting to rid himself of the dark thoughts that were plaguing him. Then, allowing his hooded gaze to run the length of her slender body, the tension visibly eased from his expression, and a slow, wicked smile curved his lips.

A primal heat filled the air between them, prickling over her skin and causing her to take an unconscious step backward.

"Yes, it might be for the best," she managed to rasp.

His smile widened as he prowled forward, his hands smoothing over her shoulders and down her arms.

"For now I have more important matters to occupy my mind," he said, his voice dark.

Her heart thundered and her breath locked in her throat. Lord, would she ever become accustomed to the thrilling excitement of this man's touch?

"What matters?" she weakly attempted to tease.

He slowly lifted her hand to his lips. Feeling oddly bemused, Talia watched as he nibbled along the length of her thumb.

"I believe that I warned you of my intentions once we were aboard the yacht."

She gave a strangled sound as her entire body shuddered in anticipation.

"Surely you must be tired?"

"Exhausted, but that does not diminish my desire for you," he assured her in low tones. "But first..."

Without warning he bent to scoop her off her feet, cradling her against his chest as he moved to push open the door that led to his adjoining cabin.

She had a brief impression of glossy wooden paneling and sleek furniture that was cleverly tucked into shallow nooks, but it was the small copper bathtub that was set in the middle of the floor that captured her attention.

"Gabriel, what are you about?" she demanded as he set her to her feet and dropped his arms.

"As much as I might want to tumble you on the nearest bed, I believe you will prefer my embrace after I have bathed," he said with wry amusement, the wicked smile still curving his lips. "Or better yet, once you have bathed me."

Talia attempted to appear offended even as a fluttering excitement raced through her body.

There was an undeniable temptation in the thought of being invited to explore his hard body in the guise of bathing him.

"You wish me to be your handmaiden?"

He pressed his lips to the center of her palm, his eyes shimmering with an unmistakable intent.

"I promise to return the favor whenever you desire," he murmured, glancing toward the copper tub. "In fact, while the tub is small we might manage to squeeze in together."

A heated color bloomed on her cheeks at the delicious image of their two naked bodies entwined in the hot, soapy water. Did husbands and wives truly do such a thing?

"Really, Gabriel," she breathed.

"Such an enchanting blush."

He gave a soft chuckle as he bent down to claim her lips in a consuming kiss. Talia groaned, her hands lifting to grasp the lapels of his robe as his hands ran a restless path down her back. A voice in the back of her mind whispered that she should be disturbed by the swift ease he managed to stir her passions, but it was a voice that she readily dismissed.

In truth she was too captivated by the glorious sensations spreading through her body to care.

Muttering beneath his breath, Gabriel pulled back to regard her with a smoldering gaze, a line of heat staining his cheekbones.

"Help me remove my robe," he commanded in thick tones.

With shaking hands she reached to tug at the belt that held the robe together, her stomach clenching with a tingling eagerness as he shrugged off the satin garment and allowed it to pool at his feet.

She licked her lips, her gaze skimming down the perfect width of his chest that was lightly dusted with golden hair and down the flat plane of his stomach. She shivered. He was magnificent.

Continuing with her unwitting inspection of his naked body, her nerve faltered as she reached the proud thrust of his erection, and she hastily lowered her gaze to the muscular legs and narrow feet.

It was his soft chuckle that had her lifting her head to meet his sparkling gaze.

"What is so amusing?"

He pressed her hand to his lean cheek. "I would like to believe you are regarding me with such absorption because you are captivated by my manly form, but I fear you are merely searching for deformities."

Embarrassed to have been caught staring like a naughty schoolgirl, Talia gave a small sniff, refusing to admit that the sight of him was making her ache with need.

"Your vanity has no need of my pandering."

"You are quite mistaken, my dear," he growled. "I am in dire need of pandering."

With a last attempt at sanity, she forced herself to step back.

"Get in the tub before the water grows cold."

He brushed his mouth along the line of her jaw. "As you command, my dear."

Steam rose from the water as he climbed into the tub, his long legs sprawled over the edge and arms set along the curled rim.

Before she could lose her nerve, Talia knelt beside the tub and reached for the cake of soap that had been left in a pewter dish on the floor. Dipping it into the water, she hesitantly smoothed it along the strong line of his shoulder

Gabriel groaned his approval, allowing his head to rest on the back of the tub and his eyes to slide shut.

Without his piercing silver gaze to watch her every movement, Talia felt her awkwardness ease, and her touch became bolder as she soaped the strong column of his neck and then the width of his chest.

He was astonishingly...hard, she realized as his well-toned muscles rippled beneath her touch. Although Gabriel had never been one of the effeminate dandies that pranced about London, his graceful movements and elegant attire had disguised the sheer strength of his body.

Her blood heated as she soaped his broad chest and felt his heart racing as she sensuously stroked his slick skin. In this moment she was in command of this dance of seduction, and she was heady with the rare sense of power.

She turned her attention to his nearest arm when a wave caught the yacht and water splashed from the tub onto the floor. Talia hastily began to rise, only to be halted when his fingers encircled her wrist, and his lashes lifted to reveal a smoldering heat in the depths of his silver eyes.

"Paradise," he murmured. "I could become accustomed to having you play handmaiden." His gaze lowered to the lace that did little to hide the low scoop of her bodice. "Of course, you would have need of proper attire."

Talia sucked in a deep breath, acutely aware that her nipples were hardening beneath his heated gaze.

"Proper attire?" she croaked.

"Hmm." His thumb stroked her inner wrist, no doubt able to feel the rapid beat of her pulse. "Perhaps a pair of those gauzy harem pants that are preferred by the sultans."

She narrowed her gaze. For all her enjoyment in playing the role of handmaiden, she would be damned if she would dress as a concubine.

"You attempt to put me in harem pants and I will drown you," she warned.

He chuckled, his gaze flicking over her flushed cheek. "Do you oppose the notion because you are a prude or because you possess the heart of a bluestocking?"

She stilled, meeting his amused gaze with a somber expression.

"Would it trouble you if I were a bluestocking?"

He lifted a brow. "The truth?"

She gave a slow nod, attempting to hide just how much his answer meant to her.

"Yes."

He moved forward to press a kiss to her startled lips.

"I find the thought of a clever, well-educated woman who possesses the heart of a warrior and the lush temptation of a gypsy unbearably erotic," he said lowly.

Her heart melted. It was, of course, the perfect response.

"You do?"

"If you have need of proof..."

With a tug on her wrist, Gabriel lowered her hand beneath the water and urged her fingers to wrap around his thick arousal.

"Oh."

He hissed out a raw breath of pleasure, a shudder rippling through his body as he surged upright and out of the tub. Talia barely managed to straighten before his arms were wrapped around her waist, and she was being maneuvered toward the edge of the cabin.

"Oh, indeed," he growled, his arms tightening as he tumbled her onto the bunk, his large body following downward to press her into the soft mattress.

Her hands lifted to his shoulders, barely capable of thinking as the damp heat of his body branded through her sheer nightgown.

"You are wet," she murmured.

"And now so are you," he teased, nipping at the lobe of her ear before allowing his tongue to trace a path to the base of her throat. Her breath caught as he nuzzled lower, giving a sharp tug on the nightgown to rip the material and expose her body to his searching lips. "Allow me to be of assistance."

"Really, Gabriel," she protested, even as she shivered in growing pleasure. "There is no need to ruin my nightgown."

"I will buy you another."

He shifted to watch the movement of his slender hand as it glided over the full curve of her breast, his thumb teasing the sensitive tip of her nipple before moving down the soft curve of her waist. He smiled as her breath quickened, his hand stroking over her hip, and then with a gentle tug he parted her legs to brush his fingers up the bare skin of her thigh.

She had to swallow twice before she could speak. The excitement in her lower belly spread through her body like wildfire. Not that she desired to complain, but it was making it increasingly difficult to concentrate upon anything beyond his hand that moved ever higher.

"Would it not be more sensible to simply allow me to remove the garment?"

"Perhaps it would be more sensible, but it would not be nearly so enjoyable."

Lowering his head, Gabriel captured her lips in a kiss that demanded utter surrender. At the same time his clever fingers found the aching spot between her legs. Her hips jerked upward as he parted her to seek the slick dampness within.

"Dear lord," she breathed in shock.

"Do you like that?" he whispered.

Her eyes fluttered closed as he pressed a finger into her moist channel, his thumb easily discovering that magical point of pleasure.

"Yes."

He groaned softly, his head lowering to press his mouth against the pulse that pounded a wild tempo at the base of her throat.

"I can feel your passion. Taste it on my lips."

Talia struggled not to be swept beneath the dark, blissful tide of her rising desire. It was all happening so fast, but she could not seem to gather the will to stop the delicious assault.

Then, accepting that she was battling the inevitable, she sighed softly and allowed her hands to explore the hard planes of his chest.

He gave a low hiss of pleasure, his mouth skimming down to the curve of her lush breast before tugging her hardened nipple between his lips.

Talia's toes curled in delight as he gently suckled her nipple while his finger continued to stroke between her legs with that swift, delectable pace.

Her hands slid around to discover the broad width of his back. She could spend hours just savoring the feel of his warm, satin skin beneath her hands.

For the first time in her entire life she was not Silas Dobson's painfully shy daughter. Or the awkward debutante who was an endless source of amusement throughout society.

She was a woman who was capable of inspiring the deepest passions of her husband.

Glorying in the delicious sense of confidence, she arched her hips upward as the pleasure began to swell toward the looming pinnacle.

"I need you. I need to be within you." He lifted his head, the silver eyes filled with a yearning that made Talia's heart squeeze in the oddest manner. "Are you prepared?"

She shivered at his expression of undisguised hunger. Was there anything more thrilling than this man's fierce desire?

Even if it was only for the satisfaction her body could offer.

Her fingernails dug into his back as that shimmering, glorious peak hovered just beyond reach. At the moment she would have agreed to anything he demanded.

"Yes," she whispered.

With a growl that echoed through the cabin, he returned his mouth to her aching breast as he shifted his body over the top of her, settling between her thighs.

"Open for me, my dear," he rasped against her skin, moaning softly as she instinctively wrapped her legs around his slender hips. "Yes, that is perfect."

"Gabriel…"

Her words were brought to a shuddering halt as his erection slid into her welcoming body. A shocking jolt of intense pleasure surged through her as he began to rock his hips back and forth.

She moaned with each deep thrust, lost in his perfect rhythm as he continued to plunge inside her and at the same time used his teeth to torment the tip of her breast.

At last it was all too much.

Talia gasped as she writhed beneath his touch, her nails raking down his back. Even having enjoyed his loving more than once she was still shocked by the near violent explosion that clenched her lower muscles and brought a startled scream to her lips.

Paradise, indeed.

GABRIEL FLOATED in a haze of blissful satisfaction, his arms wrapped tightly about his wife as the yacht swayed and rocked beneath them.

It would be a simple matter to close his eyes and allow his exhaustion to pull him into slumber. He could not even recall how long it had been since he had been able to claim more than a snatched hour or two of uneasy rest.

In truth, he had not enjoyed a full night of uninterrupted sleep since he had sent Talia away from London.

But, while he was satisfied that they truly had escaped from the clutches of Jacques Gerard and that they would soon be safely tucked at Carrick Park, he found it impossible to take his gaze from Talia.

It was not just her tousled beauty that was bathed in the sunlight that peeked through the porthole, although the sight of her dark, glossy curls tumbled over the pillow and her pale face flushed with lingering pleasure was enough to inspire poets. No, it was more the unshakable, if irrational, fear that she might disappear from his arms the moment he closed his eyes.

His arms tightened around her warm curves and tugged the cover over their entwined bodies. Talia wiggled onto her side, studying him with a searching gaze.

"What is troubling you?"

He tucked a stray curl behind her ear. "What could be troubling me?"

She wrinkled her nose at his evasive response, no doubt sensing his reluctance to discuss his odd apprehension. But rather than snuggling against his chest and falling asleep as he had hoped, she continued to regard him with that all too knowing gaze.

"What are your plans for when we return to England?"

He allowed his hand to smooth down the arch of her back. If he could not coax her to sleep, then perhaps he could find another means to distract her.

"Do you wish me to describe them in detail?"

She trembled in ready response, but pressing a hand to his chest, she refused to be diverted.

Stubborn wench.

"I mean in regard to your brother."

Knowing when to accept defeat, Gabriel rolled onto his back and stared at the open beams above his head.

"I cannot keep Harry's betrayal from the King or his council within the Home Office," he admitted.

He felt her stiffen at his side. "But..."

"It is not to punish my brother, Talia," he said, overriding her predictable protest. Once he had accepted that Harry had disappeared with no intent of returning to England, Gabriel had made his decision. The only decision possible. "But while I pray that he has truly learned his lesson, I cannot risk the lives of British soldiers while Harry is still capable of causing harm."

Her hand brushed over his chest to lie against his heart, as if unconsciously attempting to ease his concern.

"I am sorry."

He turned to press his face into her unruly curls, breathing in the sweet scent of lilac and warm woman. Who could have ever predicted he would not only put aside years of inexorable control to share his feelings with his wife, but that he would actually seek her comfort?

Astonishing.

"It was inevitable that I would be forced to reveal Harry's relationship with Jacques Gerard," he admitted, his voice revealing his painful regret, "but I have hopes that his treachery will be kept a closely guarded secret."

"I do not understand. I thought you were convinced he must stand trial."

"That was my original thought. However, I believe Harry has offered me the means to ensure the prime minister will do whatever necessary to prevent word of the betrayal from becoming common knowledge."

She shifted so she could study him with a suspicious frown. "What means?"

His lips twitched as he sat upright and reached for his jacket at the end of the bunk. Did she fear he had some nefarious plot in mind?

Reaching into the inner pocket of his jacket, Gabriel pulled out the piece of parchment he had hidden. Then, leaning back, he handed it to Talia.

"This."

He hid a smile as she carefully tucked the blanket over her lovely body, as if he had not already memorized every delectable inch of her satin skin, before she unfolded the parchment to study the list.

She at last lifted her head with a puzzled frown. "I have been introduced to several of these gentlemen, but I do not recall them being particular friends of Harry. Why would they assist him?"

Gabriel snorted, well aware that at least two of the gentlemen had threatened to issue a duel with his reckless brother when they'd caught him in bed with their wives.

"I can assure you that assisting my brother was never their intention," he said wryly.

"Then why do you have their names listed?"

"I did not list them." He grinned. "Jacques Gerard did."

She silently considered his revelation, her cunning mind swiftly comprehending the impact of the names.

"They are traitors?" she asked in shock.

He gave a lift of his shoulder. "It would seem so."

"But…" She regarded him with wide eyes, struggling to accept the evidence. "Dear heavens."

"Yes," he murmured.

Her lips flattened as she tossed aside the list and gave a disapproving shake of her head.

"Is there no one to be trusted?"

"Power is too often corrupted, I fear, but we at least have the means to use their weakness to our advantage."

Her eyes narrowed. "You have a plan?"

He plucked the parchment off the bed and waved it lazily.

"Neither Jacques nor the traitors are aware that Harry stumbled across this list."

His smile widened in anticipation. He had swiftly recovered from his own dismay at the sight of the names.

Unlike Talia, he had already been jaded by his fellow members of parliament. Which meant he understood that the traitors would never come to justice, despite the fact that the bastards would be eager enough to see Harry hang for his crimes.

A knowledge he intended to use to his advantage.

"Where did he find it?"

"At the vicarage." He silently reminded himself to have the house searched from attics to cellars, as well as the church. "Harry copied the list and left behind the original. So far as they are concerned, their contemptible alliance remains a secret."

"You do not intend to expose them?"

"Actually, it will be my suggestion that the traitors are used to send false information to the French."

She pressed herself to a seated position, her hand clutching the blanket. Not that she was entirely successful in keeping the abundant temptation of her breasts covered, he was pleased to note, taking full pleasure in the glimpse of alabaster skin and a rosy nipple.

"What would be the purpose?" she asked.

Gabriel swallowed a groan. He wanted to ignore her question and press her back onto the bed. It was surely a sin to waste this precious time alone discussing spies and traitors and devious politicians.

However, Gabriel suspected that Talia would not be prepared to respond to his touch until she was fully satisfied that he had shared his every thought and feeling.

She was like the ocean tide. A relentless force that could wear away the most rigid stone.

"If we can deceive Napoleon into wasting his efforts in preparing for attacks that will never occur or plotting futile ambushes on British troops that will never arrive, then he will be left vulnerable to Wellesley's true battle plan."

"Ah." A sudden smile lit her face. "Of course. Brilliant."

Gabriel resisted the embarrassing urge to preen beneath her feminine admiration.

It was not precisely brilliant. Indeed it was a simple enough scheme in theory. Unfortunately, it depended upon the ability of war officials to offer the various traitors false information that they could pass on to the French, while managing to keep the genuine battle plans a secret from them.

Still, he intended to keep his doubt of those in command to himself. He would have need of them if he were to keep Harry from the gallows.

"Let us hope that the Home Office considers it equally brilliant."

"How could they not?"

He snorted at her naivety. "Politicians are rarely sensible, even when it comes to organizing a war. They are far too busy battling one another to actually concentrate on the true enemy."

She looked as if she desired to argue, but she simply gave a faint shake of her head.

"I still do not comprehend how you intend to prevent Harry from being revealed as a traitor," she instead admitted.

"I intend to barter for his future."

"With the list?"

"Yes." He shifted to return the precious sheet of parchment to his jacket pocket before leaning back and running a slender finger down the bare skin of her shoulder. "If they desire to keep the names of the remaining traitors a secret, then they must agree that Harry's connection to Jacques Gerard will never be revealed."

She shivered beneath his touch, her eyes darkening with a heated anticipation.

"What if they refuse to follow your suggestions?" she managed to demand.

His finger continued down her arm and toward the hand that so desperately clutched the blanket to her bosom.

"They will still be willing to sacrifice whatever necessary to keep the betrayal of these men from society."

"I do not know how you can be so certain."

Gabriel shrugged. "Because I am well aware of the hysteria that would explode throughout Britain once it was revealed that such powerful gentlemen were in secret contact with a French spy." He grimaced at the mere thought. "It would not matter if the men on this list had offered nothing more tangible than the name of Wellesley's boot-maker to Jacques Gerard. It would be assumed that the war is on the brink of failure and that all of parliament has been purchased by Napoleon."

She gave a slow nod. "Yes, I see your point."

Grasping her hand, he gently untangled her grip on the blanket, hissing in pleasure as the fabric slid down to reveal the pale perfection of her curves.

"So long as Harry avoids any further stupidity, he should be able to put his past behind him and begin anew," he said, his tone distracted as his body stirred and hardened. "Wherever he is."

A flush stained her cheeks as she lay back on the pillows, her eyes shimmering with an invitation that would tempt a saint.

"He will return when he is ready," she murmured.

"Enough of my brother." Stretching out at her side,

Gabriel curled his fingers around the soft weight of her breast. "I believe we have a better means of passing the rest of the voyage."

She arched beneath his touch, her arms lifting to wrap around his neck.

"Do you?"

He lowered his head, his gaze centered on the sensuous lips that were already parted in anticipation of his kiss.

"Allow me to demonstrate."

CHAPTER TWENTY-TWO

As was his usual habit, Hugo rose from his bed at an early hour and attired himself in a fitted blue coat and buff breeches that showed his large, muscular body to advantage. He had no patience for those fools who lay abed the entire morning, expecting a bevy of servants to tend to their needs as if they were helpless invalids.

He had to admit there were some advantages to being the first to rise. He strolled into the breakfast room that was decorated with pale green satin wall panels and gold-framed mirrors. The delicate rosewood table matched the chairs upholstered in a yellow-and-cream stripe in the center of the room.

He was not only able to enjoy his breakfast of thick sliced ham, fresh eggs and warm toast with a large dollop of honey without apologizing for his healthy appetite, but he was able to enjoy the fine view of the craggy cliffs and distant sea without being forced to make meaningless chitchat.

Polishing off the last of his food, he strolled past the sideboard that groaned beneath the brimming silver chafing dishes and out the French windows that led to the balcony beyond.

They had arrived at Carrick Park yesterday, but he had been too weary to do more than climb the steps to the bedchamber he often used during his stay in Devonshire and fall into bed. Now he leaned against the stone railing and considered his immediate plans.

He would have to return to London, of course. His abrupt departure with Gabriel would no doubt have stirred ridiculous rumors that must be squelched. Especially if they hoped to deceive the traitors into believing their treachery remained a secret, as Gabriel hoped.

And after that, he would be expected to return to his home in Derbyshire for a few weeks. His estates were not nearly so extensive as Carrick Park, but he possessed tenants and servants who depended upon him. And he enjoyed his time in the country. His father often claimed that Hugo was a farmer at heart.

But he doubted that Gabriel would be prepared to leave Carrick Park for at least a few days. Hell, Hugo doubted the man would be prepared to leave his wife's bed for at least a week.

A rueful smile at the memory of Gabriel carrying his embarrassed bride up the marble staircase, his haste to reach the private chambers above obvious to the numerous servants who had gathered in the front foyer, curved his lips.

The image had barely formed in his mind when he heard the sound of approaching footsteps. Turning, he watched in surprise as Gabriel crossed the breakfast room and stepped onto the balcony.

The Earl of Ashcombe was as elegantly attired as always in a sable-brown jacket and ivory waistcoat, with a pair of dark breeches tucked into his glossy boots. His cravat was tied in a simple Oriental knot, but the linen was crisp, and a stunning emerald stickpin glittered among the folds.

But as he neared, Hugo could not fail to notice the

hard line of his jaw or the disgruntled glint in his silver eyes.

Hugo leaned against the railing and folded his arms over his chest.

"I did not expect you to join me this morning," he murmured.

"Neither did I," Gabriel groused, his sullen gaze skimming over the untamed landscape before settling on his companion. "I assure you it was not my choice."

Hugo gave a lift of his brows. "There is no need to growl," he protested mildly. "If you thought I would be in need of your company, then you might as well return to your bride. I am perfectly capable of entertaining myself."

"There is nothing I desire more than to spend the morning with my bride," his friend informed him, "but I was very firmly turned out of her bedchamber."

Hugo choked back a laugh, unable to believe any female would actually toss Gabriel from her bedchamber. The man had been ruthlessly pursued by women since he had left the schoolroom.

"Holy hell."

Gabriel glared at him with a decided lack of humor. "This is not amusing."

"No, it is a tragic statement on your skills as a lover," Hugo readily agreed. "If you wish, I can offer you a few suggestions to assist you in pleasing your wife. Perhaps then she will not boot you out of her bed."

A startling color crawled beneath Gabriel's lean face. Was the arrogant earl actually discomfited by Hugo's teasing? Astonishing.

"I was not booted out of her bed," he snapped. "And I most certainly do not need suggestions on pleasing my wife from a man who has become a misogynist over the past years."

Hugo frowned, caught off guard by the accusation. Perhaps he had learned to avoid debutantes as if they carried the plague. And it had been a few months since he had given his last mistress her *congé*. But that did not mean that he disliked females. Bloody hell, he adored them when they were not attempting to trap him into marriage or pleading for yet another expensive bauble.

It was just...

He gave a restless shrug. It was just that he was searching for a female he was beginning to fear did not exist, a tiny voice whispered in the back of his mind.

It was a voice he was swift to dismiss as he gave a sharp shake of his head.

"Not a misogynist," he corrected. "Merely a man who has grown weary of fortune hunters and their overzealous mothers." He paused, a taunting smile slowly curving his lips. "Of course, if there were more females such as Talia I might reconsider my cynical opinion of the opposite sex."

Predictably, Gabriel narrowed his gaze in warning. "Careful, old friend."

Hugo chuckled, giving a dismissive wave of his hand. "I speak in general, not specific terms. I do not seek an early grave."

Gabriel grunted, glancing over his shoulder as if hoping his bride might make a sudden appearance in the breakfast room.

"There are no other females to compare with my wife."

"True," Hugo agreed with a faint sigh.

He had not been entirely teasing when he had wished for a female such as Talia. It was not that he was in love with his friend's wife, but she possessed a strength of character and an unwavering loyalty that he deeply admired. They were both all too rare qualities among society.

Then, with an effort, he shrugged off his peculiar mood and studied Gabriel's sour expression. He could not deny a small measure of pleasure in witnessing his friend's annoyance. Gabriel had become far too accustomed to having the world cater to his every pleasure. It did him good to have his puffed-up conceit occasionally deflated.

"She is certainly a woman of courage," he pointed out in innocent tones. "There are few who would dare to ban you from their room."

Gabriel scowled. "I was not banned by Talia, I was rousted by my own damned servants."

"Your servants?"

"They began arriving at the crack of dawn."

"Ah." Hugo shrugged. "I suppose that is not surprising that they would desire to ensure you are well and unharmed after your adventures."

"They were not concerned with my welfare, it was their beloved Lady Ashcombe whom they wished to ensure was unharmed," Gabriel said with a grimace. "For God's sake, Mrs. Donaldson was weeping in relief when I at last fled."

Hugo's eyes widened at the mere thought of the formidable housekeeper in tears.

"Astonishing."

"And to make matters worse, Talia has very firmly informed me that she intends to devote the rest of the day to visiting the tenants."

Hugo shifted so he could glance toward the side of the house where the parkland gave way to a pretty pond.

Beyond that the rolling fields were dotted with thatch-roofed cottages.

"Perhaps it is for the best," he murmured, returning his attention to his companion. He easily recalled the tenants' frantic searches for Talia when he and Gabriel had arrived at Carrick Park and their desperation for Gabriel to rescue her from the clutches of the evil French spy. "If she does not make an appearance, they will surely storm the house to reassure themselves that you have returned her as promised."

Gabriel dismissed this logic with an impatient wave of his hand.

"She is still weary from her journey. She should be resting, not gadding about the countryside."

Hugo chuckled, not fooled for a moment. "Hmm."

"What?"

"I wonder if you are annoyed because she is not being allowed to rest or because you are being forced to share her attentions with others."

With an imperious lift of his brow, Gabriel tilted his chin to glare down the length of his nose.

"I am the Earl of Ashcombe. I do not need to beg for the attentions of my wife."

"If that were true, then the Earl of Ashcombe would not be spending his morning pacing the breakfast room in a mood so foul that the Lord of Rothwell is considering the pleasure of tossing him off the balcony."

Gabriel heaved a harsh sigh. "I suppose you are right."

"Naturally," Hugo said smugly. "I am always right."

"Be careful, Rothwell," his friend growled. "My mood is still foul."

Hugo smiled, resisting the urge to continue with his teasing.

"When do you intend to return to London?"

"It must be soon." Gabriel paced the length of the balcony, seemingly indifferent to the spill of morning sunlight or the rose-scented breeze that ruffled his golden hair. "The king and his council must know of the traitors as soon as possible."

Hugo fully agreed. Every moment that passed was another moment that offered the traitors an opportunity to put British troops at risk.

"Why do you hesitate?"

Gabriel grimaced. "Talia will not be pleased when I tell her she must remain at Carrick Park."

"Why would she not be pleased? She seems to prefer the countryside to the city."

"Yes, but when I mentioned traveling to London without her, I was informed that she would not be hidden away like an embarrassing secret."

"What the devil does that mean?"

"I haven't the least notion," Gabriel muttered, "but I sense she will insist on accompanying me."

Hugo watched his companion pace from one end of the balcony to the other, a frown marring his brow.

"Then why not allow her to go with you?" he asked. "It seems a simple enough solution."

Gabriel turned to glare at Hugo. "Impossible."

Hugo paused, baffled by the frustration he could sense simmering just below his friend's fragile composure.

They had managed to rescue Talia, outwit a French spy and discovered a means to prevent Harry from being exposed as a traitor.

Surely the man should be celebrating, not looking as if he desired to smash his fist into the nearest object?

"Why is it impossible? You surely do not believe she is in danger?"

"I did not believe her in danger when I sent her to Carrick Park, but she managed to tumble into disaster."

Good God, did the man intend to flog himself forever? Anyone would think he'd deliberately sent his wife into a trap.

"You could not possibly have predicted that there was a French spy lurking in the neighborhood."

"She is my responsibility." Gabriel stubbornly refused to admit it had been an unfortunate coincidence.

"Fine." Hugo held up his hands in defeat. "But, if you truly fear for her safety, then I would think that would be even more reason to keep her close at hand so that you can protect her."

An indefinable emotion darkened the silver eyes as Gabriel stepped forward, his hands clenched at his sides.

"Pray, allow me to decide what is best for my own wife, Rothwell."

"Not when you are being a damned fool," Hugo growled in return. He had no desire to poke his nose in the private affairs of his friend, but neither did he intend to stand aside and watch Gabriel make a hash of his marriage. "Do you not recall the last occasion that you decided what was best for your wife?"

Gabriel muttered a curse as he crossed the balcony and returned to the breakfast room, clearly intent on avoiding the logic of Hugo's accusation.

"This is not at all the same," he argued.

Hugo followed behind him. "Explain how this is different."

"I cannot bear for her to be hurt."

"Hurt?" Hugo tensed, studying Gabriel's grim expression with a puzzled unease. "What do you mean?"

Before he could respond, an elderly butler shuffled into the room, his body appearing bent, as if the blue-

and-silver uniform was too heavy for his gaunt frame, and his hair a mere fringe of gray. But there was a lingering dignity in his precise movements and a shrewd glint in his pale eyes.

"Pardon me, my lord."

Gabriel glanced toward the servant with a hint of surprise.

"Yes, McGordy?"

"There is a visitor to see Lady Ashcombe."

"At this hour?"

"Yes, my lord."

Gabriel scowled in exasperation. "If it is a tenant, you may bloody well inform them that they can wait their turn to speak with the countess."

The stately McGordy did not so much as blink at the sharp words.

"It is not a tenant, my lord, it is a Miss Lansing."

"Who?" Gabriel demanded in confusion.

Hugo was equally confused. He seemed to have a vague recollection of a Sir Lansing who was a minor baronet, but he surely had no connection to Silas Dobson or his daughter.

McGordy gently cleared his throat. "She claims to be a friend to her ladyship."

"Oh." Gabriel's frown only deepened as he seemed to be struck by a sudden realization. "Yes, I have a vague recollection of her."

Whatever his recollection of Miss Lansing, it obviously was not a pleasant one.

"Shall I inform the countess?" the butler inquired.

Gabriel gave a decisive shake of his head. "No, that will not be necessary. I will tend to Miss Lansing."

"As you wish."

"In fact, I prefer that my wife not be bothered with the knowledge that Miss Lansing was ever in Devonshire."

Confusion briefly rippled over the servant's face before he offered a stiff bow.

"As you wish."

Waiting until they were once again alone, Hugo whirled to stab his companion with a black look.

"What the blazes is the matter with you?"

Gabriel folded his arms over his chest, his expression set in stubborn lines.

"I will not have Talia bothered."

Hugo snorted. He did not consider himself an expert when it came to understanding the complicated female mind and what pleased them, but he was fairly confident that his mother and sisters adored receiving visitors, no matter what hour of the day.

"I doubt she would consider a visit from a friend as a bother."

Gabriel shook his head, his features hardening with a frigid anger.

"My wife is too kindhearted to turn away a guest," he said in lethal tones, "but I was witness to those females who pretended to be Talia's friends when it was discovered she had been jilted by my brother." He caught and held Hugo's gaze, a shimmer of grim determination burning in the silver depths. "They filled her gardens and drank her champagne even as they laughed and mocked her humiliation."

Fury raced through Hugo.

By God, he would ruin anyone who dared to insult the Countess of Ashcombe, he silently swore, refusing to recall his own scathing opinion of the shy, stammering Miss Dobson who had forced his friend into an unwanted marriage. Whatever his opinion in the past, he

adored Talia. Those who thought they were at liberty to
continue with their nasty ridicule would swiftly discover
the error of their ways.

"This Miss Lansing mocked Talia?" he growled.

Gabriel shrugged. "Not within my hearing, but I will
not take the risk of my wife being upset."

Hugo fully agreed. No shrill-tongued harridan was
going to disturb Talia while she was still fragile from
her recent adventures.

"Leave it to me," he announced.

Gabriel glanced at him in surprise. "You?"

"I will rid you of the vermin who seek to enter your
home," he promised, waving a hand toward a side door
that led to a back staircase. "You join your wife and accompany her on her visit to the tenants."

"Very well." Gabriel did not hesitate to accept the generous offer, crossing the room to lay a hand on Hugo's
broad shoulder. "I am in your debt."

Hugo smiled. "I assure you that I am keeping tally."

Gabriel managed a strained chuckle, although it was
obvious he remained troubled as he left the room. Hugo
watched his friend's retreat before leaving the breakfast
room and heading down to the front salon.

He straightened his cuffs as he casually strolled into
the long room with high arched windows that overlooked
the circular drive. For all his dislike of society games,
he was a master of playing them when the occasion demanded.

With the same nonchalance, he moved over the black-
and-white tiled floor, strolling past the walnut marque-
try bureau that matched the ornately carved cabinet and
inlaid library table. Out of the corner of his eye, he took
note of the elderly lady nearly lost among the layers of
her black bombazine gown and veiled bonnet. She ap-

peared to be napping in the corner of one of the small
velvet sofas. It was not until he leaned against the mantel
lined with marble busts of previous Earls of Ashcombe
that he took a full survey of the female pacing the floor
in obvious agitation.

His first reaction was one of surprise.

He had been expecting the typical society chit attired
in a modest gown, with her pale curls perfectly groomed
and her expression one of shy flirtation. He had been introduced to a hundred of them over the years, and they
all seemed to be exactly the same, with only their names
to offer a way to tell them apart.

This female...

His gaze narrowed as he skimmed over the wrinkled
carriage gown in a dark shade of amber and the plump
face that was stained with an angry color. She had clearly
not bothered to rest or change before arriving after a long
journey, which would explain the unruly brown curls that
had tumbled from the knot at the base of her neck and
the shadows beneath her dark eyes. And equally evident
she was not pleased to have been kept waiting.

Peculiar.

This woman did not appear to be the sort of conceited,
heartless jade that would seek out Talia to cause her pain.
In truth, she appeared genuinely distraught as she glow-
ered at him with evident impatience.

A portion of his simmering outrage eased, and he
stepped forward to offer an elegant bow.

"Miss Lansing?"

She bobbed a stiff curtsy, not seeming especially
pleased to be confronted by an eligible bachelor who
was considered one of the finest catches in London.

"Lord Rothwell," she muttered.

He straightened, lifting a brow. "Have we been intro-duced?"

"We have, although it is obvious you have no recol-lection of the momentous occasion," she said dryly.

Hugo stiffened. Had the audacious female just repri-manded him?

It was unthinkable. Females devoted themselves to fawning and preening and generally making a pest of themselves in order to please him.

"Forgive me, my lamentable memory…"

"Oh, never mind, it is of no account. You certainly are not the first gentleman who cannot be bothered to remember me," she interrupted his smooth apology, giv-ing a wave of her plump hand. "I am here to speak with Lady Ashcombe."

"Where?"

It was her turn to be caught off guard. "I beg your pardon?"

He took a step closer, forgetting the reason he had agreed to meet with Miss Lansing as he studied her pale features that were unremarkable until one really looked. Her heavily lashed brown eyes were filled with a rest-less intelligence, and the hint of a dimple danced near her full, kissable lips.

"Where were we introduced?"

"What does it matter?"

"Because I find it incomprehensible that I would have forgotten. You are quite…" He struggled for the appro-priate word. She was not a beauty. At least not in the traditional manner. And he had yet to see any attempt at charm. But there was something that captured and held his bemused attention. "Unique."

"It was at Lady Jersey's ball last season," she grudg-ingly revealed.

He shook his head. "I must have been in my cups not to have swept you onto the dance floor."

She folded her arms beneath her ample bosom. The sight of the pale flesh pressing against the lace edging her bodice caused Hugo to harden with a swift, unnerving arousal.

God almighty.

Thankfully unaware of his predicament, she offered a baleful glare.

"I believe you were too busy attempting to sweep Lady Sandford into the nearest bedchamber," she accused. "And, if you hope to flatter me into forgetting my mission, my lord, you are wide of the mark."

"Why? Are you impervious to flattery?"

"Enough of this foolishness." She planted her fists on her hips. "You will inform Lady Ashcombe that I have called or I will—"

"Yes?" he prompted.

"I will scream until she makes an appearance."

Would she? The fact that Hugo was not absolutely certain she would not create a scene if necessary only deepened his fascination.

"Why are you so determined to speak with her?"

Her rounded chin tilted. "Because I am concerned, if you must know."

He searched her belligerent expression, realizing that there was indeed an unmistakable concern beneath her bluster and even a measure of fear. Whatever Gabriel's assumption about Miss Lansing, she had not traveled to Carrick Park to harm Talia.

"You were concerned for her welfare?"

"Yes."

"That is absurd."

"Is it?" She stood her ground, her eyes flashing with

dark fire. "Talia disappeared from London mere hours after her secretive wedding to the Earl of Ashcombe. And despite the numerous letters I have written over the past month pleading for her to reassure me that she is well, I have heard nothing from her."

Hugo cast a brief glance toward the female still sleeping in the corner before stepping close enough he could capture her chin between his forefinger and thumb.

"And what is it you fear, Miss Lansing?" he asked in low tones. "Do you suspect that Lord Ashcombe has locked his vulnerable young bride in the dungeons? Or perhaps you imagined he had thrown her off the cliff?"

The color beneath her skin darkened, and he was struck by a savage need to know if the flush was a mere reaction to her anger or a display of the same arousal that plagued him.

"Who is to say?" she challenged. "I was with Talia when the earl forced his way into her private chambers and demanded that I leave. He certainly seemed angry enough to wish her harm."

Hugo shook his head, caught between indignation that she would believe for a moment that Gabriel was capable of violence toward a woman and amusement at her bold claim.

The only other female who could have dared to stand before him, bedraggled from her long journey and spitting fire, was Talia.

It was little wonder the two had been drawn to one another.

"There is no gentleman who has not been angered at some time or another," he pointed out, his thumb tracing the line of her full lower lip. "That does not necessarily lead him to commit a heinous crime. We are, after all, a civilized society."

She made a sound of disgust and pulled away. "Being civilized does not stop gentlemen from behaving as barbarians."

How could Hugo argue with her logic? He had ample proof that supposed noblemen were as capable of treachery, cruelty and shocking brutality as any savage.

Still, he found himself piqued by her obvious disdain for the opposite sex. Was it an all-encompassing contempt for gentlemen as a whole, or specifically noblemen?

"Tell me, my kitten, are you a reader of novels?" he gently mocked.

Her chin tilted a notch higher, revealing her taste for melodrama.

"Why?"

"Because not all men are the villains portrayed by the current rash of female authors."

Her lips flattened with displeasure at his teasing. "This is not amusing."

"Actually, I have to disagree," he argued. "It is rather humorous that you would suspect Ashcombe of murdering his wife."

"I have endured enough of your mockery," she replied angrily, abruptly turning to march toward the door.

Hugo was in swift pursuit, barely managing to dart in front of her before she could barrel through the doorway.

With her escape route blocked, she regarded him with a gaze that warned she was considering boxing his ears.

"Move aside," she snapped.

In response, he leaned a broad shoulder against the doorjamb, careful to ensure his large form managed to consume the entire entryway. He suspected she intended to slip past him the moment he was distracted.

And oh, it would be so easy to distract him, he ac-

knowledged, his gaze lingering on those full, sensuous lips.

"Where do you think you are going?" he demanded.

"If you will not bring Talia to me, then I will find her
myself."

His gaze lifted to meet her furious glare. "Why are
you so concerned?"

"Why?" She appeared briefly baffled by his question.
"She is my friend."

"Forgive my confusion, but it is my understanding that
Talia's *friends* have made her life in London a misery."

She stiffened, clearly offended to be included among
those who had bullied Talia.

"If you speak of those spiteful vipers who make a
sport of tormenting the less-favored females, they were
never Talia's friends, nor was she ever foolish enough to
consider them as such," she retorted sharply. "It was her
father who forced her to spend time in their company."

"And you?"

"I think it should be perfectly obvious that I was a
fellow wallflower who endured a similar fate as Talia,"
she said, a hint of resolute pride in her voice. "We are
friends because we comprehend what it means to be out-
casts from society."

A strange, distinctly alarming emotion flared to life
in the center of his heart. An emotion that Hugo was certain was far more dangerous than all English traitors and
French spies combined.

Attempting to ignore the sensation, he reached to
straighten the cameo that was pinned to the amber ribbon encircling her neck, his fingers lingering on the satin
heat of her skin.

"Forgive me," he murmured. "I should not have teased
you."

Her pulse leaped beneath the light brush of his fingers. But with an obvious effort not to be diverted, she reached up to bat away his hand.

"I do not desire your pity," she informed him sharply. "I wish to see Talia."

He shrugged. He no longer believed that Miss Lansing was anything but a concerned friend who had traveled to Devonshire to make certain that Talia was not being mistreated by her husband. But he had promised Gabriel that he would be rid of the female.

He intended to keep his word, although he was willing to offer Miss Lansing the assurance that Talia was alive and well.

"I fear that is impossible at the moment. However, I promise—"

He cut off his soothing words as she parted her lips, her eyes dark with warning. Bloody hell, she actually intended to carry out her threat.

Without conscious thought he swooped his head downward, locking his mouth over her parted lips to prevent her determined scream.

He had no intention beyond stopping her from alarming the servants and disturbing Talia. At least that was what he told himself as he deepened the kiss, his tongue slipping into the warm cavern of her mouth.

The convenient excuse, however, did not explain why he wrapped his arms around her waist and tugged her against his stirring body. Or why he closed his eyes to savor the tangy scent of lemons that clung to her soft curls.

Despite her short stature, she fit against his large form with startling perfection, he mused, enjoying the sensation of generous curves filling his arms rather than the wispy fragility of most society women. A man of his size disliked the sensation he was about to crush his lover.

Lover...

The word teased the edge of his mind, sending a jolt of warning through his aching body. Dammit, what the hell was he doing?

A gentleman did not seduce infuriating virgins in the front salon of his best friend's home. At least not before luncheon.

With a low moan, he forced himself to release her enticing lips and lifted his head. Before he could let her go, however, she reached up to slap his face with enough force to make his teeth rattle.

"How dare you!"

His lips twisted as he studied her astonished expression with a brooding gaze. She was naturally outraged at his bold caresses, but he did not miss the heated awareness that burned in the back of her dark eyes.

She was not entirely impervious to his touch.

"It was my intent to prevent you from causing an unpleasant scene," he murmured. "But I believe I have just been hoisted on my own petard."

He sensed her hesitation before she wisely decided to ignore his wry confession. Now was not the time to discuss the powerful attraction that had struck him like a bolt of lightning.

Of course, he was not especially pleased when she placed her hands against his chest and attempted to wiggle from his grip.

"Release me," she commanded.

"Do you promise not to scream?"

"No, I most certainly do not."

His lips twitched. Stubborn vixen.

"Miss Lansing, I assure you that Talia is in perfect

health and that she is in no danger from Gabriel," he said, attempting to ease her fears. "In fact, he happens to be embarrassingly besotted with her."

"Then why has she not answered the letters I sent?"

Hugo shrugged, regretting that he and Gabriel had yet to discuss the story they intended to invent in explanation of their sudden disappearance.

How the hell was he to put off this female with vague lies and bluster?

And of course it did not help that he was perilously distracted by the feel of her palms that remained pressed against his chest and the curvaceous hips that were perfectly fitted between his thighs.

"She has spent the past weeks away from Carrick Park," he announced.

"Really?" She narrowed her gaze in disbelief. "Where did she go?"

"She was sailing with her husband upon their yacht."

"Sailing?"

"It is customary for newlyweds to enjoy a honeymoon trip," he retorted with the thought it would be unshakable logic. "And what better place to find privacy than in the midst of the ocean?"

Naturally she leaped upon the fatal flaw of his story.

"And you joined them on this supposed honeymoon trip?"

"Of course." His smile was closer to a grimace. "I am a devoted sailor."

She rolled her eyes. "I do not believe you."

And why should she? Hugo ground his teeth, his usually clever wits refusing to cooperate as he searched for an explanation. Then, like a gift from God, he caught sight of Gabriel and Talia strolling toward the stables beside the manor house.

Perhaps his luck was changing.

"Then believe this," he muttered, grasping her hand and towing her toward the window. "Does Talia appear to be frightened or unhappy?"

She jerked from his grasp, but as she caught sight of the couple strolling arm in arm her belligerent expression softened, the tension easing from her luscious body.

As well it should, he wryly acknowledged. Not even Miss Lansing could fail to notice the devotion in Gabriel's expression as he gazed down at his wife, or the manner that she snuggled into his side, as if she could not be close enough to his larger form.

In silence they watched as the two disappeared through the stone archway leading to the stable yard. Then, clenching her hands at her sides, Miss Lansing turned to stab him with a puzzled glower.

"Why do you refuse to allow me to speak with her?"

He considered a variety of clever lies before heaving a sigh. She deserved at least a portion of the truth for her obvious loyalty to her friend.

"Gabriel has never been in love before," he said. "He has yet to overcome his rather primitive urge to jealously guard his bride from the world."

"Oh." Miss Lansing faltered, something akin to longing briefly rippling over her plump face. The same longing that had tormented Hugo since his return from France. "She is...content?"

"She is content," Hugo readily assured her. "And once she has properly trained her stubborn husband, I suspect that she will be deliriously happy."

"Good." Hugo watched as she squared her shoulders. "If you will call for my carriage I must return to London."

Hugo's brows snapped together. He had presumed that

she was staying with friends or family in the neighborhood. Now his blood ran cold at the thought of her journeying such a distance without protection.

Had the female taken leave of her senses? The roads were overrun with highwaymen and smugglers and bloodthirsty cutthroats. Not even coaching inns were safe from overly forward noblemen who would press their advances on any vulnerable young lady.

"You are traveling alone?" he demanded, moving so he could stand directly before her.

She appeared confused by the question, waving a hand toward the slumbering crone on the sofa.

"Obviously not. I have a companion."

"Companion?" he snarled. "Not even the most lenient of guardians could consider that..." He struggled to temper his description of the woman. For all he knew, she was some sort of relation to Miss Lansing. "That ancient female a proper companion."

She sniffed. "Thankfully you are not my guardian and who I choose as my companion is none of your concern."

"You are mistaken." The words tumbled from his lips before he realized what he was about to say. "I have decided to make it my concern."

She appeared as startled as he was by his overbearing declaration.

"Excuse me?"

He hesitated. It would be simple enough to retract his arrogant claim. Or to chuckle and pretend it had been nothing more than a feeble jest.

Then he could pat Miss Lansing upon the head, send her and her lethargic companion on their way, and perhaps find his lost sanity.

But even as the thought passed through his mind, he dismissed it.

Miss Lansing was not stepping outside the door without him at her side.

"It just so happens that I was about to leave for London," he announced, his firm tone warning he had made his decision. "We shall travel together."

She took a hasty step backward, horror spreading over her face.

"We most certainly shall not."

He smiled, moving to cup her cheek in his hand. "Kitten, you will eventually learn to simply concede defeat once I have made my decision. It will make our future together far more pleasant."

She shook her head in disbelief. "Have you gone utterly mad?"

He gazed deep into the wary brown eyes, his chest so tight he could barely breathe.

"There is a good possibility."

CHAPTER TWENTY-THREE

TALIA STRUGGLED TO catch her breath as Gabriel rolled off her trembling body and wrapped her tightly in his arms.

They had spent most of the day traveling about the estate to meet with the tenants who had been inordinately pleased to see her. For goodness' sake, one would think she had been gone for years rather than days the way they had fussed and fawned over her.

Not that she had protested. Their ready warmth and displays of affection had made her feel as if she were coming home. A feeling that she would never have dreamed possible only a few short months ago.

So, ignoring her humble instincts, she'd allowed the women to feed her their favorite seedcake and drink their cider while the children had crawled into her lap and the men had hovered in the background with wide grins on their weathered faces.

At last Gabriel had declared that it was time to return to the manor house. He had turned a deaf ear to her protests that she was not at all weary, and loaded her into the carriage.

He had continued to insist upon her need for rest once they had returned to the house and had even caused the servants to twitter in shock as he had swept her off her feet and carried her up the polished oak staircase to the master bedchamber.

Once alone, however, he'd seemed to forget his insistence that she enjoy a nice nap as he had laid her on the massive four poster bed that consumed a large amount of the peach-and-silver room.

Talia had attempted to chastise him, but she had soon forgotten why she should be annoyed with him as his mouth had crushed her lips in a hungry kiss and his hands had tugged at her clothing with a satisfying haste.

In truth, she had reveled in his obvious passion.

It was perhaps ridiculous, but she had harbored a relentless fear that once they returned to England, Gabriel would return to the cold, condemning man whom she had first wed.

There was something deeply reassuring in the heat of his kisses and his groans of pleasure as he had at last entered her with a slow, exquisite thrust.

At last regaining command of her breath, Talia turned her head to cast a glance toward the ormolu clock set on the mantel. She heaved a rueful sigh as she forced herself to sit up, realizing that she would have to hurry if she were to be presentable before they were to meet Hugo in the library.

"And where do you think you are going?" he demanded.

She glanced over her shoulder, excitement fluttering through her stomach at the sight of Gabriel's naked body sprawled over the sheets. In the firelight his hair shimmered like the finest gold while his eyes had darkened to a mysterious smoke.

He surely must be descended from Greek gods. No mere mortal should be so beautiful.

Resisting the urge to smooth her hands over his broad chest in an effort to prove he was flesh and blood and not some figment of her imagination, Talia nodded toward the clock.

"We must get dressed for dinner if we are not to be late."

Gabriel made no effort to postpone his exploration of her naked curves, his hand running a path down her hip and over her thigh in a blatant invitation.

"Why bother?" he murmured. "We can request a tray be sent from the kitchens."

"Really, Gabriel, you are a dreadful host," she chastised even as she shivered in delight. "We cannot abandon Lord Rothwell. He will be expecting us to join him."

His fingers drew aimless patterns on her sensitive skin as he leaned forward to plant a kiss on her lower back.

"Actually Hugo left earlier today for London."

She stilled, caught off guard by the casual announcement. Despite Hugo's initial animosity, she had been certain that they had become friends during their dangerous journey together. The thought he would simply disappear was oddly hurtful.

"He left without saying goodbye?"

"It was a sudden decision." Gabriel leaned back to meet her wounded gaze. "He left a message stating that he recalled urgent business in town that he could not delay."

"And he could not wait until we returned to tell us of this urgent business?"

Gabriel shrugged, although Talia did not miss his guarded expression.

"Hugo is a reasonably intelligent gentleman who understands that I prefer to devote my attentions to my new bride, not keeping an unwelcome guest entertained," he said smoothly. "He obviously wished to slip away without causing a fuss."

A chill of suspicion speared down Talia's spine.

Knocking aside Gabriel's arm, she rose from the bed and pulled on a satin robe in a pretty shade of rose.

She was well enough acquainted with her husband to know when he was lying to her.

Tying the belt of her robe, she turned to study Gabriel with a narrowed gaze.

"I do not doubt Hugo's intelligence, but I am quite certain that he told me he intended to remain at Carrick Park until you were prepared to travel to London."

Gabriel shifted until he was leaning against the carved oak headboard, his expression unreadable.

"It would seem that he changed his mind."

"*He* changed his mind or you convinced him to change it?" she challenged.

He held up his hands in a gesture of innocence. "I swear I had nothing to do with his abrupt departure."

"Hmm."

There was no mistaking her lingering distrust, and Gabriel heaved an impatient sigh.

"What is troubling you?"

"I am not entirely certain." Her features settled into a stubborn expression. "I simply sense you are keeping something hidden from me."

He gave a sharp, humorless laugh. "An impossible task, as I am quickly discovering."

It was an impossible task, but that was precisely why an unpleasant sense of trepidation settled in the pit of her stomach.

"Fine." She wrapped her arms around her waist, feeling suddenly cold despite the cheerful fire that burned in the white marble fireplace. "I suppose I shall be able to question Hugo once we arrive in London."

He shrugged, angling to the side so he could reach out to grab the fabric of her robe.

"If you insist, now…"

Talia danced backward, tugging her garment from his fingers.

"And when will that be?"

He scowled at her persistence. "Really, Talia, you should not be putting your husband through the Inquisition when he is attempting to seduce you."

"You may seduce me all you desire once you answer the question," she promised, refusing to be distracted. "When do we leave for London?"

There was a long silence before Gabriel folded his arms over his chest and heaved a resigned sigh.

"In the morning."

Her lips parted in shock. "For goodness' sake, when were you intending to tell me?" she chided. Really, did men have no notion of how difficult it was to prepare for such a long journey? "I promised Mrs. Grossman I would call in the morning with a poultice for her weak chest and then I intended to spend a few moments with Mr. Clark, who requested that I write a letter to his sister in Yorkshire whom he has not seen in the past fifty years." She waved a hand toward the large armoire set between two windows overlooking the cliffs. "And, of course, I must pack."

His hooded gaze skimmed over her flushed cheeks. "There is no need to excite yourself, my dear."

She shook her head. No doubt he expected to climb onto the nearest horse and gallop down the lane. A mistress of a house, however, had a great deal more to consider.

"I will never be prepared to leave tomorrow if I do not tend to at least a few tasks this eve," she muttered, already making a list in her head of what she could finish before retiring for bed and what must be left for the morning.

"Talia, listen to me."

Talia waved a hand, pacing the floral carpet. "I do not have time to waste, Gabriel."

"You will not be traveling with me tomorrow."

Preoccupied with her thoughts, it took a moment for Gabriel's words to penetrate. Finally, she slowly turned to study his inflexible expression.

"I beg your pardon?"

"I intend my journey to London to be a short, excessively discreet visit," he said, his tone carefully stripped of emotion. "The fewer people who realize that I have sought a meeting with the king and prime minister, the less chance that I will arouse the suspicions of the traitors."

It was a reasonable explanation, and yet, she was not convinced.

Perhaps it was only her bothersome insecurities that made her certain that he was deliberately attempting to keep her from traveling with him to London.

But it did not matter.

She was not going to settle for being hidden away like a nasty secret. Not again.

"It does not matter how careful you might attempt to be, the word of your arrival is bound to become known."

He shrugged aside her warning. "Even if it does, I shall be gone before word can spread."

Talia forced herself to pause and consider her words. There was no use in directly accusing him of trying to keep her at Carrick Park. He would only deny her claim. No, she must be clever enough to outwit him.

She forced herself to move forward, perching on the edge of the bed and deliberately allowing her robe to gape just enough for a small glimpse of her breasts. Predictably his gaze shifted down to linger on the soft mounds, and Talia hid a small smile of triumph. She was not above using what few weapons she might possess.

"You must know that it will only cause more speculation if it appears you are attempting to sneak about."

"And what do you suggest?" he demanded.

"Society will find nothing suspicious in the arrival of Lord and Lady Ashcombe in London."

He made a sound of disgust, but his attention remained focused on her gaping robe.

"You cannot be that naïve."

"And it will surely be expected of you to introduce me to the king." She pressed her advantage, tilting her head so that her dark hair spilled over one shoulder. "We will simply plan a soiree and invite those gentlemen you wish to speak with. No one will have any reason to question such an innocent gathering."

His gaze sharpened as he lifted his head and regarded her with an impatient scowl.

"Christ, Talia, do you have any notion the stir our arrival will cause?" he snapped. "The scandalmongers will have the entire town buzzing with rumors."

She shrugged. "Which is precisely what we desire, is it not?"

He pushed away from the headboard, his jaw clenched as he battled his surge of anger.

"Have you taken leave of your senses?"

She met his gaze squarely. What rumors did he fear? Those of their hasty marriage? Of their sudden disappearance?

Or the fact that his bride was the socially unacceptable daughter of Silas Dobson who remained a source of humiliation for the Ashcombe family?

The aching disappointment that was a familiar part of her past threatened to return as she reached to lay her hand on Gabriel's arm, her expression one of unconscious pleading.

"Just consider, Gabriel, if all of society is speculating on our return to London, then they shall be too occupied to consider who you might or might not be seeking out to speak with." She forced a stiff smile to her lips. "Surely that is worth enduring the gossips?"

The silver eyes flared with an unexpected exasperation. As if she was at fault for desiring to remain at her husband's side rather than him being to blame for wishing to abandon her.

"You want to be besieged by the vultures of society?" he rasped.

"Of course it is not what I wish, but it is inevitable."

"Not if you remain here."

Her heart felt as if it were being squeezed in a vise. After all they had endured together and for all his passion, he still wished to keep her stashed far away from society.

"I cannot avoid London forever," she breathed past the lump in her throat.

Seemingly unaware of her mounting distress, Gabriel lifted a hand to thread his fingers through her loose curls.

"Not forever, but there is no need to return until next season."

"That is months away."

He frowned, clearly expecting her to concede defeat with grace.

"I thought you enjoyed being at Carrick Park," he accused.

"I do, but..."

"And I do have more than one estate we must visit,"

he continued without offering her an opportunity to respond. "My servants and tenants will be anxious to become acquainted with the new Countess of Ashcombe."

Talia glanced away from his grim expression, accepting that he had made his decision and he would not be swayed, no matter her efforts.

"Gabriel, why do you wish to keep me from London?" she asked, her voice a mere whisper.

There was an awkward pause before Gabriel cleared his throat in obvious discomfort.

"I have told you that this is no more than a fleeting visit," he said, his fingers shifting to cup her nape, his thumb running a soothing path down the tense line of her jaw. "I intend to linger no longer than necessary before returning to Devonshire. It makes no sense for you to disrupt your plans for what will very well be a handful of days."

She kept her lashes lowered. "I see."

"I promise you will be more comfortable here and I will return as swiftly as possible."

"Of course."

At last sensing she was less than pleased with his refusal to even consider her wishes, Gabriel shifted his thumb beneath her chin and tilted her face upward.

"You do not intend to sulk, do you, my dear?"

Actually her first thought was to flee from the room and find a place to nurse her wounded heart in privacy. She had allowed herself to hope that her future with Gabriel would be one of mutual respect, if not love. Now it was even more wrenching to realize he continued to harbor a measure of embarrassment at having her as his wife.

With effort, she managed to squash the instinctive response. No. Not on this occasion.

She was no longer that fragile young woman who allowed others to rule her life, she reminded herself. Or who retreated from the world rather than confront those who would hurt her.

Over the past weeks she had discovered the ability to fight for what she desired.

And that was precisely what she intended to do.

"Talia?" Gabriel prompted, his gaze searching her pale face with growing concern.

She blinked back the threatening tears and summoned a faint smile. Tomorrow she would consider what might be done to salvage her marriage.

For tonight...

She leaned forward to lightly place her lips against his mouth.

"Certainly not."

"Good," he rasped in obvious relief, his hands lifting to frame her face. "Because I have no wish to waste our last evening together at odds."

She nibbled at the corner of his lips, pleased by his low moan of approval.

"I can imagine how you do desire to spend our evening," she teased.

"You know me so well." He pressed a possessive kiss to her mouth before pulling back to regard her with a gaze dark with need. "But first I believe I owe you a hot bath. And then we shall enjoy a private dinner in bed."

"And then?"

He chuckled with wicked anticipation. "And then I shall allow you to take full advantage of me."

LONDON HAD NEVER been more uninviting.

After a week of drizzling rain and mud, the sun had finally peeked from behind gray clouds to blanket the city in a smothering heat. Even worse, the stench of the docks tainted what little breeze managed to stir the air, making it impossible to leave the windows open.

It was little wonder that most of society had fled the city for their respective estates, Gabriel sourly acknowledged, leading Hugo from the mews behind his townhouse to a side door that led directly to his study.

God knew he would never have lingered for the past week if he'd had a choice.

Not only was London in late summer always a misery, he was desperate to return to Devonshire and the pleasure of his wife's company.

Entering the long room lined with towering bookshelves, Gabriel headed directly toward his massive walnut desk and the waiting brandy decanter.

The thought of Talia was a nagging concern that refused to be eased.

He had only to close his eyes to imagine the pale beauty of her face and the sweet temptation of her body, but it was not his incessant desire for her that plagued him. No, it was the sense that all had not been right when he left Carrick Park that festered in the back of his mind.

Thank God he had at last finished with his business.

Pouring two glasses of the brandy, Gabriel tossed the amber liquor down his throat before turning to hand the other glass to his guest.

Damn, who could have suspected that it would take him two days to simply convince the king and prime minister that the list of prominent English noblemen was not some French hoax? And another three days to gather a select few leaders of the Home Office to warn them of the potential traitors, only to listen to them haggle and barter in an effort to turn the unexpected situation to their advantage.

In a mood as foul as Gabriel's, Hugo took the prof-
fered drink and paced across the polished parquet floor.

"There are moments when I question how the British Isle does not sink into the sea beneath the weight of
those bloated buffoons," he muttered, heading for the
bay window that overlooked the cobbled street below.

Gabriel smiled wryly as his companion perched on the
edge of the window seat, his muscular form attired in a
sage jacket and black breeches appearing far too large
for the cramped room.

This study had been the private domain of his father.
Though he personally possessed no interest in Roman
coins or the pottery displayed in the long glass cases
cluttering the room, he did not have the heart to remove
them to the attics.

Not while his mother still considered this her home.

Pouring another measure of brandy, Gabriel leaned
against the edge of the desk.

"Those buffoons are our noble leaders, Hugo."

"They have spent the past three days squabbling like
children," Hugo muttered in disgust. "I do not believe
they give a damn about the threat to our troops. All they
care about is convincing one another they have no connection to the traitors, although they are all eager enough
to wish to keep the names a tightly guarded secret."

Gabriel grimaced. He wanted nothing more than to put
the hours of bickering behind him. It was perhaps inevitable that those who were accustomed to giving orders
and having them obeyed would find it difficult to compromise with other equally powerful leaders, but playing the role of diplomat had made his head ache.

"We at least made certain that the bastards will be unable to continue to hide in the shadows betraying their
country," he said, resigned that he had done everything

possible to keep the traitors from causing further harm. "Even if they never come to justice."

"Yes." Hugo polished off the brandy and set the empty glass on a rosewood table inlaid with brass. "Do you suppose they will be able to fool the traitors into offering Napoleon false information?"

"There are one or two within the Home Office who possess the skills and the intelligence to turn the situation to our advantage. It all depends on whether they can prevent the others from interfering."

Hugo looked far from impressed, but he readily turned the conversation to more important matters.

"Well, at least you have accomplished your mission."

"Yes." A grim smile touched Gabriel's lips. Whether right or wrong, he had made certain that his brother's guilt would be hidden along with the other traitors. "Harry is protected."

"Let us hope that he has learned his lesson."

"Agreed," Gabriel breathed, feeling a pang of regret at the thought of his brother.

For all of their troubled relationship, Harry was still family, and until he returned to England, Gabriel would mourn his loss.

There was a short pause as they both silently pondered the end of their dangerous adventure. Then, with a faint shake of his head, Hugo leaned against the windowsill, the fading sunlight exposing the lines of weariness etched on his face and the shadows beneath his golden eyes.

Something was keeping Lord Rothwell awake at night, and Gabriel did not for a moment believe that it had anything to do with French spies and overly stubborn Englishmen.

"When do you intend to return to Carrick Park?" Hugo demanded.

"Directly after dinner."

Hugo arched a startled brow. "You will travel at night?"

Gabriel smiled in anticipation. He would travel through the brimstone of hell if it meant getting back to Talia.

"As much as I enjoy your companionship, old friend, I far prefer that of my wife."

Hugo chuckled, pressing a hand to his chest. "I am wounded."

Gabriel narrowed his gaze. "And what of you?"

"Me?"

"When do you plan to return to your estates?"

Rothwell stiffened, his expression becoming wary as he turned his attention to the far wall.

"I have not yet made firm plans."

"No?" Gabriel pretended surprise.

"I have duties to attend to."

"What duties?"

"Does it matter?"

"I would think you would be anxious to leave London." Gabriel deliberately hesitated. "Unless, of course, there is a compelling reason for you to linger?"

Hugo made a sound of impatience, his head turning to meet Gabriel's searching gaze.

"Why the sudden interest in my travel plans?"

"You did leave Devonshire rather abruptly in the company of Miss Lansing."

Hugo's expression hardened, but he could not disguise the revealing color that stained his cheeks.

"You requested to be rid of her."

"True," Gabriel agreed, "but I meant for you to send her on her way, not to personally escort her all the way back to London."

With a sharp motion, Hugo was on his feet, restlessly pacing through the narrow space between the glass cases.

"I could have turned the stubborn minx away a dozen times and she would only have returned," he growled. "She was determined to speak with Talia. The simplest solution was to make certain she left the neighborhood altogether."

Gabriel might have accepted his friend's explanation had he not been behaving as a lunatic over the past week.

He was distracted one moment, short-tempered the next and inclined to stare blankly for hours on end, lost in the midst of a daydream.

Gabriel struggled to hide his smile. "How very generous of you to sacrifice your pleasant stay at Carrick Park to spend days on the road traveling with a tedious wallflower..."

Hugo barreled forward, grasping Gabriel's shoulders and giving him a warning shake.

"You will never speak of Miss Lansing in that manner again," he snarled. "Do you understand?"

Gabriel tilted back his head to laugh with rich amusement. Who would have thought that the mighty Lord Rothwell, the hulking brute who terrified most gentlemen of the *ton,* could be felled by a female half his size?

"I understand perfectly."

Coming to his senses, Hugo released his tight grip and scrubbed his hands over his face.

"Forgive me. I am..."

"Baffled, bemused and bewildered?" Gabriel suggested wryly.

"Yes." With a heavy sigh, Hugo dropped his hands and squared his shoulders. "Do you have any suggestions?"

Gabriel's smile faded to a somber frown as he studied his friend.

He had not forgotten his futile battle against his feelings for Talia. Nor how he had allowed his stubborn pride to harm the woman who deserved nothing but his highest regard.

How could he call himself a friend if he did not do everything necessary to keep Hugo from repeating his mistakes?

"It would seem to me that you have two paths that you can follow."

"And they are?"

"You can return to your estates and put Miss Lansing from your mind," Gabriel said, not at all surprised when Hugo's body stiffened in a silent rebuff of the reasonable suggestion. It was already obvious he was too far gone to take the sensible path. "Or..."

"Or?"

Gabriel set aside his glass to clap a hand on his friend's shoulder, his expression rueful.

"Or you can accept the inevitable with far more grace and dignity than I did."

Hugo shook his head. "You are not reassuring me, Ashcombe."

Sensing that his friend had made his decision regardless of whether he had admitted the truth to himself or not, Gabriel found his curiosity provoked by the woman who had captured his interest. He had dismissed Miss Lansing as just another society chit, but it was obvious he must have been mistaken in her character.

"Tell me, Hugo, what is it about Miss Lansing that has attracted you?"

"I am not at all certain," Rothwell admitted with a smile that warmed his golden eyes. "I find her beauty enticing and I enjoy a woman with soft curves, but there is no doubting that she is not at all the current fashion."

He paused, as if calling the image of Miss Lansing to mind. Obviously not a difficult task. "Her curls are brown rather than gold and they refuse to be properly styled. She has dark eyes that are pretty enough, but instead of gazing at a man with invitation, they hold a good deal too much censure, whether it is earned or not."

Gabriel heaved a sigh. He, better than anyone, understood the danger of becoming fond of a female who should never have caught his attention.

It was, after all, easy enough for a man to mistake lust for love. Such passing fancies were forgotten as swiftly as they struck and rarely cost a gentleman more than a few expensive baubles.

But when a man turned his thoughts to a female who was destined to lead him about like a hound on a leash... well, that was a far greater danger.

"What of her temperament?"

"She is overly inclined to speak her mind, but I prefer her blunt speech to the empty flattery of most females," Hugo said, his expression becoming defensive, as if he were bracing himself for an argument. "This much I can assure you—she traveled to Devonshire and risked being punished by her family because she was desperate to know that Talia was well. She was no false friend."

Gabriel nodded. "You relieve my mind. I am pleased to know that Talia has such a loyal friend."

Hugo's tension eased and a sudden smile curled his lips. "Of course, I am not at all certain that I have yet to convince her that you are not a villain who is plotting to do away with your wife."

Gabriel stiffened in outrage. "Is the female a lunatic? Why the devil would she believe I am plotting to do away with Talia?"

Hugo shrugged, seemingly indifferent to the thought that his friend was considered a murderous fiend.

"My theory is that she reads too many novels."

Before he could retort, the door to the study was opened and a short, portly butler with thinning silver hair and a perpetual frown entered to offer a stiff bow.

Annoyed by the interruption, Gabriel fixed the servant with an impatient gaze.

"Yes, Vale?"

"I thought you would wish to know that Lady Ashcombe arrived while you were out."

"Bloody hell." Gabriel reached for the brandy decanter, wondering if the day could get any worse. "I thought she was settled in Kent. Did she say what brings her to London?"

The servant cleared his throat, a hint of pompous disapproval in his expression.

"It is not the dowager, my lord, but the current Lady Ashcombe."

The bottle landed back on the desk with enough force to make the glasses rattle.

"Talia?"

"Yes, my lord."

Gabriel was barely aware of Hugo shifting as he clenched his hands at his sides and attempted to leash his surge of frustration.

Dammit. Had he not made it clear that he wished for Talia to await him at Carrick Park?

Not that he should be surprised that she would deliberately flout his command. Talia was no longer the timid child he had wed. She was now a woman with her own mind who was quite capable of making her own decisions.

A quality he fully admired under most circumstances.

But how could he protect her if she refused to cooperate?

"When did she arrive?"

"Shortly after luncheon." The butler sniffed, a lingering censure etched in his expression. "She demanded that her belongings be put into the master bedchamber."

A wave of fury crashed through Gabriel as he stepped forward, barely preventing himself from planting his fist in the pompous face. Only the knowledge that the servants were bound to have taken their cue of how to treat Talia from his own mother kept him from violence.

"Vale, listen to me with great care," he ordered in low, lethal tones. "Talia is not only the mistress of this house, but she is my most beloved wife. If I suspect that there is so much as one person on my staff who is not treating her with the utmost respect, I will have the whole lot of you thrown out into the streets." He waited as Vale paled to a sickly hue, his double chin quivering in fear. "Is that perfectly understood?"

"Yes, of course." He bowed deep enough his joints creaked. "My deepest apologies, my lord."

"That will be all."

Gabriel waved a dismissive hand, watching the butler scurry from the room.

It would be an easy matter to force the servants to accept Talia once it became known he would endure no less than complete deference to her authority. And in time, of course, they would come to love her as those at Carrick Park did for her own sake.

His mother, however, and the rest of society would not be so easily swayed.

Which was precisely why he had requested that she remain in Devonshire.

Turning his head, he glared at Hugo, as if this latest disaster was entirely his fault.

"What the devil was she thinking?"

"Perhaps she desired to visit the shops," his friend suggested. "Females are oddly drawn to pretty gowns."

Gabriel snorted. "Not Talia. She has no interest in fashion."

"Then perhaps she wished to spend some time with her father." Hugo grimaced. "As much as we might detest the bastard, he is her only family."

"I am her family now and if that bastard dares to step a foot into this house I will have him transported to the colonies."

"Do you intend to have me transported as well, Gabriel?"

The cold female voice had both men spinning toward the doorway.

Gabriel's heart gave a leap at the sight of his wife in a pretty sprigged muslin gown that hugged her soft curves. Her dark hair was piled atop her head with a few curls left to brush her temple. A simple strand of pearls was draped around her neck.

She looked as fresh and inviting as a spring day.

Then he registered her furious gaze, and his pleasure was forgotten. Not only had she ignored his request to remain at Carrick Park, now she had overheard his insensitive words.

Damnation.

It truly was a rotten day.

Stepping forward, he held out his hand. "Do not be ridiculous, Talia."

"Why not?" Her green eyes smoldered beneath a layer of ice. "It would be the perfect solution to be rid of your unwanted wife."

CHAPTER TWENTY-FOUR

TALIA PRESSED a hand to her heart, startled to discover she was not bleeding from the wound Gabriel had just delivered.

Certainly it felt as if he had stabbed a dagger to the center of her chest.

She had been a fool.

When she had left for London she had tried to convince herself that the past few days of separation would have proven to her husband that he needed her as more than just a warm body in his bed. And that once they were reunited he would have to put the past behind them and build a new relationship.

But hearing his harsh condemnation of Silas Dobson had effectively crushed her fragile hope.

He clearly had not forgiven her father for forcing him into an unwanted marriage, and if Silas Dobson was unfit to cross the threshold of Gabriel's precious townhouse, then what did it say of her own welcome?

Ignoring his outstretched hand, she allowed her gaze to skim over his lean form attired in a gold jacket and sage-green waistcoat. He looked tired. Perhaps his nights had been as restless as hers.

But then, that would mean he actually cared. And that was obviously a silly fantasy.

Cursing the fresh stab of pain, Talia jerked her attention toward Hugo, who moved forward to grasp her hand and raise it to his lips.

"Ah, a delight to see you again, my lady," Lord Rothwell murmured, the concern in his golden eyes nearly making her cry.

"Not a delight for everyone, it would seem," she muttered.

Rothwell's lips parted, but before he could speak Gabriel had reached to grasp his arm and pull him away from Talia.

"Hugo, if you will excuse us?"

"Do try not to be an ass, Ashcombe," Lord Rothwell drawled, offering Talia a last smile. "Until later."

Talia watched him stroll from the room, closing the door firmly behind his large form.

Once alone with her husband, Talia wrapped her arms around her waist and forced herself to meet his gaze. Even if her journey had not ended as she'd desired, she would not allow her courage to falter now.

"Why have you traveled to London?" he asked.

"I had a ridiculous thought that I could convince you that I belong at your side," she admitted, relieved when her voice came out steady. Her pride was battered enough without revealing how grievously he had managed to injure her. "Obviously it was a wasted journey."

Somehow he managed to look offended by her words. "What the hell do you mean? Of course you belong at my side."

"Only when we are being chased through France or secluded in the countryside."

He frowned, regarding her with a puzzled frown as if she were speaking a foreign language.

"You are angry because I did not bring you to London?"

God almighty, she wanted to slap him. Was he being deliberately obtuse?

"I am angry because you treat me as if I am a shameful secret."

Reaching out, he grasped her shoulders and glared down at her with a furious expression.

"Have you gone utterly mad?"

"Do not pretend you are not embarrassed to have me as the Countess of Ashcombe."

He hissed in a sharp breath, pretending as if he were shocked by her accusation.

"For God's sake, Talia, I could not possibly be more proud to claim you as my wife," he ground out, his fingers biting into the flesh of her shoulders.

She frowned, studying his ashen pallor and the seemingly genuine disbelief that shimmered in his eyes.

"Then why did you refuse to bring me to London?"

"Because I did not want you to have to endure the unpleasant gossip."

It was the same excuse he had given before leaving Devonshire, and she gave an exasperated shake of her head at his stubborn insistence.

"I am not a child, Gabriel. I am perfectly capable of ignoring the spiteful comments and insults." She hunched a shoulder at the painful reminder of her years spent in London ballrooms. "It is not as if I have not spent most of my life doing so."

He scowled, his grip easing so his hands could rub a soothing path down her arms.

"Well, I cannot bear the thought of you being wounded by their vicious tongues."

"And your solution is to keep me away from society?" she asked tartly.

He gave an evasive shrug. "For now."

"Why?" She jerked away from the beguiling stroke of his hands, refusing to be distracted by his skillful touch. "Time will not make me more acceptable as the Countess of Ashcombe. No matter how many months or years pass, I will always be the daughter of a baseborn merchant who bullied a peer of the realm into an unwanted marriage."

"Shh, my dear."

He reached for her, but Talia stepped hurriedly backward, bumping into one of the long glass cases that filled the room.

"No, do not touch me," she commanded. "I am furious with you."

He grimaced, but with an obvious effort he forced himself to drop his hand and draw in a deep, steadying breath.

"I surmised as much," he said, hesitating as he considered his words. "Although you are mistaken, my dear."

"Mistaken about what?"

"Most important, you are mistaken if you dare to think that I am anything but absurdly happy that you are the current Countess of Ashcombe."

She flinched at the low words, desperate to believe him even as she was terrified to endure yet another disappointment.

"I just overheard you admitting that you could not bear to have Silas Dobson step over your precious threshold," she reminded him, her voice harsh. "How can you forget that I am his daughter?"

He muttered a curse, shoving impatient fingers through his hair.

"Dammit, Talia, he is not welcome in my home because of what he has done to you."

"To me?"

"Why would you be surprised?" His brows snapped
together at her bewilderment. "You are his only child. He
should have cherished you as the precious treasure that
you are, but instead he bullied you into entering society
despite the obvious fact you were miserable among the
foolish twits."

The same thoughts had passed through Talia's mind
more than once, but Silas was her father and for all his
selfishness she would always love him.

"He was doing what he thought best for me."

"He did what was best for himself."

"Gabriel," she attempted to protest.

"No," he said in unyielding tones. "I must say this and
it will never be mentioned again."

She hunched a shoulder. "If you insist."

"Silas Dobson is consumed with a hunger to rise above
his humble beginnings, which is an admirable enough
trait until he realized he could not purchase his way in
society. His only option was to barter his daughter for
the title he longed to possess."

His hand lifted as her lips parted to inform him that
he had no need to point out her father's faults. She was
intimately acquainted with her father's lust for social acceptance and his willingness to go to any lengths to satisfy them.

Heaving a sigh, she snapped her lips shut, and Gabriel
continued.

"He gave no thought to you or your happiness when
he chose Harry as your bridegroom, who anyone with the
least amount of sense would have known would make you
a terrible husband, or when he demanded that I take my
brother's place. He treated you as if you were his property, not his only family, and to my mind that is unfor-
givable."

"I do not defend my father," she softly argued, "but he cannot change who he is."

Gabriel wrinkled his nose. "No, I suppose he cannot."

"And he is the only family I have."

"Yes, I know." His expression softened. "And if I am to be completely honest, I owe him a debt of gratitude I can never repay."

"Gratitude?"

His lips twisted into a humorless smile at her bewilderment.

"Did you never realize how often I glanced in your direction when we were in the same room?"

"Enough, Gabriel." Her brows snapped together at his poor jest. "There is no need to pretend..."

"This is no pretense," he interrupted. "I noticed you the first occasion you were introduced to society. How could I not? Unlike the other debutantes who were forever giggling and fluttering about like irritating butterflies in an effort to attract attention, you always sat apart."

She swallowed the lump in her throat, wishing he would not play with her tortured heart.

"That is because I was unwelcome, as you very well know."

"Not entirely." He took a cautious step forward, although he was wise enough not to try and grab her. She was so fragile at the moment she thought she might shatter into a thousand pieces at the slightest touch. "You are not the sort to be content with the role of a silly flirt who has no interest beyond dancing and the latest gossip." He peered deep into her wide eyes. "You were as bored at those parties as I was."

A tremor shook her as she recalled those brief moments of insight, when she had been certain she shared a bond with Gabriel, even if he would never realize their connection.

Could they have been more than mere figments of her imagination?

She shook her head. "If you truly did glance my way, you were excessively discreet," she said dryly. "I would have wagered my father's last quid you had never so much as noticed me, let alone recalled my name."

"I did not wish to admit my interest, not even to myself," he smoothly retorted.

"Why? Because I was the daughter of a mere merchant?"

"In part." He wearily rubbed the back of his neck. "I am not proud of my snobbery, but I cannot deny that it played a role."

Talia flinched, but she preferred his honesty to pretense. "And the other part?"

"I had made the decision that my wife would be chosen because of her suitability to assume the role of the Countess of Ashcombe and not because of my own wish to have her as my wife." He held her startled gaze. "Indeed, I intended to ensure that I had no feelings for her whatsoever."

She made a sound of disbelief. She had known that many members of nobility were satisfied with arranged marriages, but she had supposed that they must at least hope for a measure of affection.

Otherwise it was surely no more than a soulless business arrangement.

"You desired to be indifferent to your wife?"

"Utterly and completely."

"But..." She struggled to follow any logic that would lead a man to a loveless marriage when he could surely have any woman he pleased. "Why?"

"It is difficult to explain," he muttered, heaving a faint sigh as he studied Talia's stubborn expression. He clearly did not have to read her mind to know that she was far from satisfied with his explanation. "You know that I was young when my father died and I inherited his title?"

"Yes," she agreed slowly, searching his guarded expression as she wondered what the devil his father's death had to do with their conversation. "I know that it was very difficult for you."

"It was." Pain darkened his eyes. "I had trained all my life to become an earl, but I was still overwhelmed by the sense of responsibility that I was forced to shoulder. Suddenly I had servants and tenants who were all depending upon me to take care of them." He shuddered. "And then there was my family."

"It is a wonder you did not bolt."

He gave a sharp laugh. "Believe me, I considered the notion more than once," he admitted. "Only the knowledge that my steward would find me and drag me back by the scruff of my neck kept me from packing my bags."

Despite her determination to nurture the angry resentment burning in her heart, Talia found herself unable to ignore the glimpse of the vulnerable young man who must have been terrified by his father's sudden death.

"Whatever your uncertainty, you have obviously accepted the need to fulfill your duties," she said.

He smiled, as if genuinely pleased by her approval. "Over the years I have come to accept my position. I hope that my father would have been proud of what I have accomplished."

She blinked. Good heavens. Surely he did not doubt his skills as an earl?

"Of course he would be proud," she insisted, barely resisting the urge to reach out and brush back a lock of his tousled golden hair. "Your servants and tenants not only respect you, but they are clearly prospering beneath your care."

"*Our* care," he gently corrected. "They might respect my leadership, but they adore you. You have not only earned their loyalty in just a few weeks, but I have discovered that they truly would lay down their lives to protect you. They were plotting to invade France when they realized you had been taken by Jacques Gerard. It was only because I swore that I would return you safely to Carrick Park there was no mutiny."

A pleased blush touched her cheeks. "I hope to do what I can to improve their lives and that of their children."

He gently cupped her chin in his palm, tilting back her head to regard her with an oddly somber expression.

"Talia, you are destined to be the finest countess ever to grace the Ashcombe family."

She became momentarily lost in the silver beauty of his eyes. But she was not going to allow herself to be charmed.

Silently chastising herself for being so susceptible to this man, she shook off his hand, her expression warning that she would not be diverted.

"You have yet to explain your wish for a wife you do not love."

An obvious reluctance to finish the discussion tightened his jaw, but with a deep breath he forced himself to continue.

"As I said, I have come to accept my duties as an earl, but the responsibilities of becoming the head of the family have not been so easy to bear," he confessed.

Talia sensed that she was touching an ancient wound that he was careful to keep hidden from others.

"Because of Harry's habit of causing trouble?"

"Not entirely because of my brother," he corrected her. "Even though Harry has been a constant source of concern, he was no more demanding than my mother."

"What do you mean?"

He shrugged. "She had depended utterly upon my father, and after his death she expected me to devote myself to offering her comfort."

"Ah." Yet another dangerous surge of tenderness rushed through her heart. "And who offered you comfort?"

He flinched at her soft question, his eyes shimmering with a long-held pain.

"There was no one." He clenched his hands as he slowly glanced around the room, no doubt remembering the days when his father sat behind the desk and admired his fine collection. "I had no opportunity to mourn."

She bit her lip, blinking back sudden tears. "I am sorry."

"So am I." With a sad shake of his head, he returned his attention to Talia's sympathetic expression. "I did not realize how much I resented the demands of my family, at least not consciously. But the mere thought of wedding a female who would make even more demands upon my emotions was frankly untenable."

"Oh, Gabriel," she breathed, beginning to comprehend his fear of emotion. He had, after all, been taught that love came with cumbersome duties and little reward. "Love should never be a burden."

"So I am beginning to discover," he conceded. Then without warning he tugged her into his arms.

"What are you…"

"I was too much a coward to follow my instincts," he interrupted her protest, holding her against his chest as he gazed down at her flushed face with sudden determination. "But once your father demanded that I become your bridegroom, I was swift enough to take advantage of the situation."

She stilled, regarding him with a wary frown. "My father forced you to wed me."

"Do you truly believe I could be forced to do anything against my will?" he drawled.

"What are you saying?"

His arms tightened around her, the heat of his hands searing through the sheer muslin of her gown.

"I agreed to your father's demands because I wanted to agree."

She sucked in a disbelieving breath, trying to pretend that her heart had not given a sudden leap of hope.

"You told me that you were marrying me to avoid a scandal."

"That is what I told myself as well, but we both know that I possess the power and the resources to have destroyed your father had I genuinely been averse to taking you as my bride." He peered deep into her eyes, willing her to believe him. "I married you because that was what I wanted. Even if I could not admit the truth, even to myself."

"But...you were so cold and distant."

"It was nothing more than a pretense." His hands deliberately glided down her back, leaving a trail of fire in their wake. "Once I had accepted that you were to be my wife I was nearly consumed with my desire for you." She could feel the fine tremor that racked his body. "Damnation, the force of my need made me fall victim to my emotions which only reminded me of all the reasons I had avoided you to begin with. I knew I had to be rid of you."

"That was why you sent me to the country?"

"Yes." An aching regret filled his eyes. "It was my intention to leave after the wedding ceremony and not return until you were on your way to Carrick Park. But I could not stay away." His voice was thick with an emotion that made her heart flutter and her breath elusive. "I ached to hold you in my arms."

"You still sent me away," she reminded him.

"I had a futile hope that distance would lessen my hunger, but it only made it worse." He shook his head in disgust. "I was miserable without you."

He was miserable without her? She frowned. She could still recall his frigid expression as he had informed her she was to be sent away. And the weeks she had spent alone at Carrick Park, convinced that she was to be abandoned forever.

Did she dare to believe that he had been hiding his true feelings?

"I thought you hated me."

"Never," he rasped, lowering his head to press a tender kiss to her temple. "God, Talia, I was such an idiot."

"Yes, you were."

His chuckle was unsteady as he shifted his lips to brush a caress over her brow.

"Then it will please you to know that I was properly punished when I discovered you had been kidnapped." He pulled back, his smile fading. "I knew I would never forgive myself if you were harmed."

"You always feel it your duty to protect others," she murmured.

He made a choked sound of disbelief. "Bloody hell, Talia, if it were only duty I felt, then I would have requested the king send soldiers to rescue you. I would never have traveled to France. And certainly I would never have allowed Hugo to put his life in danger." His gaze seared over her face, lingering a long moment on her lips. "I already sensed you were claiming a place in my heart, and when you arrived in the cellars of Jacques's palace to rescue me, I was certain I could never live without you."

For a moment she thought she must have mistaken his words.

"Your heart?" she whispered.

"My heart." He shifted to grasp her hand and lift it to the center of his chest. Talia gasped as she felt the thunderous pounding beneath her palm. "You were so astonishingly courageous and you cared enough to put yourself at risk to come for me when you could have escaped."

She gazed helplessly into his handsome face. "I could not leave you behind."

"No, you couldn't." He lifted her hand to his mouth, stroking her sensitive skin as his eyes warmed with an emotion she never dreamed possible. "And that is why I love you."

CHAPTER TWENTY-FIVE

THE WORDS LEFT Gabriel's lips before he could call them back, and for a heart-stopping moment he was uncertain which of them was more shocked.

Certainly he had known his feelings for Talia went deeper than lust. Or even the mild affection many gentlemen felt for their wives. Hell, the raw, overpowering need he possessed for this woman seemed beyond mere words.

But he had never consciously considered making such a revealing declaration.

Now that the words hung in the air, however, he had no desire to take them back.

Why should he?

He was not ashamed of his feelings for Talia. In truth, he would willingly shout them to the world.

His only concern was Talia's stunned reaction.

Surely she should be a bit more pleased by his announcement?

Unless, of course, she did not return his feelings?

Had he destroyed any hope of her love...

No. He squashed the unbearable notion.

No matter how long it might take, or what he had to do, he would eventually win her heart.

She cleared her throat at last and managed to croak, "Did you just say you love me?"

He smoothed a hand up the curve of her spine, cupping

her nape in a loose grip. He did not think she intended to bolt, but he was unwilling to take any risks.

"I did."

Her expression remained wary, as if unable to accept the truth of his words.

"You no longer fear I might be a burden?"

"My feelings for you…" He faltered, unable to describe the emotions that filled his heart.

Dammit, he was not a bloody poet.

Talia allowed her hand to slide up his chest and gently placed it against his cheek as she regarded him with a pleading gaze.

"Please tell me."

He sighed, unable to deny her soft plea. "I thought they would make me weak, but I have never felt stronger," he admitted softly. "As if there is nothing I cannot accomplish with you at my side."

Her mouth parted, then with a low cry she threw her arms around his neck and flashed a dazzling smile.

"Gabriel."

He hauled her tightly against his body. He was not entirely certain what had prompted her sudden embrace. Or that smile that warmed him to the tips of his toes. And at the moment he did not care.

The sensation of her soft curves pressed against him was a delectable distraction, reminding him that it had been far too long since she had shared his bed.

"My beautiful wife," he murmured, lowering his head to press a hungry kiss to her lips.

An urgent heat exploded through him as her lips softened and parted in welcome, allowing his tongue to dip into the sweet temptation of her mouth.

He felt her shiver, and he pressed a hand to the lower curve of her back, urging her against his aching arousal.

He heard her breath catch and started planning the quick-est route to his bedchamber without being interrupted by a servant. But Talia pressed her hands against his chest and arched away from his seeking lips.

"Wait," she breathed.

He groaned in genuine pain, desperate to have her naked beneath him.

"I have missed you, my dear."

"I still need to know why you did not want me to travel to London."

He frowned, uncertain why she continued to nag upon his perfectly reasonable request that she remain in Dev-onshire.

"I have told you. I do not want you hurt."

"But…"

He shifted his hand to press a finger against her lips. It was obvious that Talia was too preoccupied to be prop-erly seduced. He had no choice but to confess his plot.

"Allow me to finish," he commanded.

She arched a warning brow, but thankfully he felt the amused twitch of her lips beneath his finger.

"Very well, my lord."

He absently outlined the full curve of her lower lip. "I cannot alter what happened in the past, but I can make certain that your future among society is considerably more pleasant."

She stilled, her eyes narrowing with suspicion. "I do not doubt your ability to browbeat others into pretend-ing they accept me, but to be honest, I would prefer their insults."

He chuckled. There were moments when he forgot just how naïve she was.

"You underestimate my skills. There will be no need

for browbeating." He paused, realizing he was not being entirely truthful. "At least not from me."

She tilted her head to the side. "Then who? Lord Rothwell?"

"His undoubted approval of you will certainly be of assistance, but your greatest weapon will be my mother."

"Your mother?" she whispered. "Good lord."

Gabriel did not blame her for her disbelief.

The dowager countess's horror in having Talia as the next Countess of Ashcombe had been the source of avid interest throughout society. The older woman had rarely missed an opportunity to bemoan the cruel fate that had brought Silas Dobson into her life, without once admitting that any blame for that fate might lie at Harry's feet.

And, of course, her dramatic exit from London on the day of the wedding had ensured that none were left in doubt of her disapproval.

Gabriel, however, understood his mother well enough to know that her flamboyant outrage had more to do with her pleasure at being the center of attention and less to do with her feelings for Talia.

"Whatever her numerous faults, my mother does happen to be the unquestionable ruler of the fashionable world," he pointed out in tones that defied argument.

"Yes, but she detests me."

He shrugged. "She does not know you."

Talia hunched a defensive shoulder, her expression darkening with unpleasant memories.

"That did not prevent her from fleeing London rather than attending our wedding."

His hand moved, stroking down her throat in a comforting gesture. Dammit. This was precisely why he did not wish to have this discussion with her. He did not want her to suffer the painful reminiscences of her awkward years among society. Or their less than romantic wedding.

"You would not have denied her such a wondrous opportunity to earn the sympathy of her friends as she was driven from her home by the evil interloper who stole her son, her title and her position?" he teased.

Her eyes flashed with emerald fire. "I do not find this amusing."

"You will become accustomed to my mother's love for melodrama," he promised, hoping that he spoke the truth. He had become resigned to his mother's excessive emotions. He could only hope that Talia would learn to be likewise tolerant. "Especially when she is given the opportunity to play the role of the tragic heroine."

She wavered, a hint of uncertainty softening her expression.

"You are saying that her anger was a pretense?"

"Who can say how much she believes and how much is a performance?" he admitted wryly. "I do know that she will soon grow weary of her self-imposed exile to Kent, and she will be eager for an excuse to return to London." He bent down to steal a swift kiss, his body still hard with frustrated desire. "I intend to offer that excuse."

Her hand curled around the nape of his neck, her fingers threading into his hair so she could gently tug his head back to meet her searching gaze.

"What are you plotting?"

"I intend for her to visit Carrick Park so she can come to know you."

"Oh." She bit her lower lip, unable to hide her flare of unease. "Are you certain that is a sound notion?"

"Of course I am. She will adore you, I promise."

She grimaced. "You can promise all you like, but I do

not believe she could ever come to adore the daughter of Silas Dobson."

Gabriel chose his words carefully. He had made a promise to himself that he would never lie to Talia again. But neither would he allow her to fear that she would never be accepted by her husband's family. His mother was…not a complicated woman.

She delighted in her excessive bouts of emotion, but they were as shallow as they were mercurial. Talia would never genuinely understand a woman who could change her feelings with the same ease she changed a gown.

For now it was enough to convince his tender young bride that she could win her mother-in-law's approval.

"She will adore you because you are generous and kind and loyal," he informed her.

She remained unimpressed. "You make me sound like a favorite hound."

"Fine." He peered deep into her eyes, smiling with all the love that filled his heart. "Then she will adore you because she will see that you are my heart, and that without you my life would be devoid of happiness."

As hoped, Talia melted beneath his low words, her fingers moving down the line of his jaw in a gentle promise.

"She will realize all that?"

He bit back a groan. His body wanted to be finished comforting Talia with words. It urged him to prove his love and commitment to her happiness in a far more primitive means.

Thankfully he was intelligent enough to realize that tossing her over his shoulder and hauling her up the stairs to his bedchamber was going to have to wait. At least until Talia was satisfied he had no nefarious plot in trying to keep her away from London.

"Absolutely," he managed to mutter.

"And then?"

With an effort he forced himself to concentrate on his scheme to smooth Talia's return to the *ton*. It was, after all, rather brilliant.

"Then she will return to London with the astonishing pronouncement that she finds her daughter-in-law an absolutely delightful young woman whom she fully intends to sponsor during the upcoming season," he said, a smile of satisfaction curling his lips. "The various hostesses will be vying for the opportunity to lure you to their gatherings."

She frowned, considering his explanation for a long moment. "You make it seem very simple."

He lifted his brows in amusement. "Talia, we have survived my brother's treachery, your father's brutish bullying and being captured by French spies. Everything else *is* simple."

She shook her head. "None of them were nearly so lethal as the *ton*."

"Trust me, we will have every one of those pompous idiots kneeling at your pretty feet before the season is over."

There was another pause, and Gabriel smothered his sigh of impatience. How could he blame her for her lingering unease? Not only was he requesting that she rely on the assistance of a woman who had treated her with blatant disdain, but she had endured years of abuse by the members of the aristocracy.

"I do," she unexpectedly announced.

"Talia?"

"I do trust you."

He trembled as her whispered words settled in his heart. Damn, he had been so terrified that he would never regain her trust. Now he pressed his lips to the hollow beneath her ear, torn between relief and the aching need to hear the words she had yet to utter.

"And?" he prompted, his voice hoarse.

"And what?"

He pulled back to regard her with a chiding glance. "Is there nothing else you wish to tell me?"

"Hmm." She pretended to consider his question. "Mrs. Donaldson insisted that I bring your favorite gooseberry jelly and several meat pies with me. She has taken a crazy notion into her head that your fancy London cook is attempting to starve you."

He lowered his head to nip at her lower lip. "That is not what I desire to hear."

"Then perhaps you wish me to tell you of Mr. Price's mule…"

"You know exactly the words I long to hear, my dear," he growled. "Do not torture me."

His tone was teasing, but there was nothing amusing about the agonizing knot of uncertainty in the pit of his stomach. It did not matter how often he assured himself that Talia would never have gone to such efforts to rescue him in France if she did not care for him. Or how readily she responded to his touch.

He was as uncertain as a young lad, desperately longing for her affection even as he feared it might be withheld.

"Very well." Framing his face in her hands, she met his gaze with a slow, breathtaking smile. "I love you, Gabriel. With all my heart."

His heart slammed against his ribs. "You are certain?"

She lifted onto her tiptoes, lightly brushing a kiss over his mouth.

"I was fascinated by you from the moment I first

caught sight of you across the ballroom," she admitted. "You were so astonishingly handsome."

Joy bubbled through him as he offered a smug smile. "Yes, well, I cannot argue."

She snorted. "Of course, you were also aloof, and cold and so impossibly arrogant that I was relieved you never glanced in my direction. You were terrifying."

"No, not terrifying," he murmured. "It was the only means I knew to keep others at a distance."

"Well, it was certainly effective," she ruefully assured him. "I assumed that you were destined to be a mere fantasy I could only admire from a distance. And then you arrived in my private chambers demanding that we be wed."

"Please." With a groan he pressed his forehead against hers, dreading the memory of how he had injured her. "I cannot bear to speak of that day."

Her fingers tenderly caressed his cheek. "I was hurt by your cutting manner, and even more by your insistence that I leave London. But in some ways the opportunity to be away from my father's constant criticism, and even your intimidating presence, allowed me to discover a strength that I never dreamed that I possessed."

He kissed the tip of her nose. "You are the strongest, most courageous woman I have ever known."

"And then Jacques kidnapped me..."

"The bastard."

She chuckled at his low growl. "And you charged to the rescue."

He lifted his head with a wry grimace. "That was my intent, but in the end you had to rescue me. Twice."

Her fingers trailed down his jaw, her eyes soft with devotion that warmed Gabriel to the tips of his toes.

"You risked your life for me, and I knew that even if

you could never return my feelings, that I would love you for all eternity."

The words seared through him with overwhelming force. Driven by a need to show his emotions in a far more tangible method, he scooped her off her feet. He moaned at the feel of her warm body cradled against his chest, her skirts spilling over his arm and her unruly curls tickling his chin.

He had barely managed to take a step toward the door, however, when she touched her fingers to his cheek to capture his attention.

"A moment."

He tilted back his head to glance toward the heavens. "Lord, no."

"I have one last question."

"You are deliberately attempting to punish me," he muttered.

"Why did you not just admit why you wished me to remain at Carrick Park?" she demanded. "You made me believe that you were embarrassed to have me as your wife."

He heaved a sigh, lowering his head to stab her with an impatient glare.

"Because I had no notion you could be so foolish."

Her lips flattened in warning. "Gabriel."

"I did not wish you to believe I was troubled by what society thinks of you, because I am not," he said in a tight voice. "So far as I am concerned, they can all rot in the deepest pits of hell. But I knew eventually you would want to return to London, and I wished to make certain they could no longer hurt you with their vile tongues. But I did it for you and your comfort. Never because I cared what they might say."

"Oh." Her fingers drifted to his lips. "I love you."

"Thank God." He cast her a pleading gaze. "Now can we please retire to our chambers?"

Her soft chuckle filled the air. "Whatever are you waiting for?"

Eight months later

THE BALLROOM on the top floor of the Ashcombe's London townhouse was a long, ivory room with a parquet floor that had been polished until it glowed. There were a dozen gilded half columns that framed the numerous double doors leading into the attached rooms that had been set up for dinner as well as card rooms for those who preferred to avoid the crowded dance floor. And overhead there was a vaulted ceiling with three massive chandeliers that were reflected in the soaring mirrors at each end of the room.

Talia stood on a dais beneath the balcony where the orchestra played a rousing country tune, dancers spinning about her in a dizzying array of brilliant satins and glittering jewels. Talia allowed a smile of pure contentment to curve her lips.

Although she had slowly come to trust Gabriel's mother as she had escorted Talia from one society event to another, she could not deny her trepidation when the older woman had insisted that she and Gabriel host their own ball.

It did not matter that she had been invited into the most exclusive homes in London over the past weeks. Or even that the frosty receptions had slowly melted to a measure of genuine welcome as she'd lost her reserve and managed to converse without her usual stammering. The fear that no one would bother to attend her first gathering had refused to be dismissed.

Now she realized that she need not have worried.

The townhouse was nearly groaning beneath the weight of the vast crowd, and Vale had recently whispered in her ear that he had been forced to turn away several uninvited guests.

Of course, her obvious triumph as a hostess was not the true reason for her contentment.

Or at least not entirely.

She was certainly vain enough to take pleasure in the sight of the *ton* filling her home. She beamed in pride as she gazed down her pretty blue satin ball gown with silver trimming about the hem. The low-cut bodice was stitched with rows of pearls that matched the strands of pearls threaded through her dark curls.

But she had far more important matters to fill her heart with joy.

Her smile widened as she recalled Gabriel's fierce relief upon receiving a note this morning from Harry. His brother was well and currently traveling through India where he had encountered several other English noblemen who were touring the country.

The assurance that his brother had fully recovered and that he was far away from Jacques Gerard and France healed a wound that had plagued Gabriel since their flight from Calais.

But in truth, it was the tiny surprise growing within her that offered the greatest sense of pleasure.

"I hope you are pleased." Joining her on the dais, Hannah Lansing waved a plump hand toward the twirling couples. "The ball is an undoubted success."

Talia nodded, her gaze running down Hannah's white tulle dress that was layered over a lavender underskirt with matching feathers in her hair. The young maiden might not be considered a beauty, but there was a fresh innocence in her round face and a ready humor in her dark eyes.

And of course, there was no mistaking the newfound confidence that only added to her natural attraction.

A confidence that came from being pursued by one of the most sought-after bachelors in all of London.

"It does appear to be well attended," she agreed.

"Well attended?" Hannah's chuckle drifted over the near deafening sounds that filled the ballroom. "I have never seen such a mad scramble for invitations. I heard rumors that even the prince refused to leave Carlton House until he was certain he had been included on your guest list."

"It is quite amazing," Talia said, recalling her breathless astonishment when the prince had arrived with his current mistress, staying long enough to kiss her hand and speak a few words with Gabriel before he was making his grand exit. "I would never have dreamed it possible only a year ago."

"Good heavens, no." Hannah pointed toward the small alcove at the far end of the room. "We both would have been cowering in that shadowed corner."

"True enough." Talia gave a small shake of her head, glancing toward Gabriel's mother, who held court among the matrons, her stately form encased in a rose satin gown and her still-golden hair smoothly knotted at the nape of her neck. "My mother-in-law is a formidable woman. Gabriel promised she would force society to accept me and she has performed nothing less than a miracle."

Hannah lightly batted her arm with an ivory fan. "I do not doubt that the dowager was responsible for ensuring you received the proper respect for your position as the Countess of Ashcombe, but it is your own efforts that have captivated them," she said, casting a rueful glance toward the same guests who had once made their lives such a misery. "The pompous fools had no notion that the daughter of a merchant could possess such charm and wit."

Talia shrugged. A large measure of her bitterness had been thankfully eased by Gabriel's unwavering love for her.

"Not that I would ever excuse their appalling behavior toward us," she said, her attention shifting to the tall, golden-haired man who still made her heart leap with excitement. Especially when he was appearing at his finest in a black jacket and gold waistcoat with white knee breeches. Reluctantly she turned her attention back to her companion. "But I was too shy and frightened of others to reveal any charm, and certainly no wit."

Hannah nodded with an understanding that only the two of them could share.

"And now?"

"And now I no longer concern myself with their opinion so I can actually enjoy myself."

"That much is obvious," Hannah agreed, studying her with a curious gaze. "You are glowing."

Talia hesitated. Thus far she had shared her news only with Gabriel, preferring to avoid the avid interest it was bound to stir among the nobles. And then there was her father's reaction, not to mention Gabriel's mother...well, she had decided she intended to be far away from London when word leaked out that she was breeding.

Hannah, however, was one of the few people she trusted in the world to keep her secret.

"My glow has nothing to do with society," she said, laying a meaningful hand over her stomach.

It took only a moment for Hannah to realize what she was implying, and with a small squeal of excitement, she gave Talia a swift hug before arranging her features into a careful mask to avoid attracting unwanted curiosity.

"Have you warned your mother-in-law that her considerable efforts to install you as the leader of London society will be brought to an early end?" she teased.

"Not yet," Talia confessed. "I am still waiting for Gabriel to recover from his shock. The poor man has been walking about as if he is in a dream, or perhaps a nightmare, for the past week."

"He is pleased, is he not?" Hannah asked in sudden concern.

Talia rolled her eyes. "Outrageously pleased, as well as maddeningly overprotective." She gave a rueful shake of her head, already sensing her time of confinement was bound to be a battle of wills. Gabriel was of a mind that she should spend the majority of her day lying in bed as if she were an invalid rather than a perfectly healthy mother-to-be with an overabundance of energy. "As soon as I shared my suspicion of my condition, he demanded that we pack our bags and return to Carrick Park. It was only my warning that I would never forgive him for forcing us to miss our own ball that kept him from bundling me in the carriage and leaving that moment."

Hannah laughed. "So when *do* you leave?"

"Tomorrow morning." Talia shrugged. "And while I have enjoyed being in London, I will not deny it will be a pleasure to return home."

"I will miss you."

Talia reached to grab her friend's hand. "You are always welcome at my home, no matter what you have been told in the past." Talia glanced toward the man who had so rudely escorted Hannah from Carrick Park months before. Attired in a dark jacket that was molded to his large body and white knee breeches, Hugo leaned against a gilded column, not bothering to hide his unwavering interest in the young woman standing at Talia's side. "Although I doubt you will be eager to leave London."

"Oh, I do not know," Hannah said, a forced airiness in her voice. "It might be fun to spend a few weeks away from the bustle of town."

"Really, Hannah, how long do you intend to torture the poor man?" Talia demanded, feeling a genuine sympathy for the nobleman who had pursued Hannah with a single-minded devotion.

Hannah's smile faded as she turned to regard Talia with a somber expression.

"It is not torture," she said, her eyes shimmering with a yearning that stole Talia's breath. "I merely need for Hugo to be certain that he will not come to regret his proposal."

"He could never regret having you as his wife."

Hannah shook her head. "I appreciate your loyalty, but we both know I have nothing to offer a man such as Lord Rothwell."

"Do not—"

"Come, Talia," Hannah interrupted, her expression troubled. "I have no lands, no dowry, not even beauty. What if he grows weary of me?"

Talia squeezed her friend's hand, knowing with all her heart that Hugo would devote his life to her happiness.

"A man that weds you because of your land or dowry or beauty would quite likely grow weary of you," she warned. "But a man who weds you because he loves you will always remain true." Giving a tug with her hand, she urged Hannah off the dais and toward the waiting nobleman. "Now go and join him before Hugo ruins my lovely ball with that dreadful scowl."

Hannah paused to send her a teasing grin. "What of you?"

Talia's gaze shifted toward the man who had stolen her heart and given her a life filled with endless promise, her heart forgetting to beat as he flashed her a smile filled with wicked impatience.

"I intend to have a last waltz with my husband before convincing him that no one will miss us if we slip away."

"Be happy, my friend," Hannah called, turning to thread her way through the dancers to Hugo's waiting arms.

"Always," Talia murmured.

* * * * *